Undue Diligence

By Paul Haughey

"Undue Diligence," by Paul C. Haughey. ISBN 1-58939-831-9.

Published 2006 by Virtualbookworm.com Publishing Inc., P.O. Box 9949, College Station, TX 77842, U.S. © 2006, Paul C. Haughey. All rights reserved. No part of this publication may be reproduced, stored in a retrieval system, or transmitted in any form or by any means, electronic, mechanical, recording or otherwise, without the prior written permission of Paul C. Haughey.

Manufactured in the United States of America.

1.

Silicon Valley, California

The whirling sound of the fan hung in the air like a dense fog. Joe Nile frowned at his watch and smeared the sweat on his forehead with the back of his hand. He was baking in his office with the late afternoon sun penetrating the blinds. Only 20 minutes to the 4 PM deadline for Express Mail pickups. If he didn't finish this patent application in time, the chewing-out Max was bound to give him for not collecting the money owed would be like a cakewalk.

"Damn!" he hissed. The description of Burak's new program didn't have any threshold. The cursor would jitter. He didn't remember Burak saying anything about a threshold, and Burak was unreachable now. The screen became blurry. He blinked several times and took a deep breath, trying to focus. He was exhausted from having stayed up most of the night the last two days. He shook his head to jar himself, and consciously widened his eyes. He glared at the screen. What could be wrong?

Was he missing something? Did some other part of the program provide compensation? Time was running out. He had to make a decision — and it wasn't just his ass on the line. The hell with it. He started modifying the patent application by typing in a description of a threshold using a combination of touch-typing with his right hand and hunt-and-peck with his left — due to a missing ring finger.

Joe peeked at his watch — there was barely time to meet his wife Sandra for dinner with her sister and brother-in-law, and afterward go to the theater show Sandra had bought tickets for two months ago. His staggered typing quickened while he typed in the last changes to the patent application for the Retinal Screen invention of his client, Telekinetics. The Retinal Screen was a key link in the fight against the deadly virus threatening the globe. It was a quantum leap improvement over Telekinetics' existing arthroscopic microsurgery tools. It had goggles with a video screen to allow the surgeon to see inside the body by the tool head. It was the only tool that could place the Sheath implant to treat the paralysis from the virus before it killed its victims.

He felt a presence behind him and looked up. His male secretary Sidney was still standing behind him.

"Oh really, Joseph," Sidney chirped. "You're screwing up the automatic claim formatting. Honestly! You may be a patent attorney with an engineering degree and understand all this electronic and software design stuff, but you can't operate a simple word processing program."

Joe shrugged. The template for automatically numbering and formatting claims — the legal terms defining the metes and bounds of an invention — was a mystery to him. That was Sidney's job to fix.

"And can you hurry?" Sidney asked. "We only have 10 minutes to get this into Express Mail and I still have a cover sheet and label to type. Not to mention correcting your formatting errors and counting the pages and claims to fill out the fee sheet. It's okay, I'm thankful for the stress. It gives me an excuse to smoke."

Joe frowned and peeked at his watch. "I thought we had twenty minutes?!"

Sidney twirled around and stormed into the hall. "Great!" Sidney bawled to no one in particular, slapping his hand on the wall as he went out the door. "He's learned the Express Mail deadline. Heaven help us now!"

"Joe!" It was Max Klein in his doorway, walking in front of Sidney. Max was the managing partner of Turner, West, Klein & Evans. "You must be excited about the upcoming partnership vote. I recall when I was up for partner . . . ."

Sidney was peeking at Joe from behind Max, frantically tapping his watch as Max droned on.

Max's cell phone rang, and he took the call. Joe used the opportunity to continue typing. Joe stopped again when Max finished his call, and continued with his story.

"Max," Joe said, "I hate to interrupt, but I've got to get this finished for the Express Mail deadline."

"Okay," Max said. "I actually came by to ask if you have a check from Telekinetics yet?"

"I haven't had a chance to call them," Joe said sheepishly. "I've been working on their patent application all day."

"I see," Max said. "This shouldn't make a difference in the vote; you've had a good career here and deserve to become the tenth partner in the firm on Friday. It's not a big deal. I would just rather not have to explain that you haven't been able to get us paid. I'm sure the question will come up."

Joe knew it was a huge deal. Telekinetics had run up a $750,000 bill defending the patent suit against its microsurgery tools by Inventech, a patent troll. That was the difference between the partners getting a nice paycheck this month, or getting nothing. If there was no paycheck before the partner meeting, it would most certainly be discussed by the partners. This was not the introduction Joe wanted to his partnership vote. But he hadn't been able to get Telekinetics to pay.

"I called yesterday, but just haven't had a chance to talk to anyone there today," Joe said. "If I don't finish this application in the next two minutes so we can meet the filing deadline, they'll sue us for malpractice."

Joe's cell phone rang. He looked at the display. It was Burak Ramaxhiku of Telekinetics.

"If that's Telekinetics, tell them we need a check," Max said.

"Can you hold a sec?" Joe said into his cell phone, and then covered the microphone with his finger. "It's my wife calling about our dinner and theater plans tonight, I have to take it."

Max's face flushed. "You know, it's not polite to interrupt a conversation for a phone call. Get your wife off the phone then finish that application. Then I'd suggest you drive down to Telekinetics and get a check right now. Remember, *partners collect*."

Max turned and sped away before Joe could get a word out. Joe sank back against the back of his chair, sighing as he tilted his head back to look at the ceiling.

"Burak?" Joe said, looking at Sidney's pleading face. "I'm glad you called, I have a question . . . ."

"Joe!" Burak barked. "I require your assistance here immediately. It is a matter of extreme importance. Can you come now?"

"What's going on?" Joe asked. "I've been working on your stuff all day, and I'm already late for dinner with my wife and in-laws.

"We have a new infringement issue," Burak said. "Another bullshit patent out of your damned patent system! You must come now. Right now."

A new infringement problem? Joe hoped it wasn't on the Retinal Screen. Had he missed something, and now Burak found out about it before Joe? He hated when that happened.

"The patent problem relates to the Retinal Screen," Burak continued. Joe slouched. "We need your help in resolving this before the Comdex trade show. As you may recall, I have to catch a flight to the trade show tomorrow."

"Okay," Joe said, deciding to wait to bring up the invoices in person, but get an answer on the patent application. "For you, I'll come down now and be late for dinner. But first I have a question . . . ."

The line went dead.

Well, Joe thought, I'll take that as agreement with my changes. He typed the last few pages then told Sidney it was his to format and finalize. He turned off his computer as Sidney raced to his. The whirl of the computer fan reluctantly dropped from the air. He packed his briefcase, signing the transmittal sheet when Sidney brought it in, and rushed out of his office. On the way, he dragged one foot across the Royaltec floor mat, and for good luck let his hand briefly feel the coolness of the stained metal bust of Thomas Edison, the greatest inventor ever. It was immediately cooler in the hall. He almost tripped, again, on the fold where the carpet had bunched up. It needed to be stretched, but it kept being put off. The firm eventually planned to make the carpet in the new space where Joe's office was match the rest of the office.

Joe had worked on defending Telekinetics against Inventech with partner Zenko Kamisaka, who was one of the top patent litigators in the country. Joe also did the patent application filing and legal opinion work for Telekinetics. Zenko had agreed to Joe's request to be the relationship attorney, to show he was ready to move from an associate attorney to partner. Joe liked the relationship attorney responsibility of seeing that the client's work got done and acting as the point of contact with the client. But it also involved collecting the bills, an obligation he was now regretting taking on. He knew what Telekinetics was doing — the company was waiting to see if there was a victory in the Inventech patent suit before paying the bills.

At least he was sure he did the right thing with adding the threshold description to the patent application. Pretty sure.

———————

Twenty minutes later Joe Nile was grinding his teeth, his pickup truck stuck in traffic on a jammed highway 101 as he made his way to Telekinetics. The Bowers Road exit was just ahead. Buildings with For Lease signs surrounded the headquarters of Applied Materials and Intel. Other than the Goliaths, most high-tech companies that survived the dot com bust had been picked off by the patent wars that followed. Telekinetics was a survivor — so far. It was ironic; innovation was being killed by patents.

A start-up would find that its own patents didn't help it because other companies didn't use the innovations or license the patents anymore, they had figured out how to steal the innovations using their own patents. The Patent Office had grown much more lax in the last 20 years. The big companies used their financial resources to obtain a portfolio of patents which the Patent Office nowadays obligingly issued on the most minor changes in technology. These companies then sued the start-up, forcing it to spend a fortune on attorneys and scaring away investors. The big company could then acquire the start-up for a song. This discouraged start-ups because these patent vultures took away all the potential upside. In addition, "patent trolls" who had no product except patents, were leeches that attached themselves to companies with real products.

Joe removed the first-aid kit from the glove compartment, dragged out a Band-Aid and pulled on the red thread to tear open the wrapper. Damn. Traffic had started moving again. With his left hand on the steering wheel, he clamped his teeth on one end of the Band-Aid while pulling the "release liner" off with the other. The little piece of white plastic that covered the sticky part of a Band-Aid was called a release liner. He learned that tidbit of knowledge from a patent application on a method for transdermal drug delivery, which was tech talk for saturating a Band-Aid-like structure with a drug and letting it soak into the skin — like a nicotine patch.

He glanced down at his cell phone and quickly spread the Band-Aid across the inside lens of the built-in camera. The cell phone had an outside lens for normal pictures, and an inside lens to send a picture of the user when a headset was used. It was stuck on the inside lens, and Joe couldn't remember how to switch it back.

His cell phone rang. He fumbled for the phone, keeping his eyes on the road. He was hoping for a call from Zenko about the jury verdict. The jury should have come back by now; it was already a few minutes past five. It would be a lot easier to get a check if he could deliver news of a victory over Inventech. He checked the caller ID; it was his wife, Sandra.

"Hey babe," Joe said, trying to sound upbeat. Best to get her in a good mood first.

"Are you in the car?" Sandra asked.

"Yes," Joe replied. There was now no chance to avoid dealing with the bad news first.

"Good," Sandra said.

"But I have to go to Telekinetics for an urgent meeting and to collect a check," Joe said. "I didn't have a choice — Max told me the partnership vote depends on this. Maybe I can catch up with you at the restaurant in time for dessert?"

Sandra was silent for a moment. "We've had this planned for two months. If you're only going to make it for dessert, don't bother to show up."

She hung up before Joe could reply. He slouched in frustration. The sensual encounters with Sandra had long since vanished, replaced with a series of boring wastes of time. If it weren't for the grief he took, he'd rather miss the dinner. Now he knew what the topic of conversation would be at dinner. He cringed just thinking of Sandra lambasting him to her sister.

He finally reached the parking lot at Telekinetics. The Telekinetics building looked like an old strip mall, mainly because it was. Telekinetics had gotten the space cheaply as a result of the commercial real estate collapse. He walked in through the unlocked front door at Telekinetics, past the deserted reception desk and through the open door to the lab. Burak Ramaxhiku, the director of engineering, sat at a lab bench taking apart a cell phone. Burak had emigrated to the U.S. from Turkey. He stood 5 foot 7, but everyone thought he was bigger. He simply carried himself taller — with such assurance. He had thick, black hair and always seemed to sport a 5 o'clock shadow.

"Sorry I'm late," Joe apologized. "Traffic."

Burak held up his hand with the palm facing Joe. "Please, seat yourself — make yourself at home. I will be through with this in a moment. I see you got in okay."

"No problem, the door was open. I'm glad that you took my suggestions on security," Joe said, pulling up a stool. "I hate to think just anyone could walk in here and steal your trade secrets."

"For your information," Burak said evenly without looking up, "we installed an automatic laser with noise detection and a retinal scan. If it had not recognized you, doors with sharp spikes would have closed and made you into a hundred shish kebabs."

Joe strained to restrain his fingers to a slow tap on the workbench as he watched Burak remove a chip from a cell phone.

"Besides," Burak said, glancing toward the ceiling, "I am sure Allah would have kept an infidel like you out if you had larcenous intent."

After a few minutes, Burak held up the chip with a tweezers, turned to Joe and moved it toward his forehead.

"I salute the prospective new partner. Should I put in a word for you?"

"A check would help," Joe replied.

Burak raised an eyebrow. "It will be easier to convince management to write a check if we had a favorable verdict to report. Any word from the jury yet?"

Joe shook his head. He had a sinking feeling he was going to leave empty-handed.

"What are you doing?" Joe asked. "Taking out a chip so you can use someone else's cell phone number?"

"Yes, of course," Burak said. "Why else would a swarthy middle-easterner be taking apart a cell phone? Actually, this is for the Comdex trade show tomorrow. There is a problem with the second prototype Retinal Screen, and I wonder if it is sabotage. I think it is this chip, so I am getting a replacement. My boss insists the good prototype must go to Comdex. I have to fix the second prototype so we can send it to Brazil. I had hoped to send it today."

Burak pursed his lips tightly while slowly shaking his head. "We have mixed-up priorities. I could have sent the good prototype to Brazil, and Ahmet would have it tomorrow, and still fix this one for Comdex. Someone must be getting a kickback." Burak removed the last wire and gently placed the tiny chip on the bench, leaning back to admire it.

"Ahmet must be going berserk," Joe said.

Burak frowned. "Odd — we have not heard a complaint from Ahmet today."

2.

São Paulo, Brazil

Earlier that day, 6500 miles away from Silicon Valley, tears were etching through the grime on Ahmet Samour's cheeks as he gazed at the hundreds of corpses littering Paulista Avenue. This was worse than any of the massacres he'd seen as an Islamic rebel fighter in his youth.

He froze. Something had moved at the end of the block, among the bodies. Keeping his eyes fixed where the movement had been, he gently stuffed his half-rolled cigarette into his back hip pocket. He started picking his way amongst the carnage, pulling out a handkerchief to protect his nose from the viscous, rising stench of bodies that had spent two days baking in the sun. The street was otherwise deserted. The few remaining residents of the elegant Cerquiera César neighborhood avoided the Avenue.

No one, least of all the police, wanted to touch the decaying bodies for fear of catching what had now been dubbed the Amazon virus. Gunfire had broken out when the crowd, protesting the paltry medical attention available, stormed the police lines. No order to shoot had been given, but every officer had read the reports about the Amazon virus spreading by contact with a victim's sweat. It was shoot to kill or die by touch. Everyone in the crowd was either shot down or fled, although some of them may have died shortly anyway.

Ahmet was startled again by a different, closer movement inside a looted lanchonete — one of the soda bars with tables set up on the sidewalk. He inhaled slowly. It was just his reflection in the shattered mirror behind what was left of the counter. Get a grip, Ahmet.

He looked down to step over a body, stopping to stare at the dead mother still cradling the corpse of her baby, maggots wriggling into view, already doing their work. He slowly swallowed to squelch the vomit trying to rise from his stomach. Then he pulled out his camera and took a picture.

Ahmet moved on quickly. The stampede two days ago had been triggered by an inability to give care to all the people who had, or thought they had, the virus. The health services were simply overwhelmed, but the rumors were that doctors and nurses were afraid to touch patients. The crowd was demanding antibiotics, unaware that antibiotics were for treating bacterial infections and would have no effect on a virus. The virus attacked the spine, and did its work quickly — the patient would become increasingly paralyzed and most would subsequently die in a few days.

Telekinetics' Sheath implant could electronically bypass the damaged area of the spine and stop the spread of the virus, which fed on the attempted neuron firings. The key was the microsurgery accuracy needed to place the Sheath around the spine. The Retinal Screen prototype had been demonstrated to do that on animals. He was hoping to get the Retinal Screen tomorrow.

Now Ahmet spotted the movement that earlier caught his eye. A woman was still alive, barely able to move her arm. He instinctively knelt down to cradle her in his arms and lifted her up. But he flinched as he felt her sweaty arm lock around his neck.

———————

Back at Telekinetics, Burak moved the chip from the cell phone aside, and leaned on the workbench with one elbow. "Joe, thanks for coming down to discuss the infringement problem I mentioned on the phone."

"Burak, about our unpaid invoices," Joe said, "I'm getting a lot of pressure from management."

"As I said, a favorable jury verdict would help," Burak said. "Zenko said it would be a slam-dunk."

Joe bit his lip. He wished Zenko hadn't used that term. Nothing was a slam-dunk, although he had to admit that this had been as close as they come. The Inventech patent was on a supposed new way for a microprocessor to access a disk drive. Telekinetics didn't do it the same way, so Inventech's attorneys had argued that the vague language of the patent claims should be interpreted more broadly, so it would cover Telekinetics. The only problem with that broad interpretation was that it covered the way disk drives were accessed before the Inventech patent was filed. So a literal reading of the patent claim meant Telekinetics didn't infringe, while a broad interpretation should mean the patent was clearly invalid, since it was not new. Either way, Telekinetics should win.

"Let us talk about the infringement problem first," Burak said.

"No, let's talk about the invoices," Joe countered. "I can't do more work until I resolve the invoices for the old work."

"My problem is more urgent," Burak said.

"No, mine is," Joe said.

"Okay," Burak said, extending his fist. "Let us settle this."

Joe sighed, and stuck his fist out too.

"One, two three," Burak said. "Ha! My rock beats your scissors!"

Joe closed his hand. "You know you're making me miss my dinner with my wife and in-laws?"

Burak pulled out a few Chinese take-out containers from below the bench and pushed them toward Joe smiling. "I saved some for you. You can thank me for saving you from that dinner with your in-laws later."

Joe plunged the chopsticks into the twice-cooked pork. "And it's almost warm, too."

"I can't go out to dinner either," Burak said. "Comdex is tomorrow."

Joe nodded. The Comdex trade show in Las Vegas was the largest electronics show. It was an opportunity to market new products. Although medical device products usually weren't shown at Comdex, the software in the Retinal Screen had potential crossover applications, such as a surgical video game. Burak had told Joe it was the crossover applications that would give the volume to bring the price down, making it affordable in the poor countries where it was needed most.

"We need that jury verdict before Comdex," Burak said. "I do not want to have to explain why it is not a problem to customers. And I do not even want to think about the possibility of losing."

"In that case don't think about it," Joe said. He knew a loss would mean that Telekinetics would have to pay royalty damages for previous sales of the existing products, and shipment of the Retinal Screen would be enjoined, so Telekinetics couldn't make any sales.

"So what is your problem?" Joe asked.

"Virtual Net sent us a letter claiming the Retinal Screen infringes their patent," Burak said. "The patent is on a common technique that has been around forever."

"When did this happen?" Joe asked.

"About a month ago," Burak replied sheepishly. "But do not worry yourself. I know about patents. I have learned from watching you. And you are a great teacher. I studied this patent very carefully. It is very broad, so there is no design-around. But it is so broad it is clearly invalid. I know of several prior products and articles showing the same thing. It is ridiculous that they got a patent. These guys must have bribed the Patent Office examiner."

"So why not tell me sooner?" Joe asked. "What would be the harm? Does A.J. know about this?"

A.J. was Telekinetic's president. Her full name was Alejandra Jimena Rodriguez. She went by A.J. for business purposes. She once told Joe that she liked the fact that people couldn't tell if she was a man or a woman on correspondence, and usually assumed she was a man.

Burak shuddered at the mention of A.J.'s name. "A.J. is nervous about patents," Burak said. "You know how patents are abused these days. I was afraid she would kill the project or delay it. You used to be an engineer, Joe. You understand. Even if she did not kill the project, you would just spend a lot of money telling us what we already know. You would say Burak, you infringe, but it is clearly invalid —

it should never have been granted. But you would give us the standard CYA speech, and say that there is a risk a jury would not understand it, and would say the patent is valid. Well, I do not mind taking risks."

Burak grabbed Joe by both shoulders. "You must cover for me, Joe. If A.J. finds out, tell her you knew about this early on, but told me it would not be a problem."

"This prior art you spoke of," Joe exhaled slowly, "the prior products and articles — was any of it considered by the Examiner?"

"Just one," Burak replied. "The Patent Office did find one of the prior art articles, but there are many others they did not find."

Joe groaned. "Well, if the one they found is like the others, they're no good to us. Virtual Net will say — correctly, by the way — that they are just cumulative. The Patent Office Examiner already looked at something just like these other articles and decided the invention was different."

"But the Examiner is wrong!" Burak said.

"Yeah, so what's new?" Joe asked. "You're surprised that a government employee is wrong? Even if the patent is invalid, we need to spend a lot of money to prove it. It has a presumption of validity after the Patent Office issues it, and courts are reluctant to reverse the Patent Office. Mainly because they don't understand this stuff."

Burak slammed his fist against the table. He just stood looking at his fist for what seemed like an eternity. Joe knew from past experience that he should just wait for Burak to calm down.

Burak stood and faced the wall. He raised his hands to his ears and then folded them, right over left, over his chest. "Allah is most great," Burak said. "Forgive me for missing Salatu-l-Fajr." Burak glanced over at Joe. "That is the early morning prayer."

Burak returned his gaze to the wall. "And for missing the noon prayer and the mid-afternoon prayer." Burak bowed down and placed his hands on his knees, then stood again. "Praise be to Allah." Burak laid flat on the floor, and then quickly sat up. "There is no god but Allah." He lay down again and immediately sat up again. "May Allah be glorified." He turned to Joe. "Peace on you and the mercy of Allah."

"Since when did you start praying again?" Joe asked.

"Since you just gave me bad news about this patent," Burak said.

Burak waved his hand dismissively, and sat down to continue his work on the prototype. "Back to the present problem. I would appreciate it if you would look at the Virtual Net patent and the prior art so you can back me up, Joe. I need to tell A.J. tomorrow. I will tell her I just recently found it, and wanted to find the prior art that I knew must be out there before I told her."

Burak started tapping on the keys of his laptop. "I am e-mailing you the patent number."

"So if I look at this, will I leave with a check?" Joe asked as he pulled his wireless notebook computer out of his briefcase and started it up.

"I'll call A.J. right now," Burak said, pulling out his cell phone.

Joe looked at his screen. "Got it." Within 15 seconds Joe had cut and pasted the number, clicked on the Patent Office web site search page and pulled up the patent. Something immediately caught his eye.

———————

Paul C. Haughey

Meanwhile, at the Inventech trial, the jurors huddled in a jury deliberation room. It was stuffy, with a musty smell that invoked memories of waiting for recess in school or watching the clock in line at the Department of Motor Vehicles. The heavy oak table looked as if it had been used as a huge cutting board. The windows were sealed shut, with the add-on air conditioner gasping ineffectually.

The jurors were beaten down by 8 hours of discussion, themselves sealed in the jury room. Carl, the foreman, looked around at the weary faces of the jurors, and could see that most were ready to make a decision just to end this ordeal. He himself was frustrated at being put in a position to vote on this case when he didn't know the first thing about technology. Dan, a mailman, was annoying everyone by holding out for Telekinetics.

"They are completely different," Dan was saying. "Look here at Figure 1 of the Inventech patent."

Carl just shook his head. He didn't understand the figure, which was a diagram of the microprocessor design. The attorneys and their technical expert witnesses had tried to explain all the blocks in the figure — the *cache memory, FIFO buffer, instruction queue, exception handling*. But they might as well have been in Greek. The patent claim was just as bad, with terms like *means for reordering operands, switchably coupled interface, means for monitoring a packet-switched bus* — and it was all in a single sentence that was half the length of the page. How were they supposed to know if Telekinetics infringed or not?

"But the plaintiff's expert said the language does cover it," Carl said. "And he sounded more confident. That's good enough for me. We're not expected to go sorting through the details of the technology, or the way this was done before the patent, or the way the patent does it, or whether the way Telekinetics does it is closer to the patent or the way things were done before the patent —." He raised both palms and his eyebrows in unison and paused for effect. "That's why they put on the expert witnesses. We just have to decide which to believe."

Resigned nods stirred the still air around the room. Carl had avoided science in school, and now he was essentially being forced to take a crash course in science. To make things worse, he was being taught by the expert witnesses for each side, and they disagreed. He was a plumber. It was a mystery why they didn't put engineers on the jury. One engineer had been a member of the jury pool, but Inventech didn't want him on the jury. Amazingly, Inventech's attorney had the nerve to say it was because the engineer might rely on his knowledge rather than what was presented in the courtroom. And the judge agreed. He'd like to strangle the idiot who came up with that law.

His mind just shut down when they started talking in technical terms. The lawyers and their experts had tried to simplify everything, but it was still over his head. And he knew that most of the other jurors had the same reaction.

"So the way I look at it," Carl continued, "it's a tie. And since the Patent Office had already looked at this and gave Inventech a patent, I think we should just allow them to enforce it. In essence, a tie goes to the patent owner."

"Wait a minute!" growled Dan. "What are you talking about? The Patent Office didn't say Telekinetics infringed — they just issued the patent." A chorus of sighs rumbled through the room as Dan launched into his arguments.

———————

Three minutes after Burak e-mailed him the Virtual Net patent, Joe spoke up. "You say it's clearly infringed? Are you sure?"

"I am sure," Burak said without looking up from the prototype he was working on. "The claim is too broad to avoid. And that is why it is invalid."

"I think you can avoid infringement," Joe pronounced.

"What? How?" Burak asked, leaning over. "You highlighted something — let me see."

"Did you talk to A.J.?" Joe asked, turning his laptop so Burak couldn't see the screen.

Burak waved his cell phone. "Yes. But tell me first."

Joe got up and grabbed Burak's shoulder, pointing to an element in the patent. He described a different way to design a chip that would avoid that element, and asked Burak if it was possible to do it that way.

Burak looked at Joe, and then looked at his watch. "How could you figure that out so fast? It took me hours to just understand what the patent was describing."

Joe shrugged. "Can you change it?"

"Yes, praise be to Allah we can change the chip that way, although it will take a couple months," Burak said. "But the claim just describes the function performed, not the details of the way it is done. You are the one who taught me that it does not matter what the description in the patent says, it is how the legal claim at the end is worded."

"True," Joe said. "But this claim is in *means plus function* language," Joe said. "They just describe the function in the claim. That type of clause looks broad, but the rules for interpreting patent claims say that it covers the particular description in the patent and equivalent structures. So it is really narrower than it appears. There are more restrictions than you would guess from the literal words in the claim."

"Can you explain that one more time?" Burak asked, looking at the claim on Joe's computer.

"It's a little complicated," Joe said.

Joe thought about all the complex rules on how to interpret claims. Each rule had been added to try to make things fairer at the time. The rules also were vague enough that no one knew where the line between infringing and not infringing was until there was a verdict in a trial. This made it extremely difficult to advise a client about whether a new product infringed a claim or not. It was like having a building code that said a house had to be set back a "reasonable" distance, which depended on what the individual building inspector felt was reasonable after the house was built.

"You should just ask me when you want to interpret claims," Joe said.

"You should teach me about patent law, so that I do not make the same mistake again," Burak said. "That will save you trouble in the future. Today can be the first lesson. Means plus function."

Joe wasn't thrilled about Burak trying to learn more patent law. Burak already thought he knew enough to interpret claims on his own, and as Joe had just shown, Burak got it wrong.

"Okay, okay," Joe said slowly, looking up at the ceiling and lightly tapping his forefinger on his cheek. "How do I describe *means plus function?*"

After a moment, Joe looked at Burak. "Well, it's like this," Joe said. "If you see the term "means" in a claim, that means the claim doesn't mean what it says."

"You are pushing my leg again," Burak said.

"No, no," Joe protested. "It's true. *Means plus function* language is interpreted to cover only the things described in the body of the patent. So it actually imports more elements into the claim than are actually in the claim."

"I see," Burak said. "So *means plus function* makes the claim narrower?"

"Exactly," Joe said. "Except that it also includes equivalents of the structures described in the body of the patent."

"So it is broader?" Burak asked. "Which is it? Broader or narrower?"

"Sometimes both," Joe said.

Burak flung his hands up in disgust. "Allah help us. Okay, no more lessons. I will just ask you next time."

"What was it you said?" Joe asked. "Don't bother looking at infringement? That you clearly infringed?"

"Okay, okay," Burak said with a grin. "I make big mistake! Oops!"

Joe finished the last of the twice-cooked pork, "About the invoices —"

"A.J. is asking me how can it cost so much," Burak said. "Your original estimate for the whole case when it started 3 years ago was one million dollars. You have billed us $750,000 in the last 3 months alone. The total is now over three million. We have already paid more than twice the estimate — why should we pay more? Shouldn't you just cancel this bill for $750,000?"

"It was just an estimate," Joe said. "We told you it could be more, and we told you there were lots of factors outside our control — like how many witnesses Inventech would use, how reasonable their attorneys would be. We've had to fight tooth and nail for everything — you know that. They've stonewalled us at every turn, forcing us to prepare briefs and petition the court to force them to give us the information they were withholding."

"I can't believe we had to spend 150,000 dollars for a testifying expert to dumb this down for a jury," Burak said, waving the opened invoice at Joe. "And after that the expert of Inventech dumbed it down to the opposite conclusion."

"These damn patents swarm over promising new products like maggots to a corpse," Burak continued. "We had a similar system in the old country."

"You had patent lawsuits in Turkey?" Joe asked.

"No, we paid mob protection money," Burak said. "Same thing here. We pay you protection money. Instead of guns, you use patents. Same thing."

"Nice analogy," Joe said. "Can we get back to the invoices? Collecting them is critical to my chances of becoming a partner, you know."

"I cannot believe some collection matter a few days before the vote would affect the chances of an attorney of your caliber," Burak frowned. "If they are saying that, they are hiding something."

"The invoices?" Joe asked.

"Hey, do you want to try the prototype?" Burak asked, his face beaming with pride.

Joe knew Burak was putting him off, but he was itching to try it. He followed Burak to another bench where the prototype Retinal Screen was set up. The goggles resembled aviation goggles. A small box on the side of the goggles housed the electronics. Burak had the goggles hooked up to a probe that was inserted in a mannequin. Joe balanced the goggles in the open palm of his hand. They weighed about as much as a thick paperback novel.

"The prototype is a bit heavy," Burak said. "The production version will be lighter."

After Joe put on the goggles, Burak started the voice recognition program in training mode. Joe recited 10 words from a list that appeared on the screen, and repeated the same words in response to a prompt.

Now he was ready to start the main program. He looked down in the left corner of the display at the "start demo" icon, and the cursor followed his eye movement. He said "start", and the demo was activated. He eased the joystick forward to insert the tool and started to move it along the route superimposed on the MRI image on the screen. It was like following a curvy road at top speed in a video game — he had trouble keeping it on course. In actual use, a surgeon would map out the best route to get to the area to be operated on, such as a tumor. The demo was taking him through the dummy's brain.

When he got to the tumor, he said "drill," which activated the drill head. He used the joystick to move the drill head around to cut up the entire tumor. He remembered that he had forgotten to start the vacuum, so he said "vacuum", which activated a suction mechanism to suck out the portions of the tumor as he cut it up with the drill.

He pushed through the center of the tumor, and realized he pushed too far — the color changed as he went through some sort of tissue wall. Suddenly there was a screeching alarm and the screen went red. He yanked off the goggles, startled.

Burak was grinning. "You cut through the artery wall. I put in an alarm and fake blood on video for the demonstration. Fun, no?"

"No," Joe said, examining the goggles. "Not exactly. Have you noticed that there is some jitter in the cursor?"

"Yeah," Burak said, furrowing his brow as he took the goggles from Joe. "There appears to be some software bug we haven't found yet, but it is good enough for Comdex."

Joe walked over to his briefcase and handed Burak a copy of the patent application, opened and tagged where he had modified the threshold. "Here," Joe said, "I noticed in drafting the patent application that you need a threshold. I think if you put this threshold in, it will take care of it."

Burak stared at the paper for a moment. His eyes slowly widened as the import dawned on him. "Joe, you are a genius!" Burak exclaimed, tossing the application and embracing Joe with a big bear hug.

"It is clear you were a good engineer," Burak continued, "even if you were an engineer in prehistoric times with obsolete technology. You should have remained an engineer, Joe, and not gone down the wicked path to become a patent attorney. Would you like a job here? It is not too late to save your soul."

"Maybe," Joe chuckled as Burak released him, "But I think I would want to work for a company that can make a cursor without jitter."

"Oh, hurt me," Burak said, grabbing his side in mock pain. "That is a low blow. OK, just more stock for me when we go public. I may invite you to my mansion after I become rich Turk."

"So this will make the Sheath practical?" Joe asked, handling the prototype.

"It will allow us to implant it much more accurately," Burak said. "So maybe we will finally get that damned Ahmet off my back."

Joe's cell phone rang. He flipped the cover, adjusted the edge of the Band-Aid that was already coming loose, and scanned down the news feed. He couldn't help but start perspiring as he read.

"The verdict?" Burak asked.

Joe shook his head. "The virus. Some soccer star is infected now."

3.

Exhausted, at that moment Cassia Cardoso slumped back from her microscope at the offices of Fundacao Nacional de Saude (FUNASA) in São Paulo — Brazil's closest equivalent to the US Centers for Disease Control (CDC). It took effort to raise her eyes to look at the TV. She couldn't stand looking at people who were sick or suffering, it made her nauseous. Becoming chief investigator for FUNASA might not seem the best job choice because of that, but she had the knack and was determined to overcome her weakness. She looked at her watch — she should have heard from her fiancé Ahmet by now. She got voicemail when she tried his cell phone.

The room had become deathly quiet except for the TV crowd noise. Even the announcers went silent as the screen filled with the image of Brito, the star striker on Brazil's soccer team, being wheeled into the hospital, visibly shaking as if he had Parkinson's disease. It was one of the first symptoms of the Amazon virus. Cassia glanced around the room through her watering eyes and saw tears on even the most machismo technicians. Brito was the next Ronaldo, expected to lead Brazil to gold and a record-breaking 6th World Cup championship.

Everyone in the room knew what this meant for Brito. The virus caused nervous system functions to fail within 48 hours. It would start with constant shaking, followed by loss of control of bodily functions, with profuse sweating and dehydration. The victim would gradually become paralyzed as the virus worked its way up the spine, and half of the victims would subsequently die. She, and everyone in the room, felt responsible. She also literally felt sick to her stomach.

It was officially called the Amazon virus because it apparently jumped species from field rodents to workers clearing grazing land in the Amazon basin in Brazil. The rare host mice were suspected to have been living with the virus in their spinal cords for tens of thousands of years. Some people called it the McVirus, since the land was to be used for cattle for hamburgers. Somehow it jumped over the mountains to São Paulo in the south, probably hitching a ride with an infected worker. It had previously been thought to be restricted to rodents, and difficult to transmit. Something had changed.

She looked at the report that had just landed on her desk. She knew what it said. Progress had stalled on a vaccine. The best hope was the Sheath of Ahmet's company, Telekinetics. With existing microsurgery tools they had been able to place the Sheath correctly by pure luck in only the first one of a hundred attempts. The Sheath bypassed the neurons near the virus-damaged area of the spine, stopping the virus from feeding on the neuron firings in some way they still didn't understand. The Retinal Screen would provide the microsurgery accuracy they needed.

Cassia wiped her eyes. It was only two weeks ago that she basked in Brazil's collective pride at hosting the Olympics. That pride had suddenly turned to anguish when the first athlete got sick the day after the opening ceremony. The next few days had been like watching dominoes. It only took a few days for the first athlete to die, with others soon following. She and the others at FUNASA felt particularly disgraced, since public health was their charge. Despite their years of preparations for the Olympics, they hadn't seen this coming.

The Olympics had first been suspended, and next were cancelled, but the athletes weren't allowed to return home because of the quarantine. A ban on return flights had been hastily put in place. Citizens in São Paulo started panicking when all avenues of transportation out of São Paulo were blocked.

People in every country watched on TV as their team members succumbed to the virus. It seemed like at least one member of every country's team had caught it so far. The vivid images were all the more painful because the cream of each country's athletes were being struck down, not to mention many of the people of São Paulo. A large number of the citizens and several of the athletes fled to the countryside before the roads were blocked. She had no idea how many had died there.

Cassia was exhausted from the long workdays, and felt a little nauseous. She looked down at her left hand — it was shaking. She caught her breath and quickly steadied it with her right hand as she glanced around.

Joe was about to ask Burak, once more, about the invoices, when his cell phone rang again. It was Max.

"Nile here," Joe answered.

"Joe, it's Max," Max said. "You still at Telekinetics?"

"Yes," Joe answered. "I'm with Burak."

Joe heard a boarding announcement in the background over the phone — Max was at the airport. Since

Joe had traveled with Max before, he knew exactly what Max was doing. Max was waiting for his flight, had his laptop out, and was reviewing the firm's financials. Joe dreaded the next question from Max.

Joe, like all the associates, knew the firm was in trouble. The partners tried to keep a stiff upper lip, not realizing the associates knew everything. The firm had taken on too many contingency cases. There was barely enough revenue from the currently paying clients, and not getting a check from Telekinetics would upset that delicate balance. So although there was a lot of work to be done on the contingent cases, the firm would not get paid until those cases were won, which would be a year or two from now.

"I don't suppose you have a check?" Max asked.

"Not yet," Joe said.

"The jury came back — we lost," Max said. "Zenko is talking to A.J. right now. Not only that, the judge bought Inventech's argument and issued an immediate injunction. The judge was afraid taking more time to consider the injunction would allow Telekinetics to ship the Retinal Screen out of the country beyond the judge's jurisdiction."

Joe held back a gasp. How could the jury be so stupid? Now the injunction would keep the Retinal Screen from being sent to Brazil.

"I have a project I need your help on," Max finally said, skipping the obvious implications of the verdict. Joe let out a breath of relief, but then felt dread. Max not yelling at him was ominous. "It's a referral from the Peterson firm. We've got a symbiotic relationship going with them; they've been giving us a lot of referrals recently. I don't want to let them down."

Max paused. "You used to work for the Peterson firm, didn't you, Joe? Did you work for Ned Stern when you were there?"

"I did a few things for him." Joe finally found some words. The idea of working for Ned Stern again did not appeal to him. Things were quickly going from bad to worse.

Max waited a moment for the elaboration that didn't come. "Good," Max finally said. "So you know him. Ned needs you at a meeting tonight for a due diligence project. He needs a review of the patent issues and a patent opinion for his client's initial public offering. "

"Tonight?" Joe said. "I'm supposed to meet my wife for —"

"Call your wife — that's what cell phones are for," Max interrupted. "Have some flowers delivered. Partners in our firm make sacrifices. Joe, I have to be honest with you. The Telekinetics loss and nonpayment just before the vote on your partnership will be a problem. It will make it easier for me to push for you if I can say you immediately jumped into this project, putting the firm's interests above family."

"Okay" Joe said. "No problem. Who's the new client?"

"Neuropt," Max said. "It's the latest venture of Gage Booth, who, as I'm sure you know, is one of the 25 richest men in the U.S. So we'll get paid for sure."

Joe was speechless. How could Max make him abandon Telekinetics while the body was still warm and go to work for their newly formed competitor? Not to mention working for Gage Booth, the King of Trolls, who founded Royaltec Enterprises and made his money with extortionist patent lawsuits.

Royaltec Enterprises was a company formed for the sole purpose of buying patents so it could go after other companies for royalties. Royaltec had no products; it didn't build anything. Neuropt, on the other hand, was supposedly a legitimate business venture that intended to develop a real product, but Joe was suspicious. He moved into the hall where Burak couldn't hear.

"You realize Neuropt is a direct competitor of Telekinetics?" Joe said.

"Yes," Max said. "One that has money, and is sending over a sizable retainer check. I won't listen to any Telekinetics complaint unless they write us a check."

"Wouldn't it be better if someone else did this?" Joe asked. "Telekinetics isn't going to be happy with me working for a competitor."

"We need to stop our bleeding with Telekinetics," Max growled. "I need you on a paying client."

"It's more than just a client," Joe said. "Telekinetics needs my help with the Retinal Screen, which they desperately need to treat the virus in Brazil."

"First of all," Max said with a tone of annoyance, "Neuropt's planned product, the Optospine, will also be a solution to the paralysis. Gage Booth is doing a good thing, going legit with all the money he made by questionable means. With the IPO, they'll have the financial resources to make and sell the Optospine, unlike Telekinetics, which is dead in the water now. Second, your background is electronics and software, which is what the Optospine is about — it uses a neural net microprocessor. Since a neural network is modeled after how the brain works, using that type of microprocessor instead of a regular microprocessor is perfect for this application. As you should know, it monitors brain waves, and activates electrodes connected to the muscles."

Max paused. Joe knew Max was trying to impress him with Max's knowledge, but guessed that Max had just recited everything he knew about neural networks.

"But the Retinal Screen is ready to ship to Brazil today," Joe protested. "The Optospine hasn't been built yet."

"My first priority is the firm," Max said. "Telekinetics can settle anytime and still ship the Retinal Screen. They just have to pay royalties they shouldn't have to. Welcome to the real world. Other countries would require bribes that are much higher. The judge and jury knew the implications when they ruled. It's not our call."

"But the judge excluded evidence about the Retinal Screen's relation to the Sheath and the virus," Joe said. "They said it was irrelevant to the patent."

"Enough," Max said. "You can take along Vishal. I understand he's a neural net expert. Joe, I gotta go. My section is almost done boarding. But if you want to have any chance of making partner, you'll meet with these guys tonight. This is what it's all about Joe. Client development, keeping the client happy — this is a chance to show you have those partner skills. Take care of them, Joe, and give me a smiling, paying client."

Joe returned to the lab, sickened by the thought of abandoning Telekinetics and working for Gage Booth, who was the grandfather of the patent trolls. He also wondered how he would explain to Sandra that his partnership chances had just been torpedoed. A.J. was there, and Joe guessed from Burak's subtle body language that they had heard the news from Zenko.

"No! No! No! No! No!" Burak was yelling, leaning on a nearby lab bench, and then abruptly sending the circuit boards on the bench flying with a sweep of his hand. Burak picked up a nearby chair and flung it across the floor. "No!"

Joe leaned against the wall, in a daze as he half listened to A.J. and Burak rant and rave. But he was trying to think of how he could still work on Telekinetics while also taking on Neuropt. The ethics rules allowed it — he was just expected to maintain each client's confidences. He wouldn't be representing Neuropt against Telekinetics, so there was no legal conflict. His experience with medical device work and Telekinetics products made him more attractive to Neuropt. That was common for patent attorneys — once they developed an expertise in a certain field, often a number of companies in that field wanted to hire the same person. The main problem was financial — Max didn't want Joe doing non-paying work.

"How could the jury rule against us?" A.J. asked. "Joe? Joe!"

Joe shook his head to snap out of his funk. "Yes?" Joe asked. A.J. was glaring at him, as if the using the jury system for patent trials was his fault. Burak was doubled over, with his head in his hands.

"How could they possibly win?" A.J. asked, her voice quivering in a struggle to keep her anger under control. "If the claims are interpreted to cover us, they also would cover products made before their invention. They can't have it both ways. Either we don't infringe, or it's invalid."

"Accordion lawyering," Joe said glumly.

"Accordion?" A.J. asked.

Joe took a deep breath. "They argue that the claim is narrow before the Patent Office to get it allowed," Joe said. "Later, when they sue someone, they argue that the claim is broad. Narrow then wide. Like an accordion."

"They must have bribed the jury," Burak said.

"Zenko said we could appeal," A.J. said, picking up the chair Burak had tossed. "But that you guys needed to get paid in full first. How can you guys lose the case, and then drop us? We're having cash flow problems, which are going to be exacerbated by this loss — so how can we pay you in full now?"

Joe felt very uncomfortable. He wanted desperately to help Telekinetics, but his boss had spoken. He had to spit out the company line. "We can't afford to. How long could you pay salaries if you gave away your products, without getting paid for them?"

"How about if we paid some now, and the rest in installments? Would that be a problem?" A.J. asked.

"That would be a problem," Joe said. "Especially if the cost of the appeal work is more than the amount you pay now. My firm won't want to get deeper in the hole with you."

"Joe," Burak said, slamming his fist on the workbench, "surely you can cut us a break. After all, you guys lost a lawsuit that was a slam-dunk. And now you will not help us on the appeal? Think of all those people in Brazil who desperately need the Sheath. Surely your firm can put aside its greed for a little bit to help humanity?"

"It's not a matter of greed, it's a question of our firm's survival," Joe said, trying to put the best face on Max's decision while packing his briefcase.

"We need your help," Burak said.

"Yes," A.J. said. "We now have to settle, and pay the outrageous amounts of royalties and damages Inventech is asking. We need an appeal filed so they still have some risk of losing, and will compromise."

"I wish I could help, I truly do," Joe said, getting up. "I have to leave — another client is doing an IPO."

Burak's eyes narrowed. "I heard that new start-up Neuropt is doing an IPO already, trying to steal our market. You are not working for them, are you? That would be a conflict, you know. Plus I know they only have vaporware, no real product. Joe? Joe!"

Joe just walked away, sick to his stomach. He didn't know how to answer.

4.

Meanwhile, in Brazil, Ahmet Samour was taking another puff of his hand-rolled cigarette and watching the few people on the streets of São Paulo scatter as the gang of kids approached. He wasn't looking forward to telling Cassia that the Retinal Screen wouldn't be coming after all. He was tired and depressed; he just didn't care anymore. Perhaps a dozen people would die tomorrow who could have been saved if it weren't for the injunction against the Retinal Screen.

He tried to get his mind off of the woman who had died in his arms last night. His shirt was stained with his sweat on this warm, humid night, and he had worn short pants to make the heat more bearable. The kids eyed him and approached. The closest looked like he had blood oozing from his eyes, and was shaking noticeably. Ahmet didn't blink as the kid came right up to him and rubbed his sweaty arm against Ahmet's bare leg.

Ahmet let a hint of a grin escape his lips, and the kid laughed, stopped shaking, and moved on with the rest of his gang. Nice try, but bleeding from the eyes wasn't even a reported symptom of the virus, and he knew the sweating stories had been debunked by FUNASA as well. FUNASA still hadn't figured out how the virus spread, but they were sure it wasn't sweat or casual contact. But that didn't stop the media from printing the rumors. Even though Ahmet knew better, he had found himself flinching at feeling the woman's sweat last night. The damn media — they got into one's head. They could get away with it by making the story the fact that there were stories about it being spread by sweat. Whether it was actually spread by sweat was neither here nor there.

The street was deserted and lifeless. Not long ago it was bustling with activity, full of humanity. The Brazilians had been so careful for the Olympics. FUNASA had succeeded in virtually eradicating several diseases that had plagued Brazil for centuries. FUNASA had even implemented a broad inoculation program against smallpox to guard against any terrorist threat — they had rushed to finish just before the Olympics. It seemed to be all for naught.

Cassia would probably be pulling another all-nighter. The pressure was intense — many people thought FUNASA was responsible, that they should have somehow prevented this. The anticipated CDC team from the US was a mixed blessing — FUNASA could use their help, but it also suggested FUNASA couldn't handle this problem.

He sighed. He and Cassia should have been sitting in a piazza in Florence sipping wine and feeding the pigeons right now. But they had to cancel their planned vacation when the virus broke out. He flicked his cigarette to the street and irritably ground it back and forth with his foot. Telekinetics couldn't even ship one lousy prototype Retinal Screen to him. He still couldn't believe there was an injunction because of some lame patent. Didn't the court have a clue what was going on in Brazil? Cassia would take it out on him; he was the ugly American working for the big US corporation. Although he considered himself a liberal, compared to Cassia he was an extreme right wing conservative. He knew he would never have the credibility of a native, even if he cared more about Brazilians dying. At least he knew Joe Nile would be trying to do something to lift the injunction.

Shortly after leaving Telekinetics Joe was stuck in traffic again, grinding his teeth. The commute went both ways. He inched forward as the SUV in front of him moved. He wished he could see around it to see what was ahead. He felt sick to his stomach over how things ended with Burak.

"Shit!" he said aloud. He hated the idea that Inventech — a "patent troll" — had won. In the old days, the invention came first — from an engineer building an actual product. After the product was designed, a patent attorney would write a patent application describing it. That's how it used to work. But these trolls would guess where technology would go, and write the patent applications with vague claims, hoping to cover future technology that others would invent. These applications issued as "paper" patents — ones where no product had ever been built. The claim language was so broad, and covered such a wide range of possibilities, that when independent engineers did indeed invent something new, they found that they were accused of infringing these paper patents.

The trolls had spawned "hybrid" firms, made up of both engineers and lawyers, whose sole purpose was to dream up and patent stuff. They had figured out that they didn't need to build products to get rich off of patents. In fact, with the new extension of patent law to business methods, they didn't even need engineers.

When the accuser was a normal company, with real products, a defendant accused of infringement could fight back with its own patents covering the accuser's products. This often happened in the electronics industry, where both companies in a lawsuit had a portfolio of patents, some of which covered each other's products, resulting in a standoff. The lawsuits would usually settle with a cross-license. But since Inventech had no products, Telekinetics' own patents were simply unavailable as a weapon.

And now Neuropt, tonight of all nights. He couldn't believe he was going to be working for the King of Trolls. What would go wrong next? Surely it wasn't enough that his wife was pissed at him, along with his client and his managing partner. He was afraid his inability to collect from Telekinetics would be a subject of discussion at the partner meeting, right before the vote on his becoming a partner. All this was happening despite busting his butt.

Plus he didn't know how he could possibly fit in another project. He was behind on everything already — he had put off a lot of work for other clients to get the Telekinetics project done, and that other work was now bumping up against deadlines. Maybe he could get Ned Stern to give him more time before he got started.

What a time for Ned Stern to enter his life again. Ned was a partner at the mega-firm of Peterson, Malone & Simon. Joe had worked for Ned before joining Turner, West, Klein & Evans. He remembered his last project for Ned Stern. Joe wrote a memo analyzing a contract for a client, and Ned said it came to the wrong conclusion. Joe still had a vivid picture of Ned getting red in the face as he angrily yelled, accusing Joe of having no common sense.

He checked his cell phone for messages. Evans, one of the name partners, wanted him to stop by ASAP for a new project. He groaned, and slowly spoke the words of Ned Stern's law firm, "Peterson, Malone and Simon."

After a moment the receptionist answered, "Ptrson, M'lne Smon." Joe was put through to Stern.

"Hello Joe," Ned Stern answered. "It's been awhile. Imagine my surprise when Max said you were the guy for this job."

"Yes," Joe said. "I can imagine."

"Hmmm," Ned said. "So here's the situation. My client Neuropt is doing an IPO. We want to file with the SEC next week, and the damned underwriters are now insisting that we get an independent patent opinion, so we can't use our patent people. I told the company that your firm is the best, and they want you to do it. It should be pretty simple; Neuropt's patent attorney already did most of the work and you basically just need to review it and give it a sanity check. I need you to come over here now so we can get started and get you up to speed. We're just 5 minutes away on Sand Hill Road."

"Are you on the speakerphone?" Joe asked, knowing that Ned was. It always used to annoy him when Ned would call with other people in the room and never introduce them.

"Yes," Ned responded, "I've got you on the box so I can keep my hands free."

Is anyone with you?" Joe asked.

"I've got a paralegal with me," Ned said. "She's helping me on this deal."

"She have a name?" Joe persisted.

"Yes," Ned snapped. "And you'll learn it when you get over here. Can you come right over?"

"Yes," Joe said, "I just have to drop by my office for a few minutes first."

"Fine," Ned said, "So can you give us an opinion next week?"

Joe inhaled deeply. This was insane! He had a ton of work to do. Despite Ned's comment on a sanity check, it could easily take several weeks to do all the work needed for an opinion. He knew that he would have to retain a patent searcher to look for prior art — prior patents and articles in the subject area of an invention — to determine if it was in truth a new invention. A searcher normally preferred a month, but sometimes would turn it around in a week if pressed. He wasn't sure if it was humanly possible to finish in a week. He'd not only be late for dinner tonight, he'd have to work the weekend — again. Sandra would not be happy. Not to mention all the other clients whose work he had put off for the Telekinetics projects.

"No problem," Joe said.

———

Ned Stern hit the speaker button to hang up the phone and looked around at the dozen attorneys and paralegals around the modern granite conference table. "OK, that's it for now folks," Ned said, wishing he could keep them around so he wouldn't be alone with Gage.

The smell of garlic lingered from the chicken brought in for dinner. Ned walked over to the containers on the credenza and put a piece of chocolate cake on his plate. He started to nibble at it as the door closed behind the last person to leave, and reluctantly peeked back at Gage Booth, the president of Neuropt.

"Why the hell didn't you tell him we need to file our prospectus with the SEC Tuesday?" Gage snarled. "Next week probably means Friday to him, and we can't afford to wait another week!"

"Don't worry," Ned reassured him, glancing up through the glass walls at a few associates lingering outside the conference room, hoping they couldn't hear. "We'll lean on him once we've got him over here. Besides, Max will make sure Nile gives us the opinion on time."

Ned had gotten used to Gage's attacks. He expected them now. It was just part of having Gage as a client. He had learned that a matter-of-fact response that ignored Gage's tone worked best.

"Is he competent?" Gage asked. "You seem worried about him."

"Yes, he's competent," Ned said with a frown. Ned wasn't sure he liked having Joe Nile work on this. He was too much of a Boy Scout. He just hoped Max could keep Joe under control.

Ned remembered the projects Joe had done when he was at Peterson. Joe was brilliant, and would finish projects with lightning speed. But he had an Achilles heel — an impatience for details. Curiously, that wasn't what finished Joe at the Peterson firm. Joe had finished in two days a project that would have taken any other associate two weeks. But he had overlooked a key case. Joe was actually still correct, legally. But he left out an argument that could have been made for the client. Granted, the argument would have failed, but it was the answer the client wanted. He hoped Joe had learned his lesson by now.

"Well, I hope he's not too conscientious," Gage said. "We just want a damn pro-forma opinion. I don't want some asshole patent attorney stalling the works because he's nit-picking stuff."

"Don't worry, he's not a nit-picker, and he won't have enough time," Ned said. "Besides, I'll have a word with his boss to make sure. Plus, there's the benefit of making sure he won't be able to help Telekinetics."

Part of Gage's business plan was to keep Telekinetics' Retinal Screen off the market. That way, the combination of the Retinal Screen and the Sheath wouldn't be potential competition for the Optospine in dealing with paralysis, whether by the virus or other causes. That would negate the disadvantage of Neuropt just getting started, and not able to have a product for at least 6 months. The goal was to show Neuropt would have the first product, since Telekinetics would be mired in patent problems.

"I imagine Telekinetics is pissed at having to pay so much to settle the suit," Gage said. "Wait until they find out what happens next, and still aren't able to ship their precious Retinal Screen."

Ned saw Gage suddenly staring past him with a lascivious grin. Ned turned and saw that one of their prettier paralegals was walking by.

"Why don't you get me set up with her?" Gage asked, nodding in her direction. "She looks like she'd be a fantastic lay."

Ned cringed. He was just thankful no one else in the firm was in earshot of Gage.

"Now, Gage," Ned said, "you know I can't do that — all the harassment rules and such we have as a law firm. If you want her to go out with you, you'll have to arrange that on your own."

"What's the matter, Ned?" Gage asked, making a thrusting movement with his hips. "Are you doing her? Is that the reason you won't set her up with your best client? You can at least let me have sloppy seconds."

Ned forced a weak smile. It wasn't right that a partner of his stature had to put up with this. But it would be over soon. He knew Turner, West would come through — he had made sure this project would be a lifeline for them.

5.

Back at the Turner, West offices, Erika Dussex, a litigation paralegal, was absentmindedly rubbing the silky underside of the turtle-shaped beanbag against her cheek as she re-read Turner's e-mail. Max Klein would not be happy with this. It looked like more sabotage to her — another Trojan horse. But why should it fall to her to do something about it? She hated confrontation. Plus Turner was not a man to be questioned.

She leaned back and closed her eyes for a moment while tapping her foot furiously. She hadn't taken lunch, and was surviving on the candy her coworkers had in bowls by their offices. She felt a little lightheaded and took a deep breath. The pungent scent of the flowers was overpowering, but their appearance softened her cubicle. She had them sent to herself and told everyone her husband bought them for her. She even had the flower shop put a nice note from her husband on the card, which she made clearly visible for anyone who walked by. She liked the way he didn't mind being so mushy.

She reached up and pulled down the collection jar for victims of the virus. There was no change from when she checked it an hour ago — $45 for the day. It was all from staff, not a single partner had contributed yet. It seemed those with the least to give gave the most.

Her heart went out to Joe. She had heard from Max's secretary about the Telekinetics loss and Joe being reassigned to Neuropt. Joe must be devastated by the loss, and mortified at having to work for Gage Booth. She was personally embarrassed that the firm was taking on Booth, as were a lot of others in the firm.

As she checked her e-mail, she saw one that she needed to respond to before confronting Turner. One of the secretaries wanted to know if anyone had an example of a petition to use when the inventor had died before signing the patent application. Erika remembered she had done one a year ago. She didn't have time to be doing this, and it was far from required — but she couldn't stop herself. It took her 20 minutes, but she finally found it.

She read Turner's e-mail again while drumming her fingers:

> *Re: Conflict check –Demodex*
>
> *Through a referral from Peterson, Malone & Simon, I have been asked to prepare a rush patent application, to be filed tomorrow, for* **Demodex, Inc.** *The technology relates to circuit boards for modems. Please advise by the end of today if you are aware of any potential conflict with taking on this new client.*

The conflict check was sent by Henry Turner, the founding partner of Turner, West, Klein and Evans. She knew that Max Klein had a client that made modems. She also knew that Max was on a flight to Los Angeles, and probably wouldn't see the e-mail tonight. Maybe some other attorney would flag it? Or maybe the records department would notice that the technology was similar? She doubted it. She had realized some time ago that she not only knew more about the law business than many of the attorneys, she had more balls than them. No one would challenge Turner.

In addition, she hadn't told anyone yet, but she had found out some things that made her suspect that Peterson was referring clients to Turner, West to conflict the firm out of future work. She had seen clients do something like this before, but not law firms. A big company would have enough legal work to spread around to all the best law firms, ensuring that none of those law firms would be available for a lawsuit against the company. If Turner took on Demodex, and there was future litigation between Demodex and Max's client, Modem Solutions, the firm wouldn't be able to represent Modem Solutions in that litigation.

She checked her e-mail again, even though it had just been two minutes since she last checked it. There was an e-mail from Cassia in São Paulo. She chewed on her fingernails for a moment, but decided to open it later. Cassia had become her friend when Cassia had accompanied Ahmet on a business trip to California last year. Erika had worked on a Telekinetics deal, and they had gone out to dinner several times and hit it off.

She reached for her toy black and white eagle — she liked the feel of its velour beak. But it flew out of her hands when she pulled it toward her, as if it had come alive. It smashed over her pencil holder, scattering pens and pencils across her desk. As she examined it, she saw that a rubber band was tied to its claw, and hooked to the desk. It was a black rubber band, so it blended in with the color of the black claw. This was clearly the work of Joe.

She separated the rubber band, put it around her wrist, and scurried toward Turner's office. She wound her way around the stacks of boxes of documents in the hallway as she took the long way through the library. On the other side of the library, she stopped in the office everyone referred to as "the invention graveyard" and started absentmindedly examining some of the prototype inventions the firm had collected over the years, procrastinating over confronting Turner. She picked up the Gosonar, which had been the subject of a lawsuit she had helped on. It looked like an MP3 player, smaller than a Walkman, with a bunch of separate plastic transducers.

Gosonar was short for Gossip Sonar. It was a perfect bug — it could be attached to the outside of a window and be monitored from a remote location via a wireless connection.

She fumbled with a few of the other prototypes. There were several pulse oximeters — devices that measured the amount of oxygen in the blood by shining light through the skin. Optical mice, eyeglasses with a miniature imbedded TV screen, a watch cell phone with the antenna in the wristband — box after box filled with different devices.

She sighed and moved on to Turner's office. She saw the gray back of Turner's head. Good — he wasn't on the phone. "Mr. Turner?"

Turner swiveled around and smiled. "Hi Erika, how's Jeffery?"

"Fine," she said. Couldn't he think of something new? He said that every single time he saw her, showing off his memory of the name of the son of a mere paralegal.

"I just saw your conflict check —"

"Yes," Turner said, "they're a referral from an old friend at Peterson, Malone. It's good to have friends like that. And the best part is that the client has a pretty good written description of the invention, I don't need to do much to it to turn it into a patent application."

"Well," Erika said, "I know Mr. Klein is out of town, so I just wanted to tell you that they're a competitor of Mr. Klein's client, Modem Solutions."

"Thanks, but I already knew that," Turner said. "While you're here, I need your help unraveling some shells."

That had become a specialty of hers. Companies sometimes put patents in separate shell companies to isolate them from a counter-suit, or just to avoid taxes. Some clients just wanted to hide from public records what patents they owned — if a competitor sued, thinking the client had nothing to fight back with, they'd walk into an ambush. She had developed quite an expertise in tracing stock ownership and winding her way through the shell corporations and offshore companies. She also was able to track the flow of license payments.

Erika hesitated. Turner clearly considered the subject of the conflict closed, and it wasn't really her place, as a paralegal. But she'd seen Klein question Turner's judgment before. "About the conflict check. It's just that I know that sometimes companies send a small piece of work to the law firm of a competitor just before suing them, so that the competitor will have to get someone else to defend them. Peterson has done that a few times."

"This is from a trusted friend," Turner said, with a hint of annoyance in his voice. "He knows I can deliver in an emergency."

"Why don't they use their own patent attorneys?" Erika asked.

"They want to just do the litigation for this client," Turner said. "This is a test of our abilities. If we do well, we'll get more patent applications."

"It's just that it seems like an odd test," Erika said, "since you don't have time to do much more than file it as they've written it."

"A little paranoid, are we?" Turner said. "Look, this could lead to a lot of Demodex work, which would help increase my billings. Any future litigation with Modem Solutions is speculative. Remember, a bird in the hand is worth two in the bush. Besides, even if there was a lawsuit, Modem Solutions might use some other firm anyway. I'm not going to give up the chance to build up a new client so Max Klein can avoid the tenuous risk of losing some work he might not get anyway."

"But . . . ," Erika started to say.

"It's none of your business," Turner snarled. "If you want to keep your job, quit bugging me. And I don't want to hear about you going to Max."

It was nearly 6 PM as Joe waited impatiently for the elevator door to open at the Turner, West offices. He was going to be late to the meeting with Ned and Gage. He let out a measured breath and leaned against the wall, dragging his fingers over his thick eyebrows, across his eyelids and onto his cheeks. The light tugging of his fingers on his face felt good. Staying up the last two nights till 2 AM, followed by getting up at 5 AM to get the last Telekinetics patent applications finished had caught up with him. He decided to quickly talk to Evans first, pick up his IPO guide to brush up on a few things before the meeting, and then find Vishal. He didn't have time to talk to Evans, but the message had said

ASAP, and just before the partner meeting was no time to disappoint a name partner. But what he dreaded most was having to coax Vishal into going to the meeting.

When the door opened, he wearily grabbed the side to pull himself through. He stiffened up as he saw who was in the reception area.

"There you are, Joe," said Sandra. She put down a magazine and quickly got up from the chair in reception. She looked striking in a black cocktail dress. "I called and delayed our dinner reservation. We'll still only be a few minutes late."

"I can't," Joe murmured as Sandra grabbed his arm to lead him back to the elevator. "I've been put on a new emergency project; I have to go to a meeting right now."

"A new project?" Sandra said, raising her voice. "It just came up? Don't you know how to say no? We've had these reservations for months."

Joe winced and glanced around. The receptionist, a waiting client and several staff members were all watching him and Sandra.

"We just got word Telekinetics lost the trial," Joe whispered. "And I wasn't able to get them to pay us. I need to jump on this new project to rehabilitate myself for the partner vote Friday. It's a project uniquely suited to my skills, and they are in a crunch and need me tonight. It will look really bad at the vote Friday if I've turned this down."

"I can't believe that after all these years of good work, it will come down to what you do in the last few days," Sandra said loudly.

"Can you keep your voice down?" Joe asked as he tried to steer her by the elbow to a nearby conference room.

"No I won't shut up," Sandra raised her voice more, digging her feet into the carpet and pulling back on Joe's arm. "They won't respect you if you don't have backbone. Now let's go to dinner. Whatever it is you can handle on the phone in the car, or in the morning."

"I can't," Joe said. "As Max told me, partners need to make sacrifices. I'll try to meet you at the theater."

"So this isn't going to end when you make partner?" Sandra asked.

Just then Joe was distracted by Erika's unmistakable silhouette behind Sandra, at the end of the hall at Turner's office. The profile of her pert breasts and perfectly curved ass were outlined against the glare from the window. He remembered Sandra's accusations that he would rather have lunch with Erika than her. The worst part was that Sandra was right. But it was innocent. He could relate to Erika — she was also a workaholic. Anyway, it wasn't that he wouldn't prefer to be with Sandra, but he and Sandra were together most of the time, and a little variety of conversation was something everyone needed.

"Well?" Sandra said, starting to turn to follow Joe's gaze.

Joe grabbed her by the waist and drew his face close to her. "Of course it will change," he said, forcing a quick kiss against her retreating lips. "Look, after I make partner, we'll start looking for a house."

Sandra instantly softened and ran her finger down his cheek. "Okay, we'll spend the weekend looking for houses. See if you can get out of this meeting soon enough to at least join us at the play."

Sandra gave him a kiss.

"Um, I can't do it this weekend," Joe said.

Sandra pulled away and gave him a frustrated slap across the chest, and hurried into the elevator, which had just opened.

"This project will be through next week," Joe said. "I'll take off next Friday."

"Yeah, right," Sandra sneered as the elevator doors closed.

He hung his head for a moment, and then hurried down the hall towards Evans' office. He glanced up at one of the framed patents that adorned the hallway. It was the original barbed wire patent. An art consultant had wanted to replace them with some modern, abstract paintings — bland, non-offensive law firm artwork. But Turner had insisted on keeping the framed patents of historic inventions.

Sandra did have a point. He didn't always have to put in extra hours, but the need for late hours had an uncanny knack for happening at the worst times. He knew that partners, especially junior partners, were expected to continue working hard. But even without the long hours, he wasn't sure he could keep Sandra happy. She was always home from teaching by 4, and always wanted to go out. He preferred his quiet time — reading, working on projects. Going out and playing all the time seemed like a waste of his life.

It had been easier when they were first married. Both of them had been willing to compromise more. Now they each were more impatient, tired of putting off what they each wanted to do. But he was sure all married couples went through this. It would be better after he made partner and the pressure was off.

As he reached Evans' door, he peeked at the computer display of Evan's secretary. It was off; she had left for the day. He used his knocks to push open the door to Evans'

Paul C. Haughey

office. It was empty, but Joe could hear the collection of trademark sounds on the screensaver going. Joe cringed when he heard the Intel Inside™ jingle for the millionth time. He decided to wait a few moments in case Evans had only stepped out for a moment. He repeatedly looked at his watch while he poked around for anything new in Evans' sensory trademark collection — products that had trademarked not just the visual name and logo, but the sound, feel, or smell. Evans had samples of perfumes, soap, shampoo, and rug cleaners that had been trademarked for their smell — but Joe's favorites were the sounds.

He opened a bag with the new fastener that had made Velcro obsolete. The sound — between that of a zipper and the ripping sound of Velcro — had been trademarked. Next he sampled the whistling sound as he opened the new Whistler plastic bags, a sound Whistler hoped would become associated with freshness. Then there were the groundbreaking trademarked feels. Evans had been the first to push the envelope of trademark law to cover these. Joe caressed the seductive silky Tricom microfiber phone. The material itself wasn't new, but Evans succeeded in registering the feel as a trademark because Tricom had the only phone with this unique texture, and customers had come to associate that feel with a Tricom phone. Thus it performed the classic trademark function — it made one think of a particular company.

After a few moments, Joe wrote on a Post-it that he had stopped by, and put it on Evans' monitor. He hurried back to his office. He glanced in Vishal's door in the office next to his. Vishal wasn't there.

"Working late?" Joe called out to his secretary, Sidney, as he headed into his office.

"Just trying to save your butt again," Sidney said.

"Oh?" Joe said as he unloaded the Telekinetics materials from his briefcase. He glanced at his artwork — an original watercolor by a local artist — no prints in his office. "Are you going to make up with my wife for me, collect from Telekinetics, reverse the verdict, make the partners vote for me and get me out of this new client meeting so I can finally get some sleep?"

"Hmmm," Sidney said. "No, I'll just stick with your butt; the rest of you is your problem. Here, sign this issue fee transmittal. We forgot this is due today."

"Can you track down Vishal for me?" Joe asked as he signed the authorization to pay the issue fee for the client's patent with one hand, while using the other to repack his briefcase. He bristled with annoyance and frustration as he looked at the Royaltec mat on the floor. He'd rather jump in poison oak naked than work for Gage Booth, the guy behind Royaltec.

Sidney was nodding, and then tapped the silver-framed picture on Joe's desk. "Your parents are going to be proud when you make partner Friday."

Joe picked up the picture and gazed at the handsome, middle-aged couple. Using his sleeve, he wiped the dust off. The man looked so confident, yet with kind eyes and a hint of a grin. The woman had a soft face, with just a few wrinkles near the eyes, which absolutely sparkled. He slowly put the picture down, adjusting its angle to face his chair. He wondered who they were. Max Klein, who was Joe's mentor, was Joe's real father figure. The ringing phone interrupted his thoughts.

He snatched the phone handset to pick it up, but it jerked back with a start — the phone and its docking charger were pulled off the desk with a clatter and the handset yanked out of his hand. He gingerly picked it up and saw that a rubber band had been attached to pull it back down when it was picked up.

He heard Sidney's laughter outside his office. Joe recognized the black rubber band and smiled. Erika. The thought of her made him flush. They had become close friends, and had this friendly flirting and practical joke routine going for the last two years. But it was all innocent, since they were both married.

As he was struggling to undo the rubber band, his phone rang. He put his head down near the phone and pried the handset open enough to answer. It was an awkward position. His nose was almost pushing the phone. His cheek was pressing against the top of his desk.

"Joe, it's Max. I just have a moment, they're about to make us turn off cell phones so the plane can push off. I just got a call from Ned, he's says you haven't shown up yet. Where are you?"

"I'm in the office," Joe said, trying not to let annoyance creep into his voice. Hadn't Max put him under enough pressure already? "I wanted to pick up Vishal and a few things for the meeting."

"Well hurry up and get over there," Max said. "And call Ned to let him know you're on the way. Gotta go."

Max hung up. Joe ignored Sidney's gaze and tried to untangle the phone.

"Who was that?" Sidney asked.

"Max," Joe answered. "I need to go visit a new client with technology to fight the paralysis caused by the Amazon virus."

"I can't believe all the companies going after this virus," Sidney said. "Where were they when AIDS broke out?"

Joe didn't answer as he struggled with the rubber band.

"Looks like you don't have experience with knots," Sidney observed.

Joe leaned back and stared at Sidney. "Would *you* like to try it?"

"Sure," Sidney said, walking over to the phone. "First," Sidney said, pulling at the rubber band and letting it snap back, "you snap it on the back. Next," Sidney started hitting the handset with a pen, "you give it a spanking while it's tied up."

Joe grabbed the phone back and shooed Sidney away and eventually undid the rubber band. He put the rubber band in his pocket.

"Vishal's in his office," Sidney said, poking his head through Joe's door just as Joe's phone rang.

Joe gingerly lifted the handset. Vishal was too lazy to walk next door?

"Joe, you're back!" Vishal Sivakumar said with unusual confidence in his voice for a second year associate. *Vishal* meant *immense* in his home country of India, a perfect match for his deep voice and his 6 foot 4 inch frame, which was draped with 260 pounds and a sizeable gut. He was quite a contrast with his 5 foot 1 inch, 100 pound wife.

"Can you come to my office?" Vishal asked. "I have something to show you."

"Where have you been?" Joe asked. "I've been trying to reach . . ."

Vishal had hung up already.

When Joe opened the door to Vishal's office, he heard the classical music as Vishal pulled off his headset — the same headset Vishal used for phone calls.

"This is urgent, and will only require two seconds of your time," Vishal said, getting up and grabbing Joe's shoulder. Joe stepped into Vishal's office, sidestepping the piles of overstuffed files with papers pouring out onto the floor. The files were just part of the mess. Every available space was filled with electronic gadgets. They were all supposedly needed to write patent applications or evaluate infringement charges. Vishal had wormed his way onto the client teams of all the companies with snazzy products. There were four different computers, one with a 30-inch flat panel screen. He had several microphones, a family of mice including optical and cordless, with and without scrolling wheels, two trackballs, three joysticks and a touch pad. He had two large and six small speakers, supposedly to check out sound programs for patent infringement. A steering wheel was attached to the desk for video road race games. Joe also counted two CD players, a ZIP drive, several PC cameras, and a bunch of other electronics components. One of the bookshelves was filled with boxes for software CDs, which didn't reflect all the software Vishal downloaded.

Vishal closed the door behind him and turned to face Joe. Vishal stopped, turned around, and put his hand on the doorknob. If Joe hadn't seen this many times before, he would have thought Vishal was about to tell him something sensitive, such as that he was about to quit. Vishal grabbed the door firmly, and gave it a couple good tugs to satisfy himself that it was shut securely. He turned to Joe and put his finger to his lips. "This is a sensitive discussion," Vishal said with a hushed, conspiratorial tone.

Vishal pointed to a picture of an SUV in a car brochure on his desk. "I need your opinion on whether to get this in black or blue."

Joe listened to Vishal's dilemma over which color to choose for a minute before interrupting him. "This isn't as crucial as your color choice, but I have a patent due diligence project that needs to be done immediately for an IPO. I need someone to go to a meeting with me."

"Oh," Vishal said, apparently surprised at the quick subject change. "I guess it depends on when the meeting is."

"Remember you are talking to a soon-to-be new partner," Joe said.

"Actually, the odds are 2-1 against that since the Telekinetics verdict," Vishal said.

Joe knew Vishal and others bet on all sorts of personnel matters at the firm; but he was surprised they had such a current bet on his partnership chances. "The meeting is now," Joe said. "Only Vishal Sivakumar can jump in and handle this technology — I don't have time to bring someone green up to speed."

"What's the technology?" Vishal asked, straightening up his 6 foot 4 inch frame.

"It's a medical application for a neural network," Joe replied.

"Say it," Vishal said.

"Vishal, I don't have time . . . ," Joe started to say.

"Say it," Vishal said.

"Okay, okay," Joe grimaced. "I need the Harvard and MIT experience of Vishal Sivakumar on this project."

"Sure," Vishal said. "I can fit it in. Don't worry about Vishal Sivakumar's time. His other main project is the QuadStar stuff he's doing for you. But he'll just put it off. Don't worry about it."

"Do them in parallel," Joe said. "They're both important."

"Boy, are you sure they didn't already make you partner?" Vishal asked. "Do them in parallel. Max Klein would say that. Well, I hope you're ready for Quadstar to be mad. You'll have to explain why their project will be late, not me."

———————

A few minutes later Vishal and Joe were silent as Joe pulled his truck onto Sand Hill Road next to Stanford University. Joe felt like a traitor to Telekinetics and he wasn't looking forward to seeing Ned again. He didn't need Ned bringing up his past in front of Vishal — it would spread through the Turner, West firm like wildfire if Vishal knew. He suddenly slammed on the brakes to avoid a bicyclist cutting in front of him against the red light.

"You should have hit him," Vishal said.

Joe looked out of the corner of his eye at Vishal, without moving his head. He never knew when Vishal was serious. He decided not to take the bait and ask why. He didn't want to listen to one of Vishal's pet theories.

But the moment of silence was brief.

"The reason why," Vishal said, "is that you are defeating natural selection. An intelligent bike rider would have looked, and not cut in front of a car. Running him over would have eliminated his stupid genes from the human race gene pool. Natural selection is what has improved the human race over the years. Survival of the fittest. But recently, we have entered a period of natural deselection. We provide welfare to people who would have died out of the gene pool in the past, and we even give them more welfare the more kids they have. Meanwhile, educated women watch too much TV and all think they deserve Mr. Perfect, and end up not marrying and having kids, and the ones that do try to limit their family size. Then of course there are all the expensive miracle surgeries for people with problems, so they can live and pass on their defective genes. California schools focus on teaching self-esteem, without giving the students the skills that would give them self-esteem, and the tests are dumbed down. We are de-evolving as a race. We have all this technology, but have to keep simplifying how to use it for the average person. As a result of this, the average person is dumber than 20 years ago, and in another generation, will be dumber yet."

"Interesting theory," Joe said.

"I've got another theory," Vishal volunteered.

Joe held up the palm of his hand toward Vishal.

After passing over the new two lane bridge by the Stanford golf course and up the hill, he noticed a new "For Rent" sign across the road. Another company had gone out of business and vacated. The few companies and start-ups in the area were fast disappearing. The law firms used to outnumber the companies only on the right side of the road, farther up toward highway 280. Now they were everywhere, with a number of them being hybrid firms.

They arrived at Peterson, Malone and walked into the reception area, which Vishal noted was large enough for a half court of basketball. Joe's eyes followed the white marble tiles on the floor to the matching marble banister on the spiral staircase, and up to the floor above. Floor to ceiling glass on the conference room adjacent the stairs allowed in light from the windows. There was a similar arrangement on the floor above, giving a skylight effect, which was amplified by mirrors on the interior wall next to the staircase. All the opulence reminded Joe of how he was abandoning Telekinetics for a richer client.

"Can I help you?" asked the receptionist. Joe did a double take — she was stunning, and was dressed like she was about to go down the catwalk in a fashion show. He quickly recovered, announced their business, and sat down in a teal blue chair. Joe skimmed through his IPO guide while Vishal scooped a binder off the glass table and leafed through the 3-inch thick collection of PR articles on Peterson, Malone.

A young man approached them. That was fast, Joe thought, starting to get up.

"Would you like some coffee?" the man asked.

"Sure," Joe said, sitting back down. He handed Joe a card. Joe grinned and showed it to Vishal. It was a menu, with perhaps a dozen different choices for coffee. Joe ordered some Colombian coffee.

"Did you hear about Brito getting the virus?" the young man asked.

Joe nodded grimly.

The young man sadly shook his head. "Brito was the best. It's a damn shame."

Vishal spoke up after they ordered. "Did you work for this guy Stern when you were here?"

"Yeah," Joe said, skimming through his IPO guide as he settled back into the sofa.

"Well?" Vishal eventually said. "What's he like?"

"He likes to make people wait," Joe said, looking at his watch. Sandra would be getting more steamed at him with each passing moment.

After a few moments Joe got a text message notification on his cell phone and slowly shook his head as he read it. "Another 50 people died from the virus yesterday."

Joe didn't have to look at Vishal to know Vishal was just glaring at him.

"Is that your idea of small talk?" Vishal asked. "I'm sick of constantly hearing about the McVirus. Every time I think about it I start to sweat."

Vishal held up a brochure from the table. "Did you know Peterson has over 1000 lawyers in 15 offices around the world? Now that is an example of proper small talk."

Joe checked his e-mail. Ahmet had sent an e-mail asking Joe to somehow help get the Retinal Screen to Brazil. Great. Ahmet had attached a gruesome picture of a woman dead in the street from the virus, with maggots visible in the shot. Joe looked up to see Ned Stern walking quickly into the room, extending his hand.

"Joe!" Ned said. "So good to see you again! Sorry I'm late, I was on a conference call."

Ned looked the way Joe remembered him; his suit fit like it was painted on. Every hair was in place, looking like a toupee, even though it was real. Ned led them up the stairs.

"Nice offices," Vishal said.

"Thanks," Ned replied. "We're expanding to a building next door. It will house our hybrid law subsidiary."

"Yes," Joe said. "I heard you are in that now."

"Everyone is, Joe," Ned said. "Turner, West should get with the program. Do you guys truly enjoy such an archaic way of practicing law? You have to be proactive. Don't just wait for the inventors to come to you. Produce patents yourselves. It amazes me that you guys are able to make ends meet. I understand you don't even take stock in the companies you represent."

"Well," Joe said, "if we're giving opinions on patent infringement, we want to be able to say we don't have a financial interest in the company. We feel that makes the opinion more objective."

As he said this, he realized there might be a conflict issue. Things had been moving so fast he hadn't had time to think about it. He had recently bought stock of ICN, a major stockholder of Neuropt. Could someone allege he gave a favorable opinion to Neuropt just to make sure his stock went up in value? Perhaps he should sell his stock. It wasn't that much anyway.

Ned stopped and looked at Joe. "No financial interest? You're being paid big bucks for the opinion, and with the expectation of a continuing stream of work if you give the right opinion. How is that different?"

"You *have* to get paid for your work," Joe said, trying hard to keep his irritation out of his voice. "It's necessary. You don't *have* to take stock. Anyway, Turner thinks it's different."

Ned laughed. "Yes, I imagine he would."

After they got to the top of the stairs, Joe followed Ned down a wide hallway, his steps softly cushioned by the plush carpeting. Joe wondered where they kept their files. The offices all had modern glass-top desks with remarkably little clutter on them. Suspended planters in front of each office spilled out lush green plants and flowers like a hanging garden. Some of the offices seemed like greenhouses with plants that were practically trees.

They approached a glass-walled conference room filled with over a dozen attorneys, paralegals and clerks.

From the hallway Joe could see through the conference room and out the windows. The 3rd floor view across Sand Hill Road included part of the 2 mile long SLAC, the Stanford Linear Accelerator Center. It stretched under highway 280 and disappeared into the rolling hills of the open space on the other side.

As they stepped into the conference room, Joe was surprised by the smell of garlic that assaulted his nostrils. He was somehow expecting a pristine, sterilized smell. Ned asked an associate to do introductions, and excused himself to fetch Gage Booth, the president of Neuropt. Before the introductions could be finished, the buzz in the room instantly stopped. Joe turned and saw a man following Ned into the room. He was perhaps 5 foot 9 inches, but was stocky, like a linebacker. His face was ruddy, like a drunk's, with a pug nose. His hair was a bushy silver gray. His nose hairs badly needed trimming.

"Joe Nile, I presume," he boomed, reaching across the table and grabbing Joe's hand. His hands were huge, and his grip was crushing, so Joe crushed back and Gage smiled. "Ned tells me you guys are the best. The frigging underwriters are holding us up with this patent opinion business. We are this close to raising $210 million." Gage held up his hand, with his thumb and finger holding the small imaginary gap, and waved it to illustrate how close.

Gage leaned on the table with both hands, bringing his face to within inches of Joe's. "Every day we delay costs us sixty thousand dollars in interest! So when can you have the damn opinion done?"

Joe was taken aback. So this was Gage Booth.

"That's sixty thousand dollars that could be put to use helping paralyzed victims walk again," Ned tactfully added.

"What sort of opinion do they want?" Joe asked as Gage sat down.

"A patent opinion," Gage said, leaning back and looking around with an exasperated look.

Real helpful, Joe thought as he simply looked over at Ned and waited. Ned slid him two stapled sheets of paper. Joe skimmed the pages, uncomfortably aware of a dozen eyes watching him. It was pages from an under-writing agreement describing a variety of representations that the underwriters required in a patent opinion to close the public offering. Part of the opinion was verifying that the statements in the prospectus relating to intellectual property were correct. This meant verifying each fact, and looking for any facts left out that might make it misleading. The usual practice was to prepare a binder that would have a separate section for each sentence, with back-up documentation to justify the sentence being placed behind it in the binder. This was a painstaking, mind-numbing process known as "due diligence." To justify the statement that the company was likely to get patents issued, for example, he had to not only study and understand the patent applications; he also had to search through all the public literature to determine if the inventions were really new and not obvious. This searching itself took a long time, to say nothing of the analysis needed after a stack of references had been identified in the searches.

Joe immediately spotted two problems — first, the opinion language was too broad; and second, they were asking him to review material not relevant to patents.

"How many applications does Neuropt have?" Joe asked, trying to figure out how much he had to review.

"Six, I think," Ned said.

"So when can you have the opinion done?" Gage asked again.

"We can shoot for next Thursday," Joe said, remembering that Ned had said they wanted an opinion next week.

"Thursday?" Gage stood back up and stared at Joe. "You just cost me $320,000! How about saving me a little money?"

Gage glanced at Ned, then around the table. Everyone was quiet, and a few people were looking at Gage as if seeing a new side of him for the first time. "This is money that will save lives," he added. "It just makes me mad to have to deal with patent problems when we're trying to save the world here."

"Joe, we were hoping to file the registration statement with the SEC Tuesday," Ned said, leaning forward and looking around the table. He seemed to relish the audience for this encounter. "And we don't need the actual written opinion until the closing. But we need to finalize the prospectus by Tuesday, and know that you will be able to provide the opinion, and have a draft that is as final as it can be. Let me impress on you the importance of speed. We have already lined up potential investors for the road show to start in about two and a half weeks. If we delay, we'll have to adjust to everyone's schedules, and that could add further delay."

Joe nodded. The IPO was basically a stock purchase agreement. Like any agreement, even a purchase of a house, it was typical to sign the agreement first. Sometime later, the closing would occur with the exchange of final, signed representations and other papers, along with money changing hands. To sell the stock, representatives of the company and the underwriters went on a "road show," traveling around the U.S. and Europe for sales pitch meetings with institutional investors and other potential purchasers.

"Not only is setting up these meetings difficult," Ned was saying, "we have several institutional investors that may use up their budget this year in other stocks for medical field investments if we delay by even a week."

"Don't forget our market window — our pricing is based on the current red-hot market, which won't last forever," Gage added, pacing the far side of the room, stopping as an afterthought seemed to come to him. "And we need the money to get the Optospine helping people sooner."

"Okay," Joe said, taking a deep breath. "We'll try for Tuesday. But it won't be this opinion." Joe tapped the pages with his hand.

"Whoa," Gage said, putting his hand up like he was a traffic cop. "You can't give the opinion?"

"They want us to make a representation that all the applications will issue as valid patents," Joe paused and looked down at the page, "*with substantially the same claims,*" Joe quoted. "And they want a representation that the product won't infringe any patents. There is no way. No sane patent attorney would give that opinion. In fact, I can give you exactly the opposite opinion right now."

"Remember we have some big companies as investors," Gage said. "They'll protect us with their patent portfolios. If anyone dares sue us on a patent, they'll get sued back."

"What about companies like Royaltec?" Joe asked before he could stop himself. He was so used to using Royaltec as an example of evil that he forgot he was talking to Royaltec's founder.

"I can assure you," Gage said with a hint of a grin, "that Royaltec won't be suing Neuropt."

There was nervous laughter around the table.

"I still have to give an opinion," Joe said. "Saying they'll get sued back isn't what your investors want to hear. They want to know if you have an infringement problem. Don't worry, we can negotiate different language with the underwriters."

"Different language?" Gage asked, leaning across the table.

"Something like — we *are not aware* of any infringement, and that the applications *have potential* to be allowed," Joe said.

"But the underwriting agreement is already signed," Gage said. "We can't change the language."

"Doesn't matter," Joe said, not believing him. It would be rare that the underwriting agreement was finished, to say nothing of being signed, this long before the closing. But he decided to just play along. "They'll waive this condition and accept different opinion language. Happens all the time. There's no need to amend the agreement."

"He *is* right, Gage" Ned said. "The language of the opinion is considered negotiable. But Joe, given the time constraints, I'm afraid negotiating the opinion will take more time we don't have."

"Not negotiating it will make the opinion take longer," Joe answered. The quiet throng around the table was beginning to bug Joe. It reminded him of a jury, with Ned and Gage being the prosecuting attorneys, and no defense attorney.

"Okay, okay," Ned said, clearly annoyed. "But negotiate it quick."

"Yeah," Gage chimed in, "none of this lawyerly pissing over details."

Joe took a deep breath. He had addressed the first problem, now for the second. But before he could say anything, Ned threw out a third problem.

"We don't want you to do any searching," Ned said. "Neuropt's patent attorney has already done searches. You can just review what he's done. That should save a lot of time."

Joe was taken aback. He had to do his own search for prior art if his opinion was to be at all independent.

"The underwriting agreement asks for an *independent* opinion," Joe politely pointed out.

"Wait a minute," Gage broke in, turning to face Ned. "Ned, the patent applications are top secret." Gage motioned at Joe. "I don't want him looking at them. We already had a patent attorney prepare them; I don't want to pay for the same damned thing twice."

Joe was starting to feel completely exasperated. First they didn't want him to do any searches, and now they didn't even want him to look at the patent applications he was supposed to do an opinion on? This was nuts.

"It's a little hard to do an opinion on the patent applications without reading them," Joe protested. "And they'll also help us understand the product for the infringement opinion."

"The product is described in the damned prospectus," Gage answered. "Here's a copy of the S-1 with the prospectus." Gage grabbed the draft S-1 registration statement and pushed it across the table.

Joe locked eyes with Gage for a moment, unable to completely restrain his annoyance. He opened the prospectus while Gage continued to complain to Ned. He was being forced to justify his need to get information from the client — this was usually a given. He had to tread lightly; the last thing he needed was Ned or Gage complaining to Max that they weren't happy with Joe. He decided to only deal with one more problem at this meeting — getting access to the information he needed. He quickly found the summary description of the Optospine.

> The Optospine will have sensors that detect the firing of brain neurons in 3-dimensional space. A neural network microprocessor analyzes the information and uses it to control electrodes that stimulate the muscles. An enormous amount of data crunching is done quickly, so the patient doesn't detect a delay between thinking about moving a limb, and it actually moving. A revolutionary optical neural network processes the sensor information at light speed, using optical logic components."

Joe realized he would not only need to review the patent applications, he would probably need to talk to the engineers to determine if these statements in the prospectus were true. He didn't see how it was possible to do what the Optospine claimed to do. He was aware of a number of technical hurdles.

"The description in this prospectus is too vague," Joe said as he continued skimming. "It doesn't explain how the neuron firings are interpreted, for example, or even how the problems I'm aware of in stimulating nerves are overcome. And the detection of synapse firing in the brain is pretty vague. I need to see the product and talk to the engineers."

He slid the S-1 over to Vishal. He already missed working for Telekinetics.

Gage shook his head and looked over to Ned. "Can't we get that underwriter fella on the horn and talk some sense into him? Why do we need two types of patent opinions?" Gage asked.

"We've been through this before," Ned answered. "The underwriter's attorney won't budge. Believe me; it is much easier to give the opinion."

"I don't like it," Gage declared. "And my engineers are too busy to teach these guys about neural nets. I don't want them taking my engineers' time."

You've already tied both hands behind my back, Joe thought. Why not just put my feet in concrete and drop me in the ocean? Why was one of the richest men in the world so concerned with these details?

"I'm already pretty familiar with neural networks," Vishal volunteered, speaking up for the first time. Joe froze and hoped Vishal wouldn't say something stupid. "I used them in my senior project in college, and I've been studying patents in that area for other clients."

"Uh-huh," Gage grunted, giving Vishal the once-over with his eyes. "Well, farting around in school is one thing — this is state-of-the-art stuff, and it ain't simple. No one's done an optical neural net before." Gage stared at Joe as Ned leaned over and started whispering in Gage's ear.

"Joe," Ned said, without losing a beat as he stopped whispering and straightened up, "We'll set you up in a conference room with one of our associates to brief you on Neuropt's business and technology. It shouldn't take more than a few hours."

Joe felt his cell phone vibrate and looked down. There was a text-message from Sandra — she wanted to know when he would be finished.

6.

At that hour in São Paulo Ahmet was finally giving up — it was time to quit putting off Cassia. She might have new information about how the virus spread. He gazed at the Sheath between his tweezers. It was in his hands, it worked, and he was denied the tool needed to use it. He tenderly pulled the sensor strip from the microscope with the tweezers, gingerly placed it back in the plastic container and slammed his fist on the table, making the container leap an inch off the table.

The Sheath was exactly that — a sheath. It was a tube placed around a person's spinal cord — basically a jumper cable for bypassing a damaged portion of the spinal cord. It had a strip of sensors that needed to be sensitive enough to detect neuron firings in the spinal cord. The detected firings would be transformed into electrical signals and transmitted down the array of wire traces in the Sheath. At the other end of the Sheath, the electrical pulses were used to activate neurons that are still functioning. Connecting to the correct neurons had proved impractical, so the Sheath simply relied on the brain being able to relearn how to control the body. A brain neuron firing that previously controlled the left thigh might instead be hooked up to the neuron downstream that controlled the big toe. But the brain should be able to relearn and sort this out over time.

By placing the Sheath above where the virus had progressed, neuron firings in the virus area were stopped. The doctors didn't understand the mechanism, but somehow the virus fed on the neuron firings. Without the energy of the neuron firings, the virus stopped spreading.

Ahmet quickly covered the two blocks to the Fundacao Nacional de Saude (FUNASA). Cassia was sitting on the steps in front of the skyscraper, slowly dragging on a cigarette. An unruly crowd of people extended from the door, down the steps and for at least a block along the sidewalk. A few nurses with clipboards were walking among them, handing out forms and taking notes.

Ahmet sat next to Cassia and they exchanged kisses on both cheeks, followed by a long one on the mouth. Cassia held out her left hand. "See how steady it is?"

"So?" Ahmet asked.

"It was shaking earlier," Cassia said. "Freaked me out. Thought I had the virus. Turned out I was just tired and needed a drag."

Ahmet held out his own hand and studied it.

Ahmet sat down next to her, and lit his cigarette from hers. "Still no pattern?"

Cassia shook her head, blankly staring across the street. "I'm hoping the CDC team that is coming will see something we missed. I had wished we could solve it first."

Ahmet savored the smoke as he slowly sucked on his cigarette. Cassia and her team had been trying to find a pattern to the virus infection. They checked for sexual partners, contaminated food and a host of other possibilities. They hadn't been able to figure out how the virus spread. The US Center for Disease Controls was sending some experts; it hadn't taken long for FUNASA to give up its hope for a quick resolution and call for help.

"You shouldn't smoke, you know," Ahmet said.

"It keeps me thin, don't complain," Cassia said. "It's just like Atkins — something toxic is OK if it keeps you thin. Besides, you smoke."

"Yeah, but I'm a man," Ahmet said.

Cassia hit him in the shoulder.

"This is the most frustrating disease we've seen," Cassia said, grinding the butt of the cigarette into the street long after it was out. "We can't seem to make progress."

"But you are making progress," Ahmet said. "Like the illustrious American inventor, Thomas Edison — the more things you eliminate, the closer you are to the solution."

"We've made no progress on the vaccine," Cassia said. "I just got the report. They tried everything. But at least we'll have the Retinal Screen tomorrow, right?"

Ahmet sighed and explained what had happened in the lawsuit.

"Who devised such a crazy system?" Cassia asked. "Endless fighting which prevents needed products from making it to the market. Is someone benefiting from this?"

"Same answer to both questions," Ahmet said. "Lawyers."

"Well, if you can't get your company to come through," Cassia said, "I'll go to the Minister of Foreign Affairs. The US government should be able to get us a lousy Retinal Screen."

"Wait two days," Ahmet said. "We are going to settle the lawsuit. Since we lost, we'll pay the royalty, even though it's extortion, and we'll get a Retinal Screen here."

"You guys shouldn't get so uptight about a little extortion," Cassia said. "It's just a cost of doing business."

Ahmet just nodded. Cassia, a native Brazilian, had a different perspective on extortion.

"These people make me nervous," Cassia said, jerking her head toward the line. "Most of them think this is a hospital, and are worried they have the virus. Nearly all are wrong. One little mistake in handling them, and we could set them off."

———

Ned rubbed his hand across the cold granite table, looking at the uneven pattern, as people filed out of the conference room.

"I'm telling ya, that son of a bitch Nile makes my skin crawl," Gage said after everyone else had left the conference room. "I don't think he likes me."

"Gage," Ned said, "no one likes you."

"Except you?" Gage asked.

"Except me," Ned sighed.

Gage laughed. "That's fine with me, I like being the hard ass. Look where it's gotten me. Did you see how quickly Nile went through that prospectus? It was uncanny, I tell ya. He got us to give him more leeway on his investigation than I wanted. And you even agreed to let him change the opinion — what were you thinking?"

"I didn't mind because while he's fooling around changing the opinion," Ned said, "he'll be distracted from digging too much on Neuropt. Don't worry; we have plenty of smarter people here."

"Yeah, right," Gage laughed. "I haven't seen a one of your people who could do anything that quickly. And your bills suggest they are even slower on the uptake than they appear in person."

Ned was sorry he made the comparison. He'd better steer Gage back to the opinion. It was the lesser evil.

"He doesn't have much time," Ned said. "That was my doing, remember? We waited until the last minute to bring him in. He won't be a problem. Besides, I'll have a word with his boss to make sure."

Ned involuntarily let out an audible groan when Gage pulled out his toy he bought at some gag shop. It was a 2 inch tall man, and when you pulled his head back, his penis jutted out. Gage started jutting it toward Ned.

"Wanna try it?" Gage asked.

"No thanks," Ned said.

"Perhaps you'd rather touch its dick?" Gage laughed.

Ned looked out the glass window into the hall. "Could you put that away before someone sees it?"

Gage pointed the toy toward the hall and made its penis jerk rapidly. "I'll tell my engineers not to cooperate with Nile," Gage said. "I want to force him to do the opinion on minimal information. That way there won't be delays or problems."

"Don't worry," Ned said. "The time pressure won't allow him to dig deep. Besides, I'm sure any problems can be dealt with."

"I'm still worried," Gage said. "He seems a bit too sharp. We just want a damn pro-forma opinion. I don't want anyone stalling the works. I think I'll arrange for a little insurance."

The next afternoon Erika twirled her scrunchie as she waited for Sidney to answer. Good, Sidney had said Joe would be out of his office for awhile. She awkwardly lifted the package and headed toward Joe's office. Abruptly, she put it down and raced back to her desk. She sat down to catch her breath, opened her briefcase and pulled out her 4-year old son Jeffrey's latest artwork to pin on the picture-wallpapered wall of her cubicle. She had forgotten about it until now. She absentmindedly picked at the yarn — it must have gotten squished in her briefcase. The bunch of yarn was glued as a glob-like skirt onto a vaguely female image on yellow paper. A scattered bunch of glitter depicted a flashy blouse, although it didn't quite align with the skirt. The pictures were proof that she was a good mother who spent a lot of time with her son. Anyone could see that. She clicked on her mouse to bring up the daycare website. The image from the web cam of Jeffrey's daycare filled the screen. She didn't see him there. He must be in the bathroom or something. She clicked again to reduce the image to its normal spot in the lower right corner of her screen.

She sprang to her feet and ran to where she left the package in the hall, lugging it to Joe's office. Sidney was blocking the door to Joe's office.

"You'll get me in trouble," Sidney complained.

"I did this when you weren't here," Erika replied, squeezing past Sidney.

Erika looked around at Joe's artwork as she opened the package. Joe rented different pieces from SFMOMA, the San Francisco Museum of Modern Art. "Which do you like most?"

"You're not going to trick me into picking one," Sidney pouted.

"In that case, this one," Erika said, as she took down the painting and hid it behind Joe's credenza. She hung the new painting she had brought in, then stepped back to admire it. She put her finger to her lips as Sidney started to laugh, but her "shhh" turned into a giggle as Sidney doubled over to stifle his laughter.

"I don't think Joseph has had a painting from this period yet," Sidney said.

"I think you're right," Erika said. "I think it's time he expanded his horizons."

"So what exactly is the era?" Sidney asked. "Late 70's?"

"Set me back two bucks," Erika said. "But Joe's worth it."

The painting was a velvet picture of a farmhouse with yarn glued on for the borders of the buildings and the fence. There was also a farmer outlined in yarn, feeding a pig made of glitter. She and Joe had been doing practical jokes on each other for two years. She enjoyed flirting with Joe, and knew that he enjoyed flirting with her. It was friendly flirting, since they were both happily married — well, they were both married.

———————

"What are you doing here?" Joe asked Erika as he entered his office.

Erika slid past Joe toward the door, grabbing his chest as she wedged by, turning Joe back toward the door. "Sidney was just showing me your new artwork."

"You brat!" Sidney reached out to tickle Erika, and she squealed as she darted away.

Joe shook his head as he sat down. He didn't have time for Erika and Sidney's antics, whatever it was.

"Hold my calls, will you Sidney? I don't want any interruptions."

Joe slouched in his chair and closed his eyes for just a moment. He was so tired. He hadn't gotten home until after midnight last night. Sandra had left a sticky-note on the closed bedroom door telling him to sleep in the guest bedroom — one of her endearing tactics when she was mad. Supposedly, it was so Joe wouldn't wake her up. Joe had left in the morning before she woke up.

He and Vishal had spent a frustrating morning with Neuropt's patent attorney. It was almost as much a waste of time as the several hours with the Peterson associate last night. If he didn't know better, he'd think they were trying to keep him from doing anything by taking all his time with pointless meetings.

The patent attorney had brought over the Neuropt patent applications, but hadn't brought the file histories — the file of correspondence with the Patent Office concerning each application. Worse, the patent attorney talked at length without saying much. The guy not only couldn't explain the technology, he didn't know what parts of the Optospine were new.

Joe had seen this type of patent attorney before — one who didn't understand the invention, who just parroted what the inventors told him. The patent attorney had apparently made no effort to determine what was novel, and how the novel parts were different from the way things had been done before in the prior art. He had commissioned some searches for prior art, but used a shotgun approach, lacking focus. He seemed to have only a superficial understanding of the technology, and was unable to articulate his prior art search strategy, if indeed he had one. Normally a patent attorney had some strategy for prior art searching. For instance, certain technology areas could be identified to look at, and key words for a computer search could be developed.

Time was running short to do the Neuropt work; the Tuesday deadline was fast approaching. And Joe hadn't even been able to figure out how the Neuropt Optospine worked yet.

Joe jerked his head with a start — he had dozed off. He blinked and took a few sips of his coffee. He needed to catch up on any fires that had popped up while he was in the meeting.

Sidney reappeared with a pile of papers. "Here's your mail," Sidney said, next handing Joe a series of notes. "Here are your messages."

"Don't they know about phone mail?" Joe asked, looking at his cell phone — there were 8 new messages, two from Sandra.

"Chiptec wants you. Three different people there left messages on your phone mail, but when you didn't respond in 5 minutes, they called me," Sidney said. "They wanted to make real sure you'd call them back soon. I also left some faxes in your inbox, and one of your messages is asking you to check your e-mail for a message. It looks like they're in trouble; there are three new infringement letters in the faxes."

Joe started to check his voicemail as he read the Chiptec faxes. "You have fifteen new messages." Joe hung up, and looked at his e-mail. There were over 80 new messages.

Sidney started gently stroking the chin of the Edison bust. Joe glanced at him, and turned to his work, shaking his head slowly. Sidney laughed and headed for the door.

Chiptec was in trouble. They had come up with a great new technology for making chips, but doing it as a start-up was suicidal in today's patent war environment. The established companies with large patent portfolios were descending like vultures. Each wanted a 5% royalty, but there simply wasn't enough profit margin for them all. Joe was under strict orders from Max not to do any more work until Chiptec caught up on its bills. It was a shame — the established companies, with their short-term profit greed, were strangling all the innovation in the market, which would only cause their products to stagnate and hurt them in the end.

Joe had hoped to spend a few minutes on a little last minute smoozing with some of the partners before the vote tomorrow on his partnership. He momentarily froze up. He didn't know what to deal with first. He put his hand on the Edison bust for a moment, and then looked at the Internet news about the new virus cases in Rio. He called Zenko but got his voicemail. He decided getting Zenko to help Telekinetics with the appeal should be the top priority.

His phone rang, and he let Sidney get it.

A moment later Sidney was at his door. "It's the inventor of the sensor chip on the camera," Sidney apologized. "He said he only needs five minutes."

Joe sighed. He didn't have time to talk right now. He picked up the phone, ready to make an excuse and call back next week. Thirty minutes later Joe was still listening to the inventor. This inventor didn't work for a start-up, and didn't have a product, and thus didn't have to worry about the big companies coming after him with their patent portfolios. Since he had no products, he couldn't infringe anyone's patent portfolio. His plan was to license a big company to make it. He would not make as much money as he could with a start-up, and the product could end up languishing, but it was better than being crushed by an avalanche of patents.

"What's that clicking sound?" asked the inventor. "You're not doing other work while I'm talking to you, are you?"

"Of course not," Joe said, clicking on another e-mail and scanning it briefly, then deleting it. "I'm taking notes on my computer of what you're saying. I don't want to miss anything."

Joe had long ago grasped all he needed, but the inventor insisted on explaining irrelevant aspects of the product. Vishal poked his head into Joe's office, and Joe waved him in. Joe excused himself to the inventor, saying he had an important meeting that was just starting.

"Ah, ah, ah," Joe said, pointing.

Vishal crinkled his nose. "Really, Joe, how long are you going to make everyone do this?" Vishal dragged himself to his feet and walked over and tapped the bust of Edison on the edge of Joe's desk, while half-heartedly dragging one foot on the floor mat that said "Royaltec."

Joe smiled. He enjoyed putting young associates through this little ritual. The Edison bust reminded them of the finest inventor ever, so he made junior associates pay tribute by touching it. Royaltec represented the dark side of patent law, so stomping on it was required.

"You may have to get rid of this mat," Vishal said. "What if your new client Gage Booth comes by and sees it?"

"He won't come by," Joe said. "And I work for Neuropt, not Booth or Royaltec."

"The odds on your making partner tomorrow have improved to 1.5 to 1," Vishal said, absentmindedly leafing through papers on Joe's desk. "I think it's because you have Vishal Sivakumar's help on this Neuropt project."

"Great," Joe said, slapping Vishal's hand away from his papers as if he were a child. "Were you able to reach any of the engineers at Neuropt?"

"Nope, I was told we only get to talk to the engineering manager, Harold Walsh," Vishal said. "Joe, there's something I think you should see."

"Hell," Joe said. "How are supposed to do our damn job? When do we get to talk to Walsh?"

They needed someone to explain the product design details so they could do their analysis. Joe had run into companies that were secretive about their planned products, but this was ridiculous. Neuropt should be anxious to move on this — after all, the IPO depended on it.

"He's not available until Monday," Vishal said.

"That's a little late," Joe growled. "They want the opinion Tuesday. How about any written materials? Design specs, manuals?"

"Nope and nope," Vishal said. "They say they haven't written any yet, they've been too busy working on the design."

"Oh for heaven's sake, they must have something written down," Joe said.

Vishal just shrugged.

"Did you say there was something I should see?" Joe asked.

"Gage Booth sent over his admin with the patent application files," Vishal said grimly. "I think you'd better see her."

"Why?" Joe asked. "What's up?"

"You'll see," Vishal said, turning to leave. "She's in a conference room. I'd bring her in here, but she might be overwhelmed by your artwork."

Joe got up and followed Vishal. He didn't know what Vishal meant about the artwork, but he had given up on trying to figure out what made Vishal tick. He refused to take the bait and look at his art. He would deny Vishal the satisfaction of thinking he was second-guessing his taste.

When they walked into the conference room the admin had her back to the door, looking out the window. She was wearing a black skirt that clung to her firm rear end and was slit just a little too high. Her stockings were black, with a subtle, white flower pattern.

"Alicia?" Vishal said.

"I was just looking at your view," Alicia said in a soft, husky voice, turning around leisurely. A stunning profile revealed itself midway through her turn. Her long, brunette hair fell to bounce lightly on her shoulders, with a few curls dangling on the sides of her face. She was wearing a half-sheer white blouse that revealed the top of a lacy bra straining to hold in huge breasts. A black vest covered the rest. She flashed a smile that radiated warmth.

"You must be Joe," Alicia said, extending her hand.

"That's right," Joe said, taking her hand.

She clasped both hands around Joe's, her eyes sparkling as they engaged Joe's. "I'm Alicia Conrath, and I'm looking forward to working with you. Gage — I mean, Mr. Booth — told me about you and your firm. I think this technical work you guys do is fascinating."

"Alicia brought over the file histories for the Neuropt patents," Vishal said, pointing to a pile of files on the table. "We were just going over the product specs and other things we'd need from Neuropt. She's going to help us get them."

Alicia was still grasping Joe's hand, tenderly caressing the nub of his ring finger. It was gone from just below where the second knuckle should be.

"I heard you lost that finger in the Gulf War," Vishal said, putting his hand to his mouth to cover a grin. "Something about a knife fight?"

"A friend closed a car door on it when I was a kid," Joe explained.

"I guess no one can tell if you're married or not," Alicia said. "Since there is no place to put the ring."

"Married," Joe quickly clarified. "Can you get us an appointment with Harold Walsh today or tomorrow?"

"Walsh is pretty busy," Alicia said, letting go of Joe's hand. "But I'll try. Mr. Booth wanted me to help you with any clerical work you need done. He said he doesn't want to see you charging him for paralegals doing things that I could do."

"You wouldn't happen to know anything about how the Optospine works, would you?" Joe asked, leafing through one of the files.

Alicia backed a chair far away from the table, sat down and leisurely crossed her legs. "I know it uses a neural network, and I know that is a computer modeled after the human brain. But I don't know how a neural network works. Do you?"

"Do you know how a standard digital computer works?" Joe asked. "With a processor fetching instructions from a memory where they are stored, executing the instructions, and putting the results into another part of memory?"

"Uh, sort of," Alicia said, tugging down in vain on her skirt, smoothing it across the top of her thighs with the palm of her hand, dragging Joe's eyes along.

"Well, a neural network works nothing like that," Joe said.

Alicia smiled. Vishal groaned.

"In the brain," Joe continued, "we have millions of neurons which are all interconnected. All of our senses — sight, hearing, touch, etcetera — are formed with neuron chains that are interconnected and extend into the brain. When we sense something, the brain remembers the *pattern* of the neurons that fired. Whenever we sense the same thing, or something similar, the same pattern of neurons is excited, strengthening the interconnections forming that pattern, and thus strengthening that memory."

"This is not intuitively obvious," Alicia said, putting one elbow on the desk and leaning forward, chin in hand, so that her blouse hung forward, exposing the top of her breasts and bra. "But keep going, maybe I'll catch on."

"The concept of the neural network computer is the same," Joe continued, uncomfortably aware of Alicia staring at him as his eyes were drawn to the top of her blouse. "Instead of storing data in a memory that has to be addressed to retrieve that data," Joe continued, looking away, "the *memory* is the pattern of interconnections within an array of nodes. Each time a node receives an input, it increases the amplification of the signal output to the other nodes to which it is connected. This mimics the action of a neuron. There is no separate memory in a neural computer. Instead of storing data in a memory, you train the array to respond to certain patterns."

"How can you store data without a memory?" Alicia asked, looking down at the top of her blouse and belatedly giving it a little tug.

"This is where I'm a little fuzzy," Joe admitted with a clearing of his throat, wondering if she knew that her tug had exposed more of her breasts, not less. "As I understand it, you don't read the contents of the memory in the classic sense — that is, you don't get an output of the stored pattern of interconnections. But if you apply the same input that generated the pattern, you'll get an output signal that will be different than the output you'll get if you apply a different input. And that distinct output will be the same every time you apply that input. You just have to remember which output applies to which input."

Alicia was staring at him blankly.

"Well," Joe paused. "All you need to know is that it works like the brain and it's good for image recognition. Other typical uses are tasks where comparisons of patterns are important, such as speech recognition, detection of possible fraudulent credit card transactions by buying pattern variations, etcetera."

Joe wondered how he ended up giving information instead of getting it. "Can you find us any written description of the Optospine? Draft specifications, notes, figures, anything."

"Sure," Alicia said, pulling out her cell phone. "I'll get right on it. I'll make some phone calls. Let me know if you need anything else. Mr. Booth wants me to be at your disposal."

"Thanks, Joe said. "Can you also see if Neuropt has gotten any letters accusing them of infringement? Neuropt doesn't have a product yet, so this is unlikely, but sometimes these patent owners are aggressive. In particular, I know that Royaltec claims to have a patent on a neural network, and has been sending out threatening letters to a lot of companies."

Alicia smiled. "You want me to check if Gage sent a letter to himself?"

"I'm just being thorough," Joe said.

"Or anal," Vishal added.

Joe stared at her as she turned to the window and started talking on the phone. He couldn't put his finger on it, but something didn't seem quite right.

———————

Meanwhile, Zenko was slouched in his leather chair, running his hand along the smooth armrest. He started to call A.J. then hung up. Max had told him to stop work for Telekinetics, that he needed to be generating collections — now. Max had even told him to help other partners on their cases as second chair (second in command) instead of trying his own cases as first chair. Zenko cringed — that would be like death.

Zenko moved his hand across his clutter-free desk. Other than the receivables report, the only items on his desk were a notepad, his golf trophy and an 8 by 10 of his wife. She looked stunning in the slinky dress she was wearing, and had a mischievous smile. Too bad she didn't look like that anymore. And she seemed to have lost her cheerfulness with her battle against weight. Zenko found it hard to feign attraction anymore — with the loss of her figure the mask over their other differences vanished as well. It was mostly the kids who kept them together, and they were almost ready for college. Zenko spent most weeknights at his condo in Palo Alto, rather than their home in San Francisco. Ostensibly, it was because he had to work late.

The phone rang. It was A.J. from Telekinetics. "We need an appeal filed ASAP so we have some leverage in settlement negotiations," A.J. said. "Have you got a draft yet?"

Zenko cleared his throat. "My managing partner won't let me work for you anymore unless we get paid."

"Look," A.J. said, "you lost a case you said was a slam-dunk. Now you want to abandon us? No way. If you don't file an appeal for us, we'll sue you for malpractice."

"There was no malpractice," Zenko said. "The jury just screwed up. Companies often have to go to an appeal to get justice. I explained that possibility at the beginning."

"Yeah, but we should have gotten to the appeal about a million dollars ago," A.J. said. "And you said it was a remote possibility."

"There's no malpractice, and you know it," Zenko said.

"It doesn't matter what I know," A.J. said. "It's about how much money you'd have to spend defending a malpractice charge. It's about the affect of such a charge on your reputation, right after losing a case. It's about how many other clients you'd be able to attract when they hear about the malpractice charge. It's about whom a jury would side with in a malpractice suit — someone like them, or the attorneys. I hate to be so blunt, but I have to do what it takes to protect the Retinal Screen. Think about it."

A.J. hung up before Zenko could reply.

Zenko opened the drawer and looked at the bottle of Sake next to a bottle of Johnnie Walker Black Label Scotch Whiskey. The sake was the finest, reputably made from rice chewed on by virgins. He pulled out the whiskey. After slowly untwisting the cap, he gently tilted the bottle to fill a shot glass. He waved the glass under his nose, inhaling slowly. He opened a bottle of Effexor anti-depressant pills, tossed a couple in his mouth, and sipped the whiskey with his eyes closed. Then he called Max to give him the bad news about A.J.'s threat. Max said A.J. was bluffing, and he would call her on it. It didn't matter anyway if she sued them for malpractice, because if they kept working for Telekinetics, they'd go out of business before the malpractice trial. The firm at least had a chance with paying clients. Max said he'd send Trevor West to talk to Zenko.

Zenko still couldn't believe it. Two losses in a row. After years of nothing but victories, he lost a case last year when one of his witnesses changed his story on the stand. It wasn't his fault, but all anyone remembered was that he lost the case. Since then, he had been forced to scramble for litigation clients in the last year. He wasn't able to attract top clients; his reputation seemed to only go as far as his last case, even though his record was 25-1. Well, 25-2 now. Although he had gotten a number of smaller clients with good cases, they all had trouble keeping up with the bills. In previous years he wouldn't have taken them on because of their shaky finances, but he needed the work this year. They would pay when he won the cases — the firm just needed to hang on.

Zenko set the glass down and picked up the receivables report. Telekinetics was his biggest client. Max's main complaint was the costs advanced. In addition to the firm not collecting on its fees from his clients, they were paying out of the partner's pockets for a variety of services — everything from expert witness and consultant fees, to deposition transcript fees, copying, and travel costs.

Half an hour later there was a knock at the door, and he quickly put the whiskey back before partners West and Ferguson walked in. "Can we have a minute, Zenko?" West asked.

"Sure," Zenko said, rising, giving a short bow out of habit and pointing to the guest chairs. He couldn't put his finger on the connection between these two, but it made him uneasy. Were they both on the same case? What was it?

"Sorry about the verdict, Zenko," Trevor said, still standing. "That was a bad break."

"Yes," Zenko said, studying their eyes. "We should have won. And we will. There's no way it would stand up on appeal. As Buddha said, wisdom is ofttimes nearer when we stoop than when we soar."

While West slowly sat down, Zenko fidgeted with his pen, trying to project outer nonchalance. As Ferguson turned back to close the door, Zenko realized what the connection was between the two — they were both on the Partner Compensation Committee.

"We'll get right to the point," West said, leaning forward in his chair as Ferguson was sitting down. "At the Executive Committee's request, the Compensation Committee has met to make some adjustments before year end. Emergency adjustments, so to speak. We're dropping you 5 levels, Zenko. Effective immediately. Sorry to lay this on you so suddenly, but you know the state of the firm."

Zenko swallowed slowly. 5 levels! That would put him one level below an entry-level partner! Just like that he went from making over a million dollars to just one hundred thousand. Was he being forced out of the firm? Could this really be happening after 15 mostly successful years, including getting listed in California

Lawyer Magazine as one of the top 10 litigators in the state?

"What happened to averaging collections over 3 years?" Zenko asked. "And all my years of service to the firm? My reputation? Surely these count for something? My 25-2 record is still better than anyone else's."

"Your reputation isn't what it used to be," West said. "And you've talked to Max — we can't afford to gradually adjust. The firm is in trouble, and we need significant steps now."

"Oh, for Christ's sake," Zenko said. "That's like trying to cut expenses at a retail store by tossing out all the inventory simply because sales were slow one day."

"You might as well hear the rest of it now," Ferguson added. "We're also reassigning the three associates working on your cases."

"But I only have part of their time anyway," Zenko protested. "Why? Why are you doing this?"

Zenko's stomach knotted up. This was practically a deathblow to his cases. He was vastly undermanned with only one associate on each case as it was. The opposing counsel in each case had at least two partners and half a dozen associates.

"Well," West explained, "we think you should find a way to disengage Telekinetics, and drop your other cases, but we're not going to force you to since you're a partner. The clients can't pay, Zenko, so you're using associates for non-paying work. We need to have them on paying clients. If you want to continue pro-bono for those guys, that's your business, but no forced pro-bono with our associates. Once you get your collections back up, we can reconsider your level. In the meantime, Alex Yurkowski needs some help on one of his cases; I suggest you work with him."

"You want me to become the assistant of a junior partner?" Zenko said.

"It doesn't matter to me," West said. "It depends on how much you want to get paid."

After Ferguson and West left, Zenko opened a locked drawer and pulled out his tanto dagger — allegedly actually used by an ancient Samurai to commit hara kiri. He turned it in his hand for a moment, put it aside and stared at the revolver in the drawer.

———

A few minutes later, Joe entered Zenko's office and closed the door behind him.

"Are you working on the Telekinetics appeal?" Joe asked.

"Nile-san, there is nothing I'd rather do, believe me," Zenko said, closing the drawer. "But Max told me not to work for them until they pay."

"He told me the same thing," Joe said. "But we both know people are dying each day the Retinal Screen is enjoined from shipping to Brazil. We'll do it under the radar. Don't tell anyone you're working on this. I'll draft some arguments for the appeal. I just need you to present it in court."

"I just can't," Zenko said. "Your work could be under the radar, but a court appearance by me will be noticed."

"I can't do it without you," Joe said. "I'm taking a big risk. My partnership is on the line if I get caught," Joe said.

"So is mine," Zenko said.

"Somehow, I thought you had more honor than that," Joe said.

Zenko sat up ramrod straight in his chair.

Two hours later, Joe e-mailed his arguments for an appeal of the Telekinetics verdict to Zenko and joined Vishal in the conference room. Alicia had left already. After another hour of going through the applications and doing research on the Internet, Vishal and Joe both put down the files.

"We're getting nowhere," Joe said. "When are they going to call back and set up an earlier meeting with their chief engineer? Should we e-mail again?"

"We've e-mailed twice and left messages twice," Vishal said. "Not to mention e-mailing and calling Ned Stern. I've asked Alicia, but she said we'd have better luck calling than she would. I think we just have to wait."

"We don't have time to wait," Joe said, tapping his fingers. "I'd like to say we'll give a negative opinion unless Walsh meets with us now, but they'll complain to Max. I don't need that before the partnership vote."

"OK, let's go over what we do know," Joe said. "I guess we learned a little about the Optospine — tell me if you agree with this. Sensors are to be mounted around the head, and could be in an ordinary hat to disguise them. The sensors would be wirelessly connected to a pager-sized device on the user's belt. This device on the belt is to contain the neural network processor and other electronics. It would transmit signals to electrodes implanted in the user's legs. This is also to be done wirelessly, on a different frequency."

"That's right," Vishal said.

"The sensors will supposedly detect the brain neuron activity pattern when the person thinks about moving a leg. The neural network processor will compare this pattern to all of its different stored patterns. An output corresponding to the match would control which of the imbedded electrodes is activated. Because the neural net is made of optical components, it will literally operate at light speed. And that's about all we know. Did I leave anything out?"

Vishal shook his head. "No."

"Okay," Joe said, leafing through a Neuropt application. "Let's start at the beginning. To make this work, they need sensors. What do they have?"

"Why are you worried about whether it will work?" Vishal asked. "We just need to opine on whether they'll get patents, or infringe someone else's patents."

"Have you forgotten we opine on a prospectus that says they'll ship in 6 months?" Joe asked. "Besides, I'm curious."

Vishal sighed. "The overall system application simply said they could use any number of commercially available sensors, such as an MRI or EEG. But there were no details."

"Doesn't an MRI require putting the patient in a huge machine and taking a half hour for the scan?" Joe asked.

"As far as I know," Vishal said. "The same goes for the EEG. I don't think normal EEGs are sensitive enough to pick up anything more than a general state of the brain, not signals to move a leg."

Joe pushed the Neuropt application aside and stared out the window. It was becoming apparent that the new sensors were a key part of the Neuropt design. Yet he hadn't seen any detail in any Neuropt materials on the sensor design. Not the patent applications, not the prospectus. Although the Optospine sounded feasible to a layperson, Joe had been an engineer himself, and he couldn't see how the Optospine could possibly function. How was Neuropt going to make this work?

Joe stood up and put on his coat.

"Where are you going?" Vishal asked.

"To do some research on sensors," Joe said. "You keep working on the rest of the system."

A few minutes later Joe walked across the parking lot to the entrance to the Rose and Crown bar. He looked up at the façade. It was very exotic — a second floor balcony with ivy vines twisting their way up to it, suspended flower boxes with colorful flowers in bloom, and windows with white shutters opened against the wall. There was only one problem — it was just a painted scene on the bare stucco wall.

"Jesus, Joe, you're late again!" Hank's voice boomed from somewhere in the back as Joe eased past the crowded bar. "Wendy," Hank called out to the waitress as Joe approached, "this round's on Joe."

The TV at the bar was showing the video clip of Grito shaking from the virus. They had apparently slapped together a documentary on Grito's career as an excuse to continually repeat the shocking clip, interspersed with video of crying fans.

Joe nodded to the group as Hank pulled out a chair for Joe. He didn't have time for the Thursday night get-together at the bar, but Hank should know what types of sensors were available. Hank had held all types of odd jobs, some of questionable legality. Hank was currently consulting for medical equipment giant Healthtronics, having somehow convinced them he was a marketing expert. The others thought Hank was a con artist, but put up with him because he was Joe's friend. He was certainly a master bullshitter.

"Hank, I was hoping you could help me with . . .," Joe said.

"In a minute," Hank interrupted, pushing Joe down into the chair. "I have something to show you first. This is important."

Hank hadn't changed much since college days, when he first got the nickname Hanker because he would hanker after so many things — cars, women, you name it. Becoming a manager hadn't curbed his childish ways. Joe looked around the table. It was mostly associates from Turner, West. Zenko, the only partner there, was at the end of the table. Joe had hoped Zenko would be working on Telekinetics, but instead he was getting drunk.

"It looks like every group in your firm is represented now," Hank said. "We only had lizards and bio-phds before, but now we've got a chiper!"

Joe looked around. He was the only one from the electronics group there — nicknamed chipers by the associates because they dealt with semiconductor chips. He was proud to have come up with the name "bio-phds" for the Biotechnology group — a reference to biology and the fact that many of them had PhDs. He wasn't sure who came up with lizards — he believed it came from "gator" being part of litigator, and a gator being a big lizard. It seemed to fit the sliminess and reptilian nature of many litigators.

"We're playing Liar's Dice," Zenko shouted from the other side of the table with a heavy slur. "Wanna join?"

"Hanker!" Wendy shouted from the bar. "Don't let another attorney join. They have an unfair advantage at Liar's Dice."

"Very funny," Joe shouted back. "Keep working on that tip, Wendy."

"I thought you liked to pay for abuse?" Wendy hollered.

"Okay, Joe," Hanker said, pushing a spreadsheet across the table to Joe, "here's the plan. We all chip in and buy this house and the mineral rights to a nearby plot. It's in the gold country on the way to Lake Tahoe. We'll use it as a combination business venture and vacation home. We'll pan for gold occasionally, or just hang out at the cabin, or go fishing. We can deduct all sorts of stuff since it's a business venture. My contribution will be mostly putting this together and managing it."

Joe shook and rolled his dice, then looked at the spreadsheet. It didn't list Hank's financial contribution, probably because he thought he could get away without making one. It not only listed the property, but a boat, mountain bikes, windsurfer, skis — the list went on and on. "What's all this other stuff?" Joe asked. "Is it on a lake?"

"Amenities, Joe," Hanker said, grabbing Joe by both shoulders and giving him a shake. "Amenities. Ya gotta have the amenities. There's a lake a half-mile away. It's perfect."

"Three fours," Zenko said, announcing his claimed roll of the dice.

"I don't know," Joe said, tilting his cup back to look at his dice. "I mean, how often would we use this? Why not just rent a place for the few times a year we want to go up? It's gotta be cheaper. Three fives."

"Wrong, wrong, wrong," Hanker said. "Look at the spreadsheet. It's a bargain. And you'll go up more if you don't have to hassle renting each time. You can just go. It'll always be there. Look, the others were skeptical at first too, but I've got them convinced now."

Joe glanced up. The others were shaking their heads "no."

Hank looked at his dice. "Four fives."

"Hank," Joe said, "are there any sensors available today that can detect brain activity accurately enough to know what muscle the brain is trying to move? Like an EEG or MRI?"

Hank looked at Joe carefully. "Do you even know what an EEG is?"

Joe nodded. EEG stood for Electroencephalography. It used electrodes on the scalp to detect different brain waves — alpha waves indicating relaxation, beta waves produced during REM (rapid eye movement) sleep.

"Well," Hank said, "in that case you should know they just detect alpha or beta waves. That's enough to tell if someone is relaxed or stressed, but not if they're moving a muscle. An MRI won't do that either. They're working on advancements and combinations, but no one is anywhere near close to that level of detection as far as I know."

"Call," said the bio-phd next to Hank. Hank reached under his cup and tossed a die into the middle of the table, and everyone shook their dice again.

"How about making the sensors small enough to be portable," Joe said, frowning at his dice, and then smiling at Hank. "Four fours."

"An EEG, sure," Hank said, tapping his fingers as he studied his dice. "But an MRI machine is huge. I don't know of anyone working on miniaturization. Four fives."

"None of my clients are," piped in a bio-phd, Andrea Whitaker, PhD. "They're all working on a cure for the virus. This whole virus thing has also raised awareness of other possible diseases that may get out of control, so everyone figures the potential for profits has gone through the roof. At least since there is a threat of the virus coming to the US, where the profits are to be made, unlike Brazil."

"Well," Zenko slurred, "to be fair, someone might be working on miniaturization even though there aren't the same profits. They could be keeping it secret."

Joe twisted his face into an expression of shock. "A lizard being fair?"

"Yeah," Zenko replied. "I see your point. That's like a chiper writing something that is intelligible to a normal human being."

"You give us too much credit," Joe said. "The biophds have a monopoly on that — we don't even come close."

"Hey," said Andrea. "At least our clients don't throw their portfolios around and extort money from everyone in the business like the big electronics companies."

"Uh-huh," Joe said. "But in electronics, companies at least license their patents. They don't freeze out competition to prop up outrageous drug prices."

"What B.S.!" Andrea said. "Years of research are required for biotech. And many of the projects fail, or don't get FDA approval. So all of that needs to be covered by profits on the few successful ones. Unlike computers, where you guys patent vaporware that hasn't been built yet. How much can that cost? Minimum wage for a teenager for a weekend?"

"What do you mean, cover by profits?" Joe asked, making his way toward Zenko. "They don't seem to have trouble raising tons of money in IPOs. Investors seem willing to throw money their way without knowing if it will be successful."

"The only reason investors throw money their way," Andrea slowly spoke, as if to a dense child, "is because they can charge a lot and make a lot of money."

"Huh?" Wendy said. "They can raise a lot of money because they can make a lot of money? Why do they need to raise money?"

"It takes money to make money," Hank said.

"Zenko," Joe whispered, sitting down next to Zenko, "About the Telekinetics appeal, have you . . ."

Zenko leaned over and threw up on Joe's shoes.

7.

Erika pressed the send button the next morning, Friday. Well, that project was done. She closed her eyes and smelled her flowers. They were still pungent. She looked at them and noticed that two were dying already. She pulled them out and threw them in the trash.

She looked around nervously, biting at her fingernails, then opened her drawer and pulled some papers out. She had enough work to do; she knew she shouldn't be dabbling in this. But she couldn't stand the idea of the firm falling apart. She was apprehensive about looking for another job; she didn't think other places would give her the same flexibility in hours she had at Turner, West. The top paper was a report from accounting. She had asked her friend in accounting to check the accounts of all the clients referred by Peterson, Malone in the last year. Almost all of them were significantly behind on their payments.

Sidney had just called her back with news from his friend, a secretary at the Peterson, Malone law firm. Erika had asked Sidney to call his friend after Zenko came by Erika's cubicle this morning to complain. He had lost a beauty contest — the sales presentation to a potential client for a new lawsuit — to Peterson. Her hunch paid off. Sidney's friend had opened up about how they got the case, since Sidney appeared to know about it anyway. The Peterson attorney falsely claimed that Turner, West only had two litigators who had ever tried a patent case, that they usually tried to settle, and that Zenko hadn't won in years and had a losing record.

She decided to use this as an excuse to talk to Joe. Joe had barely looked up by the time Erika had walked around his desk and stood right next to his chair, picking up a Neuropt patent application on his desk. She sat on the corner of Joe's desk, running her hand along the smooth edge.

"Nice looking admin your new client sent over," Erika said.

"You saw her?" Joe asked. "Now that you mention it, yeah, I guess she wasn't too bad looking."

"There's something not right about her," Erika said. "She looks more like a stripper than an admin. I'd watch out for her — she's up to something. I'd be careful what I say around her if I were you."

"I already figured on that," Joe said.

She didn't believe him, and was annoyed that he was trying to pretend he was suspicious like her.

"So how's Sandra?" Erika asked, leaping back to her feet, and shifting from one foot to the other.

"Fine," Joe said. "She'll be better after I make partner today. How's Ray?"

"Fine," Erika said, sitting back down.

"I'm jealous," Joe said. "I see he sent you flowers again. It must be nice to have such an attentive husband."

"Yeah," Erika said, looking away to resist the tears that wanted to well up in her eyes.

She quickly changed the subject and explained what she had found out about the Peterson, Malone competition — the bad-mouthing at the beauty contest, referring financially troubled clients, the suspicious referral to Turner. This followed another tid-bit she had discovered this morning. She knew the work from Federated Semi-conductor had fallen to a trickle in the last few months. One of the litigation case clerks was a soccer mom friend of the wife of an in-house attorney at Federated. The case clerk found out that Peterson was having attorneys give free presentations about patent law to Federated. They also sent an attorney down there once a month, at no charge, to talk with inventors about possible inventions.

The Peterson firm must figure that if they did that for free, they would get the paying patent application and other work. It appeared to be working. Erika would have normally dismissed that as a normal, aggressive business generation technique. But she knew Peterson usually charged through the nose, and would normally not do anything for free. But for some reason, this particular client was made an exception.

"I think they're trying to ruin our firm," Erika said.

"That does sound odd," Joe said. "Maybe they figure we're their toughest competitor and have targeted us?"

"Do you think Klein would listen to me?" Erika asked, carefully watching his face. She knew Joe often didn't say everything he thought, trying to be diplomatic. But his face usually gave him away.

"Sure," Joe said. "I think you should talk to him. Even if it's not a conspiracy against us by Peterson, he should know about this stuff so it can be dealt with."

Joe crinkled his forehead. He didn't believe it.

"You don't think it's a conspiracy," Erika said, drumming her fingers on Joe's desk.

"Well," Joe replied, "they did just refer the Neuropt work. And that can't be a bad AR risk since Peterson is also doing a lot of work for Neuropt."

He had a point. If Peterson were also working on Neuropt, the Account Receivable (AR) must be collectable. Was she wasting her time? Was she seeing things? "You just don't believe it because it's coming from a woman," Erika teased.

"No, no," Joe said. "I don't believe it because it's coming from a *beautiful* woman."

"Hmmm," Erika said.

"What?" Joe said.

"I'm trying to decide whether to scold or thank you," she said. She walked out, stopping to pat the wall near the picture frame. "Nice painting, Joe. This one is much more appropriate for your office than the others."

She paused long enough to see Joe's eyes widen in realization as he looked at the painting, then scurried away to dodge the rubber-band that came flying from Joe.

She sat back down at her cubicle, wondering if Joe was right. Well, just in case, she decided to start sending out her resume.

———

A little later that morning, Max Klein was adjusting his tie while looking at his self-image in the corner of the screen. He was uneasy about the rumors that some partners were about to bail out of the firm. This client trip to L.A. forced him to participate in the partner meeting by videoconference from his hotel room. It seemed strange — the client had insisted he dress casual. But he went back to his hotel room to put on a suit and tie for the partner meeting. Most of the partners didn't wear suits anymore, unless they were going to court or meeting a new client. But Max wanted to project an image of professionalism as managing partner, especially in view of the content of the presentation he was about to give.

Max presented the dismal financial results for last month. In addition to the video, back in the Turner, West conference room the PowerPoint slides were being projected on a screen. The bottom line was that there wasn't even enough profit for the normal minimal monthly distribution to the partners, and there would be no quarterly distribution at all.

It wouldn't take much to push the firm over the edge. Max had seen some other patent firms crumble with much better finances — the psyche of a firm was more important. All it took was a couple of key partners deciding the future was iffy and leaving. It would start a crisis of confidence with a resulting race to the door. Even the Brobeck mega-firm had managed to disintegrate with amazing speed.

Turner spoke first, breaking the long silence after Max's presentation.

"Well," Turner said, "I think we should suspend partner distributions until we get our house in order."

Max leaned back and waited for the onslaught from the younger partners. Turner was out of touch — maybe he would get an education today.

"Some of us have high mortgages to pay," piped up one of the younger partners, whom Max noted had lost their fear of publicly opposing Turner. "We just bought houses recently, at high prices. You bought a long time ago, at a low price. You've also had a long time to put money away, and don't have young children in school.

So I have a better idea — lets leave the lowest draw for the young partners unchanged, and cut the draws of the more senior partners to the same level as the junior partners until we get our house in order."

Max knew that was unworkable. The partners who were paid more were worth it — other firms would pay them that much more, and Turner, West had to pay market rates. Otherwise, they'd leave, with their clients, and the firm would be even worse off.

Max could see in the video the portraits on the wall behind Turner — portraits of all the previous managing partners. He didn't like the associates' nickname for the conference room. They called it the Mug room, a disrespectful reference to the portraits as mugs. The portraits went back 75 years, and there were 12 painted portraits on the wall. Soon, his would be added. He had just made an appointment to pose for the portrait in a few weeks. It had been suggested to use a photograph, but he liked the tradition of a painted portrait.

Max's cell phone rang. He put the video on mute, and took the call from his client.

"You're already being paid an ungodly amount," Turner was saying. "What are you doing with your money?" Turner asked. "Obviously spending it all on expensive homes and cars and vacations when you should have been saving."

"Jesus!" said one young partner. "Let me give you a reality check. I have interviewed at several other firms recently, and I can tell you I'm not the only partner who has done this."

So there it was, Max thought, looking up at the screen. It was out in the open now. He had heard rumors, but didn't want to believe them.

"A number of them are willing to guarantee $300,000 a year," the partner continued. "So we can quit arguing over what's a lot of money. That is simply the going rate for a new partner."

"That's the problem with you young partners," Turner said, "you have no loyalty — if things get tough, you're willing to leave at the drop of a hat. You're clearly in it just for the money."

"Everyone works for money," Max broke in, after putting his client on hold. "We all love the law and this firm, but we have to feed and clothe our families. We need to pay competitively if we want to remain in business. I propose we cut the amount of money we distribute until we get caught up on our collections. But I would insist on a minimum floor of $10,000, even if we have to borrow. We simply have to continue paying our partners."

"But that's less than our youngest associates make," said one of the younger partners. "And now we'll have to split profits with Joe Nile as well."

"It's only temporary, for a few months," Max said. "By the end of the year, everyone will have made much more than the highest paid associate, I'm sure. As for Nile, we're not going to vote on him for partner. We can't afford another partner at this time. We need to wait until next year when our finances are back to normal. But don't anyone tell Joe that finances were the reason. We can't have associates panicking and leaving. We clearly need most of them."

Max noticed a commotion on the screen, and saw a broadly smiling Trevor West walking in. "Sorry I'm late," Trevor said. "I was waiting for the jury verdict. We won!"

Max let out a breath and relaxed. He saw the partners change their mood instantly and actually applaud Trevor. This meant another feather in the firm's cap, enhancing its litigation reputation. More importantly, the sizable receivable the client had built up would be paid.

"Hey Trevor," a partner called out, "why couldn't you have stretched out the trial? Now we'll probably have to lay-off the two associates you had working with you since we don't have new work for them to do." Max knew the partner was only half-joking. A number of the partners started worriedly nodding. It was ironic that such a victory for the client could be disaster for the firm.

"Don't worry," Trevor said. "Just because we got a verdict from the jury doesn't mean its over. Those associates will be busy for a few months fighting the inevitable post-trial motions to set aside the verdict, followed by the appeal after the judge denies the post-trial motions." The partners murmured among themselves, relaxing.

"The down side of that," Trevor continued, "is that we won't get paid until we win the appeal. It turns out our client has been late paying not because they wanted to see how the trial turned out, but they simply don't have the money. But at least the judgment will be bonded, so we will be certain to collect when we win, with interest."

Max saw the partners tense again. He knew it could be quite a while before they saw any money, and the associates working on the case wouldn't be generating any collections for a while. It was because of the potential for endless appeals, in addition to a chance that the appeals court would reverse, that lawsuits sometimes settled *after* the trial was won.

"Trevor," Max said, "settle that suit any way you can."

A few moments later, at the Turner, West offices, Sidney was knocking on the wall next to the door of Joe's office. "Joe, the partner meeting is over. Mr. Klein wants to see you."

"I thought he was in L.A.?" Joe said.

"He is," Sidney said. "He's on the video link in the conference room."

Joe crossed his fingers on both hands as he made his way to the conference room. He saw the last two partners leave the room. They glanced at him, and Joe smiled, hoping for congratulations. But instead, they quickly looked the other way and walked away.

Joe grimaced as he entered the room. Max was on the screen, talking on his cell phone, but waved Joe in.

After a few minutes Max hung up. "I'm sorry Joe, but we decided not to make you partner this year. The partners just didn't feel you were quite ready. It was close. You need just a little more seasoning. Next year should be a shoe-in."

Joe felt like his breath had been sucked out of him. Worrying about it was one thing; hearing it was another. This couldn't be happening again.

He finally forced his vocal cords to work. "But that's what you told me last year. You said you'd push for me. What happened?"

"I did push for you," Max said, "but even though I'm now the managing partner, I still have only one vote. The fact that you weren't able to collect from Telekinetics didn't help."

Joe couldn't shake the feeling that this was a dream. His heart was in his stomach. He prayed that Max couldn't see the sweat he felt beading up on his forehead.

Max droned on for a few minutes, reciting the requirements for partnership and suggesting Joe work on all of them. Joe only half heard him.

"I'm afraid I don't have a lot of time to discuss this now," Max ended. "I have a meeting I have to go to. Perhaps you can talk to one of the other partners."

Joe got up and walked out into the hall in a daze. He wondered if anyone other than the partners knew yet. He could tell by the looks of pity he encountered that they did.

He sneaked past a group of associates near his office and closed the door. He picked up the picture on his desk. What would they think?

"Sorry about the vote," Sidney said, cracking open the door. "I guess it's going to be hard to tell your parents, huh?"

"Harder than you know," Joe said. Sidney hesitated, as if about to say something, and headed back to his cubicle.

Another year before partnership. Maybe. Joe put the picture face down and slid his elbows onto the table, his head folding down on top of his arms. After a few moments, he shifted his head, lifting it with some effort onto his folded hands. He picked up his firm mug and slowly swirled the last drops of cold coffee.

He shakily got to his feet, the self-pity turning to anger, and flung the mug against the wall. It shattered and left coffee staining the wall. Sitting back down, he looked at his hands, which were convulsing as if around someone's neck. He took a deep breath and tried to will the rage to leave his body. This wouldn't do him any good. He had to keep his poise and figure out what to do. Tomorrow he would think about it. Today, he had work to finish. He picked up the phone to call Sandra, but decided to wait until he got home to tell her.

———————

Joe paused after he put the key in the door to his apartment that night. He wasn't looking forward to telling Sandra he didn't make partner. He had been rehearsing what he'd say all afternoon. His stomach was in knots when he opened the door. Something seemed amiss. He noticed the large Post-it on the wall in front of him.

"I can't believe you didn't call — I had to call your secretary to find out you didn't make partner — again. I'm tired of waiting, and I'm not going to put up with another year of your not being here, just to have you not make partner a 3rd time. I'm not putting my life on hold anymore for you. You're on your own."

Joe crumpled the note in his hand as he walked into the living room. At that point he realized what was amiss — there was no furniture. She had taken it all. He walked into the bedroom, the bathroom and the kitchen. Everything was gone. The pots and pans and dishes were gone. All that was left were his clothes, his personal stuff and his computer — sitting on the floor. She'd left him one towel and one washcloth. Not even a pillow or blanket was left. The partner vote was just hours ago — how did she get movers to show up so fast?

He folded up a jacket for a pillow, grabbed his bathrobe for a blanket, and lay down on the floor to sleep. But he couldn't sleep despite how tired he was. He felt empty inside. Things had been rocky with Sandra, and he was angry that she had just screwed him over, but he still missed her. Was this really the way it was all going to end?

The next morning at the Turner, West offices, Erika walked up to Max Klein's office. She was annoyed at having to come in on a Saturday, but at least it improved her chances of being able to talk to Max without fighting her way past his secretary. Plus, Max had left her a message asking for a D&B, so she knew he'd make time to talk about that. Just as she stepped in the open door, Max flung a book toward her. It smacked the wall right next to the door.

"Dammit!" He shouted.

She stood tentatively in the doorway, shifting from one leg to the other.

"Uh, perhaps I should come back later?" Erika asked.

"No, no," Max said, circling his hand to wave her in and forcing a smile. "It's okay."

Erika guessed he had just seen Turner's conflict memo. Demodex had sued Max's client Modem Solutions yesterday. Modem Solutions was a solid client that would have no trouble paying the bills. Max had sent an e-mail to Erika that morning asking her to do a Dunn & Bradstreet report on Demodex, starting the information-gathering process. But since Turner had filed the application for Demodex yesterday, Demodex was already a new client, and the firm couldn't be defense counsel for Modem Solutions in the lawsuit by Demodex.

"I just discovered that we've been conflicted out of the case I left you a message on," Max groaned. "And it could have been avoided. So I guess you don't need to do the D&B."

"Too late," Erika said, holding up one of the two binders in her hands. She hadn't moved from the doorway.

"Please, sit down." Max gestured at the chair.

"It's the D&B on Demodex you asked for," Erika said as she glided into the chair. "I also did one for Modem Solutions. I figured you'd want to check to see if your own client can afford this litigation."

Max smiled. "You have better business sense than most of the attorneys."

"I saw Turner's conflict memo," Erika continued, while twirling a lock of her hair around her finger, "but I thought you might make Turner drop the client. I know there's a hot potato rule that says it can still be a conflict if you drop one client to take on someone adverse, but I know the rule is fuzzy and thought you might want to risk it. So I did the reports anyway. I also printed out the web pages for both companies, and pulled up a few articles. They're all indexed and tabbed."

Max leafed through the binder Erika gave him, nodding and smiling. Erika could tell he was pleased. Max looked over at the second binder Erika had on her lap.

"Max, I know you're busy," Erika said, rapidly tapping a finger on the binder. "But I thought you should know about something."

Max smiled. Erika knew he like everyone to call him Max instead of Mr. Klein. She guessed it not only seemed friendlier; it made him feel younger. She imagined he especially liked the familiarity coming from a young woman.

"Shoot," Max said as he leaned forward.

Erika pulled her chair closer to his desk, opening the binder on top of the papers cluttering Max's desk. She opened it to the first tab from her upside down viewpoint. It was an overdue accounts receivable report with nearly half of the clients highlighted in pink.

"The highlighted clients are referrals from Peterson in the last year," Erika said. "As you can see, over half of our major AR problems are due to Peterson referrals."

"Are you saying Peterson is deliberately sending us work that won't pay to sabotage our business?" Max asked.

"At first I thought it was just natural," Erika said. "It would certainly make sense for them to send us work they don't want to do because they're worried about creditworthiness. They have an IP group, if the work was good, you'd think they'd keep it for themselves."

"Sure," Max said. "But I think our partners are savvy enough to suspect that a referral may be coming because of credit problems or a business conflict."

She knew a business conflict was not really a conflict — it was usually just a decision not to take a client because it would piss off another client that was a competitor. A legal conflict, where the attorney was forbidden to take on the client, happened when the prospective client was legally adverse to an existing client, such as being in a lawsuit.

"But what if they have a legal conflict?" Erika asked.

"That would indicate it is more likely to be a good client," Max said. "A good credit risk."

"Right," Erika replied. "All of these were presented as conflicts, not credit problems. *All* of them. I checked. Either legal or business conflicts. So the partners didn't worry about credit, or they were just anxious to get business regardless of the credit. And most of these were presented to us as business conflicts where they were supposedly worried about annoying another client in the same business. It seemed a little strange to me. Peterson is well known to skirt close to the line on legal conflicts all the time. So why would they all of a sudden get real worried about business conflicts, which are even less of a concern than legal conflicts?"

"Actually, Peterson skirts over the line most of the time," Max chuckled.

Erika nodded. She knew, as did Max, that it was unheard of for Peterson to refer clients because of business conflicts.

"I have sources at Peterson," Erika continued, annoyed that Max seemed to be brushing her off. "And I also checked with our contacts at these clients. Only one had a true legal conflict. The rest that were presented to us as legal conflicts weren't. And when I checked with the clients where there was supposed to be a business conflict, I found that almost all didn't see the business conflict, and would have liked to have Peterson representing them. I have notes on all my conversations here." She pointed to the tab in the binder.

Erika went on to point out some bad-mouthing of Turner, West she had heard about, and a few other things. She didn't like the reaction on Max's face. She could see he thought these were simply the acts of a zealous competitor fighting for the same IP market. She turned to different tabs in the binder. As she went through it she got more nervous. Max must think she was obsessive, and had just documented a bunch of gossip and even second source gossip.

When she finished, her fears were realized. Max patiently explained that this was just competition, not a conspiracy. Besides, Peterson had just referred the Neuropt work. She had no answer to that.

She nodded, quickly rose and excused herself, saying she had taken enough of his time. Max handed her the Demodex binder back. Unfortunately, he wouldn't need it. She paused at the door and looked back over her shoulder. "Did you notice who referred the Demodex work that conflicted you out of this?" she asked, patting the binder with the palm of her hand, catching Max lifting his eyes from the back of her jeans.

"No," Max said. "Who?"

Erika met his gaze for a lingering moment. "Peterson."

———

Joe tried to take his mind off Sandra by immersing himself in his work Saturday. He alternated between being angry with her and ashamed of himself. He felt empty, but surprisingly had no desire to go after her and beg her to come back.

The judge had agreed yesterday to partly lift the injunction until the JNOV was decided — Judgment Notwithstanding the Verdict. That meant the judge could overrule the jury if the jury clearly screwed up. Telekinetics could show the Retinal Screen at Comdex, but still couldn't sell it or ship it to Brazil. The judge was still concerned about losing control over the manufacture of the Retinal Screen if it was shipped out of the country.

Zenko had also filed the Telekinetics appeal yesterday. Meanwhile, A.J. was in settlement discussions today with Inventech. They not only had the appeal as leverage, Burak had a new design that would use flash memory instead of a disk drive. Telekinetics could use the threat to go to this design-around unless Inventech was reasonable in settling. So today Joe concentrated on the Neuropt work.

By 7:00 P.M. that evening Joe was extremely frustrated. He had been working all day trying to do an opinion with no help from Neuropt. Ned had called that morning and promised to get Harold Walsh to call today, but Harold never called. Joe finally left a message for Ned that they simply couldn't do the opinion unless they had a meeting with Walsh this weekend. Still there had been no reply.

His cell phone rang. It was Vishal calling from his car. "Joe, I had to leave, but I'll keep calling Walsh tonight to see if we can set up something for tomorrow. I'll let you know on your cell phone or Blackberry if I hear anything."

Joe got up and wandered around the building. The Neuropt admin, Alicia, was working in the small conference room, organizing several boxes of Neuropt files she had brought over.

He stopped as a thought occurred to him, and returned to the conference room. "Alicia, do you know much about Neuropt? Not the technical stuff, but perhaps you can fill me in on how many people work on what, things like that."

Alicia leaned back and grinned. "Sure, I know stuff. How 'bout if I spill over dinner?"

"Okay," Joe said. "I'll order in some pizza."

Alicia grimaced. She reached into her purse and stood up, cocking her hip outward so it strained against her leather skirt. She was holding up a credit card.

"I have the company credit card," she said. "Let's eat somewhere nice. I'll drive."

Joe hesitated. It was work, but he was a married man. At least he thought he still was. It wouldn't help reconciling if he was caught out with a beautiful woman. On the other hand, what were the odds of someone seeing them? Besides, it was going to be a working dinner. Hell, Sandra didn't want anything to do with him anyway. He could use some cheering up after yesterday's double whammy of the partnership vote news and Sandra's Post-it.

"Okay" he finally managed to mumble.

Her car was a bright red Alpha Romeo Spider. It was a warm night, so they drove with the top down. She drove to highway 280, and got off on Woodside Road.

"So we're eating in Woodside?" Joe asked.

"You'll see," Alicia said.

After they passed through Woodside, Joe guessed she was heading to a restaurant on Skyline Boulevard at the top of the hill. Good, the farther away from work, the less chance of running into someone from work. Although he was starting to worry about how much time this was taking — time better spent working. As they wound up the hill, he caught glimpses of the peninsula. To the north he saw the distinctive metallic blue green cylinders that were the Oracle towers. Closer by was Hoover tower near the Stanford quad.

When they passed Skyline and kept going, he guessed La Honda as the destination. Alicia wouldn't say. Over an hour and a half later they ended up in Santa Cruz. The ocean waves sparkled in the moonlight along Highway 1, sending up flashes as they crashed on the rocks.

Even though it was past nine by the time they got there, they still had to wait for a table. They sat down at the upstairs bar, and he got a scotch and soda while she had a margarita. There were brightly colored surfboards dangling from the ceiling, and flags hung above the windows with a view of the ocean bathed in an eerie moon glow. They sat near the metal, freestanding fireplace. The bar was full and noisy compared to downstairs. It was an unusually clear evening with no fog, and they could see the lights of Monterey in the distance from the bar.

"So what can you tell me about Neuropt?" Joe asked.

"Over dinner," Alicia said. "This is drinks. Time for small talk first."

That worked for him. He wasn't feeling too loyal to the firm at this point, or to his marriage. His cell phone rang, but before he could see who it was, Alicia grabbed it out of his hand.

"I can see you've been overusing this," Alicia said, "since you had to put a band-aid on it." Alicia turned it off and put it in her purse. He shrugged and ordered a second drink.

Their table was finally ready, so he followed her downstairs to the main dining room, hypnotized by the rhythmic straining of her rear against the leather skirt as she descended the stairs. He was jolted by the sight that greeted him at the bottom of the stairs. The hostess was leading them right past a table where Trevor West and Roger Borland of the Peterson firm were sitting, along with their wives. What were they doing here? Joe looked away as they walked by, hoping he wasn't seen. The hostess stopped 3 tables away, by the window, and Joe quickly reached for the chair that would put his back to Trevor West. Alicia tugged on her skirt as she sat at their table. The moonbeam stretched across the water right up toward their table.

She ordered the most expensive bottle of Chardonnay and talked about movies, restaurants, anything but work. After five minutes he had forgotten about West and Borland being behind him. He flinched but quickly relaxed when her stockinged leg rubbed his. She gave a weak apology. The next time, the apology was even less sincere.

Joe gazed at her shoulder. The neckline of her sweater had slipped over her shoulder, exposing a black bra strap. Alicia saw Joe's gaze and looked down at her shoulder.

"Do you like my sweater?" Alicia asked, adjusting it so her bra strap was no longer exposed.

"I especially like your black bra," Joe answered, swirling his wine.

Alicia blushed, adjusted her sweater again and got up. "If you'll excuse me," Alicia said, "I'd better go to the women's room and straighten up."

Damn, he shouldn't have mentioned the bra strap. He watched Alicia's hips sway elegantly. The leather skirt was overmatched trying to restrain her assets as she walked to the restroom. Both male and female heads swiveled as she passed them — like the wake of a boat.

"Joe," said a familiar voice next to him. He looked up. Trevor West and his wife had come over to his table.

"Mr. West, Mrs. West," Joe said, getting up in an awkward half-stand since his chair had pushed up against the chair behind him. "What a pleasant surprise to see you here."

Undue Diligence

"I was playing golf at Pebble Beach with Roger Borland today," West said, gesturing toward Borland.

"Whipped his ass pretty good, too," West said with a grin. "Seriously, Joe, my wife and I couldn't help but notice you, and we just came by to urge you not to do this."

"Do what?" Joe asked.

"It's not worth risking your marriage," West said, putting a hand on Joe's shoulder. "Don't do it."

West turned and returned to his seat before Joe could think of anything to say. Mrs. West just glared at him for a moment, then spun around and followed her husband. Joe sat down and picked up his menu. His embarrassment slowly turned to annoyance. Why was West assuming something untoward was happening? It wasn't any business of West's anyway, and West had no idea what was going on with Joe's marriage.

He didn't look up from the menu when he sensed the wake returning, until she sat down. Her sweater was sliding off her shoulder again, but he couldn't see the bra strap. She reached across the table.

"Give me your hand," Alicia commanded. He glanced over his shoulder back toward West, and slowly put his hand out. She quickly grabbed it. She gazed into his eyes for a moment, and asked him to close his eyes. He complied, feeling a tingling sensation just from holding her hand, which was replaced by the feel of lace. He slowly opened his eyes and saw her bra in his hand.

"Since you liked it so much," Alicia said, "I thought you'd like to have it."

His face flushed and perspiration started to build on his forehead as he glanced around and saw several men at different tables looking at them. He didn't dare turn around to see if West was watching — he hoped West's view was blocked. He quickly pulled the bra down to his lap, but couldn't resist rubbing the cup between his fingers before stuffing the bra in his coat pocket. Alicia's nipples, visibly pushing against her sweater, confirmed this wasn't a dream.

Joe's blackberry startled him with a beep, and he pulled it out to see what the message was, grateful for the distraction. But Alicia reached over and grabbed it. "Any more toys I need to confiscate?" she smiled.

Her smile flashed into a devilish grin as she reached over to drop her black thong on his salad fork. Without taking his eyes off hers, he grabbed his covered salad fork and brought it to his lap, where he glanced down to inspect her thong before stuffing it in his pocket.

It was a struggle to concentrate on their conversation for the rest of the dinner, knowing she had no underwear on and that the men glancing their way also knew. With waning determination, he tried to pump her about Neuropt. He didn't learn much, although she did say that most employees left at 5, which seemed strange for a start-up about to go public. He also found out that Gage Booth didn't do much; he mainly used an office there to monitor all his other businesses. After Alicia plopped down her company credit card, he looked around and saw to his relief that West and Borland were gone. He and Alicia took their glasses of wine out on the deck. She wobbled down the 3 steps to the deck, clutching his only slightly steadier arm.

The cool breeze bit a little, but was refreshing. The halyards of the sailboats in the harbor clanged against their masts in an exotic rhythm. She forced his back against the rail with her breasts pressing against his ribs, and her hips against his. Her hand eased into his coat pocket, pausing to caress his rear through the cloth. She pulled out the thong and rubbed it softly against his cheek, with her lips a tantalizing inch from his and their eyes locked. He was vaguely aware of eyes on the deck watching him, and was sure they were a show for those having dinner inside.

"So," she whispered, "since we've had too much to drink, I don't think it would be prudent to drive home. I think the responsible thing to do is to get a motel room nearby."

He forgot about work as her lips gently eased onto his. He briefly thought of Sandra for the last time that night.

At one AM that night, Ahmet was standing next to Cassia's Chevrolet Corsa in the FUNASA parking lot, waiting for Cassia to come down. Ahmet had just dialed Burak's cell phone number when Cassia came out the door.

"Who are you calling?" Cassia asked.

"Burak," Ahmet said. "Is the CDC team still working?"

"Yeah, they know there is no time for sleep," Cassia said. "Isn't it late to be calling?"

"No," Ahmet said, "it's only nine PM in California."

Cassia lit two cigarettes and handed Ahmet one. Ahmet looked at the card he kept in his wallet with all the time variances for Telekinetics' offices. One AM in São Paulo was 11 PM in Austin, Texas where Telekinetics got its microprocessors. Software and system design was in Santa Clara, California. Mechanical design was in Taipei, Taiwan where it was noon. It was also noon in Kuala Lumpur, Malaysia where circuit board assembly was done and in Shanghai, China where mechanical assembly was done. In Germany, where electrical design was done, it was 6 AM. The idea was to take advantage of the lower costs and particular skills of each region, but he wasn't sure that the communications problems didn't cost more.

"Who is calling?" answered Burak's irritated voice.

"It's me," Ahmet said. "Any luck on settling?"

"I have bad news," Burak said. "We were on the verge of a settlement when Gage Booth did a deal to buy the Inventech patent. Booth wants to shut down the Retinal Screen so the Sheath isn't competition for his Optospine product. That way he can raise more money in his IPO. He has told us he won't settle on any terms. So the injunction is still in place."

"He doesn't care that people are dying?" Ahmet asked.

"If he cannot make money off the deaths, he does not care," Burak said.

"I've got an idea," Ahmet said. "Don't fix the second prototype — just send it to us. Since it doesn't function, it's not really a Retinal Screen, so you haven't violated the injunction. You can tell A.J. honestly you weren't able to fix it. I'll fix it here."

"You know I cannot do that," Burak said.

"Well, dammit, do something!" Ahmet yelled. "We need it now."

"I am working on it," Burak said. "We're doing a redesign that will take out the disk drive entirely, and use flash memory. It will be expensive as hell to make, but we will avoid the patent and the injunction. I think we can have the prototype Retinal Screen retrofitted in a few weeks."

"We don't have a few weeks," Ahmet said as he took a drag. "People are needlessly dying every day here."

"Look," Burak said, "Let us talk about this tomorrow. I've got other problems to attend to at the moment."

"Sure," Ahmet said. "I'm sure those other products are more important than the Retinal Screen."

"For your information," Burak said, "A.J. cancelled two products today so we could focus resources on the Retinal Screen."

"Which ones?" Ahmet asked.

"The Sonic Defribulator and the Stroke EWS," Burak said.

"Damn," Ahmet said. "I thought the Early Warning System had promise?"

"Each of them had attracted a number of patent infringement lawsuits," Burak said. "We simply do not have the budget to fight a multi-front war right now. So we are focusing on the Retinal Screen. If you want to complain, why do you not call those product managers? I am sure they will be very sympathetic."

Ahmet knew this was killing Burak. Burak was employee number 5 at Telekinetics; and with A.J. and the other founders had sunk his savings into getting the company started.

"The Retinal Screen will help stop a plague," Ahmet said. "I think it is different. People need it. Someone else will produce a Sonic Defribulator and Stroke Early Warning System."

"We were actually the last on the EWS," Burak said. "As you know, we had some competitors. The products were not as good, of course, and we introduced first. But they dropped out when they started getting hit with incoming lawsuits. The parasite patent owners got too greedy and forgot they need someone living to suck blood out of. At least there is some justice in that."

"What kind of a crazy legal system is this?" Ahmet asked. "All this money, all this effort is spent on arguing and endless fighting in the courts. No one has time to actually make the products — all the money and effort goes to the lawsuits."

A loud explosion interrupted Ahmet. He looked up to see fire and debris shooting out of one of the windows several stories up. He grabbed Cassia and started to run when he was slammed to the ground by something hitting him in the back. It felt like his back was broken. He couldn't move. After a few moments he felt Cassia roll him over on his back.

"I can't breathe," he hissed.

"You just got the breath knocked out of you," Cassia blubbered, shaking noticeably.

She looked to the side, turned away and vomited. Ahmet followed her gaze. There was a burned torso near him, severed at the waist. He could still see the blackened letters "CDC" on the back of the lab coat.

"I guess you can't rely on the CDC now," Ahmet said.

8.

Joe sluggishly opened his eyes the next morning. There was a pair of breasts a few inches from his nose. He slowly remembered, and nuzzled between them. Suddenly he sat up – he felt uneasy for some reason. He looked at the clock, but it was turned away from him, so he got out of bed and turned it around – it was already 11:30. He searched for his cell phone and Blackberry, finally finding them in Alicia's purse. There was an e-mail from Vishal and a voice mail – the meeting with Walsh had been set up for 9 AM this morning.

He woke Alicia and said they had to go now. She wanted to spend the day in Santa Cruz, pointing out that he had already missed his meeting anyway. Joe was insistent, deaf to her pleas for brunch first, or at least a shower. He grabbed her keys and she was forced to follow.

Joe made it to the office at 12:30. He walked the long way from reception to his office, so he wouldn't have to go by Max Klein's office. He noticed Vishal's door was closed.

He pushed the door open when there was no response to his knock. Vishal had a headset on listening to music, and was reading something. Vishal looked up at Joe, looked down to read for a few moments, then slowly took the headset off and leaned back.

"Where were you?" Vishal asked. "We finally got our meeting with Walsh this morning. I tried calling your cell phone last night, and copied you on the e-mail he sent. I thought you constantly had the handheld on?"

"She took my cell phone and Blackberry!" Joe blurted out, before realizing that he'd given himself away.

A broad grin slowly worked its way across Vishal's face, his eyes brightening. Joe realized he had said too much. "She? Would that be a certain admin?"

Joe just rolled his eyes. "How'd it go with Walsh?"

"Fine," Vishal said with a tone of annoyance. "No problems. You're lucky I was here to cover your ass. How'd it go with the admin?"

Joe ignored the question and quizzed Vishal for half an hour about what he learned, reviewing a folder of documents and notes. Vishal insisted that everything checked out.

"There was one minor thing," Vishal said, "a couple of their patent applications did seem pretty thin. They have more sales talk in there than substance."

Vishal picked up one of the Neuropt patent applications and waved it at Joe. "But I expect this garbage will make it through the Patent Office, since they hand out patents like candy on Halloween. It's like handing out guns to terrorists. Jefferson would roll over in his grave."

Joe nodded. Thomas Jefferson had originally opposed adding patent protection to the Constitution, but eventually agreed reluctantly, and only for truly new and useful advancements. He would be shocked at the minor changes patented these days. Permitting patents on minor changes allowed all sorts of mischief by unscrupulous people manipulating patents. Patents were like chemotherapy — a little bit is a good thing, too much will kill you.

"Oh there you are, Joe," it was Max Klein at the door. "I thought you would be in early working on Neuropt. I was glad to see Vishal here working away on it." Max walked around the desk to stand behind Vishal.

Great. The first Sunday he hasn't been in early in months, and the managing partner notices. And not only that, Joe is supposed to be working on a project for him. And there was Vishal grinning ear-to-ear as Max put his arm around his shoulder.

"Well, as a matter of fact," Joe said, "I was offsite going over some things with the Neuropt admin they sent over to help." Joe saw Vishal smirking.

"They sent over an admin, huh?" Max looked surprised, but only for an instant. "Well that's useful. Glad to hear you're on top of things." Joe was glad Max was behind Vishal and couldn't see him covering his mouth to keep from laughing out loud.

"So how's the Neuropt investigation going?" Max asked. "I got a message from the underwriter's counsel. They want to know if we've come up with any issues."

"Well, Vishal went over their technology today," Joe said, "and it appears to check out." Vishal nodded when Max looked at him.

"Their own applications look a little thin," Joe continued, "but we haven't found any show-stoppers yet."

"As far as infringement issues, I have Bernie Sloan working this weekend," Joe said. "I'm expecting early faxed results today, and hopefully should have everything Bernie finds in his prior art search by Tuesday. I haven't finished going over everything yet, but I think the opinion they want is too broad."

"How's that?" Max asked.

"They have us opining on a couple sections of the prospectus that talk about more than patents," Joe said. "Things like likelihood of success for the product and expected introduction date. I'd like to see our opinion limited to patent matters. Also, they have a few statements that bother me. Like they aren't aware of any patents they infringe. As you know, they probably do infringe something."

"Yes," Max answered, "but they *aren't* aware of it. So the statement is correct. Look, you can ask to change it, but if they say no, don't push it. I know we normally don't give such opinions, but I don't want to jeopardize this project. Understood?"

Joe nodded, disappointed. Usually it was Max insisting that the opinion be limited.

Vishal grinned at him after Max left. "I'd love to see your billing time entry for this morning," Vishal said. "What will it say, oral conference with admin? Or perhaps *all hands* meeting?"

Joe waved Vishal off, and went back to his office satisfied that Vishal had covered the meeting, but then started having second thoughts. Vishal was a junior associate, and Ned was expecting Joe to either do the work, or to supervise it carefully. He went back to Vishal's office, and asked to borrow the folder. He started reviewing it carefully. The more he understood the details, the more gaps there appeared to be. Vishal wasn't able to answer his questions, so he tried calling Harold Walsh and left a message. He later got an e-mail from Walsh saying he missed his opportunity at the meeting this morning, and Harold didn't have any more time to explain.

Joe looked through the materials again. There wasn't any justification for the 6-month product introduction target — other than Walsh saying that was the schedule. No explanation of how Neuropt expected to overcome the design hurdles that still screamed out at Joe. There was no more information on sensor designs than what he had found in his own brief Internet search. The main Neuropt patent application was written as if the optics and the neural network were completely separate sections, while the invention was supposed to be the way the optics and neural net were uniquely combined. The combination of the two was only written about very generally.

After awhile, his stomach started growling, and he realized it was after 9 already. He tried Sandra's cell phone again, got her voicemail and hung up. Then he clicked on his Blackberry to a web site he had saved. The site did software simulations on the Amazon virus spreading, allowing the user to put in different assumptions. It was both fascinating and morbid. He picked their worst-case assumptions and entered 6 months. At that moment his cell phone rang.

"I can't believe you're still there on a Sunday night." It was Alicia. "I thought you might be there when you didn't answer at home."

Joe clicked "go" and leaned back and watched while he talked to Alicia. The series of red dots in Brazil spread throughout South America, momentarily stalling near Panama, probably because the Darien Gap was built into the model. It was called the Darien gap because the border area between Panama and Colombia is the only gap in the 16,000-mile (26,000-kilometer) Pan-American Highway, which stretches from Alaska to Patagonia. The Pan American Highway construction stopped at the Colombian border in the 70's because of protests by environmental groups trying to protect the

Darien National Park, one of the largest protected areas in Central America. There were also fears that a completed highway would allow hoof and mouth disease from Colombia to spread to the U.S. Hoof and mouth disease was eradicated in Colombia by 1991, but the highway remained uncompleted. Now it might stall a new disease.

After a pause, the red dots started growing again. A group of dots appeared at port cities in the US — Los Angeles, San Francisco, New York. The dots spread inland from there. The rate accelerated at 5 months. By 6 months, the US was almost entirely red.

His office phone rang and he put Alicia on hold — it was Arthur Gursky, underwriter's counsel for the Neuropt deal. Everyone had lawyers in an IPO, including the underwriters.

"So how's the due diligence coming?" Gursky asked.

"Okay," Joe said. He wasn't prepared to talk about this. He didn't want to say anything bad, yet he didn't have much good to say. Neuropt would be pissed if he said something that bothered the underwriters without being completely sure and checking with Neuropt first. Although the opinion was independent in theory, Neuropt was his client. Attorneys were always expected to be advocates for their clients. "I'm still waiting for search results."

"Don't you have any yet?" Gursky asked.

"I've gotten a few articles, but not much," Joe replied. He wanted to talk to Neuropt and their counsel, Ned, before he said anything to the underwriters. But he didn't want to say that to Gursky, it would sound like he was trying to hide something.

"Anything close?" Gursky asked.

"I haven't had a chance to completely review it yet," Joe said. "So far, the articles look like pretty generic stuff." As does the invention, he thought.

"I see," Gursky said. He sounded like he had concluded something from what Joe was saying. But Joe hadn't said anything. Maybe that was it.

"You used to be an engineer," Gursky said. "You've seen the product descriptions. Do you think they'll have it ready in 6 months like they say?"

"Well, I'm not an engineer anymore," Joe said. "And that is out of my area of expertise as a patent attorney." He had no clue how they'd make it in 6 months, but he wasn't about to tell Gursky that.

"How about these new sensors?" Gursky asked. "Have you seen the prototype in operation? I saw it, but I can't make heads or tails of it. All I know is that they gave me a write-up by an outside expert raving about it, and the feasibility of miniaturizing it."

Joe winced. He *hadn't* seen the prototype in person, and he never saw any expert report. This was the first he'd heard of it. Why hadn't Harold Walsh mentioned it?

"Well, that's not going to be part of the patent opinion," Joe said. "I'm hoping to limit the opinion to exclude that."

"Because you don't think they'll make it in 6 months?" Gursky asked.

"Because we're experts in patent law, not product schedules," Joe said.

"Well, I don't think they'll make it," Gursky said, pausing while this sunk in. "So do you have anything to say to prove me wrong? How can they make it in 6 months?"

"Have you asked the Neuropt people that question?" Joe asked, letting a hint of irritation slip out.

"No," Gursky said. "They don't know it's a concern of mine. I was hoping to get some answers from you before they had a chance to whitewash your opinion. But I see I'm not going to be successful."

"No one whitewashes our opinions," Joe said. Why the hell was he suggesting this?

"We'll see," Gursky said. "Goodbye."

Joe hung up and took Alicia off hold. "Still there?"

"Yes," Alicia said. "Have you eaten yet?"

"No," Joe answered.

"Good," Alicia said. "Meet me at my place in 15 minutes — I'll get some take-out. Then we can make-out."

Joe was initially reluctant. He had more work to do tonight, and he knew he wouldn't get anything more done at Alicia's. Then he realized how Alicia could help him.

———

At about the same time in São Paulo Ahmet was calling Cassia on his cell phone as he approached the back door of the FUNASA building. With the extra security guards since the bombing, he couldn't get in unless she vouched for him. Most of the FUNASA personnel had been dispersed to other government offices to make it difficult for a terrorist to locate them, but Cassia was part of a skeleton crew still at FUNASA headquarters, two floors above the bombed out floor. She was just inside the door, smoking, when he arrived.

"How are you holding up, working this late?" Ahmet asked, as they got in the elevator. The walls of the elevator were covered with mover's blankets from workmen hauling out debris during the day. He was worried about her. Cassia was normally very cool and deliberate, but now she seemed frazzled.

"I've stayed up later," Cassia said curtly. "Since your company is unable to deliver the Retinal Screen, I asked the Minister of Foreign Affairs to have the US Ambassador make an emergency request to the US White House."

"My people are doing the same thing," Ahmet replied defensively.

As they got off the elevator at the FUNASA offices, it was buzzing with activity — an odd sight at 4 AM. The small amount of office space that hadn't been damaged was crowded even with the reduced number of workers. She walked over to a desk covered with stacks of papers and showed Ahmet some printouts.

"Still no pattern that we can see," Cassia said in frustration. "We have been eliminating more stuff. We don't know how it spreads, but it must spread like AIDS, or maybe by mosquitoes — something requiring bodily fluid contact. We've isolated the virus, and it dies quickly outside the body."

"Is either of those two possibilities supported by how it spreads?" Ahmet asked.

"Unclear," Cassia sighed. "We've got a few cases where there appears to have been no possibility of sexual contact, and no exposure to mosquitoes. But you can never be sure of that. We did find a strong correlation to the smallpox vaccinations. We suspended the smallpox vaccination program just in case. I don't think much of it, since there have been a number of cases where the patient didn't have a smallpox vaccine. For example, the Olympic athletes. But I am beginning to wonder. Maybe there is some other link between the athletes and the smallpox vaccinated victims. The smallpox vaccine might have weakened people, making them vulnerable to the virus. But again that doesn't explain the athletes. I just don't know. Whatever it is, it is beginning to smell. It just doesn't look natural to me."

As Joe drove to Alicia's place, he felt guilty — last night he was drunk and basically seduced. This was premeditated. Sandra hadn't returned his messages, but if he were really in love with her, he knew he would be making more of an effort.

When he arrived, Alicia was lounging in her red Alpha Romeo Spider, her feet up on the passenger seat. A couple of young guys were leaning over, chatting with her. When she saw him, she got out quickly with a bag of take-out and led him to the front door. She was in her version of casual, he guessed. Jeans, but bright yellow ones. A loose cotton top with a bare midriff. And white high heels. He looked back at the two guys gawking as she fumbled with her keys with one hand while caressing his butt with the other.

Then Joe's eyes opened wide in amazement. Sandra pulled up in her Mercedes convertible. How did she find out about Alicia, and where Alicia lived? And how did she know he'd be here now?

"I can't believe it," Sandra yelled from the car. "Two days after I move out, and already you're shacking up with another woman. And a cheap slut at that. Now I have divorce grounds that are your fault, asshole!"

"What are you talking about?" Joe yelled back, his embarrassment turning into boiling anger. "You're the one who had movers already lined up before the partnership vote."

"I think I'll give you a little time with your wife," Alicia whispered, slipping inside the house. Joe was puzzled at Alicia's non-reaction to being called a cheap slut.

"Yeah?" Sandra yelled back, as she started to pull away. "Try proving it."

Joe felt like his insides were all twisted up as he stepped inside and slammed the door closed behind him. Alicia was just smiling at him, and shook her head when he headed for the dining room table. She pointed to the coffee table. He noticed it was nicely decorated, antique furniture and pricey paintings. She put the Chinese take-out down on the glass coffee table, and patted the floor in front of the couch, pulling a lace-bordered cushion down. He sat down, and she pushed his legs apart and sat between them, slouching down and leaning her head back against his stomach.

"Forget about your wife," she said. "Try to relax."

She filled a plate and handed it up over her head to him with some chopsticks, then filled her own plate.

"So how's the due diligence on Neuropt coming?" She asked.

"Okay," Joe said, relieved to be talking about work. "I got a couple of articles from my searcher today. And Vishal went over the prospectus statements with Walsh."

"So what do you think?" Alicia asked, stabbing at some shrimp.

He hesitated for a moment. Deep down, he had hoped he was wrong about Alicia just wanting to pump him for information. It was now clear to him. At least this was something he could use to his benefit, but he had to play it right.

"We still have more work to do," Joe said. "It's too early to tell."

Alicia tilted her head back to look up at him. "So what more do you have to do? Didn't you get all you need on the prospectus already? At least that must be okay, right?"

"I want to do more follow up on the product release schedule," Joe said. "We haven't gotten enough information yet to verify that Neuropt will have a product in 6 months."

"Why are you looking at that?" Alicia asked. "What does that have to do with patents?"

"Nothing," Joe said. "We shouldn't even be covering that in our opinion in the first place."

"Hmmm," Alicia murmured. She held some shrimp up to his lips with her chopsticks. He took a bite.

"So how about infringement issues?" Alicia asked, looking down at her plate. "Any problems?"

"Nope," Joe said. "Haven't gotten any patents back yet. Don't know yet."

"I thought you said you got something from your searcher," Alicia said.

"Articles," Joe said. "Not patents."

"So what do articles have to do with patents?" Alicia asked. She had put her hand on his back and moved downward inside the back of his pants.

"Well, if the articles show the same thing that Neuropt is trying to claim in its own patent applications," Joe answered, "then Neuropt probably won't be successful in getting patents."

"Oh," Alicia breathed, giving his butt a squeeze, and leaning in so her lips were an inch from his. "So are the articles a problem?"

"They're fairly close," he said, trying to stay focused. She was talking work, but was positively breathless with her words, as if she were talking dirty. "But that may just affect whether Neuropt can get broad claims or narrow claims. They *may* still get a patent."

"*May* still get one? That doesn't sound real positive," she said with a purr as she put down her food and started unbuttoning his shirt.

"That's what makes it difficult for us to give that opinion," Joe said. "And I don't see why the underwriters need that opinion. Most of the value should be coming from the technology and marketing anyway, not from the patents."

"I see," Alicia said, giving his chest a few caresses. "Well, I think it's just wonderful that you're working so hard, even on a Sunday, to get this opinion done soon so they can do the IPO. You're playing a part in fighting the Amazon virus. It's like you're part of a crack team that is saving the world."

Alicia sat up and started picking up her food again. They finished up the Chinese food. Alicia insisted that he stay seated while she cleared the containers. She opened her purse and then closed it again, as if she decided not to pull something out. "I'm going outside for a few minutes — I need a cigarette."

Joe smiled. She had taken the bait.

"Here," Alicia said, tossing him a bottle from her bag. "You get started; I'll join you in a moment. And don't worry about the smoking, I have mouthwash."

He watched as she walked to the front door, her hips hypnotizing him. She paused and grinned back at him from the door, then gave her rear a couple quick wiggles. In an instant she disappeared outside. What was he supposed to start? He looked at the bottle. It was bubble bath.

Max was fuming the next morning by the time his computer beeped, signaling that Joe's card key had activated one of the locks in the office. Ned had called to complain over an hour ago. Max had been trying to reach Joe on his cell phone for over an hour, but Joe had it off. Max had set the notification alarm for the building doors, which was one of the perks — or rather tools — of management. He looked at his watch. It was nearly nine A.M. Monday morning. He got up and headed down the hall towards Joe's office.

Max took a deep breath as he approached Joe's office. He would have to appear calm and diplomatic. Although what he in fact wanted to do was skin Joe alive.

He saw Joe before Joe saw him. Then he saw a woman sitting in Joe's client chair. She turned and noticed Max first. Wow. She was too pretty to be a client, and she wasn't Joe's wife.

"Joe, you have a visitor," she said.

Joe looked up. "Max," Joe said. "How are you doing?"

Max nodded. "Fine."

"Max, this is Alicia Conrath," Joe said. "She's the admin from Neuropt who's been sent over to help us with the due diligence. Alicia, this is Max Klein, our managing partner and the partner in charge of the Neuropt project. He the smartest lawyer in the firm, and approves everything I do on this project."

Max smiled broadly, succumbing to Joe's flattery and Alicia's admiring gaze. "Pleased to meet you," Max said shaking her hand.

"The pleasure's all mine," Alicia exhaled, holding onto his hand a little too long. "I've heard about you. Ned Stern speaks quite highly of you."

"Really?" Max smiled again. "Joe, do you have a minute?"

"I'll head to the conference room," Alicia said, grabbing a file and vanishing out the door. Max shot one more quick glance at her as she went out the door. It was as if she knew what Max wanted to talk about.

Max's cell phone rang — it was a client. "I'd better take this."

Joe nodded as Max sat down in Joe's guest chair. It only took a couple minutes for Max to deal with the client.

"Joe, I got a call from Ned Stern this morning," Max said as he hung up. "He tells me you've been talking to the underwriters."

He watched Joe's face. Joe just nodded, apparently oblivious that he had done anything wrong. That wasn't good.

"He tells me you told the underwriters that you didn't think the Neuropt applications were any good, and that you had doubts whether the product would be ready in 6 months," Max said.

Joe appeared surprised. "I never told Gursky that!"

"Well," Max continued, "they got that impression. You must have said something. These guys are experts at reading in between the lines when you talk to them. You have to be real careful what you say. I would have preferred that you talked to me first. When we talked yesterday, I didn't have the impression from you that there were any problems."

"Anyway," Max continued, looking at his watch and getting up, "they're expecting a call from me in 20 minutes. So come down to my office then with your stuff."

———

Shortly thereafter, during the call, Joe listened as Ned and Max kept referring to the "misunderstanding," which of course meant they blamed Joe for the underwriter getting the wrong impression. Joe was getting more aggravated as they talked.

"Joe," Ned said, "we want to do all we can to help you give the opinion. I told Gursky that we should exclude the 6 month shipment date and other non-patent information from the opinion. It's asking too much in a short time, and will allow you to focus on the patent stuff."

Joe nodded. Alicia had indeed taken the bait. If he had directly asked Ned or Gursky, the underwriter's counsel, for this change, he may have been rebuffed. But if they thought it was their idea to move things along, they were agreeable.

"Also," Ned continued, "Gursky agreed to exclude any opinion on the likelihood of the patent applications being allowed; on the basis that most readers of the prospectus would assume that an application filed would be allowed. We're going to add a risk factor instead."

"Good," Joe said. Both problems he mentioned to Alicia had now been addressed. It had been easier than he thought. Almost too easy. He felt good about successfully manipulating Ned, but had the uneasy feeling it was really the other way around. He had begun to wonder if it was Alicia who tipped off Sandra, as a ploy to put more pressure on him, to distract him. But distract him from what?

Half an hour later, Joe scanned the draft prospectus language Ned had e-mailed. If the prospectus had just said there might be a problem with the Neuropt applications, it would be a red flag that would concern anyone reading the prospectus. But Ned had added such a list of horribles that could happen, stretching on for two paragraphs, that it just looked like cover-their-ass boilerplate: there was no guarantee any of the patents will issue; the Company may not be able to stop anyone from copying the technology; the Company may not be able to file any more patents; an unforeseen technology could be developed by a competitor making the patents useless; etc.

This was unlikely to be noticed, it was in the middle of pages of other risk factors. The Company may not be successful in developing new products. The FDA might not grant approval. There may be consolidation in the health care industry that can adversely affect the Company. The Company may not be able to attract or retain the highly skilled employees they need. Product liability claims can adversely affect the business. Regulatory changes can adversely affect the Company. The management has no experience in managing a public company.

It was funny — the longer and more draconian the list of things that could go wrong, the less scary it was. It sounded like they didn't believe there was any problem; they were just listing everything that could possibly go wrong because their lawyers said to. It looked like just standard boilerplate.

Vishal Sivakumar materialized in Joe's office holding some papers and plopped down in a chair looking tired. "I think we have an infringement problem," Vishal said, weakly waving a patent in his hand. "We just got an initial group of patents from the search Bernie Sloan did. The Neuropt design appears to infringe one."

Joe sighed and went over the infringement analysis with Vishal for 10 minutes — it appeared to be right. The patent appeared to cover the surface-emitting laser in the Neuropt design. Joe turned back to the front page of the patent and suddenly sat up straight.

"No!" Joe said. "Why the hell didn't I notice that before?"

"What is it?" Vishal asked.

Joe pointed to the part of the patent that listed the attorneys who prosecuted the patent application. It was Turner, West, Klein & Evans. A patent of one of the firm's other clients covered the Neuropt design.

At that moment, Burak was sitting in a conference room at the offices of Telekinetics corporate attorneys after delaying his flight to Las Vegas — again. Jacob Zimmerman, the lead partner for Telekinetics matters, was talking. Burak looked nervously at A.J. in the hall, where she had gone to take a call. She should be hearing this. The government wasn't going to step in to let them ship even one prototype Retinal Screen to Brazil.

"Gage Booth has a lot of pull," Jacob was saying. "The politicians won't admit it's because of Booth's contributions. We're being told that Brazil doesn't respect patent rights, and they aren't about to overrule the independent judiciary."

"But people are dying," Burak protested.

"People were dying of AIDS when Brazil had to threaten compulsory licensing of AIDS drugs to make them affordable," Jacob said. "The politicians didn't care then, and more people died. Plus, Brazil now has a black eye for that threat to usurp patents."

"Great news," A.J. said on entering the conference room. "The University of California just placed a large order for Retinal Screens for all their hospitals. They can wait a few months until Burak's flash memory re-design is done, so there won't be any patent problems."

"That's great," Jacob said. "But what will happen when they find out about this new Royaltec suit?"

Burak looked at his worn wingtips through the glass of the conference table. Jacob was returning to the original reason for the meeting. Royaltec had just sued them for patent infringement. Royaltec had the gall to say this patent, on what looked like an erector set, covered the neural network chip in the Retinal Screen. They didn't claim to have invented all neural network chips, just *imbedded* neural networks — ones that include a neural network processor on the same chip as a standard micro-processor. Everyone was using them, Telekinetics wasn't the only one. Telekinetics didn't even make the chip, but Royaltec was going after Telekinetics instead of the chipmaker supplier.

"Do you know this company, Royaltec?" A.J. asked. "I understand they always settle for low amounts, less than attorney's fees for trial."

"Yes," Jacob said. "They are the original patent trolls. They filed a bunch of paper patent applications decades ago on Rube-Goldberg type devices. Then they watch what new technology is being developed, and amend the claims with vague terms they claim cover the new technology. Which, of course, they didn't invent.

They get the patent to issue, then sue, forcing the company that actually developed the technology to pay a lot to fight them, or settle. No one wants to risk going before a jury that doesn't understand the stuff. Plus it costs a fortune to fight a patent suit. So they settle."

"That's like legalized extortion," Burak said.

"They've been called that, and worse," Jacob said. "They've spawned a whole industry of copycats, which we refer to as patent trolls or patent assertion firms. Recently, hybrid firms have popped up — law firms that file their own patent applications."

"The other thing Royaltec does," Jacob continued, "is a bunch of PR. They sponsor an inventor of the year award and have established a charity called the Royaltec Art Institute. The Art Institute has a small ownership interest in the patents so they can make them a plaintiff in the lawsuit. Then it looks to the jury like this poor non-profit charity against this big, bad corporation."

"But don't these guys always settle?" Burak asked.

"That's right," Jacob said. "Since patent suits cost millions to defend, they settle for less than the attorneys fees would be to fight them. Since they go after a lot of companies, it adds up."

"So can you help us?" A.J. asked. "I know we owe you some money on unpaid invoices, but we'll give you a retainer."

Jacob looked away for a moment. "Look," Jacob sighed, "We can't take this on. We don't think you can afford it. The retainer will be used up in the blink of an eye, and we'll be in the hole again."

"But I thought they settled quickly" A.J. objected.

"I don't think they will this time," Jacob continued. "They're not using their usual lawyers. Some different game is up. They've gone out and hired Roger

Borland of Peterson, Malone. He's a real scorched-earth, hard-ass litigator, and he's got a big firm with lots of resources. They wouldn't do that unless they had something other than a small settlement in mind. Maybe they intend to make you the guinea pig to establish a high royalty rate for this patent."

"Guinea pig?" Burak asked.

"They make an example out of you," Jacob said. "Show they are willing to go to court. Then they can say that since Telekinetics had to pay this high rate, everyone else should pay the same rate. It's a way of setting a high price."

Jacob had a look Burak had seen before — the look of someone who had made up his mind not to do a deal. He didn't seem to care if this caused his firm to lose Telekinetics as a client.

"I've been up against Roger Borland before," Jacob continued, tapping his pencil on the conference table. "He believes in wearing you down with unrelenting motions, discovery and simple harassment. They picked you for a reason. They correctly figured you are vulnerable."

"I don't think they want us as guinea pigs," Burak said. "This is a Gage Booth ploy to keep the Sheath off the market so it won't be competition for Neuropt's public offering."

"If that's the case, you're really dead," Jacob shrugged.

A.J. turned to Burak.

"I guess we should go talk to Turner, West," A.J. said.

Burak nodded.

"A little off-the-record advice," Jacob said, leaning forward and lowering his voice. "You may want to interview some other firms, and not just go with Turner, West."

"Why?" A.J. asked.

"Turner, West is a good firm," Jacob said, pausing as he looked around at his associates. "If you go with them, I'd try to get Trevor West. Zenko hasn't won for a while, as you painfully know, and the others aren't of the same caliber. But even with Trevor, they just aren't hard-asses. They still practice — what should I call it? They practice the old fashioned way. They are good to their word. They treat the opposing lawyer with respect. They don't fight things just to fight them. They'll actually answer interrogatories the first time and produce documents they are asked for in discovery. They focus on the substance. They don't engage in dirty tricks."

"Okay, okay!" Burak said, raising both arms. "Enough already! I see what you mean. I am surprised the bar association has not taken away their license to practice."

"I also understand Turner, West is having financial problems," Jacob continued. "They may not be around to finish the case."

———————

Joe picked up the phone that evening when Ned called from the printer. Ned and his team were at the offices of the printer putting the finishing touches on the prospectus. It was customary for the legal team to move into a conference room at the printer for the few days before filing. They would go over proofs of the prospectus and work the phones from there to finalize everything they needed.

"Joe, I've got Gage on the line," Ned said, "I understand that you found a Turner, West patent that's a problem."

"That's right," Joe said.

"Crap!" Gage said. "You attorneys are such whores. You wrote a patent that covers us?"

"Joe," Ned said, "we can't get a new attorney at this point just to evaluate one patent. Isn't there any way you can deal with this?"

Joe's cell phone rang. "Let me get rid of this other call," Joe said, opening his cell phone.

It was Hank. "Hank, I'm on an important call, I'll have to —"

"Joe, this will just take a sec.," Hank said. "It's about the vacation home. I found a great deal in Santa Cruz. This is much better than the one near Tahoe I showed you."

"I'll call you back," Joe said.

"No, listen to this — ," Hank said.

Joe hung up and returned to the call with Ned and Gage.

"Well," Joe said, "you don't have to get separate patent counsel if you can take out all references to the surface emitting lasers in the prospectus. We can say that since the design isn't finalized you might use another sensor. If the surface emitting laser isn't mentioned, we don't have to deal with the patent."

"Done," Ned said.

Joe later sold the solution to the underwriter's counsel, Gursky, by emphasizing the difficulty of getting another patent firm up to speed at this late date, since the prospectus was to be filed tomorrow. Joe didn't feel good about it, though.

Joe tried calling Sandra again. Still no answer. He was feeling both angry with her and guilty about his fling with Alicia. He was dying to get Sandra to say how she heard about it.

He blinked his drooping eyelids to try and focus on his work. It was 10:30 at night, and Joe was running out of steam. He still had a few things to check out on Neuropt, and he had a patent to look at for another client. The intercom announcement was like a splash of cold water.

"John Doe, pick up line 212," blared the paging system. Joe got up and walked into the hall and looked around. He returned to his desk, picked up the phone, and dialed 212. "This is Nile," Joe said. "No John Does here." John Doe was code for partners. If no one reported any partners in the office, then it was clear for a chair race challenge. It had been almost a month since the last challenge. They would have to pick tonight, Joe thought. He was sure they did it on purpose because they knew he was busy and tired. Savages.

He had to accept a challenge at any time he was in the office and there were no partners around. Those were the rules. He was the three-time defending champion. "All clear!" announced Vishal's voice on the paging system. "Racers and judges report to the reception area." He sat in his chair, turned it around, and pushed it backwards out into the hall and down to the reception area. He was glad he'd greased the rollers on his chair last week.

When he got to the reception area, he could see the challenger was a bio-phd, Andrea Whitaker, PhD. She was built like a linebacker and played on a soccer team. A formidable challenge. The double doors on both sides of the elevator lobby were braced open. When the whistle was blown, both would race backwards, side-by-side through the elevator lobby to the hallway on the other side. Since the hallway was too narrow for two chairs, he would go one way and Andrea would go the other.

Vishal walked into the reception area. "The course is all clear," Vishal said officiously. "No obstacles. And we have a fully officiated race, with spotters at both checkpoints."

There were two checkpoints along each route, equidistant from the start. They would be manned only if enough people were around. There was a big crowd tonight. The spotters picked up phones in the secretarial stations at the checkpoints, and got a conference call going. Then they connected to the paging system. This way, they could give reports on the progress of the racers.

The whistle blew, and they were off. Andrea tried to bump him as they made their turns past the elevator. She didn't affect him much. That would cost her, he thought as he accelerated. Andrea probably slowed herself down by kicking Joe. "Joe at one!" announced the paging system, followed immediately by "Andrea at one!"

He took the corner too fast and bumped into the secretarial partition. Damn, that would cost him. "Andrea at two! Joe at two!" announced the spotters. He slid down in his chair to extend his legs a little more and picked up the pace. He kicked off the wall as he went around the last corner. The finish was a secretarial cubicle. Whoever turned into it first was the winner. He sideswiped Andrea right in front of it, but he had the front edge, and smashed past her into the cubicle first.

"For the fourth consecutive time, in a new record course time of 15.4 seconds, it's Joseph Nile by a whisker," announced Vishal. "The chipers retain the title!"

Andrea held up her hand and he slapped it. Everyone crowded around for a minute offering congratulations, and some pizza was brought out. "You know, Joe," Andrea said, "you're just a little too good at this. Me thinks you spend too much time here."

He laughed. "You're right."

"You coming in early tomorrow?" one of the other associates asked Joe.

"Yeah," Joe said.

Joe was handed several card keys. He knew what to do. He'd run them by the scanner in the morning so that if management checked the database, it would look like all these associates came to work early. The associates would come in later, after reception was manned and they didn't need their key, and would collect their card keys from Joe.

"So what nasty partner is keeping you here?" Andrea asked.

"Neuropt," Joe said.

"Ah, the company going public," Andrea said, then frowned. "You know, not only are they going after the paralysis, instead of a cure for the virus, they seem to be making an odd choice. It sounded to me like old technology that didn't work. These days, most people see the future as bioengineering to regenerate nerve cells, or using stem cells. There has been promising research in that area. They are implanting cells containing genetically engineered growth factors into injured spinal cords. They have found a class of proteins that can spur the growth of spinal cord axons. There's also some promising research on PEG — polyethylene glycol — a polymer similar to molecules in antifreeze."

"Are you sure this isn't just bio-phd jealousy of an electronics solution?" Joe asked.

"Yeah, right," Andrea said. "Have these guys made anything work?"

"Not yet," Joe said.

9.

It was the next morning, Tuesday, in São Paulo. Ahmet was watching the surgeon use the Retinal Screen on a virus victim. Burak had shipped the Retinal Screen in pieces in defiance of the injunction. Burak said he would claim, if asked, that it was just parts, not a Retinal Screen, and it didn't work anyway because of the bug. A subsequent e-mail to Ahmet told him a solution for the bug, and Ahmet had assembled it.

The hospital, Israelita Albert Einstein Clinic, was reputed to be the best in Brazil. The surgeon administered Methylprednisolone to limit the demyelination of the nerves by limiting the swelling. Ahmet opened the case with the Sheath, and the doctor carefully extracted it with tweezers and inserted it into the vacuum tube. The tube went all the way into the patient near the spine, where the surgeon had positioned it using the Retinal Screen. The far side of the tube was temporarily closed, and connected from a return tube to a machine which would apply the vacuum. When the surgeon turned on the vacuum, the Sheath was sucked up to the tool head. The surgeon then turned off the vacuum, and used the Retinal Screen controls to open the end of the tube, using the tool head to pull out the Sheath and position it around the spine.

Ahmet would have felt he could contribute more if there were some glitch with the Retinal Screen that required his technical knowledge, or the surgeon had some questions about how to operate the Retinal Screen. But the surgeon had learned quickly, and performed a flawless arthroscopic insertion of the Sheath. Ahmet called Cassia on his cell phone while he watched the surgeon through the window in the door.

"The surgery is going well," Ahmet said. "What are you up to?"

"I'm looking through my microscope," Cassia answered. "I'm looking at a tissue sample from a victim's stomach lining. There is the same residue of a plastic I found in another victim — the type of plastic used for time-delayed delivery of drugs."

"You told me before that the smallpox vaccination program was cancelled," Ahmet said. "So if you are still getting victims, it must not be the smallpox vaccine, right? Since the virus is continuing to spread?"

"Hardly anyone here thought the smallpox vaccine was contaminated," Cassia said, "but we had to eliminate it as a possibility. Or maybe someone behind this has switched from contaminating the smallpox vaccine to something else?" Cassia paused as she considered this. "We didn't find the plastic in an early Olympic athlete victim I just checked. Only in the most recent cases. It also wasn't in other earlier ones — we've been going back and checking."

"You're sounding a little paranoid, dear," Ahmet said. "Doesn't the evidence just show it wasn't the smallpox vaccine?"

"That's what everyone here says," Cassia sighed. "We've identified the thermoplastic material as what is used in new time-release drugs — it sticks to the walls of the stomach and gradually releases the desired drugs. The plastic is used in all sorts of vitamins and drugs."

"Wouldn't most people have that in their stomach anyway?" Ahmet asked.

"Again, that's what everyone here says," Cassia said. "But I've got a hunch and I'm getting desperate here. I'm going to visit the homes of some of these victims."

Thirty minutes later the surgeon was finished. "We can't get the Sheath much closer than that," the surgeon said. "It's wrapped around the spinal cord like cling-wrap. It's up to the therapist now."

The next patient was wheeled into the operating room as the first patient, Liberio, was wheeled out. Ahmet followed and observed the physical therapist. They had only used a local anesthesia during surgery, but Liberio had fallen asleep. He was already paralyzed from the waist down due to the virus, and apparently didn't feel the surgery. Within half an hour the shaking had stopped, and Libero was able to wiggle his toes. Ahmet called Cassia to report the success.

———

Erika was a few steps from Joe's office that same Tuesday morning when Vishal brushed past her, cut into Joe's office and closed the door. She had finally screwed up her courage to talk to Joe about what was going on with her husband, Ray. She decided to talk to Joe's secretary, Sid, and wait to see if it would be a short visit with Vishal. She knew Vishal bugged Joe, and Joe would usually try to keep it short.

"Bonjour, Sidney," she said.

"Erika darling," Sidney said, looking up from digging through his recycling box. Erika could smell his cologne more as he sat up. His cologne, as usual, had the upper hand over her own perfume in the battle of the noses. "It's always a pleasure to see your smiling face. Ohhh — and you're wearing your cashmere knit dress again, I see."

Erika blushed, caressing the fluffy outside of her dress. She knew why Sidney thought it was so special — it clung tightly to her and she'd seen the approving smiles of men — including Joe.

"I like the way it makes your butt look," Sidney continued.

"Best butt in the firm?" Erika asked, doing a half turn.

"After Joe's," Sidney smiled.

"I have to agree," Erika said. "Going through your garbage to practice for your next career?"

"Ha, ha, ha," Sid said. "I just threw out the last draft by accident. And of course it's one of the few times Joe says he wants to compare the latest draft to the prior one. I don't know why he gets into these moods. Something to do with my getting the wrong name on that letter, I suppose."

Joe's door opened and Vishal went back to his office. "Gotta go," she said, and swooped into Joe's office before he could get on the phone. Joe was standing by his desk, glancing up at her from the file he picked up.

She closed the door behind her, and then tested the latch. "I had better secure the door, Joe," she whispered in her best husky imitation of a male voice. "This is extremely sensitive stuff, I mean, uh, complex data and information, — that Vishal and his PhD have to converse with you about."

She tested the door latch, and then turned to face Joe, who was grinning and shaking his head.

She took a step, then paused and turned back to the latch and very gingerly tested it again. "Can't be too careful," she said in a barely audible voice. She turned to face Joe again and took a step toward him.

She paused again, and then turned to stare at the door again, as if it might explode open of its own will.

"Okay, okay, already!" Joe laughed. "You get the Oscar."

"Sorry about the partnership vote, Joe," Erika said. "Are you okay?"

"Fine," Joe said, picking up the picture on his desk. "I just don't know how I'll tell them."

Erika groaned. "I'm starting to worry about your obsession with those fake parents."

Joe stared at the couple in the picture. She knew that he didn't know who they were. He had said they looked like the ideal parents when he saw them in the frame in the store. So he just left the picture in there and put it on his desk. He never lied to anyone about them being his parents — he didn't need to. They just assumed. No one at work knew they weren't his real parents. Except her — she knew his mother died of a drug overdose and his father was a drunk who was wandering the streets of Miami the last Joe knew, 5 years ago.

"I heard Sandra moved out," Erika said.

"Yes, she was her usual, supportive self," Joe said with a forced smile. "I just wish she'd let her true feelings out and get angry with me, just once."

"You don't want to talk about it, do you?" Erika asked, losing her nerve to have a serious discussion about their respective marriages.

"Not really," Joe said.

She moved one foot toward Joe and then stopped, looking into Joe's eyes, which met her unflinching gaze. She looked aside to quickly tap the Edison bust and graze the Royaltec floor mat with her toe. She took another tentative step and stopped again within less than a foot of Joe. Then she rushed past Joe to sit in his chair. Without looking back at Joe, she switched his computer to the games application.

"What game do you want to play, mon cher?" She asked, turning her head to look back at Joe and smiling mischievously.

"I don't have time for a game," Joe said, moving behind Erika and putting both hands on the back of her chair to lean over her and look at the screen.

The door suddenly opened, with Sidney knocking only after it was mostly open.

"You just got a fax from Ned Stern," Sidney said.

Erika stood up and put a hand on Joe's shoulder as she leaned over to look at the fax. Sidney was doing the same thing on the other side of Joe. Neuropt had just been threatened with a lawsuit on some patent. The patent was alleged to cover a software routine for analyzing image data. The company was appropriately named SoftImage Data Inc. The three of them skimmed through the letter claiming that the Optospine would need to have such a routine in its software. There was also an enclosed Complaint which SoftImage was ready to file suit if Neuropt didn't settle immediately.

"Ned and Gage must be apoplectic over this," Joe said.

Erika knew the timing wasn't coincidental. It was a common trick to threaten to sue a company about to go public. The company wouldn't want to disclose in the prospectus that they were being sued since it could make it difficult to sell the stock. There wouldn't be time to investigate the patent. So it was an extortion situation — if they paid off the patent holder, the suit would be dropped, and they wouldn't have to disclose it in the prospectus.

Erika sat down again at Joe's computer while he continued reading and Sidney went back to his desk. She checked the Patent Office web site for the patent number. The file history wasn't there. It must be an older one they hadn't gotten around to scanning yet. She looked at her watch — the Patent Office would be closing soon. She dialed Bernie Sloan's number on Joe's phone, while switching Joe's computer to the games menu.

"I've got to deal with this," Joe said. "I can't play a game now."

"Okay," Erika said. "We'll just have to make it a quickie! And I'll keep it simple so it won't hurt your head."

She felt Joe's hands gently squeeze around her neck in a mock strangle. She took the opportunity to push her hand behind her against Joe's stomach. She liked the feel of his rippled stomach muscles. She really wanted to slide her hand inside his shirt, but resisted. She quickly looked back at the screen. "We'll make it tic-tac-toe, Joe," Erika said, marking her O first.

Bernie Sloan answered and she asked him to get a copy of the patent's file — the file history, while she responded to Joe's X.

The first two games were cat games.

Joe's cell phone rang — it was Ned.

Erika could hear Ned's loud voice. "Why didn't you find this in your search, Joe? Why are we finding out about it at the last minute?"

"We didn't have much time and — ," Joe started to say.

"I don't want to hear excuses," Ned said. "We need to deal with that patent *now*. We have only a few hours to finalize the prospectus so we can ship it tonight. I think we can get them down to $5 million to settle if you can come up with some reasons to throw doubt on its validity or their infringement claim."

"I'm on it," Joe said, marking his next X. Erika knew there were only a handful of patent attorneys who could determine if a patent was not infringed or invalid in a couple of hours. Joe Nile was one of them.

The next X's and O's went quickly. Erika tried to keep the mouse from Joe on the last move. "I know what move you want," she said, "I'll just make it for you since you are in a hurry." She tried to move to a losing square for Joe's X, but he grabbed her hand on the mouse and moved it back.

"So have you heard any gossip about partners leaving the firm?" Joe asked, looking down at her. "I've heard rumors, but no names. The word is that collections are weak."

"I prefer not to call it gossip," Erika said, leaning her head back to look up at Joe. "Think of it as a sophisticated intelligence gathering effort. We have our people everywhere. We watch who closes what door, compare different overheard comments from partners and piece them together at our headquarters, and double-check our conclusions with active intelligence gathering efforts, formulating key questions to ask certain partners."

"I thought some partners were just blabbermouths to their secretaries," Joe said.

"Yes, well, that too!" Erika laughed.

Undue Diligence

There was a knock at the door, and then Vishal opened it without waiting for an invitation. He looked at the tic-tac-toe game on the computer. "Okay, quit playing games you guys! Joe, Sidney got a couple copies of the patent, I figured we could go over it together in the conference room."

Joe turned to follow Vishal. "As long as you're at my computer, Erika," Joe said, "why don't you do some of my work?"

"I would," Erika said, "but I don't have the five minutes to spare that it would take to do all your work." Joe just grinned and shook his head.

"Well, I guess I can do some," Erika said, moving papers around on Joe's desk. "Here, this stack is to find some junior associate to dump on, this is to do mañana, this is to get an extension of time on — "

Joe stopped just as he was in the door. "So you really haven't heard anything?"

"I've heard stuff," Erika sighed.

———————

Bernie Sloan's arthritic knee protested as he got off the Metro at King Street in Alexandria, Virginia. He still had some searching to finish for Joe Nile, and now a file history to copy. Other than Joe, his work had really slowed down. Everyone seemed to want to use the young guys who were more comfortable with computers. He liked Joe, but everything was always urgent. Joe always offered to pay an "expediting fee," but Bernie just couldn't bring himself to charge it — heck, he just had to rearrange the order of his searches a little. Joe just owed him a lunch the next time he came to Washington D.C.

Paul C. Haughey

He walked into the middle of the U-shaped group of buildings that was the new Patent Office. He made a small detour. Not really a detour, since he always visited the Patent Office museum. It was to the right, inside the 10 story atrium. He didn't like it as much as the old museum. It was now a wall of TV screens, with glass-covered exhibits mixed in with the TV screens. The exhibits always changed; he didn't like that either. The next change was to be on Thomas Edison's birthday, February 11. They had a few gadgets for sale, but it wasn't the same as the old Invention Store at Crystal City. He used to stop there to see if they had any gadgets that had recently been patented. They sold a few things and also had a billboard with newspaper clippings describing other recent inventions that they didn't carry. Bernie liked to get things for his grandchildren there.

He had to admit he liked some of the museum exhibits. He still got a kick out of Lincoln being the only US President to be awarded a patent — Pat. No. 6,649 for an inflatable bellows system for helping a boat over shoals — something he invented when he was working on the river. Then there was the display about Thomas Jefferson acting as a patent examiner before he became president, while he was Secretary of State. And Clara Barton, before she started the Red Cross, had been a clerk at the Patent Office. Another display talked about how the Patent Office was the one building not burned to the ground when the British invaded and burned Washington during the War of 1812. The British officer in charge of burning the building had been convinced by the pleas that the contributions to science inside should not be destroyed.

Undue Diligence

Bernie left the museum and asked for Tang Nguyen at the security check in. Tang Nguyen was a primary examiner in group 2300, which handled computer systems applications. Tang told the guard to let him in, and he went through the metal detector and up the elevator. As a primary examiner, Tang had signature authority on office actions. Thus, Tang not only handled patent applications himself, he reviewed the work of some junior examiners. Tang should be able to give him some leads on where to look for this search. The elevator was crowded and stopped at every floor. Bernie never ceased to be impressed by the number of people who worked at the Patent Office — around 4000 examiners. Over a thousand patent applications were filed every single day. Every Tuesday the Patent Office issued nearly 4 thousand patents. The classification manual was 2 inches think, and all it did was list the different subject matter categories of the patents.

Tang was in his office, but he was with someone. Bernie waited patiently outside. It looked like a patent attorney was interviewing a case. Bernie knew it wouldn't take long. It was near the end of the quarter, and Tang probably was behind on making his quota. Each examiner had a quota of points to make each quarter. Points were awarded for two things — the first "office action," which was the initial written response of the examiner to the inventor, and disposals — which were either allowing or finally rejecting the application. This meant it was rare to have additional office actions, even if the patent attorney brought up new arguments, since there were no points for them. Instead the attorney had to file a continuation application, and pay a new fee, to have the patent application considered again. The attorney soon got up and left, and Bernie knocked on the door jam as he entered.

"Bernie! How are you doing?" Tang said.

"Fine, fine," Bernie said, looking back at the departing attorney. "An interview?"

"Yup," Tang said. "I let him have some narrow claims, and he's going to cancel the rest. So I get a disposal, and two more points. I'm almost there. He'll file a continuation on the broader claims, of course, but that just means more easy points, and also more filing fees for the good 'ol U S of A. Ca-ching!"

Tang moved his arm as if he were pulling on a slot machine. Bernie knew the patent fees had gone beyond making the Patent Office self-sufficient — they were a source of general revenue for the US budget. The more patents granted, the more revenue. It was no surprise that the number of patents being granted had skyrocketed.

"What have you got?" Tang asked. Bernie told him about the Optospine, and Tang explained where he should look for prior art.

Bernie headed into the Patent Office public search facility across the atrium from the museum. It was much larger than the old facility. There were 57 cubicles with computers downstairs, and that was only part of them. There were 260 upstairs. He was glad they still had microfiche machines. The old patents hadn't been put on the computer yet. There were a number of searchers at work. Al Chan was on the phone. Al used the search room as his office. Al had his cell phone as his office number, and the search room was a wireless hot spot, so he could use his laptop. Bernie used his search room card to go through the security gates — they were just like the Metro gates. He touched the bust of Thomas

Jefferson as he went by, then sat down at a computer terminal, typed in a few search words and got a list of patents back. He found it frustrating to look at the patents on the computer. Switching back and forth between the text and the figures was a pain.

He missed the old shoes. The "shoe" was a box cut away in front so you could see the front page of the patents and flip through them. The front page had the abstract and the most significant drawing so you could quickly see what it was about. Legend had it the name came from when Thomas Jefferson used to store patents in a shoebox under his bed, back when the Patent Office was a one-man operation. Bernie sighed after he looked at the first patent and sneaked a peak at the next few. They were pretty complicated — this was going to be slow going.

"Damn," Bernie said, sitting bolt upright. He had forgotten about Joe's file history.

Burak groaned and pulled back his sleeve to look at his watch a little later that afternoon. 4:00 PM. He had been on the phone in his office most of the afternoon. He heard a sound like ocean waves as he rocked the tip of his pinky finger in his ear to dig at the earwax. He didn't hear as well out of his left ear anymore. Maybe he should shift the phone earpiece to the right ear. But it just didn't feel natural.

He felt like a pariah. Between him and A.J. they had talked to a half dozen law firms. No one even wanted to have a meeting after hearing about the suit. One firm indicated interest, then called back to say no. Usually law firms would be clamoring for a new lawsuit.

It must be discrimination against Muslims. Or a conspiracy against his company.

He sighed. There was another possible explanation. An article about the lawsuit had been posted on the Internet in the morning, shortly after Royaltec's press release was posted. Several other articles had followed in quick succession. They all picked up on the theme that Telekinetics was financially on the ropes, and everything depended on the new Retinal Screen, which had just been unveiled at the trade show this morning. All the articles speculated that even if the recent verdict could be stayed and overturned on appeal, sales would be crippled by the new Royaltec lawsuit. They all had the same take as Jacob. It would be a long, expensive fight against Borland and Royaltec, and they figured Telekinetics couldn't afford it. They were right. Telekinetics couldn't even afford the $50,000 retainer some law firms were asking for. They were already delaying paychecks to the employees.

Burak heard his door open behind him, and looked around to see a US marshal, another man, and A.J.

"These guys have a court order," A.J. said. "Give them access to your computer. Your laptop, too."

"What is going on?" Burak asked.

"Your little stunt of shipping the Retinal Screen has won us a court order," A.J. said. "Gage Booth gets to have all our networks, shipping, everything monitored to make sure we don't violate the injunction again. We can't ship product, software or even send e-mails without it being monitored."

"How did they find out so fast?" Burak asked as he watched the man, who was a computer technician, load some software on his machine.

"The success of the Retinal Screen is all over the Internet," A.J. said. "What did you expect?"

"I expected," Burak said, "that when the judge saw lives being saved, he would lift the injunction."

Ten minutes after they left, Burak's computer beeped. It was the team in Brazil trying to set up a Net-Meeting. Burak added them into the videoconference. When the video came through, he could see Ahmet. He looked frantic.

"What is going on?" Burak asked.

"They destroyed the Retinal Screen," said Ahmet.

"What?" Burak said.

"Word got around, and the hospital was flooded with virus victims," Ahmet said. "We couldn't operate on them all, and some were dying while waiting. We had only one Retinal Screen. They started rioting, broke into the operating room, and ended up trashing everything in there, including the Retinal Screen. Fools."

"Allah help them," Burak said.

"You have to send another Retinal Screen," Ahmet said. "Send the second prototype and get more built ASAP. We're arranging for better police protection this time."

"I am afraid it will not be so easy this time," Burak said. "We have a new problem."

Joe anxiously looked at the clock display in the corner of his computer. It was almost 5 PM that afternoon. The Patent Office had closed hours ago, and still no file history from Bernie. He clicked on the next article in the list pulled up from his keyword search on the Internet. He was desperately searching the Internet to show the invention in the patent had been thought of before the patent was filed, to show the patent was invalid. He knew Ned would blame him for not finding out about this patent in his due diligence. Max would believe Ned, and might feel that Joe had to be fired to save face. Nevermind that Neuropt didn't give him sufficient time to find it.

Joe could just imagine Neuropt refusing to pay the firm's bill because the failure to find the patent earlier forced them to spend $5 million to settle. It was worth a lot to have the prospectus clean — it could cost a fortune in a lower stock price or fewer buyers if Neuropt was trying to go public under the cloud of a patent suit.

"Joe," Sidney called out from his cubicle, "Ned Stern is on the phone. Why do you have your phone on Do Not Disturb?"

"Joe, it's nearly five o'clock," Ned said when Joe answered the phone. "We need to ship off the prospectus, and this SoftImage Data asshole is still asking for twenty million dollars. Please tell me you have some good news."

"We just got faxed pages from the file history a few minutes ago," Joe lied. "I need to go through it, and finish my online search. I'll have something for you soon."

Joe hung up, called Bernie again, and got voice mail again. He struggled to focus his eyes on the article he had turned up in his online search. It took all his powers of concentration to wade through the engineer speak and figure out what the article was about. He finally decided it was no help, and clicked on the next article.

"Here's the fax from Bernie," Sidney interrupted as Joe waited for the page to come up on his screen. Sidney dropped a stack of pages on Joe's desk.

"He kept screwing up the fax," Sidney volunteered as Joe leafed through the pages. "I had to call him twice to have him resend some of the pages. He doesn't know how to scan and e-mail? I don't know why you keep using this guy."

Joe looked up and waved the pages. "Results and timeliness. Well, results."

Sidney sniffed, did a half spin and headed for the door. "That makes your job easier, not mine."

"Right," Joe said. "Let's switch to someone who sends us the wrong stuff, but can fax it perfectly."

"Now you're talking," Sidney said.

Joe quickly scanned the faxed pages from the SoftImage Data patent file history. The Examiner had made some comments on how he interpreted the language of the claims. It was helpful for half of the terms in the claim. SoftImage couldn't try to interpret the vague language in those claims any broader than what the Patent Office examiner had said they meant. But the other half of the claim was still a problem, and time had almost run out.

He went back to the online search he was doing. The next article wasn't any help, nor was the next. His phone rang again — it was Ned.

"We're out of time," Ned said. "We need to ship the prospectus, so we need to settle right now. Do you have anything or not?"

Joe was scanning the next article as Ned was speaking. Paydirt! It showed that the elements in the second half of the claim had been thought of before.

"We've got them between a rock and a hard place," Joe said, quickly explaining what he had found.

"What do you suggest we settle for?" Ned said.

"Don't," Joe said. "Call his bluff. Disclose it in the prospectus. Say we think it is either invalid or not infringed. We can wrap some language around this to explain this happens all the time, and that it appears to be an extortion attempt at the last minute. Of course we'll use nicer language than that."

"I need Max to sign off on this," Ned said.

"I'll conference him in," Joe said. Joe held his breath, but luckily reached Max on his cell phone. He conferenced in Max, explained what he had found, and Max thankfully agreed with Joe's assessment.

"That's what I wanted to hear," Ned said. "Can you draft some language and e-mail it in the next 15 minutes?"

"No problem," Joe said.

Joe set the phone down. He knew the prospectus would be printed within the hour, then would be hand carried on a red-eye flight to Washington D.C. for filing with the SEC tomorrow. The prospectus was being shipped, he had cleared it, and he still didn't know how the hell the Optospine worked.

10.

Max was steamed the next morning. He couldn't believe the Executive Committee had even agreed to listen to Zenko's proposal to take on a new case for Telekinetics when they still hadn't been paid for the last one. He was determined to derail this.

Max slouched in his chair and glanced at the other Executive Committee members as Zenko put his laptop and projector on the faded mahogany table. Max looked at his watch while Zenko pulled down the projection screen and then adjusted the window blinds — a slide show seemed excessive.

Thankfully, Zenko only had a few slides outlining the merits of the Telekinetics case. Zenko claimed there was no way a jury would go for Royaltec. Indeed, the side-by-side pictures of the cabled contraption from the Royaltec patent and the neural network semiconductor chip used in the Retinal Screen showed that they couldn't have been more different. Zenko said that no matter how many experts they paraded out to confuse matters, he'd make mincemeat out of Royaltec at trial. Max groaned.

"What's the problem, Klein-san?" Zenko asked. "You don't think I can win?"

"I think you can win," Max said. Zenko bowed his head slightly at the affirmation. "I just don't think Telekinetics can last until trial. Not to mention all the money they still owe us. Why on earth would we work for a client we know can't pay? I've heard they shopped this to a half dozen firms, which have all turned them down."

"How about the fact that their product might end up saving all our lives from the virus?" Zenko asked.

"That's pretty speculative," Max said.

Evans spoke up. "But they're *our* client, have been for years. We built this firm on defending the little guy. Plus, Zenko pointed out to me that if we don't defend them, they'll go under and will never be able to pay what they owe us. We'd be protecting our investment in them."

"Did you ever hear the expression *sunk costs are ir-relevant?*" Max asked. "Our AR is sunk costs — sunk like the Titanic. We need to cut our losses."

"Honorable Executive Committee," Zenko said. "I believe so strongly in this case, and that Telekinetics will be able to pay, that I'm willing to forgo my partner draw until we get paid. Any money Telekinetics pays before the trial is over will go to the firm, but I won't take a dime of it."

Turner leaned forward and looked around. "Well, that clinches it for me. Besides, it's not like we have a lot of choice here. If we don't take it, Zenko and a couple associates won't have any work to do. It's better than having to let some people go."

Evans spoke up. "It's too bad the litigation associates don't have the skills for patent prosecution. We have tons of that kind of work."

Max shook his head. "No, no, no. You guys just don't get it. If we take work that isn't going to pay, that is worse than having no work and laying people off. If we lay people off, the ones left will have work, we'll be able to afford to pay them, and the firm continues to exist. If we take work that doesn't pay, we can't afford to pay everyone because our overhead is too high — we have too many mouths to feed and not enough money coming in. The money that does come in from other paying work gets spread out more, having to pay more salaries, and it just won't be enough. We end up destroying the firm. We can't pay salaries, people leave, and the firm unravels and goes bankrupt."

Max looked around at the blank faces of the Executive Committee members. He could see he was losing this argument — and probably losing the firm with it.

———

That same morning in Las Vegas, Burak was slamming on the brakes. He could feel his pulse racing and had to catch his breath. That was close. The strip in Las Vegas was crowded for a Wednesday, with rental cars driven by out-of-towners, interspersed with crazy taxi drivers. Only an idiot would be talking on a cell phone. He tentatively applied the gas again as traffic began to move.

"Now wait just a minute," Burak said into his cell phone to the University of California representative. "You cannot cancel an order just because some lawyer for Royaltec threatens you. If you wait to buy the Optospine from Neuropt, you'll be waiting forever. They have vaporware, with no prospects for a real product anytime soon. Plus, you will have the same problem. Royaltec or someone else will eventually come after them too. And it is not a problem. This Royaltec patent is bullshit. They are just trying to get to us through you."

"That's not what he said," the customer replied. "He said if I buy, he would sue me. I asked what would happen if I bought from Neuropt. He said they wouldn't sue — Neuropt will be licensed."

Burak slammed on the brakes again, and then felt his car get bumped by the guy behind him. Damn. He put the car in park.

"He is bluffing," Burak said. "He is just trying to scare you off. They want to ruin us financially so we will be forced to settle. They will not sue you."

"It's not that we're scared," his customer said. "But how can I justify taking on this risk when I can get another product — granted, perhaps not as good — somewhere else without the risk? Are you willing to guarantee we won't get sued? Will you indemnify us for any loss we might suffer?"

Burak walked to the back of the car while still talking on his phone, and checked out the bumper. The other driver was also talking on his phone as he looked at his car. Burak didn't see any damage. He looked at the other driver and shrugged, and the guy shrugged back. They both went back to their cars without saying a word to each other.

"Maybe so," Burak said. "I will talk to my lawyer. We may be able to indemnify you. So do not cancel. Wait for me to get back to you, OK?"

"I'll wait 'til tomorrow," said the customer. "I can't wait any longer." Shit, Burak thought. He was hoping to buy more time than that.

"Your secretary said you wanted to see me right away," Joe said later that morning as he stepped into Zenko's office.

"I've got Burak and A.J. on the phone," Zenko said. "They've been sued by Royaltec."

"The masters of the paper patent," Joe groaned.

"Paper patent?" Burak asked.

"One where they never built the invention," Joe said. "The Patent Office doesn't require that an invention be built, just that it be described on paper. Inventors used to build something first, but nowadays most patents are paper patents — on things that have never been built."

"Great," Burak said. "What a wonderful patent system your country has. And why are you talking to us, Joe? Shouldn't you be helping your new client, Gage Booth, keep his injunction against us?"

"I heard about that," Joe said. "I think it's ridiculous. I'm working for Neuropt, not Gage Booth or Royaltec. They're completely separate. And I'd have to get my managing partner's approval to work for you, since you haven't paid your bills. The only reason I'm here is because Zenko didn't tell me it was to talk to you."

Joe paused, wondering if he had gone too far in responding to Burak's trash talking. "I presume," Joe continued, "that you are trying to get the Feds to intervene on the Inventech injunction?"

"With about as much luck as you guys had in the Inventech trial," Burak replied.

"So about Royaltec," Joe said. "I guess they sued you on their robot patent?" Joe asked.

"How'd you know?" A.J. said.

"They've been waving it around," Joe said. "This one's actually not a paper patent. Royaltec just bought it from a company called AutoSmart. Royaltec also does data mining of patents. They look for existing patents with vague language that sounds like new technology. This patent is on a robotics system for applying tension to cables. The cables connect a number of arms of some convoluted robot that looked like an erector set. Royaltec is now claiming it covers a neural network microprocessor. The patent attorney had happened to use vague enough language, and the right terminology, so that in addition to covering the robotic system, the claim, if looked at in isolation, seems to also describe aspects of an imbedded neural network."

"I still don't get it," Burak said. "How can a patent on robotics read on a neural network?"

Joe smiled. Burak had learned some patent law. *Read on* is a term patent attorneys use to mean the claim language is read broadly enough to cover a product.

"The nodes of the cables can be read on the nodes in a neural network," Joe explained, looking at the patent that Zenko pushed in front of him. "The claim also says that the stress applied to the nodes is detected, and the cables attached to them are strengthened by increasing the tension. But the claim doesn't mention that it is stress applied to *cable* connections by increasing *tension*, it just says the connections are strengthened. It doesn't even use the word *cable* in the claim. So if you didn't know what patent this was in, it would sound like a neural network. And the claim talks about a computer as part of the system, so Royaltec can say the system is a chip, with the computer being the standard microprocessor, and the connection system being the imbedded neural network.

"The patent figures and description talk about strengthening the connections, or cables, when excessive pressure was applied to nodes, to take up slack. They clearly meant cables, not electrical connections in a neural network. But the claims aren't clear."

"I know a little bit about this patent. It was actually filed *after* the first neural networks were developed, but before *imbedded* neural networks were developed. As you know, an imbedded neural network is a chip with both a regular microprocessor and a neural network microprocessor — the neural network microprocessor is *imbedded* on the regular microprocessor chip."

"This sounds nuts," Burak said. "Surely a jury would see right through this crap."

"How'd the jury do on the last lawsuit?" A.J. asked.

"Point taken," Burak said.

"Look at the people standing in line at the grocery store," A.J. continued. "That's your jury. They won't be engineers who understand this stuff."

Zenko finished the call saying he'd get back to them with a plan for the lawsuit, and then looked over at Joe.

"Nile-san, you know I consider you the most talented attorney at this firm," Zenko said.

"Cut out the Nile-san crap," Joe said. "What do you need?"

Zenko bowed his head — he couldn't look at Joe. "I need your help again on the Telekinetics defense. As you know, the management committee approved my handling it, and they said I could have a quarter of your time, after you finish the Neuropt work. But I can't wait. I need a non-infringment opinion for Telekinetics, to block Royaltec from charging that Telekinetics willfully infringed. I know you're busy and aren't finished with Neuropt, but I was hoping you could start this one thing in stealth mode. You know the technology and the patent. It'll probably only take you a few days. Hell, you're so efficient, you might even be able to do it in a day."

"I'll get in trouble," Joe said. "Even though Neuropt filed its prospectus, I still have to draft the opinion and put all the documentation together. Max said that takes priority over everything. As far as stealth mode goes, you know that they can monitor the network. Max might check to see what documents I'm working on to see if I'm only doing Neuropt. Plus, I don't have the time. I was up to my eyeballs in work before I took on Neuropt, and now those clients are clamoring to have their projects finished."

"So you'll do it?" Zenko asked.

"Of course," Joe said. "I'll do the work on a laptop so it can't be traced."

"Remember that it's okay for you to work on it, Zenko said, "just not now. So save up your time entries, and post-date them after you finish the Neuropt project."

Joe nodded. "You're not going to OD on antidepressants and miss a court appearance again, are you?"

"No way," Zenko said with a bow, extending his hand to Joe, "Deal?"

Joe grasped Zenko's hand firmly for a moment.

"Zenko," Joe said as he was almost out the door, "there's no way it will take me a whole day to do that opinion."

———

Joe looked at the clock as he clicked the e-mail to send the completed opinion to Zenko. Just after 5:30. Not bad, it just took an afternoon to complete the opinion. A moment later Sidney came into Joe's office, knocking without stopping, and dropped a large manila envelope on Joe's desk.

"You know," Joe said, "most people knock *before* they come into an office."

"I'm in a hurry," Sidney said, shifting from one foot to the other while looking idly out the window.

The envelope had a Neuropt return address, but was marked "Personal." It was stamped received yesterday. "Why didn't I get this yesterday?" Joe asked.

"I forgot," Sidney shrugged. "You had me too busy with other work."

Joe grabbed a pen, put the tip under the exposed flap, and started to rip it open. He stopped and stared at Sidney.

"Oh, all right," Sidney said, twisting around and hastening out the door.

Joe reached in and pulled out some black, lacy panties. He recognized them as Alicia's. There was a note:

> Since you seemed to like them, I thought you should have them. Feel free to put your hand inside them and feel around! Love, Alicia

Joe smiled, reached inside the panties with his hand, and gently caressed the silky material between his thumb and forefinger. He put the panties back in the envelope and shoved it to the edge of his desk. He had work to do.

After about five minutes, he became aware of a presence at his door. He looked up. Erika was standing there.

"I've been watching you for about a minute," Erika said. "You sure know how to concentrate."

He nervously glanced at the envelope with the panties as Erika pushed the door mostly closed and approached his desk. She stopped with her legs against the edge of his desk, practically touching the envelope. He kept looking at her face, avoiding looking at the envelope.

"Joe," Erika said softly. "There's something I've been meaning to tell you, but I haven't found the right time. And you have to agree to keep it secret."

"Deal," Joe said.

Erika looked down, absent-mindedly pushing the manila envelope back and forth. She jerked herself straight up and looked at Joe and whispered. "Okay, I'll just blurt it out. Ray left me for someone else. We're getting a divorce. He finally left a few months ago, but he had been cheating on me for some time. I found out almost a year ago, and we tried to work it out. But it was clear he wanted her more, so that went nowhere. I didn't want anyone at work to know my business, and I didn't want men coming on to me while I was sorting this out, so I didn't tell anyone."

"I had no idea," Joe said, feeling a bit slighted that Erika didn't tell him.

"No one knew," Erika continued. "We had problems before that anyway. Ray was just too unstable for me. He'd get involved in one start-up after another, and they'd always fail, and he'd end up without work again. So I could never quit my job to spend more time with Jeffrey. Not that I would do that, I like my work too much. But it would be nice to have the security of that option."

She looked down and started fidgeting with the manila envelope again. "There," she said softly without looking up, "I said it. I just thought, and I know it's soon, but since Sandra left you, and since both of our marriages have broken-up —"

As Erika continued to push the manila envelope around, the panties poked out. He watched as she pulled them out, as if in slow motion. He tried to grab the note, but Erika snatched it and spun around to read it.

"Well, I guess I'm too late," she said, her voice rising. "And I thought I was too early. You just separated from your wife a few days ago, and already you're sleeping with someone else? You slut."

"Uhmm," Joe managed to eek out. He was tongue-tied.

"Well, I guess I've just made a fool of myself," Erika said as she hurried to the door. She hesitated at the door and looked back at Joe. "Did you know that Trevor West was sleeping with your wife?"

Joe's mouth dropped open.

"I didn't think so," Erika said. "I'll let you get back to working for the King of Trolls. Maybe you can help him keep other products from being used to save lives." She stuck out her tongue then spun and hurried away.

Joe sat stunned for a few minutes, absorbing the two body blows from Erika. He slowly got to his feet then hurried over to Erika's cubicle. She had gone home already. He got her home and cell phone numbers from the office manager, claiming he had an emergency question on a conflict. He called and left her several messages, until she called back directly into his voice mail and said she just didn't want to talk about it. He had no idea she was available. That would have changed everything. He shook his head — things were happening too fast.

His heart jumped as his phone rang, and then sank. It wasn't Erika. He recognized the number displayed as Morton Silverman from Golden West Ventures. Morton was an angel investor whom he had worked with before on a few projects. The projects usually involved evaluating the patent position of some company Morton was thinking of funding.

Angel investors were rich individuals who took on companies that the venture capitalists were not willing to touch, usually because they were too early in the development cycle. There was a pecking order on who got a shot at the best companies. The established venture capitalists got first shot because they could offer an experienced and respected businessman on the Board of Directors, and had other connections of value to the company. They could open doors. Next came the lesser known venture capitalists, and then angel investors.

"Hey, Mort," he said, "What's up?"

"Well, I don't have a project for you this time," Morton said. Although I will likely have one in a few weeks."

"No problem," he said. "We're busy, but we'll find a way to fit it in for you."

"That's what I like about you, Joe," Morton said. "Your can-do attitude. I actually just called to say I'm pleased to be able to get your patent analysis for an investment of mine without paying you for it. When I realized that was happening, I was just tickled pink!"

"Really?" Joe asked, perplexed. "How's that?"

"I'm investing in Neuropt," Morton said. "I was planning to pay you to analyze their patent position, but then I was told you were already working on an opinion for the company. So I figured, if you're able to give that opinion, that's good enough for me. And I get the benefit of your advice without paying for it."

"I was about to invest in a gene-therapy start-up," Morton continued, "they called themselves Spinal Tap, of all things. They were just spun off from an incubator. But Neuropt sounds like they have a much better solution for treating paralyzed people, and farther along, too, if they'll have a product in six months. I think our money is also safer there, since they have some big investors with patent portfolios to protect Neuropt. Spinal Tap is more of a sitting duck for patent suits."

"Shit!" Joe said aloud after Morton hung up. His opinion wasn't an endorsement. Neuropt going bust would be one thing, Morton losing money would be worse. He wondered which incubator was spinning off Spinal Tap. He didn't recognize that name, and he had worked on a few incubators — companies whose purpose was to come up with ideas, put together a management team, and get them far enough along on development to spin them off as an independent company, with the new company's stock being held by the incubator's investors.

Joe felt a renewed urgency to pin down whether Neuropt was all hot air, as he was beginning to suspect. He was supposed to just finish the opinion, but decided to investigate a little more. He looked up the inventors' home addresses on one of the Neuropt applications he thought was iffy. His previous efforts to contact the inventors at work had been thwarted. Harold Walsh had insisted on answering all technical questions to avoid taking the inventors away from their work, and the inventors' admins had redirected his calls to Harold Walsh.

Paul C. Haughey

As he got the four inventors' home phone numbers from information, he worked on his excuse. He could say he called them at home to avoid taking them away from their work. Weak — but good enough.

The first inventor answered, but said he didn't have time to talk, and referred him to Harold Walsh. The second inventor simply said he was too busy to talk about it. He claimed to be working at home, and perhaps he was. The third inventor was pay dirt — Nigel Frederickson was more than willing to talk. Nigel was young, and was apparently listed as an inventor for a minor contribution. Joe apologized for calling at home, but said he had finally gotten a quiet moment to work on this, but it was too late to call at work. Joe then explained that he was just checking on how this invention might work, emphasizing that it was common to file patent applications on speculative inventions that the inventors weren't sure they could build. This got Nigel comfortable talking about how little they had done. Nigel didn't know about the sensors — his area was the optical neural network. But he knew he hadn't seen anything concrete on a sensor design, and they weren't anywhere close to knowing how to build the optical neural network. There was no way they could have a product in 6 months.

Ned slowly paced the room later that evening, looking alternately at Roger Borland and the three-sided boomerang-shaped speakerphone in the middle of the marble desk. Gage's voice had stopped for the moment.

Gage had learned that Zenko was handling Telekinetics' defense. He had checked with some of his buddies in the business, and hadn't liked what he heard. Ned could hear the flipping of pages and figured Gage was looking through articles he had obtained on Zenko. Ned hated it when a client got involved like this, and tried to second-guess the lawyers. He looked across the conference table at Roger Borland. Roger was leaning back in his chair with his arms across his stomach, staring at the speakerphone with a bemused look.

"The best damn trial lawyer they've ever seen," Gage continued. "I heard that from two different executives whose companies got *destroyed* in lawsuits they thought they should have won easily."

There was a long silence. "The best trial lawyer they've ever seen. Did anyone pull their head out of their ass enough to check to see who Telekinetics' attorneys were before we filed the damned suit? Couldn't you assholes have found out ahead of time that this guy Zenko would be defending him? How could this have happened?"

"Calm down," Ned said. He knew Gage could turn on him in an instant. If the money weren't so good, he wouldn't have anything to do with him as a client.

"First of all, that's old news," Ned continued. "Zenko lost his last two cases. He's a has-been. Besides, Zenko won't be a factor."

"Not a factor?" Gage yelled. "How can you say that? He's handling the damn case for them. It seems to me he's a huge factor."

Ned smiled. "I know Zenko. And, yes, he's an impressive trial lawyer. He's quick on his feet in front of a jury. But," Ned paused a moment for drama, "and this is a big *but* — he's not very good at preparing for trial."

Ned paused again to let this sink in. "And he'll never get to trial. The trial won't be for years. We'll make sure of that."

"And if you check around," Ned continued, looking over at Roger, "you'll find that the best attorney around for *delaying* a trial and burying someone with discovery and motions is Roger Borland." Roger gave a slight bow of his head.

"Telekinetics will be history long before then," Ned said. "And Zenko doesn't have the skills to stop it."

There was not a word from the phone for a moment, then a chuckle that got louder and evolved into a long belly laugh. "I love it!" Gage said. "They hire the best fighter around, but we never let him into the ring."

"I also happen to know," Roger spoke up, "that Zenko's firm won't give him the associate help he needs on this case. In fact, he's been frozen out of assigning new work to any associates, and has had some associates taken off his cases because his management is concerned about his case selection."

"And don't forget we have practically destroyed his firm," Ned added. "We could finish them off if we needed. The bankers for Turner, West are one of our clients. We know that Turner, West has drawn down all of their credit line and is behind on repayment."

The laughter from the speaker continued. Then it slowly stopped, and the line was oddly silent for a moment before Gage asked, "If they aren't giving him associate help, who the hell is working this case for him?"

Jeff raced bare-chested down the hall of Erika's apartment the next morning, snapping his shirt against the wall — the one Erika had just struggled to put on him. His pout was so exaggerated it was comical. She just sighed — he was in one of those attention-demanding modes. She knew from experience that there was no substitute for her spending some extra time with him. She was going to be late again.

She sat down and clicked on her home computer, logging in remotely to the Turner, West network. At least she could get a little work done between her pampering of Jeff. She gave him his Pokeman cards. They had a little game they played so she could check her e-mail. She would say something about what the e-mail message said, and then ask Jeff to tell her how to respond. Usually it was simple yes or no. But Jeff had an elaborate technique of putting cards down and pretending to read them to get an answer. He was distracted long enough for her to read the message, and start working on a response. She also called her voice mail, and put it on the speaker. Since Jeff could also hear the messages, he didn't feel left out. Usually.

An e-mail from Cassia had come in. Cassia expressed her frustration with the virus, and described all the people dying. Erika's eyes welled up with tears. Cassia said she didn't think the virus was natural, and was going out in the field today to check her theory. She couldn't say anything more right now.

Erika cocked her head to the side. What did she mean, not natural?

There were several phone messages from Joe. She deleted them all without listening to them. Joe had also sent an e-mail. She was about to delete it when she realized it was a work project. Joe wanted Erika to do a Dunn & Bradstreet report on Neuropt and any related companies, and a report on Gage Booth and any companies he was previously involved with. Then he wanted her to search for articles on him and those companies.

She pursed her lips, while running her hand across the spongy softness of the Daffy Duck mouse pad. Why was he asking for a D&B on his own client? She asked Jeff if she should get the D&B for him. Jeff put down several cards, rearranged them, then looked up and said yes.

She requested the D&B over the Internet. After half an hour, she was finally able to get Jeff to keep his shirt on and load him into the car. He then proceeded to throw a minor fit when she left him at daycare. Her patience was gone by now. Daycare would just have to deal with him. She left him wailing.

She felt okay about Jeff as she drove to work. He had to learn that his crying wasn't going to get him out of daycare. But by the time she stepped in the elevator, she was feeling guilty. She turned on the computer, and then went to get some coffee while it went through its turn-on routine. Her computer was as bad as she was in the morning.

She printed out the D&B and glanced through it, noting the names of the related companies. She was about to start the literature search Joe requested, then stopped. She pulled up Joe's e-mail and replied she was too busy; he should get his girl Alicia to do it. Then she threw the D&B in the trash.

———

That afternoon in São Paulo, Cassia bounded up the stairs to the victim's apartment with her assistant, a computer expert. It was the fifth one she had visited today. Her exhaustion was overcome by the adrenaline that came with her frantic desperation to stop the virus.

"Have you seen Jorge's new Porsche?" asked her assistant as he gasped for breath near the top of the stairs.

"He has a new Porsche?" Cassia replied, suddenly interested.

"Yes, bright red," the assistant said, stopping to catch his breath. "Loaded with extras."

"I'm surprised he could buy it on his salary," Cassia said.

The assistant shrugged. "I heard Jorge say he inherited some money from an uncle who died."

"Wasn't Jorge working on the smallpox vaccine distribution?" Cassia asked.

"Yeah, why?" the assistant asked.

"Nothing," Cassia said, pushing aside the quarantine tape. The stench hit her immediately, the nausea almost overcoming her. She could see the body in the middle of the entryway. The first police on the scene had refused to touch the body, and the coroner was backed up and hadn't gotten there yet. Sometimes it would take days to remove a body. She covered her nose with a handkerchief, and leaned against the wall as she edged by. The wooziness subsided slightly when she no longer had the body in sight.

By now, she knew what she was looking for, and headed straight toward the bathroom. The victim had been a packrat — there were piles of magazines, papers, letters and pictures everywhere. The place was a pigsty. She continued to hold her hand to her nose to ward off the nausea. She went through the medicine cabinet, but didn't find what she was looking for.

Her phone rang. It was an assistant in Foreign Affairs. The US was stalling on responding to the request for intervention against the injunction of the Retinal Screen. She turned beet red when she heard the reasons. She had been involved in the campaign to threaten the big drug companies with compulsory licensing on AIDS drugs. They let people die then, she didn't doubt they'd let people die now. "What spineless, inhuman assholes!" she shouted into the phone. "We should cancel the damned quarantine and let the virus spread to the U.S. You tell them that!"

She hung up, knowing the U.S. would be told no such thing. The Americans were useless. She'd have to handle the virus on her own.

She met her assistant in the kitchen. He just shook his head no. She looked in the drawers of a nightstand by the bed. O bicho! It was a bottle of Adbil Cold & Sinus, partially consumed. Adbil was an Advil generic, produced by one of the main drugstores in Brazil. She held the label close to her eyes, next to a plastic bag with the other two bottles she had found in the second and fourth homes they had visited. The font was the same. She looked again at the label on the bottle of legitimate Adbil in her pocket — the font was different, all right. Looking closely, she could see all three counterfeit bottles had frayed ink around the edges of the lettering. Even generics were counterfeited.

The previous victims had no computer, and no record of the purchase. They could have bought the Adbil anywhere, in any flea market in town or at a kiosk.

She showed the bottle to her assistant. "Okay," he said. "I'll check out the computer."

Cassia started looking through the wastebaskets, then in the drawers, hoping to find the package the Adbil had been shipped in. There was at least some advantage to this victim being a packrat — he didn't seem to throw out anything.

"Found it!" her assistant yelled. She rushed into the bedroom and looked over his shoulder. The victim had gone to a website to buy the counterfeit Adbil. There was even a record of an e-mail acknowledgement of the order.

"Can you track the website to a company with an address?" Cassia asked.

"Maybe," the assistant said.

"I'm heading back to the office," Cassia said. "After you're finished with the computer, check through the mountain of trash in this house. Then visit some kiosks and flea markets."

———————

Joe grabbed his gym bag and headed out at noon that day. He was already running late for the volleyball game. He and Burak used to go to the same pick-up game every Thursday. But Joe hadn't made one in weeks. Burak had gotten him to agree to go today, even though he didn't have time. Burak said if he could get back from Vegas to make it, Joe could make the drive. By the time he arrived at the gym and changed, the game was already going.

One side was short one person, so he jumped into the middle of the court, after grabbing one of the sandwiches on the sideline. The duty to get sandwiches for everyone rotated each week. He took a few bites, and then quickly stuffed it in his pocket as he saw Burak grinning at him from the other side. The other side set Burak up for a spike, but he hit it too hard, and it went out of bounds.

"Afraid to hit it my way?" Joe called out.

"Next one is right at you!" Burak shouted back. Joe lifted his hand, palm up and waved his fingers toward himself, signaling Burak to bring it on. It was all part of the game. Joe had to act like he wanted Burak to spike it his way, and that he would enjoy digging it out. In truth, Burak had a monster spike, and Joe felt like his arm was almost broken the last time he tried to hit Burak's slam back. Most people in this pick-up game would just get out of the way when Burak spiked.

Sure enough, on the next set, Burak spiked it right at Joe's feet. He dove for it, and managed to dig it out. Unfortunately, he sent it out of bounds where his teammates couldn't get to it. Burak was beaming.

After a few rotations, Joe finished his sandwich with bites between rallies, and found himself opposite Burak at the net.

"Joe," Burak whispered. "You have done it again. I read your opinion. Zenko sent me the draft. It is excellent. I am glad you are so confident we will win against Royaltec. They are dead meat. Allah has answered my prayers."

Joe was perplexed for a second. "Uh, Burak," Joe whispered, looking around to be sure no one else was listening. "That opinion is a willfulness opinion — it's just so you can say you relied on the opinion to avoid a charge of willful infringement. It protects you against punitive treble damages for knowingly infringing, in case you lose at trial. It doesn't mean you'll win — we are not actually that confident that you will win."

"What?" Burak asked. "What are you telling me? You gave me an opinion that is not true?"

The ball came Burak's way, and he set it to another player. Joe shifted over and leaped up to help his teammate try a block. By trying to avoid the block, the spiker sent it sailing out of bounds.

"The opinion is correct," Joe said. "But this goes in front of a jury that doesn't understand the stuff. It's a crapshoot. And it's determined by things other than who's right. It's determined by which expert comes across as more believable to the jury, whose attorney the jury likes more; things like that. So you could still lose this thing."

"I see," Burak said. "So you give me one opinion in writing, and another orally, that you just gave me. I am familiar with things like this in the old country. This is like two sets of accounting books. One for real, one for the IRS."

Joe cringed. "No, it's an opinion of what we think the right result is. But, like an engineering design, there's a margin of error of 50%. But we don't want to say that in the opinion, or Royaltec will argue that it is no good, and you knew you were infringing."

"I see," Burak said. "Now you slam engineers just because I compared a lawyer to an accountant. We never sell a product if there is a 50% degree of error. I must have hit a nerve."

"Burak," Joe said, getting annoyed, "It's just that there is a lot of risk that the jury will screw up and get it wrong. In fact, juries get it wrong as much as they get it right."

"Okay, okay," Burak said. "I get the point. But I am beginning to wonder why we have patent attorneys who give us an opinion that is no good. If you were a car maker, you would be out of business. We may have to send suicide bombers after Royaltec now."

"Turks don't do that," Joe said.

"What do you mean?" Burak said. "All Muslims are the same."

———

Joe found it hard to concentrate on work that afternoon after the volleyball game. Burak's comment didn't bother him, but Neuropt still gnawed at him. He tried Alicia's number again and got her voicemail — again. She hadn't returned any of his messages since the prospectus had been filed. How could he break up with her if she wouldn't call him back? Even though he and Alicia were a farce, he wanted to be able to say he broke it off so he could go after Erika, hopeless as it might be. He knew that Erika would judge him, like any woman would, on whether he broke it off face to face.

He headed off to the bar at 7 PM — late, he knew. Only Zenko and Hank were still there.

"Nile-san!" Zenko called out loudly enough for the whole bar to hear as Joe sat down next to him. Zenko put his hand on Joe's shoulder. "I was just telling Hank-san about that hot admin you are going out with."

"Time to spill," Hank said. "Do you have pictures? How is she in bed?"

"You guys are disgraceful," Joe said. "Would you tell me that stuff about your wives?"

"Sorry," Zenko said. "I know it must be hard on you, with Sandra leaving you."

"Have you heard from Sandra?" Hank asked.

"No," Joe replied, surprised at how he felt nothing. Their love really had died long ago.

"Nile-san," Zenko said, "you are better off having Sandra leave before you make partner. If you were a partner, they would value your partnership like it was some asset you didn't have to work for every day. Sandra would get half of that in the divorce, and you'd have to sell whatever else you have to pay for it."

"I can't believe you hooked up with someone else so quickly," Hank said with a frown. Then Hank grinned and gave Joe a high five. "You the man."

"Actually, I didn't hook up with her," Joe said. "She was just trying to milk me for information. So I let her try, and used her to report to her bosses what I wanted them to hear. It was never going to be a relationship, and we both knew it. Except she didn't know that I knew."

"Okay," Hank said, "since you don't want to talk about this hot admin, I want to tell you about this great place I found in Cabo San Lucas. It's great — on the beach, near the bars, and we can store all our toys in the garage — the windsurfer, jet ski, ATV. And the price is great."

"Okay, okay," Joe said. "I'll talk about the admin."

Hank leaned forward. "So what was she like? Did you do anything kinky with her?"

Joe grinned.

———————

Joe returned to the office at 9 PM. He walked down the hall to his office in the dark, with lights popping on behind him after a delay for the motion sensors to activate them. He couldn't get Erika off his mind. Maybe if he focused on Neuropt. He was determined to see if he could figure anything out. When the lights in his office came on, he stared at the picture of his fake parents. He had this odd desire to make them proud, whoever they were. Try as he might, he didn't feel that strongly about his foster parents — after all he'd been shuffled among 4 pairs before he went off to college. He had been a bit of a rebel as a kid.

He dragged his hands through his hair with his elbows on his desk, closing his eyes. A vision of Erika's sweater popped in his head, so he immediately opened his eyes again. He thought about the main Neuropt patent application. It may be irrelevant to Neuropt's success, but it was his job, so he was going to look at it with renewed determination. It was the only thing he could sink his teeth into.

The Neuropt patent application continued to gnaw at him, even though he had a solution of not dealing with it in the prospectus and his opinion. He decided to do some online searching. He guided his mouse to first use Lexis and Dialog, and subsequently went to the web. He had developed an ability to quickly scan through very technical articles and figure out the gist in just a minute or two. He went through 100 in just 2 hours. Then he decided to change tactics. The searchers were looking for the *combination* of optics and a neural network. What if he just looked for the two, as described, separately?

After searching fruitlessly for half an hour, he found an article on a neural network that looked familiar. The diagram on page 3 of the article looked awfully familiar. He went into Vishal's office and came back with a copy of the Neuropt patent application.

"Deja vu," he muttered, holding the figure from the patent application next to the diagram on the screen. They were nearly identical. Some of the text caught his eye as well. It appeared that sections of the article had been lifted for the patent application. The ordering was changed, and wording had been modified here and there, but it seemed to be just copied from the article — not a description of something Neuropt had invented.

He returned to his searching, this time looking for optical computing prior art. This time he hit pay dirt in 20 minutes. This article also sounded familiar, describing an optical switch array. It also had a drawing nearly identical to one in the patent application. Again, it looked like sections of text had been lifted without much modification.

After marking the sections and drawings that had been lifted, there wasn't much else in the patent application. Mostly the claims, and some very general language about how the two could be combined.

He then reviewed the list of references on the Information Disclosure Statement that had been filed with the Patent Office by Neuropt's patent attorney, listing the relevant prior art they were aware of. Neither article was listed.

Joe struggled to keep his eyes open and collect his thoughts. The application was manufactured without *any* real design work being done by Neuropt. He wasn't allowed to see anything on the sensors, or verify their prototype miniature MRI. And the stuff he was allowed to see was an illusion. He looked at the clock — it was after 2 AM. What the hell were they doing at Neuropt?

11.

Max burst into Joe's office the next morning. "Joe, I'm taking over the Neuropt deal. I just got off the phone with Ned Stern. They aren't happy about your contacting inventors, especially at home, and especially after you should already have all the information. I'm putting Vishal in charge of doing the opinion and finishing up."

Joe sank back in his chair. Well, it was now or never.

"Max, I think we need to be careful about our involvement with Neuropt, and I wonder about our ethical obligation with respect to some things going on there."

"Oh?" Max said, sitting down.

"As you know," Joe said, "we got out of having to opine on their patent applications. Which is good because I found two public articles they basically just pasted together for the application. They haven't invented anything."

Joe leaned forward. "In fact, they don't have any idea how to make the Optospine. I've talked to engineers who have told me they still need to figure out how to do it, and that there is no way they can do this in 6 months. As I'm sure you know, there are no miniature EMI machines that they would need, and they have no plans on how to make one. And the engineers aren't working on it — they are doing busy work on projects for Gage's other companies, with the excuse that they need to wait for the design to be figured out. Well, the design isn't going to be figured out."

"You know what I think is going on? They have no intention of making the Optospine. They are going to make money from the IPO and run with it. They just have to keep some buzz going for 6 months, so their holding period expires and they can sell their stock. What else would explain the lack of any concrete design along with the vague plagiarized patent applications and their not wanting me to talk to anyone?"

Max's phone rang, and he raised his hand to stop Joe while he took the call. "Yes, Ned we're on it," Max said. "Don't worry; I'm with Vishal right now, that opinion will be done on time. Don't worry."

Six months was the holding period for Gage and the other people at Neuropt. The SEC made the insiders hold their stock, and not sell it, for six months after the public offering. Joe was convinced they purposely scheduled the product release for after their holding period expired. That way they could sell their stock and cash out before they had to admit that they didn't have a product. He could see how that would be under the SEC radar. So many companies had gone public on the promise of developing a new product, and then failing, that it would be difficult to tell whether it was simply too difficult a product to develop, or if it was sinisterly planned.

"You were saying?" Max said as he snapped his phone shut.

"They have refused to let me visit their offices," Joe continued. "Everyone there goes home shortly after 5

PM. Does that make sense for a start-up struggling to get a product completed to deal with a global plague?"

He gazed expectantly at Max. Max didn't look at him, instead turning to look out the window with his chin in his hand, deeply in thought. It was obvious that Joe's presentation had made an impact on Max.

"Joe, the client wants you off the deal," Max said, continuing to look out the window. "So I'm going to have to take you off Neuropt. You know how it is. It's politics. The client is always right, and sometimes we have to shuffle the team because for some reason a client doesn't get along with a terrific associate here."

"I see," Joe said. "But you can see that I'm right, can't you?"

Max still was looking out the window. What was he thinking?

"Even if I personally don't have to struggle with this," Joe said, "something has to be done. There is still the issue of the firm's malpractice exposure."

"Joe," Max said, turning and looking directly at him, "even if I did agree with you, you've taken care of any malpractice exposure with the changes to our opinion and the prospectus. Even if the company was a fraud, you've isolated us from any malpractice exposure. There is nothing to worry about. And it's not our concern. It *certainly* isn't your concern anymore."

"But Max, there is more to this," Joe said. "They're not only defrauding investors, they're attracting investors to a technology that won't work for the Amazon virus, and away from a proven solution — the Retinal Screen. This has an impact on whether people in this country will be alive or dead when the virus gets here."

"Now you're being over-dramatic," Max said. "There's plenty of government money being thrown at possible vaccines."

"But they're not . . . ," Joe started to say.

Max held up his hand. "Enough," Max said. "You're out of line, Joe. Remember, they're our client, not our adversary. I think you've forgotten that."

Joe's heart sank, he felt sick to his stomach. Max either didn't believe him, or worse, didn't care.

———

Zenko was uneasy as he made his way to Judge Albert's chambers later that morning — Zenko hoped the judge would be reasonable enough to deny Borland's expedited discovery request, or at least delay and limit it. Borland had asked for so many depositions and documents in such a short time it would be impossible for Zenko to handle them. It was very unusual to have that much scheduled so soon after the complaint was filed.

Borland had asked for a preliminary injunction hearing in about a month. Telekinetics was working on a Retinal Screen design-around to avoid the Inventech injunction, and now they were threatened with a preliminary injunction by Royaltec. If granted, it would stop Telekinetics from shipping the Retinal Screen even though there hadn't been a trial yet. Preliminary injunctions weren't usually granted — it required Royaltec to prove that the evidence was so overwhelming that Royaltec was likely to win. It also required that Royaltec would be irreparably harmed by waiting until a trial to stop the infringing product. To present sufficient evidence, Borland had to do discovery in a hurry. But Zenko suspected Borland didn't really care about winning a preliminary injunction — Borland probably just wanted to harass Telekinetics, forcing them to spend money and time until they cried uncle and settled.

Judge Albert had been assigned to the Royaltec v. Telekinetics case. Albert was a good judge to have if you were the patent owner. Albert had been trying to make a reputation as an intellectual property expert, and always wanted the patent cases, even though he wasn't the best qualified. Some thought he had political aspirations and wanted to show he was pro-business, which he thought meant pro-patent. Thus he was a bad judge to have if you were on the other side, accused of infringement.

The Peterson attorneys were already there. Albert's chambers looked like a study. Supreme Court Reporters from the 1800's lined a bookshelf along one wall, dusty since they contained court decisions too old to be referred to anymore. Another wall seemed to have every one of Albert's diplomas and awards. Zenko had counted them once; there were over 20, including Albert's grade school diploma. Behind Albert's desk was a picture of Albert with President Bush, blown up to life size in a gaudy gold frame. It was as if the president was blessing everything he did.

Judge Albert had called Zenko and Roger Borland into his chambers. Borland brought two associates; one of them handed Zenko a thick stack of papers that contained Royaltec's proposed discovery requests — interrogatories and document requests. The judge put down his copy and looked at Zenko.

"I'm inclined to grant this request," Judge Albert said. "Any reason I shouldn't, Mr. Saka?"

"It's *Kamisaka*, your honor," Zenko said, somewhat incredulous. The judge merely nodded. Zenko hadn't expected the judge to immediately side with Royaltec on what was clearly an overreaching request.

"Well, your honor," Zenko began, "I believe these requests may be reasonable over the course of a year for a trial. But this is for a preliminary injunction, which requires evidence of a substantial likelihood of success. If they need to take the deposition of every employee of my client to get the evidence they need, I submit that the evidence simply cannot show such a substantial likelihood. If there is overwhelming evidence, they should find it quickly."

"Also, your honor," Zenko hurriedly added, fearing that he would be cut off by the judge at any moment, "it is clear there is no need for a preliminary injunction. Where is the required substantial threat of irreparable injury? They just acquired this patent — how can waiting for trial hurt them? They aren't even in the business. The purpose of this burdensome expedited discovery is clearly to tie up my client so they can't do business, and drive them into bankruptcy regardless of any merits of this lawsuit."

"Alright already," Judge Albert said. "I've heard enough. What would you suggest, Mr. Kamisaka?"

"I'd limit them to depositions of only two Teleki-netics employees, one document request and one inter-rogatory set, both limited to 5 pages, and required to be specific, not a fishing expedition," Zenko replied. Zenko held up the thick stack of papers. "These — ," he started to say.

"Your honor," Roger interrupted. The judge held up his hand, and Roger stopped.

"I think your suggestion is unduly restrictive," Judge Albert said. "But I do think, Roger, that you shouldn't need to depose all 55 of the Telekinetics employees in less than 30 days, especially since you have noticed many of them for several day depositions. I don't see how it could be physically accomplished. Why, you'd need 3 attorneys simultaneously taking depositions constantly for the month."

"We are willing and able to do that, your honor," Roger volunteered, "to put a quick end to this piracy."

"Alright," Judge Albert said. "I'll give you 15 depositions. You chose which ones. And I will not limit the interrogatories and document requests. If you think they are overly burdensome when you study them, Mr. Saka, call Roger and arrange a compromise. If you can't, you can always make a motion to me. And I won't be scheduling the hearing in 30 days; I have another trial on my docket then. It will probably be in 45 days. I'll let you know."

"Your honor," Zenko said. "Have you looked at this patent yet? They are trying to read a cabling system on a microprocessor."

The judge held up his hand. "You'll get a chance to address the merits at the preliminary injunction hearing, Mr. Saka." Zenko knew it was fruitless to try more. Even the most blatantly ridiculous patent infringement claims wouldn't be thrown out until after many months and up to hundreds of thousands of dollars in attorney's fees.

———————

Zenko saw Burak, A.J. and Joe in the conference room when he got back to the office. He hurried past the conference room before they saw him, and closed the door to his office. He sat down and tapped his fingers on his desk for a few moments, then used his key to open the locked drawer. He pulled out the bottle of

Johnnie Walker Scotch Whiskey. He ran his finger along the edge of the diagonal black label for a minute, and then slowly twisted off the cap. He held it under his nose, taking a deep breath. He frowned, screwed the top back on and replaced it in the drawer and headed out the door to the conference room.

"They're going after our customers," A.J. said as he was pushing open the door. A.J. slid a piece of paper across the table. "This is a copy of a letter Royaltec has been sending to our customers. A number of our customers have brought it to our attention, and asked what our response was. I told them I'd get back to them after meeting with our attorneys this morning."

Zenko put his laptop on the table, and looked back at the paper as he went to the credenza to pour some coffee. Both A.J. and Burak shook their heads no as he waved the coffee pot in their direction.

"As you can see," A.J. continued, "they are saying that our customers risk being sued for infringement if they buy the Retinal Screen or any product with a neural net processor from us. Can they do that? How can they single us out? They don't mention other neural net processor users."

"They haven't even talked to us about a license," A.J. added. "They just sue us, and they try to scare our customers into going to our competitors. If they buy from us, they're going to get sued. This stinks something fierce. There must be something you can do about this, right? Don't tell me it's legal to pull this kind of crap?"

"Unfortunately," Zenko said, looking up from the letter, "it's perfectly legal, unless they are lying about their belief that you are infringing. And if there is any colorable basis for suggesting you infringe, no court is going to hold they are lying. Any colorable basis."

"Colorable?" Burak asked.

"Plausible, believable, credible," Joe said.

"Can you do a letter to our customers saying the patent is not infringed?" A.J. asked.

"That is easy," Burak said. "Just show them the damned patent. It is clear it is on cables, not a neural network. Show them Joe's opinion — maybe it is good for something after all."

"Thanks a lot," Joe said.

Zenko nodded as his secretary interrupted with copies of the Royaltec interrogatories and document requests for everyone.

Burak started reading through the interrogatories and groaned. "This is no good," Burak said. "We cannot do this. These questions will take forever to answer. Look at this."

Burak pointed to interrogatory 3. They all leaned over and read it together.

3. Describe every product designed, manufactured or sold by the Company that uses a neural network design in any way. For each product, identify:

a.) the name of each person participating in any decision, conference, or conversation or writing relating to proceeding with the manufacture, sale, assembling or distribution of each such product and the position held by each such person, whether or not such person is employed by the Company;

b.) the information upon which the actions in a) were based;

c.) the names of each person supplying said information or any part thereof and their posi-

tion, if and, with the Company or their relationship to the Company;

d.) identify any document directed in whole or
in part to said actions and the reason there-
fore, or related to the information relied upon
in such actions.

"Allah help us," Burak said, "It would take a whole week just to answer this one question, it is so broad. And it is just one of hundreds of questions." Burak flipped through the document to illustrate.

"And the document requests are just as bad," A.J. said after grabbing that pile of papers. "Here is one, look at this."

15. All documents relating to the design, development, circuitry, testing, manufacture, acquisition,
and operation of Company's products, including,
but not limited to, all product specifications, brochures, change orders, drawings, schematics, net
lists, program listings, technical, service and operation manuals, and component lists.

Burak shook his head in disbelief. He pointed to another one, his eyebrows furrowing in disgust.

26. All documents relating to the marketing, pro-
motion and sale of Company's products, including,
but not limited to, all advertising, product an-
nouncements, press releases, customer solicitations,
articles, sales presentation slides or programs, product brochures, catalogs, including any drafts thereof.

Undue Diligence

"We need to give them every document the company has to comply!" Burak complained. "I need to be working with my team on the Retinal Screen redesign so we can stop the needless deaths in Brazil, not dealing with this crap. Surely you can object to the judge?"

"I already did," Zenko sighed.

Joe was tapping his fingers on his desk later that afternoon. He had to do something, but what? How many people would die while waiting for the false promise of the OptoSpine? How many people would be mad at him for his involvement in the Neuropt opinion when Neuropt went belly up in 6 months and the stockholders lost all their money?

But what could he do? He could go to the media, get disbarred for betraying his client's interests, and probably not be believed because someone else would give the opinion Neuropt wanted. If only he could make a clearer case. It was clear to him, but someone without engineering training would be confused, and Neuropt could find – no, they had found – engineers willing to support its position.

He just sat there looking at Arthur Gursky's name, the underwriter's counsel, on the front of the draft Neuropt registration statement on his desk. Gursky had been bugging him, as if he was suspicious that something was wrong with Neuropt. So Joe was sure he'd get a sympathetic ear from Gursky. But how could he justify calling Gursky without Neuropt's OK, especially since he was now off the project? There was no good way he could think of to blow the whistle that wouldn't cost his job – and more. He'd have to choose.

His handheld beeped. He checked the update. It was about how Brazil was making progress in educating the public that the virus was not spread by sweat. He rested one hand on the Edison bust as he called Erika and asked her to come to his office.

She came and stood just inside his door, with her arms folded. "This had better be real work," she said with a look of defiance.

Joe walked over and shut the door. She scurried to the window as Joe got close to her. Joe leaned back against the closed door — she was still mad at him. He gave her the same explanation he had given Max about Neuropt — that he thought they just wanted to make money on the stock, and had no plans to make a real product.

"I think Gage Booth is trying to destroy Telekinetics," Joe was saying. "A company with a legitimate shot at preventing the Amazon virus, just so he can get rid of competition and make more money on his scam company, Neuropt. Why else would Royaltec target Telekinetics? They aren't the most obvious target. And why not open discussions to settle, like they usually do, instead of pushing a lawsuit?"

Erika just looked out the window without saying anything.

"Joe," Erika said, "I'm seriously starting to wonder if you've lost it."

"I think I can stop them," Joe said.

Erika whirled around. "No! I don't know what you're thinking, but don't do it. You can't do anything without violating your client's confidences, which would mean disbarment. And you'd be doing this on a hunch. A *hunch*."

Joe smiled. She still cared about him.

Undue Diligence

An hour later Arthur Gursky called Joe back. Joe got up and stretched out to push his door closed.

"Hello," Gursky said. "I got a message you wanted to talk about your opinion for the Neuropt IPO. What's up?"

"I'm not going to be working on the Neuropt project anymore," Joe said, "so I thought I'd bring you up to speed on where we are."

"Oh?" Gursky said. He seemed genuinely surprised. He must not have been told Joe was off the project.

"First," Joe continued. "Just so you are aware of all the circumstances, one reason we took out the language in the prospectus about the product being ready in 6 months is that the engineers I talked to at Neuropt didn't think it could be done. They aren't anywhere close to demonstrating a viable design. And they won't show us anything on the sensors, so we have no evidence that they'll work, or that they even have a design in mind."

Joe paused. Gursky said nothing. He would have preferred some reaction. Well, it was too late to stop now.

"We also took out the details of the surface emitting laser because we found a patent that would probably be infringed," Joe resumed. "By taking out that language, we could still give an opinion that we weren't aware of any potential patent infringement. And as far as their own patents, we are changing our opinion to not say anything about the likelihood of patents issuing because I don't think Neuropt will get a patent. The Neuropt patent application seems to have been written by copying from two different articles. I also suspect that's all the design is, they don't know how to combine them to make something work. They just described a combination that sounds like it would work."

Joe stopped and waited for a reaction. After a few moments, there was a low whistle from Gursky. "Wow!" Gursky said. "That's a lot of shit. I suspected something was fishy with Neuropt, but I had no idea."

Gursky was silent for a while, and Joe let him digest the significance.

"So tell me, what are the likely scenarios here?" Gursky finally asked. "As I understand, you're telling me that Neuropt is unlikely to get its own patents, and it might be sued for infringement. When are these likely to occur?"

"Well, let's see," Joe responded, "a lawsuit would probably happen when Neuropt introduces its product. There isn't much point to suing until there is a product to stop and sales to recover damages from."

"And you just told me a product isn't going to be introduced," Gursky said. "At least not anytime soon. Not in six months, probably never. And no one would be surprised at some delay for such a cutting-edge product. Products often have their introduction delayed. And Neuropt's own patent applications?"

"It will be longer," Joe said slowly, the significance of these questions starting to dawn on him. Since they were just filed, and it will be at *least* a year, more likely one and a half or two, before there is a final rejection. And they can file continuations and appeals and keep it alive for many years before having to admit they can't get a patent. He was beginning to see how this could work for Gage.

"Good!" Gursky said. "Just as I thought! Since nothing is likely to happen within six months, I'm not actually worried about liability. Traditionally, a shareholder will have a tough time pinning a stock price drop on a failure to disclose when more than 6 months have passed. Too many intervening events will have occurred, and they will have had an opportunity to sell in the interim. Basically, the prospectus will be too stale for them to sue on."

"Hmmm," Gursky said, "In addition, as long as you guys sign it, I'm off the hook. I can point to relying on you guys if Neuropt gets sued, and the investors can go after you. So I'm not sure I care whether the opinion is correct or not, as long as your firm gives it."

Joe tried to convince Gursky that the underwriters should pull the plug on Neuropt, but Gursky didn't care if they were a fraud. He only cared about his liability. Joe dropped his head to his desk after Gursky hung up.

———

Ned watched the video monitor intently that evening while he talked on his cell phone. He was sitting on his disheveled bed in his hotel room, dressed in boxers and an "I love N.Y." T-shirt. It was nearly midnight Friday. He could see Gage Booth in the background in the video, pacing by the conference room window. The only others with Gage were one of Ned's partners and a trusted senior associate. He had the videoconference on mute, and the camera on his side turned off. He pulled the blanket up over his bare legs.

He looked up to see Max Klein walk into the conference room. He quickly ended the other call, and turned off the mute on the videoconference.

"What's going on?" Max asked. "I got a message from my secretary to head over here as soon as I got in."

"Your asshole Nile has caused us a shitload of trouble," Gage growled. "He told the underwriters' counsel that our IPO was a fraud."

"What?" Max gasped, grabbing a chair shakily and sitting down. Max looked around for a few moments, at a loss for words. Finally he spoke. "He had no authority to do that! I took him off the deal. I told you I took him off the deal."

"Fortunately," Ned said, "the underwriters only want to use that to extort a larger fee. But we are concerned about who else Nile will talk to."

Max sat absorbing this for a few moments, then leapt to his feat. "I'll have him fired immediately! We are still giving that opinion. We'll take care of it."

"I'm afraid it's not quite as simple as that," Ned said calmly. "Gage and I have been discussing it. If Nile is fired now, he may go to the media, and it will look like we're trying to cover something up."

"No," Gage said, "we must totally discredit Nile."

Ned swallowed and looked at Max, who was red in the face with poisonous eyes.

"What if I told you," Max said, "that I happen to know that Joe had stock in International Computer Networks, and recently sold it? ICN is a major shareholder of Neuropt, as you know."

"Why would he do that?" Ned asked.

"He was worried it might be considered a conflict," Max said, "if he owned ICN stock and was doing an opinion for a company they had a major stake in."

"Really?" Gage said, nodding vigorously and starting to laugh. "That could prove very useful, very useful indeed."

12.

Joe sensed a presence in his doorway mid-Monday morning and looked up from the file he had been studying. Erika was standing there, a vision of beauty. He loved everything about her — except her folded arms and angry look.

"Working on your resume?" Erika snarled.

"Why would I do that?" Joe asked.

Erika looked at the ceiling and blew her hair away from her eyes. "Well, there's your bonehead move with Neuropt, and the news about West."

"What about West?" Joe asked. This was it, Joe thought. He had been waiting for repercussions from his call to Gursky.

"Don't you hear anything?" Erika asked. "How do you function?"

After a brief pause, Erika continued. "Trevor West is jumping ship to the Peterson firm."

"I hadn't heard that," Joe said, straightening up in his chair. This wasn't the bad news he was expecting.

"They say he wasn't happy with the financial situation here," Erika continued, leaning across Joe's desk. "Apparently the Peterson firm threw some enormously big bucks at him to get him to jump. They also say we didn't get paid on a number of receivables, and the partners had their draws cut."

Joe clicked on his e-mail while Erika was talking. The e-mails were flying already. The associates were speculating about which associates West would take with him. It was assumed West would take several, but West wouldn't recruit them until after he was gone to avoid breaching his fiduciary duties to his partners. The associates also traded tips on what firms to send their resumes to. Everyone was assuming the worst.

"I don't know about you," Sidney said as he knocked on Joe's open door and dropped some mail in Joe's in-box, "but I'm sending my resume out right now."

"Have you seen the Neuropt press release?" Erika asked coldly as Sidney left the office. Joe checked the Internet and found the Neuropt press release. He quickly skimmed it — Neuropt had withdrawn its public offering!

"I hope you're happy," Erika said.

Joe grimaced. His goal had been attained after all, but something was wrong. The purported reason was that Neuropt couldn't get a patent opinion from their patent counsel. The article made it sound like the patent counsel was being a hard ass — there was no mention of anything about the company not having a viable product. The article also mentioned that International Computer Network's stock had fallen 3 points on the news, since ICN was a major investor in Neuropt. Joe wondered what had happened, since he knew Max was still planning to give the opinion. Had Gursky decided not to accept it?

"Hi Vishal," Erika said.

Joe looked away from his computer to see Vishal standing at his door grinning ear to ear.

"Why are *you* so smug?" Erika asked.

"I won a hundred dollars on my bet that West would leave this month," Vishal said. "Joe, the odds are 5-1 against you still having a job by the end of this week. Want to get in on the action?"

Joe shook his head and waved Vishal away. "Erika, can we talk over lunch? Or dinner?"

"Ohhh," Erika said softly as she leaned forward over Joe's desk and smiled. "Are you asking me out?"

"Actually, that's what I wanted to talk about at lunch," Joe said. "Or dinner."

"Well forget it," Erika said sharply as she spun around and headed for the door. She paused and turned. "Why would I want to go out with some jerk who sleeps with some whore just days after separating from his wife, and is about to lose his license because he violated the attorney-client privilege?"

Joe stared at the empty door after she sped away. Erika was starting to piss him off.

He returned to his work, being apprehensive several times at the sound of approaching footsteps, expecting Max to darken his door. But Max never came by. By the time he saw Max's e-mail trying to reassure the firm about its stability, he had received four calls from headhunters. They were descending on the firm like vultures impatient for the carcass to die.

Joe shivered in his office the next morning — the air conditioning was always too cold in the morning, then it was too hot in the afternoon. The smell and taste of his coffee gave him a jolt as he sipped, and he savored its warmth going down. He smiled as he read the Royaltec patent. Maybe things were finally going his way. He now had time to work for Telekinetics again.

As he tried to concentrate he sensed someone's gaze. Sidney was leaning against the doorway. "Joe, there's an article on the Internet I think you should see."

Sidney walked behind Joe's chair and leaned to click on the Internet browser. He navigated to a news article in a couple clicks, patted Joe gently on the shoulder, and then went back to his desk.

Gage Booth was quoted as saying a new patent attorney had contradicted the earlier opinion of Joe Nile. Gage said his team became suspicious when Nile's opinion contradicted the analysis done by Neuropt's previous patent attorney. Some checking revealed that Joe Nile had sold his International Computer Networks' stock, and then bought puts on ICN. ICN was a major stockholder in Neuropt, and when Neuropt's offering was called off, ICN's stock declined, and Joe Nile avoided a loss on the stock he sold, and made 100,000 dollars on the puts. After discovering this, Gage had asked to have another attorney at Turner, West review the analysis, and they contradicted Nile's opinion. Gage also found out that Joe Nile had just been turned down for partnership, which may have been another motivation for Nile. Representatives from the SEC and the California state bar commented that they would initiate investigations.

"Jesus," Joe said, feeling suddenly queasy and slumping in his chair. The draft opinion didn't contradict anything — and it hadn't even been given yet. Was Gage referring to his oral comments to Gursky as his opinion? How come the reporter knows about this investigation before he's informed? And what's with these puts? He didn't buy any puts. Hell, he'd heard of them, but didn't even know what they were. Where was the due process? Then he remembered — due process didn't apply to the media.

Vishal poked his head through Joe's doorway, munching on a doughnut. "Joe, I just want you to know I think this is bogus, what they're doing to you. All the other associates I've talked to agree with me."

"Thanks, Vishal," Joe said. "I can't believe this is happening. But it's pure bullshit. I'll be able to show that."

"We're having an associate meeting at lunch to discuss this," Vishal said, taking a bite out of his doughnut, causing white powdered sugar to fall on the floor. Joe deliberately let his eyes follow it to the ground and stared at it. "Maybe we can put some pressure on the partners or something," Vishal continued, oblivious to Joe's stare.

"Pressure on the partners?" Joe repeated. Something didn't sound right. "What do the partners have to do with this?"

"Well, I'm sure they've signed off on this," Vishal said. "You don't lay-off associates without getting partnership approval."

"Lay-off?" Joe asked. "Who's being laid off?"

"Uh-oh," Vishal said. "Gotta go."

"Wait a minute Vishal," Joe said, rising from his chair, "what's this about —." Joe stopped mid-sentence. Max Klein walked into his office.

"Do you have a minute, Joe?" Max asked, sitting down.

"Sure," Joe said, leaning back in his chair. Joe no longer felt that sinking feeling. Everything now seemed like a bizarre dream. He strangely felt amused at Max telling him something he had already learned from Vishal. Max looked uncomfortable, shifting in his chair, giving Joe some small pleasure.

"Joe, I'll get right to the point," Max said. "As you know we don't have enough work, and we have to lay-off someone. Unfortunately, you got the short straw." Max paused, waiting for Joe to say something.

After an awkward silence, Max continued. "We did it on the basis of matching work skills to the types of work we had. Unfortunately, most of our work isn't in your technical area, and we need lower level workers for existing projects, not someone with your higher, management type skills. Your billing rate is simply too high for the work we have. There were also some performance issues, such as your working on Telekinetics after I told you not to."

Max stopped for effect. "Yes, I found out about that. We also have video of your chair races. Our IS group came up with an override to counter the associates hacking to turn the webcams off."

Max paused again. Joe didn't get it. What was Max talking about? He kept waiting for Max to mention the Neuropt opinion and the ICN puts. Max never did.

"Well, I guess that's about it," Max said, getting up to leave. "You'll be paid through today, so you'll have to pack up your things this afternoon. I'm sorry it had to happen this way." Max extended his hand. Joe looked at it blankly. Was it possible they had decided to lay Joe off before the article came out? Maybe Max hadn't seen the article? No, that wasn't possible.

Joe didn't make any move to take Max's hand. "Excuse me?" Joe said. "What about Neuropt? Are you saying you're not firing me for that?"

"No," Max said, withdrawing his hand and absentmindedly placing it over the Edison bust, his fingers in

Edison's eyes. "You're being laid off. At this point, as far as we're concerned, the article just contains allegations. The bar investigation has just begun."

Joe sat quietly for a moment as this sunk in. So that was it. The firm's labor lawyer must have told them to drum up some other excuse. Or maybe they were afraid Joe's defense would show that Neuropt was a fraud. Max let go of Edison and started moving briskly through the door.

"Wait a minute," Joe said. "I've got a huge backlog of work. How can you say there isn't enough work for me?"

"We're reassigning that to litigation associates with a lower billing rate," Max said.

"They don't have the technical training for my projects, and you know it," Joe said.

"That's what we're doing," Max said. "If I were you, I'd start packing my desk and hire an attorney."

Max quickly disappeared out the door.

Erika appeared out of nowhere. "Do I have to say I told you so? Or have you figured that out?"

Erika waited for a second, and then left when Joe didn't immediately respond.

Joe slapped the article on his computer monitor with the palm of his hand. "I must be a complete idiot to do this for $100,000. I should have gone for at least a few million."

Sidney eased across the threshold of Joe's door a moment after Erika left. "You okay, Joe?"

"Yeah," Joe said softly, "I'm okay." He tapped a single finger on his desk, glaring at the article. "But I'm starting to get a tad annoyed."

Ahmet blinked several times, trying to keep his eyes open that night. Ahmet leaned forward on the stone wall around the edge of the fountain, with the metal horses spitting water out of their nostrils behind him. He turned to the next page of the Folha newspaper as he took another sip of his cappuccino and glanced over at the old man coming out of the café — the only customer in this normally crowed venue, especially at prime time — 11 PM.

His phone buzzed. On the third buzz, he reluctantly answered. It was Cassia.

"Any update on the Retinal Screen design-around?" Cassia asked.

"Burak expects to ship the first one in a few days, and several more after that," Ahmet said. "That's all I know. They are pulling all-nighters trying to debug it."

"And it will avoid the injunction?" Cassia asked.

"Yes," Ahmet said. "It uses flash memory, so there is no disk drive."

"I thought you'd be interested," Cassia said, out of breath. "We've found a correlation for the non-smallpox vaccine victims — Adbil."

"How's that?" Ahmet asked.

"We've done a total of 15 autopsies in the last week on people that didn't have the smallpox vaccine," Cassia said. "We checked all the drugs and vitamin bottles they had, and all of them had the same type of black-market Adbil."

"Find anything in the Adbil pills?" Ahmet asked.

"No," Cassia said. "We're checking to see if some substance in the pills might be affecting the nervous system, making it susceptible to the virus. But we haven't found anything yet, and I don't think we will."

"What are you thinking?" Ahmet asked.

"I think one pill might have been added containing the virus in a time release plastic," Cassia said. "The label is a black market counterfeit of Adbil, with generic ibuprofen inside. It didn't look like these bottles had any safety features — there is no evidence of a seal or plastic covering. It would have been easy for someone to add a pill, and it would only take one. We'd only find victims who had taken that one pill, and the one pill would of course be gone."

"You think someone is deliberately spreading the virus?" Ahmet asked. "Is that enough proof?"

"My superiors don't think so," Cassia groaned. "They're worried about getting sued by Adbil's manufacturer, even though these are in an Adbil knock-off. Adbil would be concerned it would affect their sales as well. They have a lot of power in Brazil, you know. But I got them to agree to put out a warning not tied to the virus. We're just going to say we've found tainted pills that can have *unwanted* consequences, without explaining. We hope to get people to turn in unopened bottles for a new Adbil bottle — we might get lucky and find a pill still in one of them."

"What about the smallpox cases?" Ahmet asked. "Are you saying someone did this deliberately, and used some other delivery system in the smallpox cases? A contaminated vaccine?"

"That's what it's looking like to me," Cassia said. "But I can't get anyone here to agree. I'm looking into something, but I don't think I should tell you."

"So no warning on the smallpox vaccine?" Ahmet asked.

"No," Cassia said. "It's still pure speculation. Plus, since we suspended our program and symptoms turn up in a day or two, there is no risk."

"But people can still get it through the black market," Ahmet said.

"It's not my decision," Cassia said. "And I think only the official program was compromised, not black market vaccines."

"Isn't the Adbil speculation?" Ahmet asked.

"Yeah," Cassia said, "but the Adbil knock-off is black market stuff that shouldn't be sold anyway. If we release speculation on the smallpox vaccine, we'll never be able to have a successful vaccination program again in this country."

"Well, I'm breathing easier now," Gage said, clicking his glass with Ned's at the same moment in an earlier time zone. Gage leaned back in his chair and surveyed the patrons at the crowded Boston airport bar. "Now that we have that asshole Nile out of the way, and we've stuffed Telekinetics back down."

Ned grinned weakly, taking a sip of his whiskey. He didn't enjoy seeing Nile get fired, and he had mixed feelings about Telekinetics. By the time they finish their redesign to avoid the injunction, the cost of the Retinal Screen will be too high and the Royaltec lawsuit will scare off all competitors. He was glad he was heading back to California instead of accompanying Gage to Europe on the road show to pre-sell chunks of the Neuropt stock offering to institutional investors. A junior partner would take over from here.

"So are our patsies still on board?" Gage asked, studying his whiskey as he swirled it in his glass.

"Who?" Ned asked.

"Our patsies," Gage repeated, looking over at Ned. "Max Klein and the Turner, West firm."

"I wouldn't call them patsies," Ned protested, fixing his eyes on the table. He sometimes hated the way Gage would put things.

"Uh-huh," Gage said. "And you'd call a fart perfume? Are our *patsies* on track to give us the patent opinion we need?"

Ned took a deep breath — he could just strangle Gage sometimes. "Yes," he said, "the draft is completed; it's simply a matter of getting it signed for the closing. Max is giving us just the kind of opinion we want."

"But we're not making them patsies," Ned said deliberately, lowering his voice. "We're just asking them to give an opinion on the prospectus. They've had the opportunity to review whatever they want, do all the due diligence they need, even ask us to change the language in the prospectus. We hired an expert, not a patsy."

Gage laughed. "I love the way you attorneys make everything seem sooo damn proper! You and I both know we don't have the Optospine or any damned sensors. And since the Optospine doesn't exist, we had to dream up some bullshit stuff to patent. But our patsy patent firm wasn't able to figure it out; certainly not in the short time we gave them. Except for Nile, but we took care of him. So we got them to be the patent experts and they give the opinion that everything's okay. Then, if it blows up, they get sued, not you and your Peterson, Malone partners. Turner, West is your fall guy. If that's not being our patsy, I don't know what the hell is!"

Ned bit his tongue. Neuropt *didn't* have the Optospine.

"I wouldn't say they're bullshit," Ned said slowly after a pause. He was uncomfortable with Gage speaking about this in such a public place. He looked around, but didn't see anyone obviously listening. The others in the bar were glued to the TV, where commentators were speculating on the cause of the virus, and how the quarantine had been successful so far. No flights were allowed into Brazil, and only ships with crews from other countries were allowed in and out. The authorities figured that if any of the crew caught the virus, it would be apparent before they reached another port.

"We're just playing by the rules," Ned said. "If the SEC didn't want companies to go public until they had a product, they'd have a rule to that effect. If the Patent Office doesn't want to issue B.S. patents, fine. But as long as they issue them to your competitors, we'll recommend you file your own B.S. patent applications."

"Beautiful," Gage chortled, clutching the front of his flannel shirt and bursting out in a belly laugh. Gage couldn't stop laughing. Ned looked around. People were watching Gage, but probably didn't know what he was laughing about. After a few moments, Gage contained himself. "You are so damned good at this bullshit," Gage said. "I love it!" Gage started laughing again, and Ned shifted uncomfortably in his chair. He couldn't believe it — Gage had to wipe the tears from his eyes, he was laughing so hard.

Ned slammed down the rest of his drink, trying to ignore the eyes of the other patrons on them. He picked up the menu and pretended to study it. He had to peel his finger off as he opened it. He didn't want to know what the sticky stuff was on it.

"Hey," Gage choked out the words, "you can laugh too."

Gage abruptly stopped laughing when Ned didn't respond, as if a sharp pain suddenly seized him. "And don't act high and mighty on me, fart-breath," Gage snarled. "Your firm is making a butt load of money on this deal — you're laughing your way to the bank just like me."

It just annoyed Ned more when Gage was right. An initial public offering was the ultimate cash cow for a law firm's business practice. An IPO required hordes of attorneys and paralegals spending incredible hours over several months doing due diligence and putting together documents — from hundreds of thousands of dollars to more than a million in fees. Since they got paid when the deal closed from money raised from stock purchasers, and since the client was getting a boatload of money at the same time, the client didn't care about the bills. When Neuropt closed, the payment would return Ned to his normal status as number one biller in the firm.

Ned's cell phone rang. It was the managing partner of Peterson, Malone.

"Ned," the managing partner said, "Congratulations on getting Neuropt back on track."

"Thanks," Ned said.

Gage stood up and signaled to Ned with a twisting of his cupped hand. Ned shook his head, he didn't want another drink. He knew Gage just wanted an excuse to hit on a stewardess who had just sat at the bar.

"I'm sure you'll end up number one biller again," the managing partner said. "But you won't be doing the most for the firm."

Ned didn't like the sound of this. "Oh?" he said, sitting up a little straighter. "How's that?"

"Hybrids," the managing partner said. "We've made more money from our patent licensing this year than from client billings."

"Including litigation?" Ned asked incredulously.

"Yes, including litigation," the managing partner said.

"That would mean the patent licensing returned an average of over a million dollars per partner this year," Ned finally said.

"That's right," the managing partner said.

"Well, I may not have brought in that much licensing revenue," Ned said, "but I'm keeping plenty of associates busy."

"Actually, your keeping associates busy is the problem I wanted to talk to you about," the managing partner said.

"What?" Ned said. "How can that be a problem?"

"Because that means those associates aren't available to work on our hybrid business," the managing partner said. "Hybrids that generate patent licensing revenue. That made more money for us than regular legal fees this year."

"I want you to fire Neuropt after they go public," the managing partner continued.

"What?" Ned exclaimed, suddenly finding himself standing in indignation, although he had to hold back a smile looking over at Gage chatting up some stewardess at the bar and thinking about firing him. "Fire my best client? Are you nuts?"

"Do it diplomatically," the managing partner said. "Suggest another firm with more expertise in handling public companies should take over. He'll think you're doing him a favor, looking out for him instead of your own firm. Use it as an opportunity to try and get more work from Royaltec, with a piece of the action."

"You're not serious?" Ned said as he slowly eased himself back into his chair.

"I'm perfectly serious," the managing partner said. "And you will be too, when you see that the Compensation Committee knocks you down a level because you haven't brought in enough licensing revenue, and have used associate time that we could have put on hybrids. Look, I'm not ordering you to do this. But if you don't, the Compensation Committee will take note."

Early the next morning, Joe was having a nightmare. Gage Booth was hitting Joe in the face, and Ned Stern hit him in the stomach. They pushed him roughly to the ground, face first, and tied his hands behind them.

"What are you doing?" Joe pleaded.

"We're going to put a gun in your mouth and blow your brains out," Ned said. "Then, after you're dead, we'll untie you and put your hand around the gun."

"We already have a note," Gage chimed in, patting his pocket. "We had samples of your handwriting duplicated. It seems you were despondent about your scheme being uncovered and the prospect of being disbarred. You couldn't face the humiliation."

"I especially enjoyed your confession," Ned added. "That was a nice touch."

Gage beamed. "That was my idea."

The sound of the gun went off like a bell. No, it was a bell — the doorbell. Joe realized he was in his own bed, and it was Wednesday morning — it had been a nightmare. He put on his bathrobe and went to the door. As he started to unlock it, he paused, remembering his dream. Through the peephole he could see some young, clean-cut kid with some papers — not a mobster. Probably had a petition to save the whales or something.

"Joe Nile?" the kid asked.

"Yes," Joe said, "that's me. What can I do for you?"

The kid handed him the envelope. "I have a sub-poena for you," the kid said. He turned and started to walk away. "Sorry to wake you," the kid said over his shoulder, "but they want us to deliver these early to make sure we catch you."

Joe tore open the envelope. So was it the SEC, or the bar? Joe looked at the papers. It was Neuropt. They were suing him for malpractice.

He looked down the hall. His landlady was standing in her doorway looking at him. "Problems with the law?" She asked. "I don't cotton to criminals in my building."

Jeffrey turned over the baggie of Cheerios and dumped them on the floor of the back seat of Zenko's BMW that night. He then gave Erika a defiant look. She took away his toy, which set him off wailing. Zenko didn't turn around. It was as if he just didn't want to know what was going on in the back seat. She looked out the window and ignored Jeffery.

When they arrived at Joe's apartment they saw a notice taped to Joe's door. It was from the SEC. Erika tore it off. Joe answered the door wearing sweats and a T-shirt. He looked happy to see Zenko, but gave her a scowl. She stuck out her tongue at him and handed him the note. "Troubles with the SEC?" she said.

"Yeah, the SEC was here," Joe said, waving the note. "They took my computer. But they were nice, they left this note."

Erika stood behind Zenko holding Jeff and his bag, along with her briefcase. She watched Jeff to avoid looking at Joe.

"I could have told you that," Zenko said. "They would want to preserve evidence before you could destroy it."

"I didn't know you were going to bring anyone else," Joe said to Zenko.

"Erika is helping me with Telekinetics," Zenko said. "The Executive Committee said I could get associate help, but Max has made sure they are busy on other work and told them I'm a low priority. So I essentially have no help."

"Zenko," Joe said, "I told you I talked to Burak about helping. I can work on this full time now. You don't need Erika."

Erika glared at Joe. Didn't he have any idea of all the work she did? There was no way Joe could duplicate it. Why was he angry at her now? She was the one angry at him — he should be repentant, and on his knees begging forgiveness.

"Nile-san," Zenko said. "You need to spend some time on your own defense. You have bar and SEC investigations to worry about. If you need money, I can loan you some."

"I don't need the money," Joe said. "I have saved $60,000 in stock. Joe opened the door wide and led them in, waving his hand at his apartment. Erika could see that there was no furniture — just a blanket on the floor, and a keyboard and monitor next to it, but no computer.

"I'm afraid you don't have $60,000, Nile-san" Zenko said. "Your whole account has been frozen. They claim you have tainted money in there from illicit stock gains. Good luck getting out the untainted part anytime soon."

Joe spun around. "What?" Joe said. "How do you know that?"

"I called the police investigator," Zenko said. "He assumed I was your attorney, and I didn't see the point in telling him otherwise. The good news is they have no immediate plans of issuing an arrest warrant."

Erika stepped into the apartment and put down her bag and briefcase near the door. Jeff was beginning to whine. "I presume Sandra took the TV?" Erika asked. "So Jeff can't watch a video while we talk?"

"It was hers anyway," Joe said with a shrug. "I didn't watch it, don't miss it."

She noticed that Jeff let Joe pick him up without a struggle.

"So," Joe said, "does your mom talk about me a lot?"

"I don't know," Jeff said.

"Uh-huh," Joe said, "she swore you to silence, I see. Is that because she always says how handsome I am?"

Jeffrey giggled, shook his head side-to-side, and in a staccato giggle said, "no-o-o."

"Does she say how smart I am?" Joe asked.

"No-o-o-o-o-o!" Jeffrey said, laughing and shaking his head more violently.

"Does she say —," Joe started to say, but Jeffrey was already shaking his head. "Hey," Joe said, "you're already shaking your head, and I haven't even asked yet!"

Jeffrey stopped shaking his head, but held it cocked to one side in anticipation.

"Does she say how much she admires me?" Joe asked.

"No-o-o-o-o-o-o-o-o-o-o-o-o-o-o!" Jeffrey said, shaking his head rapidly.

"OK," Joe said, "does she say I'm her favorite patent attorney?"

"Uh-huh," Jeff said, "You're her favorite. – Not!"

Joe handed Jeff back to Erika.

"Nice try," Erika said.

Joe reached into a box and pulled out a raccoon puppet. He then sat on the floor, and started making the puppet perform for Jeff. She set Jeff on the floor, and he went over to Joe, laughing at the puppet and trying to grab it. She was amazed. Jeff never took to strangers, yet he seemed to develop an instant rapport with Joe.

Zenko sat down cross-legged on the floor, putting his briefcase next to him. He looked disappointed when Joe said he didn't have any tea. Erika sat on the blanket, rubbing the smooth border of the blanket between her fingers.

"You're very good with that, Joe," Zenko said. "Where did you get that? Is it one of your nephew's?"

"It's mine," Joe said, picking up a wind-up toy bug, pulling it back across the floor on its wheels to wind it up, and letting it race across the floor. "Mine too."

"You guys don't think I'm guilty, do you?" Joe asked, looking back and forth between Zenko and Erika.

"You sold the ICN stock," Erika said, hopping up and pacing the room. "You told me. That saved you some money in losses."

"But I didn't buy any puts," Joe said, realizing how lame this sounded as he said it. "And I sold the ICN stock because I thought it would go up with the IPO, and I'd be accused of giving a good opinion to make money, not the other way around. I did that before I started on the project, before I knew what was going on."

"I don't know about the Neuropt patent position," Zenko said. "But I don't believe you intentionally bought puts to take advantage of Neuropt, and I don't believe you made up something about Neuropt that you didn't believe in."

"But it sounds like you don't believe I was right about Neuropt," Joe said.

Zenko looked at the floor for a moment, and then looked right at Joe. "No," Zenko said. "I don't. Of course I don't know all the details, but from what I know, I think you were being a little naïve. Companies with weak positions go public and fail all the time. Those aren't conspiracies; they're simply greedy people pushing the envelope on when they can take a company public. It's perfectly legal."

Erika exchanged a glance with Zenko as she plopped on the blanket again, and said nothing. This was getting awkward.

"I know it looks bad," Joe said, letting the zoom bug go toward Jeff. "But I didn't buy any puts. Someone must have tampered with my account somehow."

"Do you have any idea how contrived that sounds?" Erika asked.

Joe returned her gaze for a moment, and then looked away. "Yeah," Joe said. "I do."

"So maybe I should change my story to aliens tampered with my account?" Joe asked, reaching over to help Jeff wind up the zoom bug.

"I don't think this is something to joke about," Erika said.

"So let's talk about the Telekinetics defense," Zenko said. "Are you in?"

"I'm in," Joe said as he wound the zoom bug. "Do you think Burak is concerned about these Neuropt allegations?"

"Burak?" Zenko snorted, "I think he likes this. He thinks he has some leverage over you now. He wants you to charge half your Turner billing rate. He figures you'll keep all the money now instead of it going to the firm to cover all its overhead."

Joe laughed. "That sounds like Burak, all right."

Zenko started to laugh, and then Erika found herself laughing too. It wasn't that funny, but it felt so good to laugh, and it just seemed funny that they were laughing at a time like this. Jeff even started to laugh at all the adults laughing.

"Nile-san," Zenko said after the laughter subsided, "I don't want Max Klein to find out that you are helping on this, and I don't want Royaltec to try to use your legal problems as some sort of disqualification defense. I want you to work closely with Erika, and funnel everything through her."

"No!" Joe and Erika said in unison.

"Don't make me report to her," Joe said.

"Don't make him report to me," Erika said in unison.

Meanwhile, in São Paulo, Cassia was shaking with anger as she watched Jorge through the one-way window as the federal police investigator questioned him. One of her own betrayed her, betrayed Brazil. They wouldn't let her in the room. Just because she had threatened to strangle him. Jorge had been scanned for weapons, and they took his shoes, saying they wanted to X-ray them. Jorge was in no mood to cooperate.

"I want to see an attorney," Jorge was saying.

"Where do you think you are?" the investigator laughed. "In the United States? Why don't you just tell me where you got your money? We've checked, and you don't have any uncle that recently died."

"That's just a rumor at work," Jorge said, sweat beading up on his forehead. "I don't have to explain where I get my money. I've saved for years, worked multiple jobs — that's all you need to know."

"You've sure saved a lot," the investigator said. "You have several hundred thousand dollars in cash in a U.S. bank, and we're still checking for stocks. The bank account was just opened a few weeks ago."

"That's private information," Jorge protested. "What right do you have to get that?"

They were interrupted by an assistant who gave Jorge his shoes back.

"They were clean," the assistant said. "We didn't find anything in them."

"And it seems you've been on a buying spree," the investigator continued. "The Porsche, a condo in escrow, and there are several prostitutes getting rich off of you."

Cassia checked her e-mail on her cell phone. She knew all about Jorge's spending, and Jorge wasn't talking. There was an e-mail from her computer expert assistant. He had found a mailer in the pack-rat victim's house. It was from a company in Saudi Arabia: Abdulla Al-Jameel Pharmaceuticals.

"Okay," the investigator was saying. "Let's move on to your work. We know you helped distribute smallpox vaccines. We did a little checking, and it turns out that quite a number of the patients who took the vaccine that you distributed came down with the virus. There were only a few cases for patients of other distributors. How would you explain that?"

Jorge shrugged.

Cassia looked at the "x-ray" assistant when he joined her. "Well?"

"No problem," he answered. "We put the tracking device in his heel."

She nodded, but doubted it would do any good. Jorge had obviously already been paid and done his work. There was probably no need for him to meet whoever put him up to it. Probably.

13.

Erika held the beanbag turtle in her left hand the next morning and rubbed its smooth belly as she turned back and forth the pages of the file history of the AutoSmart patent Royaltec had bought. The file history was the Patent Office file, and contained all the correspondence back and forth between the Patent Office and the patent attorney during the application process. She had already gone though and double checked all the pages against the index. There were missing pages, alright. She squeezed the beanbag with annoyance, digging her fingernails into its belly. This sort of thing happened a lot with Patent Office files. Sometimes the entire file would be lost. There had been a number of times that Turner, West had to give the Patent Office copies of its files because the Patent Office has lost its copy.

She checked her e-mail. Joe had already sent a claim chart, with relevant descriptions from the Telekinetics product in one column, lined up against another column with the elements of the claim from the Royaltec patent. A third column showed how Joe thought the claim language for each element should be interpreted narrowly, pointing to particular sections of the description and figures in the patent.

Erika switched to her online search program. She restricted her search to a 3-year window before and after the filing date of the AutoSmart patent, and searched the inventors' names. There were a half dozen hits. She scanned through them and came across an article published the same month the patent application was filed. It had one of the inventors as an author, and another individual, named Cecil Bridges. The article was about a new robotic product. She scanned the article. She didn't understand the technology, but she recognized enough feature descriptions to realize it was the product the patent application covered. It was some sort of robot with multiple arms connected by a maze of cables.

She did a separate search for anything listing Cecil Bridges, without any date restrictions. One other article turned up, 5 years later, and he was listed as working for another company, Triscope. She called directory assistance for Triscope, but they had no listing. She did a search for articles on Triscope, and found that it had gone out of business. She also found out about a new company that had spun off from Triscope before it went out of business, and she checked with them. No luck. She then checked the phone books for all the cities around where AutoSmart and Triscope were located. No luck.

She decided to put aside searching for Bridges for a while. She was hitting dead ends. She had also been unsuccessful in her call to AutoSmart that morning, trying to get information on sales at the time the patent was applied for. If they had sold a product covered by the patent more than a year before the patent application was filed, the patent would be invalid. This surprisingly wasn't that rare, since marketing and engineering and legal didn't usually communicate very well, and finishing the patent application often got put off.

She called Joe. "Any progress?"

"No," Joe said.

"Figures," Erika said. "Why not? Trying to find another slut to give you her panties?"

"Yeah?" Joe said. "What have you found?"

Erika sighed. "I'm hitting some dead ends. I got the brush off from an admin at AutoSmart."

"Really?" Joe said. "Must be that new charming personality you've adopted. What did you do, call her a slut?"

Erika slammed the phone down. She stared at it for a good five minutes, twirling her hair in her fingers. She couldn't help but be mad at Joe, even though she still loved him. Why couldn't he just apologize? She'd given him enough openings.

She finally picked up the phone once more and called AutoSmart. She reached the marketing manager's admin again. "I'm sorry," the admin said. "Like I told you this morning, she's real busy today. It doesn't do any good for you to keep calling."

"I thought I might have missed a call when I was away from my desk," Erika lied, looking at the pencil she was making do acrobatics between her fingers.

"Are you sure I can't help you?" the admin asked. Couldn't hurt at this point, Erika thought.

"Well, I'm looking for information on sales of a product covered by an old AutoSmart patent," Erika said.

"Oh," said the admin. "Is this in connection with the Royaltec suit?"

Erika knew this couldn't be good. "Yes."

"Well," the admin said, "I think I can save you some time. We signed some deal with Royaltec, and we can't answer any questions about anything related to the suit unless we run it by their lawyers first. So I'm sure you'll just get referred to their lawyers."

"So what do you think of the suit?" Erika asked, trying to probe for information on the relationship between AutoSmart and Royaltec.

"Not much," the admin said.

"How so?" Erika asked.

The admin didn't reply.

"Sorry," Erika said. "I don't want you to talk about the suit itself, since I know you can't. I was just wondering how you *felt* about it. I was just curious. Nevermind."

"I guess you're right," the admin said. "Talking about how people feel about it — that's not talking about the suit, right?"

"That's right," Erika answered.

"Well, most people here aren't happy with it, to tell you the truth," the admin said. "They think we got hoodwinked into selling a patent that Royaltec is using against stuff not covered by the patent. And they've muzzled everyone here with the agreement."

"Yeah," Erika said. "I'd be pissed too. Say, how long has your boss been with AutoSmart?"

"Five years," the admin said.

"You don't happen to know who was in her job when the patent was filed, do you?" Erika asked, tapping the pencil on the desk.

"No," said the admin, apparently realizing what Erika was up to. "But if you hold on a minute, I can look it up."

Meanwhile, Joe walked into Zenko's favorite restaurant at lunchtime, hoping to catch him there at a lunch break from the deposition he was handling. Bingo. Zenko had just picked up a bite of uni sushi with his chopsticks when Joe found him.

"What are you doing here?" Zenko asked, looking around.

"I had some things to tell you about," Joe said. "I just took a chance to see if you were here. I know you didn't want any calls or e-mails."

"But Max comes here sometimes," Zenko said. "This is too close to the office. Go tell Erika what you have. She'll get it to me. And she'll organize it."

"Fine," Joe said, backing away and feeling miffed. He wasn't going to be able to avoid Erika after all. "So how's the deposition going?"

"I swear these two Peterson attorneys are trying to bore me to death," Zenko said. "That's the only explanation for the lame and pointless questions they're asking. This reminds me how much I hate doing depositions. Max is trying to torture me by denying me associate help."

Joe knew that unlike Royaltec, Zenko didn't have the resources to cover a large number of depositions or to go through lots of irrelevant documents to annoy Royaltec. For Zenko's discovery on behalf of Telekinetics, he focused in on what he absolutely needed to know to show the patent didn't cover the Retinal Screen. He asked for only 3 depositions, and had only 5 pages of interrogatories and 2 pages of document requests. The requests were narrowly focused, rather than open-ended.

Zenko's cell phone rang, and Joe's rang immediately afterward. It was someone from the state bar. They wanted a "voluntary" interview with him regarding Neuropt.

As Joe was leaving the restaurant, his cell phone rang again. It was Erika.

"So where are you?" Erika said. "You haven't responded to my e-mail."

"I was trying to have lunch with Zenko," Joe said.

"Well, while you're chowing down on sushi," Erika said, "I'm working my butt off and skipping lunch. I could use a little help. My back is getting a little sore carrying this team. I need you to call one of the inventors on this patent, Doug Chang. That is, unless you need to rendezvous in some hotel right now with that Alicia slut."

Joe would normally have assumed Erika was just yanking his chain with this talk. But now he wasn't sure. "If you hadn't been sending flowers to yourself," Joe retorted, "and pretending to still be happily married, I would never have gone out with her."

"That's right, try to blame your screw-up on me," Erika said. "Lighten up and call Chang."

Joe quickly scribbled down the phone number Erika rattled off before abruptly hanging up. What did she mean by lighten up? Had she just been teasing him about Alicia all along? No, not possible. Maybe she was trying to transition to it being teasing? He could drive himself crazy trying to figure it out, and doubted that asking her straight out would get a straight answer.

Joe called Chang right away. When Chang answered, he explained who he was, that he was calling about the patent.

"So what can I do for you?" Doug asked.

"Well," Joe said, "I'd like to know what you think of this. Did you think you invented a robotic cabling system or a neural network?"

"Both," Doug said.

"Both?" Joe asked. "Then why isn't a neural network described in the patent?"

"At the time," Doug said, "I didn't appreciate all the applications of my invention."

"And when did you appreciate that it might apply to a neural network?" Joe asked. He knew what was coming.

"After Roger Borland, the Royaltec attorney, called me," Doug replied. "Look, let's cut through the bull. We both know what you want. You want me to say I didn't invent a neural network. But if I say that, I give up my royalty."

"Royalty?" Joe asked. "Didn't you assign all rights to AutoSmart at the time? I thought that was standard practice?"

"Yeah," Doug said. "It's standard practice. Every engineer is hired to invent, that's part of the job, and the company owns all the rights. That doesn't keep it from rubbing you the wrong way if the company makes a lot of dinero off your invention."

"Okay I'll bite," Joe said. "If AutoSmart owned all rights, how are you getting a royalty?"

"I'm glad you asked," Doug said. "It seems this Roger Borland and Royaltec are real stand-up people. They just didn't feel right making a lot of money without sending some the way of the inventors of the neural network. So they're giving me a percentage."

Joe hadn't expected this. Royaltec owned the patents it bought from AutoSmart, and had no obligation to pay anything to the inventors. It was a shrewd move, though.

By voluntarily paying some small royalty to the inventors, they insured that the inventors would testify favorably. What other mischief had Royaltec been up to?

Max looked around the conference table that afternoon. He could smell the fear in the air. Turner had a look of stubborn self-righteousness, while Evans looked exasperated. The rest of the partners just looked scared. The only ones who looked calm were the framed former managing partners staring down from the wall.

Riley, Ferguson and Wang had announced on Friday that they were leaving to join Peterson, Malone, and were taking at least two associates with them. Rumor had it more would be leaving. The firm was unraveling. The partnership meeting was to discuss what to do, and whether to layoff further staff.

"In all the years I have been with this firm," Turner was saying, "we have never laid off a secretary because her attorney left. That is not the kind of firm we are! We would find some overflow or other work for the secretary to do, and when we hired the next new attorney, she would work for him. To do otherwise would cost us all the goodwill with our staff we have built up over the years."

"What does it take to get through to you?" Evans asked. "We don't have the money to pay the secretary without the attorney generating billings. And more attorneys will leave before we ever get around to hiring a new one. If we wait, the extra costs will drag the firm down. We'll go out of business. Then everyone will lose their jobs. For Christ's sake, Turner — we're in a desperate situation here."

The partners were divided. The optimists sided with Turner, and most didn't like firing people, so they were willing to believe anyone who told them they didn't need to. A number were clearly more concerned about the viability of the firm, and their own paychecks, and demanded that some action be taken immediately. Tempers were flaring.

As if by some unspoken command, Max noticed all eyes turned to him as the room quieted down. The debate had played itself out, and it was time for a decision.

"Well," Max said, standing up and slowly walking to the end of the room, touching a number of the partners on the shoulder as he walked by. "I've been listening to this discussion, and I think everybody is right." Everyone started nodding, apparently happy with this conciliatory wisdom, whatever it was.

"I have just two points to make," Max continued. "First, I don't think we need to lay anyone off, because I understand half the staff has resumes out anyway, so we're going to lose some people regardless — and this way we won't need to pay severance."

"The second point," Max continued, "is that the firm may completely unravel with people leaving. If it does, any savings from layoffs would be dwarfed by the losses of the business folding. Our best bet for avoiding that is to outwardly project confidence that we are here to stay. Announce we aren't laying people off, that we are bullish on the firm, and will hire attorneys to replace those that left. Part of the problem is a self-fulfilling prophecy, so we need to rewrite the prophecy."

Evans seemed genuinely intrigued by Max's analysis. "So," Evans said, "if I understand you correctly, the best way to save money is to not do the layoffs. Do you in truth think it will work? Do you think a couple secretaries will leave in the next few weeks anyway?"

"Yes, I'm certain of that," Max said. "I think half-way measures will fail. As to whether the firm will be able to survive, that depends on what each of us in this room do."

———————

Later that Thursday afternoon, Erika crossed her fingers as she listened to the phone ring. This was wearing on her. Everything she tried on the Telekinetics suit had led to a dead end. But she had finally gotten what she believed was Cecil Bridges' phone number. She had tracked it down through a number of former Triscope employees. Each had pointed her to another that might still be in contact with Cecil until she hit pay dirt. Bridges had quit the rat race, and was working at a boat rental operation in Tonga, in the south Pacific. She was told he would work on sailboats, and sometimes go out on a cruise as a skipper for some group. It should be tomorrow morning there right now.

"Tonga Yacht Charters" said a man on the end of the line.

"Hello," Erika said. "Is Cecil Bridges there?"

"Yeah," he said. "He's out on the dock. Hang on a minute." She could hear him yelling for Bridges, then explaining there was some woman on the phone.

She could almost smell the sea air. She pictured a rickety office on the second floor of a shack built out on a dock. The man must have leaned out an open window to call Bridges. She closed her eyes and could practically feel a warm sea breeze lifting her hair from her face. Bridges was probably bare-chested and tan. He was a bit old, but still in good shape, with a sinewy body hewn from hard work on the docks. He was wearing tattered jeans, torn and frayed at the bottom.

"Yeah, hello?" It was Bridges.

Erika explained who she was and that she was investigating an AutoSmart patent he might know about, since he was listed as an author on an article discussing the product.

Bridges laughed when Erika was done explaining. "I have to tell you," he said, "that I'm relieved. I thought you were a collection agent. They always get pretty women to call us old farts, since they know we're suckers for a pretty young woman."

"Well, I'm not a collection agent, Mr. Bridges," Erika said, taking the scrunchie out of her hair and twirling it around her finger. "But how did you know that I'm pretty?"

"The voice," Bridges said. "Please, call me Cecil. How can I help you?"

"Well," Erika said, "first of all, I'd just like to know whether you remember anything about that AutoSmart patent or product?"

"I was thinking it was funny you should ask about it," Cecil said. "Because I do remember it. I was one of the inventors, but I left for another job before the patent application was filed, but after the article was submitted for publication. Since I no longer worked there, they didn't list me as an inventor. Maybe they thought I wouldn't sign the paperwork, I don't know. It wasn't a big deal to me. I would have liked to have a patent in my name, so I would have signed it. I guess they were afraid I'd cause trouble since my leaving wasn't on the best terms. They would have probably tried to take my name off the article, too, if it hadn't already been submitted."

"Uh-huh," Erika said, busily scribbling notes. "Did you think that what you invented covered a neural net processor?"

"A what?" Cecil asked.

"A neural net processor," Erika repeated.

Cecil snorted. "Hell, no. It was a robotic cable tensioning system. What is a neural net processor?"

Meanwhile, Joe was walking into his apartment when his cell phone vibrated.

"Joe, help!" Burak said when Joe answered the phone. "They are driving us nuts. If this goes on, I will not be responsible for my actions. I will need a murder defense attorney."

"What's going on?" Joe asked, flopping backward onto his mattress on the floor.

"We had all the papers ready for the Royaltec attorneys," Burak answered. "Just like A.J. wants, we are being cooperative. Everything they should need, in one room. But they are not satisfied. They want to look at everything, whether it is related or not. They say they will decide if it is relevant. They are disrupting everything, going through files all over the place. We cannot get any work done."

Joe groaned. A.J. had instructed him not to object to the document requests, since she didn't want to pay attorneys fees for fighting over it. She thought they could just be reasonable, and give Royaltec's attorneys access to the documents they needed. It was becoming clear that Borland didn't just want what he needed — he wanted to make life difficult for Telekinetics.

As soon as he hung up, Joe saw that a message had come in. It was from Erika. She wanted him to prepare a declaration that she could fax to Cecil Bridges and have him sign. At last, some progress! Cecil was willing to say he hadn't invented a neural network. He replayed the message twice. The sound of Erika's voice filled him with desire for her, and he wanted to listen to her sign off again.

"So can you fax that to me within the hour?" Erika had asked. "Or do I need to send you some of my underwear to get you to perform for me?"

———————

By the end of the day, Erika had finally tracked former AutoSmart CFO Alex Wineeson to a company he joined just a year ago. Hopefully, he was still there. He had certainly moved around a lot. Things were finally starting to go her way. First she found Cecil Bridges, now perhaps Wineeson.

"Alex here," answered a voice on the phone.

"Mr. Wineeson," she quickly said. "I'm a paralegal at the firm of Turner and West. I wanted to talk to you for just 5 minutes about some AutoSmart products at the time you were at AutoSmart."

"Is this about the Royaltec lawsuit?" Alex asked.

Uh-oh! Had Royaltec already talked to him to? Maybe he just kept up on his old company.

"Because if it is," Alex said before she could respond, "I can't talk about it. I've been hired by Royaltec as a consultant on the lawsuit."

"Is that right?" she asked, her annoyance getting to her. "Are they keeping you busy?"

"It's more of a contingent consulting arrangement," Alex said. "In case anything comes up."

Clever, she thought. She was somewhat surprised he said the arrangement was contingent. Borland had gotten the guy to agree not to help Telekinetics without having to pay him anything.

"I see," she said. She tried to keep him talking. Maybe he'd let something slip. She was constantly amazed how much people would tell a stranger over the phone if she just asked. "Can you at least confirm you were at AutoSmart . . . ."

He hung up before she could finish.

———————

Early that evening Ned was adjusting the framed picture of himself and the SEC commissioner. He had needed to walk around, do something, to keep his mind off wanting to scream at Gage. He looked across the desk at Roger Borland, who held up his palm in a signal that he was in control. Good. Litigators are more used to this abuse, he'd let Roger handle Gage.

"A paralegal?" barked Gage from the speakerphone. "All of this is being done by a paralegal?"

"That's right," Roger answered. "We checked her out with attorneys who have been on the other side of litigation where she was involved. She seems to be smarter than most of the associates at Turner, West. She was working with Zenko the last time he won, and now they're teamed up again."

"And she's beating you guys to the punch!" the voice laughed. "I guess your asshole attorneys aren't such damn hot-shots after all, huh?"

"She hasn't beaten us to the punch," Roger said, a tone of annoyance slipping into his voice. "I said she has gotten close. Too damn close. I would just feel better with her out of the picture, that's all."

"So what do you want me to do about it?" Gage asked. "Rub her out?"

Ned was dumbfounded. He wasn't sure if Gage was joking.

"No," Ned said. "Have Neuropt hire her away from Turner, West. Without her, Zenko is lost."

"I can't just be hiring people I don't need," Gage said. "Why don't you hire the bitch?"

Ned grimaced. This should be obvious. "Because she's on the other side of the suit from us," Ned explained. "If our firm hires her, Turner will claim we have a conflict of interest since we have access to the confidential information she has about Telekinetics' defense. The judge would disqualify us from representing you. That's the same reason Royaltec can't hire her itself. Besides, not needing her isn't an excuse. Neuropt doesn't need any of the people it has, you know."

"Shit," Gage said. "What the hell am I supposed to do with her?"

"She's a paralegal," Ned said, moving his mouse to the picture he wanted and clicking on the mail function. "And a damn good one. Surely you can find a use for her."

Ned hit send. "I just sent you some information we've pulled together on her. Along with a picture." He winked at Roger and waited.

"Holy shit!" said the voice. "This is one hot broad. Why didn't you say so in the first place? We'll find a place for this babe, don't you worry."

"You'll have to make it an offer she can't refuse," Ned said.

14.

Zenko put down the Time magazine and looked at his watch. It was 4:15 the next afternoon – he had been waiting 15 minutes. He had gone through People magazine in the first five. He looked around for something else to read. The table was mostly strewn with PR pieces on Peterson, which he refused to pick up. The young receptionist stood up and leaned over the counter. "Would you like some coffee?"

He shook his head and took out his phone to check his phone messages again. Roger finally strolled into the reception area, casually joking with a young associate. Zenko knew the game – annoy the other attorney anyway you can, and make him bill more time to his client.

"Zenko!" Roger said, extending his hand. "Good to see you again! We haven't gone head to head for a while. I'm looking forward to kicking your butt this time."

"This time, huh?" Zenko said, standing up with a short bow and smiling at the memory of their last suit and shaking his hand. "I see you still haven't forgotten our last encounter, Borland-san."

Roger got quiet. He must have realized his error in bringing up the last time they met. Although it had been over 5 years, Zenko had kicked Roger's butt big time.

Roger led Zenko up the staircase to a small conference room adjacent the main conference room. "I'm going to enjoy this suit," Roger said, grinning broadly and gesturing for Zenko to take a seat. "We've got a rock solid patent, a client that doesn't know anything better to do with its money than to throw exorbitant amounts at us for this lawsuit, and your client caught with its pants down."

So it begins, Zenko thought.

"As Buddha has said," Zenko shot back, "a dog is not considered a good dog because he is a good barker. The rock your patent is made of is pumice — it's full of holes. Your client is going to be plenty pissed at you when I get your patent declared invalid by the court. All those potential royalties from big companies down the drain because you decided to go after the wrong small player first. So I'm going to save your sorry ass, Roger, I'll let you dismiss this suit and walk away with your patent intact without asking for Rule 11 sanctions for suing without any basis."

Roger sat down at the conference table and pushed a piece of paper at Zenko. Zenko glanced at it. It was a standard letter agreement confirming that the settlement discussions were confidential and information exchanged in the settlement discussion could not be used in the lawsuit. Zenko read it carefully to make sure Roger hadn't snuck anything in there, then signed it and pushed it back.

"Why don't you start," Zenko said, "by telling me what royalties your client would accept in settlement."

Zenko knew it was always best to get the other side to commit to a number first. A negotiation was like a game of chicken. Whoever went first betrayed weakness.

Unfortunately, the side that needed the settlement most was usually forced to start, but it was worth a try.

"I'd be glad to," Roger said. "We'd accept 90% of your profits."

"I see I am going to have to go first, since you are not being serious," Zenko said. "I'll just cut to the chase. Telekinetics would consider the same deal you gave Neuropt."

"Oh?" Roger said. "What makes you think Neuropt is licensed?"

"Because that is what Neuropt is telling Telekinetics customers," Zenko said. "So I'd be just as happy if you told me they weren't licensed, because then I could sue Royaltec for trade libel and unfair competition."

"Uh-huh," Roger said, turning his chair to look out the window for a moment. "Well, you needn't bother, because Neuropt is licensed," Roger said.

"You might as well tell me the Neuropt license terms now," Zenko said, "since we're entitled to find out in discovery."

Roger turned to look at Zenko and smiled. "Yes, but you're not entitled to it *now*. You have to make the discovery requests, wait the requisite time we're given by law to answer, put up with our stonewalling a reasonable time, and then file a motion with the judge to compel us to give you the information. At that time we'll give you something that's not quite complete and you'll have to make another motion to the judge."

Roger leaned back in his chair. Zenko was a little surprised. Everyone knew that was the game, but no one *said* it. Even if there was no one else in the room and it was his word against Roger's.

"And by that time," Roger continued, "I'm betting your client will be out of business."

Zenko laughed so he wouldn't give away his concern. "You'll have to license Telekinetics on similar terms to Neuropt or face antitrust and discrimination charges."

"There is no antitrust violation, no unfair competition," Roger countered, "Royaltec doesn't have a monopoly on neural nets or these helmets, so the antitrust laws don't apply. And you'd have a tough time showing any type of unfair competition. Surely you don't think we did a straight license with Neuropt. You should know that other business aspects of a deal can make the royalty rate not applicable to other companies — such as a license back of their technology, a distributor arrangement, a purchase contract, etcetera, etcetera, etcetera. All those things are reasons for reducing a royalty rate for Neuropt that won't apply to your client."

"You still have to value the other aspects," Zenko said, but knowing that he was had. What Roger described was a common technique to justify screwing whomever you want with a higher royalty rate than other licensees, and still claiming it's a non-discriminatory royalty rate. He'd lost count of the companies he'd seen agree with a standards board to charge a fair and non-discriminatory license to anyone, and then use bullshit like that to charge different rates. It's like everyone selling PCs with different combinations of features so you can't compare prices because you can never find two systems with the same feature set.

Roger shook his head, then leaned forward over the table and looked directly into Zenko's eyes. "You may think I just want to waste your time," Roger said. "But I don't. So I'm going to give it to you straight. And if you tell the judge what I say, I'll deny it. We want to make an example of Telekinetics so the rest of the industry is afraid of the same thing happening to them and signs up for big royalties. We are not only going to win the suit; we are going to put Telekinetics out of business in the process. Even total capitulation and stopping sales won't make us drop the suit. We wouldn't settle on *any* terms. We'll go after treble damages on the sales that were made and consequential damages because your client caused the market to expect a lower price. No matter what you do, your client will be out of business before the judge would consider dismissing the suit. And since your client won't be able to pay you, I suggest you drop them, or Turner, West will go down with them."

Roger leaned back in his chair. "By the way," Roger added, "I understand finances aren't so good at your firm these days."

Zenko smiled broadly at Roger. There was only one way to respond to such hubris.

"Is that so?" Zenko said, leaning forward. "Okay, I'll be candid too. If that's what you're planning to do, we have no choice but to fight to the end. The court probably won't let us withdraw from representing Telekinetics even if we wanted to until after the preliminary hearings and motions, because the short notice wouldn't give them time to find other counsel. Telekinetics will owe us a bunch of money by then, and they won't be able to pay us. So we'll have to win to get our fees, and we'll bury Royaltec and its patent in side-by-side graves."

Zenko was making this up as he went, but he found himself believing it. "We'll keep representing Telekinetics even if they end up being in bankruptcy. And we won't stop until we get the court to declare this bullshit patent of yours to be invalid. And then you'll have nothing. Nothing, that is, except a suit for malicious prosecution because I think you already know the patent is invalid."

Zenko smiled and leaned back in his chair. Not bad for off-the-cuff, he thought. Roger just smiled back.

"Well, I wish you a lot of luck with that," Roger said as he stood and walked toward the door, signaling that the meeting was over.

Joe saw the message waiting light blinking as he shuffled slowly into his apartment at 6 PM that evening, dropping his papers on the floor where his desk used to be. Now there was just a pile of paper, books and pens. He closed the door behind him, and then leaned his head against it. Researching at the county law library to defend against the SEC or State Bar investigation had been frustrating.

He checked his messages. Zenko had been calling all afternoon, complaining about Joe having his cell phone off. Well, that was exactly why he had it off — so he could get some work done without interruptions. There was also a message from Hank.

"Joe," Hank said. "I heard about your problems. Talk to me next time so I can give you some tips on how not to get caught. Anyway, now that you have time on your hands, call me. Think Scottsdale, Arizona. It's warm like Mexico and they speak better English. I found a place right on a golf course. It's perfect."

Joe ended then saved the message. He'd listen to it later. The phone rang as soon as he hung up.

"You're there!" said Zenko. "Where the hell have you been, Nile-san? I've been trying to get a hold of you all afternoon."

"I was at the library," Joe said, rolling onto his back on the floor. "Doing some research on a case near and dear to my heart. Mine."

"Joe," Zenko said, "you've got to help us full time. I can't get good help, and I need you on this. Royaltec wants to put Telekinetics out of business — Borland told me to my face that they won't consider any settlement. I'm beginning to think that part of their strategy is to put Turner, West out of business so we can't defend Telekinetics."

Joe was conflicted. He desperately wanted to help Telekinetics, but he also had to look out for himself. Couldn't Zenko understand he was doing both? Didn't Zenko encourage him to do that? He listened as Zenko briefed him on his meeting with Borland. This wasn't like Royaltec. They would usually settle these for less than the litigation costs — that was how they got people to sign up for such B.S. patents. What did they have in mind here?

"Zenko," Joe said. "Do you remember that you're the one who advised me to work on my own defense?"

"I know," Zenko said. "But then I met Borland today. I guess he was right."

"Right about what?" Joe asked.

"In our meeting I put up some bravado and told Roger Borland we'd beat their sorry asses," Zenko said. "I told him that I had the best patent attorney in the business — *you*. Borland just laughed at me, and said Ned had told him that you were a screw-up when you worked for Peterson, and now you are so mired in your own problems you wouldn't be able to do a thing. And even if you had time, he said you were a second rate patent attorney who would get his nose bloodied if he mixed it up with the big guys."

"Borland said that?" Joe said, flushing with anger.

"Yup," Zenko said. "That's what he said. So will you meet me at Moe's for dinner to go over the case?"

"I'll be there," Joe said.

———————

At that moment in São Paulo, Ahmet was squishing a gooey material between his fingers. It was called a mesh amplifier — it was embedded with thousands of electrically conductive strands. When packed against the spinal cord, the engineers thought it would have the effect of amplifying the signals from the neuron firings — or at least making them more visible to the sensor. The plan was to pack the material inside the Sheath. It should make the Sheath work better. The Sheath had proved effective in stopping the virus, but it was spotty in overcoming the paralysis. He hoped it would work.

The new prototype Retinal Screen with flash memory was due to arrive tomorrow. This time, there would be sufficient police protection.

Ahmet clicked his mouse again with his other hand. There was another one. The rumor was spreading through the chat rooms faster than he could follow them. There was speculation that the unnamed tainting was in fact the virus, and people thought Adbil itself put out the speculation about black market Adbil. They thought that the maker of Adbil was taking advantage of the crisis to try and kill off its black market competition.

Ahmet was suspicious — he didn't think this was just people's mistrust of drug companies. Whoever was planting the virus in the pills could be going to different chat rooms and starting the rumor. Or perhaps it's the black market manufacturer — afraid of losing sales? Even in a disaster, someone's always trying to make money.

His cell phone rang — it was Cassia. They talked for a few moments about the rumors. She sounded nervous and preoccupied.

"I have a favor to ask," Cassia said.

"Yes?" Ahmet answered.

"I got a call from an informant who claims to have vital information about the virus," she said. "We've gotten crank calls before, but this one knew to call me, and something tells me he is different. But what bothers me is the guy wants to meet me alone."

"Don't do it," Ahmet urged.

"I don't intend to," Cassia said. "You know the restaurant Cabana Gaucha?"

"In Santo Amaro?" Ahmet said. "It's a Churrascaria."

"That's the one," Cassia said. "I'd feel better if I knew you were there where you could watch."

———

Erika and Zenko arrived at Moe's at the same time and sat down at a table that still hadn't been bussed. Moe's was a new Menlo Park restaurant on Santa Cruz Avenue that was basically a copycat of the old Sam Wo's in San Francisco — a cheap Chinese restaurant that had an offbeat reputation for friendly abuse. Erika looked out the window and saw Joe parking his truck.

The entrance was through the crowded kitchen, with pots and pans in disarray all over. There were a few haphazard mats on the floor, and various pieces of food littering the floor. She heard the cooks giving out the usual abuse as Joe came in.

"Hey, look," said one cook, "another sucker."

"Don't order the hot and sour soup today," said another said. "We've had this batch of leftovers going for 2 weeks, it's dreadfully foul now."

"Nile-san," Zenko said as Joe made it through the gauntlet to their table. "You're late. You must follow the teachings of Buddha — It is better to travel well than to arrive."

"You can sure pick the right atmosphere," Joe said, looking at Erika. She didn't look up, constantly turning the menu over in her hands. She was still uncomfortable with Joe, her mind a flurry of mixed feelings.

"How's your personal defense going?" Zenko asked.

"Fine," Joe said, "just fine."

Before Joe could sit, the Chinese waiter, Desoto, appeared. "Not okay," Desoto said, looking at Joe and wagging his finger. "Not okay. You keep beautiful lady waiting. Bad, bad. You should be here first, so she not have to deal with obnoxious Chinese waiter."

Desoto was a plump, jolly waiter with a dirty apron. Everyone who had eaten at Moe's knew Desoto. Desoto handed a basin and a towel to Joe. "Here," Desoto said, pointing to the table. "You bus table. Put the dishes in here, then wipe table good."

Joe cleared the table. Desoto then pointed him to the silverware bin and made him set the table. Then Joe sat down across from Zenko. The place was cheaply decorated. The tables seemed like long card tables with plastic tablecloths. The walls had tacky yellow wallpaper with a few velvet pictures hanging in a slapdash arrangement. Joe picked up the flower vase at the end of the table so Zenko and Erika could see the water swirl. It had a plastic flower in it.

There was a sign taped to the wall at the end of the table: "We serve soda and tea. If you want beer, go across the street and buy it." On the table was a triangular cardboard that said: "You can order the shrimp if you want, but it is expensive and the portions are small."

"Well, Zenko," Joe said, "this is perfect for the occasion. What's a little more abuse?"

Desoto came over and handed Joe a paper and pen. "Write down your order," Desoto commanded. "And be precise. No errors. You make nice lady wait; now you take orders. Nice lady must be confused, thought this was Stars. She dressed too nice for Moe's, and too nice for you," Desoto turned and left.

"Ya know," Erika said, "that Desoto is pretty sharp."

"Yeah, yeah," Joe said, holding the pen poised over the pad. "So what was it you wanted, Erika? The tofu wrapped in seaweed with jellyfish?"

Erika screwed up her courage to break the news about her job to Zenko and Joe, but Zenko spoke before she could open her mouth.

"So Erika," Zenko said, "what's the story with Bridges? Were you able to get his affidavit?"

"No," Erika said. "By the time I faxed it, Bridges had taken off on a cruise. Apparently it was some last minute thing he got assigned to — just a little suspicious, if you ask me."

"How's that possible?" Zenko asked. "I thought you sent the fax within a few hours of talking to him?

"I did," Erika said. "But I had to send it to a copy place, the Marina didn't have a fax. And they were closed, so they didn't get it until the middle of the next day. Things are a bit more relaxed in Tonga."

Joe saw Desoto working his way over to their table. He hurriedly got the orders written down.

"You not ready?" Desoto said. "You make Desoto wait?"

"No, no, oh most mighty waiter-meister," Joe said, "I'm just about finished." Joe scribbled some more and handed Desoto the paper.

Desoto squinted as he read. "What letter this?" Desoto said, pointing at a word.

"That's a g," Joe said.

"No, no it looks like a p," Desoto said. "We don't have no *sprinp* rolls. You must be thinking of somewhere else."

Desoto handed the paper back to Joe, who made the letter into a clear g, and handed it back to Desoto. "Oh, *spring* rolls!" Desoto said, walking away. "Poor choice, but you can have it if you want."

"I called the two experts whose names you e-mailed me," Zenko said to Erika. "And both had already been retained by Royaltec. The second one was surprised when I told him the other had also been retained. They clammed up pretty quickly, but it was clear both had just been retained."

"I'm beginning to think we're being watched," Zenko said.

"How so?" Joe asked.

"Erika e-mailed me over the Internet about the experts," Zenko said. "I was working at my condo. I think they intercepted the names and contacted and retained them before we could. I'm starting to think Borland bribed someone at my internet service provider."

Zenko turned toward Erika. "You left a message on Joe's machine about Bridges, didn't you?" Zenko asked.

"Yes," Erika replied.

"No e-mail?" Zenko asked.

"No," Erika replied, "just the one phone message." Zenko nodded.

"You don't think Bridges decided to contact Royaltec on his own after talking to Erika?" Joe asked.

"That seems unlikely to me, given what he said to Erika," Zenko said, and Erika nodded. "And, with the expert thing, I think someone's tapping into our communications. I see two probable possibilities with the Bridges thing. Either they eavesdropped on Erika's or your phone, Joe, or they got your remote activation code for your home phone. Or they could have bugged your place, or done any number of other things. Who knows?"

"Zenko," Joe said, leaning forward across the table and lowering his voice, "don't you think you're just a little paranoid?"

"Yes," Zenko said, "I do." Zenko picked up his fork and examined it. It had some gunk on it. He tossed it aside. "I think I'll use chopsticks."

"Yes, Nile-san," Zenko continued, "I am being paranoid. And, I might point out, Nile-san, that you're out of job, and being investigated by the SEC, and the bar, and your client is being sued out of business by a ruthless company with even more ruthless lawyers. Don't you think you should be a little more paranoid?"

"Point taken," Joe said, leaning back.

"So new ground rules," Zenko said. "No Internet e-mail about anything sensitive, unless it's encrypted. And nothing sensitive on voice mail. Just leave a message to call back. Especially on cell phones or wireless handsets. I doubt they tapped the Turner, West line, but Joe, yours might be. Is there a pay phone you could use instead?"

Everyone stopped talking as Desoto approached. Desoto showed up with the spring rolls and set them down by Joe. Desoto put his hands on his hips and looked around the table. "Why you stop talking?" Desoto asked. "Top secret business conversation? You afraid Desoto is industrial spy?"

Desoto slapped Joe's shoulder with the back of his hand. "Why you talk business?" Desoto asked, looking at Erika. "You have beautiful woman here. You should be getting her phone number. Telling her jokes. Telling her what a nice body she have. What the matter with you?"

"Won't work," Joe said, "something about her being married or something."

Erika looked away from Desoto, but held out her hand, waving her ring finger. Desoto leaned over the table and grabbed Erika's hand, pulling it close to his face and forcing Erika to lean across the table and half stand up. Desoto examined the diamond carefully, then grimaced as if he smelled something rancid, and pushed her hand away. Desoto turned to Joe, putting his hand by his mouth as if to block the others from hearing what he was saying, but clearly speaking loudly enough for them to hear, "Cheap diamond. Husband must be cheap. She can't be happy. You have a good chance. Go for it — get her bigger diamond."

Desoto quickly retreated to the kitchen.

Erika scowled at Joe's grin. "He clearly wouldn't have made that joke if he didn't realize it was a real diamond."

After they discussed the case for a while, Erika interrupted. "I know this isn't a good time, but there's something I need to tell you guys."

"What?" Zenko asked.

"I'm going to quit," Erika blurted out.

Joe and Zenko just stared at her.

"Neuropt offered me a position today," Erika said. "They need a paralegal right away. Apparently that slut Alicia told them that I was brilliant or something."

"Whatever they offered you, we'll match it," Zenko said.

"They're giving me a ton of stock options," Erika explained. "And I think they're basically back-dating it or something, because they said they can give them to me substantially below what they expect they'll go public at. And as you know, they go public in less than a month. So I'll make a lot of money real quick. You guys couldn't match it, and I owe it to my son to take it. Besides, we all know Turner, West is falling apart. Even with all that, it wasn't an easy decision. I know you need me, Zenko. It's tearing me apart to do this. But I have to. I have to think of Jeffrey."

"Erika," Joe said, "the stock isn't going to be worth anything."

"To be honest, Joe," Erika said, "I just don't buy your crazy theory. Sorry. Besides, they are giving me some stock that I can sell in 90 days. Surely it will still have some value in 90 days, even if your theory were correct."

Zenko turned away and followed Joe's gaze out the window.

"I have to take it," Erika pleaded. "The stock and options will be worth *seventy-five thousand dollars* at the offering price. That's only a few weeks away at the most. And if the stock increases in value, if it triples like they expect it to — well, you can do the math. I can't afford not to take this. Besides, they're working on something that will fight the virus. It's something I want to be a part of."

Erika felt torn apart inside. She didn't dare tell them the truth. It was better that they think she was a traitor. Just like it was better that Joe think she hated him.

Later that night at his apartment, Joe still couldn't believe that Erika was doing this. It was one thing to leave Turner, West — but to go to Neuropt? That was like a slap in the face to him. Was that why she was doing it?

He struggled to put Erika out of his mind and focus his weary eyes as he looked at Bernie's e-mail. He was impressed that Bernie was searching at this time of night. Midnight here meant 3 AM in Washington D.C. Bernie reported he still hadn't found useful prior art on the Internet. Joe continued searching himself, but to no avail. His eyelids had started to droop when the doorbell rang. What nut would come around at this time of night?

Burak's mug panned into view as Joe swung open the door. "Burak," Joe said. "This is a surprise. Come on in. Are you here to haggle with me on my consulting rate?"

Burak smiled as he entered. "It is good that you kept your sense of humor," Burak said. "I was close by; I thought I would come see you."

"Good to see you," Joe said.

Burak grabbed both of Joe's shoulders and peered intensely at Joe. "I will pay you a higher rate if you need the money. I acted tough to Zenko. I acted like it was just business. But it is not just business. You are my friend, Joe. I want you to know that I do not believe the lies they made up about you. I know you, Joe. You have honor. You could not do what they say."

Joe just nodded. His throat was suddenly too dry to speak.

"I am here," Burak continued. "To tell you that I stand aside you."

Joe smiled. He grabbed both Burak's shoulders, and they collapsed in a bear hug. "It is good to have a friend," Joe said, shaking Burak's shoulders as he released his embrace.

"So," Burak said, holding up a bottle. "I think we should have a drink to drown your sorrows."

"I don't need a drink," Joe said. "I need to keep my focus."

"Then you should drink to keep me company," Burak said. "I will drown my sorrows. I did not come here to not drink. It is a tradition in my country. If something bad happens, we drink. I have a bottle of the finest Raki freshly smuggled from Turkey."

"And if something good happens?" Joe asked.

Burak grinned wildly. "We drink. Good system, no?"

"Doesn't Islam prohibit drinking alcohol? Joe asked.

"Not in Turkey," Burak said, pouring both of them a drink.

"Do you not think you have overdone the decorating?" Burak asked, looking around at the empty apartment.

"I like the minimalist approach," Joe said. "Besides, I can't afford the place now. Zenko's going to let me move into his condo for awhile."

"It will not stick," Burak said, as he clinked Joe's glass. "And Neuropt knows it. They just want to distract you, force you to spend your time defending bar investigations, SEC investigations, and malpractice suits. He only needs to stop you for a short, crucial time."

"Stop me from what?" Joe asked.

"From helping us," Burak said.

Joe laughed. "So this is really about you? Well, I can see why you need a drink, if it is you they are after, and not me, as it would appear."

"Not me," Burak said. "The Sheath. We need to stop the virus."

Joe stared at Burak for a moment, and then threw his head back as he downed the shot.

"You know Zenko already stopped by," Joe said. "You don't need to pressure me as well. I'm on it."

"I appreciate your help," Burak said. "Do not forget that you are in a dangerous spot."

"Dangerous?" Joe asked. "Well, I'm sure there are more dangerous spots in Turkey, right?"

"You are in the most dangerous spot in Turkey," Burak said.

"What are you talking about?" Joe asked. "I've never even been to Turkey, and I'm not there now. How could I be in the most dangerous spot in Turkey?"

"The most dangerous spot in Turkey," Burak said solemnly, "is the most dangerous spot everywhere. Between a man and his money. You have gotten between Gage Booth and his money."

A few hours later in Santo Amaro, a barrio of São Paulo, Cassia looked across the tables before entering Cabana Gaucha. She could see Ahmet reading a paper. He had a window seat. She went inside and recognized her informant immediately by the corncob pipe he said he'd have. He had dark eyes and a two-day old beard.

He clearly wasn't Brazilian, although he had spoken perfect Portuguese on the phone. He had eastern European features.

After they sat down, he talked about the weather, then about an article in the paper, as if they were old friends. The casualness of his conversation put Cassia on edge, and she edged back as he reached into his coat pocket. The waitress came, and he ordered a pizza, while she chose the Frango com polenta.

"So why did you ask me here?" Cassia asked, eyeing his hand coming out of his pocket. "I'm a busy woman."

"I know," he said, pulling out a pipe-cleaner. "My name is Vladmir. I know a lot about the virus."

"Like what?" Cassia asked.

"I know that you've figured out it isn't natural," Vladmir said, pushing the pipe cleaner down the pipe. "You've also figured out that it was distributed in small-pox vaccines and counterfeit Adbil pills. You've traced it to a company in Saudi Arabia — Abdulla Al-Jameel Pharmaceuticals. And, by the way, I know that you've shared this information with your boyfriend, and that he is sitting two tables behind me watching us."

"So you're a clever busybody," Cassia said, taking a sip of the latte the waiter brought. She actually felt more relaxed, rather than threatened. She didn't have to play any games. "Tell me something I don't know."

"I used to work for the KGB in Russia," Vladmir said. "The virus is a Russian biological weapon. They developed it by modifying a virus found in rodents in the Amazon rain forest, not far from here, coincidentally. It was stolen from a Russian lab."

"Now that is interesting," Cassia said, leaning forward. "Do you know who took it?"

"No," Vladmir said. "But we suspected some Muslim extremists."

"Do you know where they are?" Cassia asked.

"No," Vladmir said.

"Do you know why they are doing this?" Cassia asked.

"No," Vladmir said.

"Do you know if they are putting this virus in anything else?" Cassia asked.

"No," Vladmir said.

"How much was stolen?" Cassia asked.

"I don't know," Vladmir said.

Cassia leaned back in her chair and pushed her latte cup to one side. "Well, what good are you? Do you know anything that will help me?"

Vladmir leaned forward, and glanced around. "The Russians have an antidote."

15.

A few days later Ned was picking up a call from Gage.

"They're like zombies," Gage said. "Why won't Turner, West simply die? We hired away that hot paralegal, hired away a bunch of their partners, and I'm reading in the paper how they are still confident and planning to hire replacements."

"Well," Ned said, "we've limited the resources they can throw against Royaltec."

"Not enough," Gage said. "I want the bastards dead. Nuke them. I thought you said you could get their biggest client to leave. Do it. And call their bank."

"Now Gage," Ned said. "I don't think that is really necessary."

"Call them," Gage said, "or you're fired."

———————

The next day, Zenko nervously looked at his watch as he walked past the framed patents in the hallway to meet Burak at reception. It was already two o'clock. Burak was having his deposition taken tomorrow, and Zenko needed to find out what Burak knew in order to prepare for questions Borland would ask. Zenko knew Borland would try to make Burak mad so he'd talk too much, and would try to put words in Burak's mouth. A few hours simply wasn't enough time to go over Burak's testimony. But Burak had refused to come in earlier, claiming he was too busy. A.J. was there with Burak and they had already settled into the conference room. Zenko called Joe on the speakerphone. He didn't have Joe come in so Max wouldn't know Joe was helping.

"Burak," Zenko asked, "I presume you watched the video I sent you?" He had sent Burak a video on deposition preparation that went over some of the basics — not to volunteer information, keep answers short, take your time, etc. He used the video all the time for witnesses — it saved him a lot of time in preparation. But he knew Burak hadn't looked at it.

Burak was avoiding his eyes. "I am afraid I did not have time," Burak said. "I promise I will watch it tonight."

"Zenko, this stinks," A.J. said. "Not only do you take Burak away for what you say may be several days of depositions, you want him for days in advance to prepare him. Thank God we got that down to one afternoon. I can't spare him that long. Burak is my top manager."

Burak was leaning back in his chair and beaming at Zenko.

"We cannot afford all these distractions," A.J. said. "Our work is grinding to a halt at this critical time."

"Do you think we can get a technical person on the jury this time?" Burak interjected, "someone who can explain to the other jurors that this is bullshit?"

Zenko shook his head. "If we get any technical people in the jury pool, Royaltec will object and won't want them on the jury for exactly that reason."

"Object?" Burak asked, his face distorted in the incredulity of a two-year old. "How can they object? That is exactly the type of person who would understand the product."

"That's exactly why they'd object," Zenko said, "and exactly why the judge would agree with the objection. That happened in the Inventech suit — didn't you know? Someone who knows the technology has *preconceived* ideas about what the result will be. Preconceived is considered bad, because they won't decide solely on the evidence. They consider that person to be prejudiced."

"Prejudiced?" Burak said. "It is knowledge. Is someone who understands English and can add two and two prejudiced? I have never heard of anything so crazy. How can such a jury possibly understand the technology to decide this case? Do they throw people off juries for a hit and run because they have driven a car before? No. This is crazy."

"Well," Zenko said, "the theory is that they can be taught enough to figure out who the bad guy is. What happens is that each side hires a technical expert as a witness to explain to the jury why their side is right. The jury decides which technical expert is more believable, and they decide accordingly. You know this."

"I just still cannot believe it," Burak said. "Surely you are pushing my leg. If the jury does not understand the technology, how can an expert teach them in a short trial? It would take a several year trial to teach that. And how does the jury know which expert is the correct teacher?"

"That's easy," Joe said over the phone, "the jury decides which expert dresses more professionally, sounds more confident, and is friendlier."

"Very funny," Burak said. "But this is not a joking matter."

Zenko checked the phone number of the call that just rang on his cell phone, and then looked up again. "Joe is only partly kidding," Zenko said. "The system isn't fair, and although Joe exaggerates, there is a lot of truth to it working that way. I didn't make up the system, I just work with it."

Burak scowled. "It is a system to keep lawyers and experts busy and rich. That is what it is. How can you work with such a system?"

"So," A.J. interrupted, putting her hand on Burak's forearm, "our strategy will be to pick jurors who would best understand our technology even though they are not engineers?"

"No," Burak interjected, "we pick people who are prejudiced toward our expert. If they pick a German expert, and ours is Chinese, we want Chinese on the jury. It does not matter what they understand."

"Burak," Joe said, "you're picking up on this exceptionally quickly. Have you had some legal training?"

"This system," Burak grunted, "is like having ice skating in the Olympics, and each skater hires their own judge. The judges then recommend a winner to the audience, and the audience votes. Of course, each judge says their skater is the winner. And the audience is screened, to eliminate anyone who has seen ice skating before."

"I think there is a better analogy," Joe said. "It is more like a wine tasting, where the judges don't taste the wine, they just watch the faces of the people tasting it. And the people tasting it are actors who are experts at facial expressions, and have been hired by the different wineries."

"I know another one," Burak laughed, "how about a film critic who does not watch the films, instead watches the audience and rates the films based on audience reaction."

"That sounds more like politics," Joe said. "Besides, to make it a true analogy, half the audience would have to be plants by a competing director."

"You are correct," Burak said. "We had a better justice system in the old country. And much faster, too. The judge would put a chicken in between the parties, and cut its head off. Whoever the chicken ran toward would lose, and they would get beheaded, too."

"Right," Zenko said. "They don't do that in Turkey. It would constantly be in the papers if they did."

"That because no one sues in the old country," Burak said. "No one wants to lose their head. It is a good way to limit the number of attorneys."

"OK, enough already," A.J. said, slapping both palms down on the table. "I understand how the system works. But how about this: can we explain to the jury that the Patent Office made a mistake? I've heard Joe describe how the examiner only has a limited amount of time to deal with a patent application. We could show that these are just government employees, give some examples of other B.S. patents that the Patent Office handed out, only to have them invalidated. We could show that they are worse than the Post Office."

Zenko was shaking his head. "I would like to do that, but we can't. That was confirmed in a Federal Court case out of the Western District of New York in January 2000 that said you couldn't have testimony about how the Patent Office works. They thought it would undermine the presumed validity of the patent. It was Bausch & Lomb versus Alcon Laboratories, I believe."

"This becomes more and more ridiculous," Burak said. "What about the O.J. trial? They introduced evidence of how the police are incompetent, and mishandled the evidence. It is done all the time. Why cannot we do the same here?"

Zenko shrugged. "I don't make the rules."

"Zenko," A.J. said, getting to her feet, "the main reason I'm here is to tell you that you have to find a way to end this soon. In one month we won't be able to pay our employees and we'll be bankrupt. Customers are canceling orders, and we can't get any new orders. We were counting on the Retinal Screen to generate revenue, and now it seems dead on arrival."

Zenko said nothing for a few moments. "I hear you," Zenko finally said. "I don't know what to do about it, but I hear you."

"I know you'll come up with something Zenko," A.J. said. "But whatever you come up with, you'd better come up with it soon. Real soon."

Silence descended over the Turner, West Executive Committee meeting that afternoon. Turner had stood up and was slowly walking around the conference room, pausing in front of the portrait of each previous managing partner. Max couldn't help but think that now his portrait would never make it up there. It seemed a little silly, perhaps, but the row of portraits ranging back over 50 years had an aura of permanence. He had thought his own portrait would be there for future generations. Now it wouldn't even be there.

Turner, West had been hanging on by its finger-nails, and the positive attitude towards hiring new attorneys, rather than laying-off the staff of departed attorneys, seemed to be working. But one of Turner's biggest clients gave notice yesterday that they were taking their work to Peterson, Malone. They gave the reason that they believed Turner, West didn't have the quality attorneys it used to have, and that they were concerned about the stability of the firm.

The client defection was featured in an article about the decline of Turner, West in one of the legal rags this morning. Max had his suspicions about who gave the reporter this information, but it didn't matter now. Rumors had begun flying again, and panic was starting to spread through the firm.

Then, at noon, the bank called Max. They were calling Turner, West's loan since they hadn't maintained the required profit ratios. He still couldn't believe what they told him. The bank was threatening to start repossessing the assets securing the loan — not only the computers, desks and other equipment, but also the office leasehold and the receivables remaining to be collected. This would not only eliminate Turner, West's ability to meet its payroll, it would leave them with no place to work and nothing to do work with.

"So what do we do now?" Evans finally asked.

Max spread his hands. "We start looking for other jobs."

Burak ran his hand across the marble table again late the next morning. His headache was getting worse. He had started the morning with butterflies in his stomach, now it felt completely knotted up. These Peterson, Malone attorneys were intimidating. Roger Borland was looking through his notes on his yellow pad, while one of his partners was whispering in his ear. There were also two associates, a clerk and a paralegal. He glanced sideways at Zenko. It was the two of them against 6. And Zenko looked tired.

Burak was thankful for the break. Roger had started out asking a lot of questions about Burak's address, position, experience and responsibilities at Telekinetics. Burak found it uncomfortable answering even these simple questions with a court reporter taking down everything that was said. Then Roger had launched into a series of questions about Telekinetics' product development, giving an accusatory tone every once in awhile, such as when Burak had to admit they hadn't done a comprehensive patent search. Even though Joe and Zenko had both told him it wasn't required, Roger made it sound like he should have done that.

Roger leaned back in his chair. "So," Roger said, "tell me generally how this neural-net processor in the Retinal Screen works."

Burak glanced over at Zenko. Zenko had his elbow on the table and his chin in his hand. Two of his fingers extended up his cheek, forming a V. Burak recognized that as the signal for "volunteer," as in *don't*. Zenko didn't want him to volunteer information not specifically asked for. Burak was thankful Zenko had only made him memorize a few signs. But he liked the way it made him feel — like he was a baseball player.

"You will have to be more specific," Burak answered.

"Just generally describe it in your own words," Roger continued. "You don't have to go into a lot of detail."

"I object," Zenko said. "The question is vague and ambiguous and open-ended. I'm instructing the witness not to answer."

"Okay," Roger said, turning the pages of the Telekinetics data sheet he had downloaded from Telekinetics' web page and introduced in evidence as an exhibit. Roger started asking a lot of questions about diagrams in the data sheet — what did this control line do, what happened to data here, how was data stored. Burak silently cursed his team for putting all that detail on the web. Roger went on for about an hour, and Burak was starting to get tired. Then Roger started asking general questions about basic physics and the tension forces in a cable.

"So it sounds like cables," Roger was saying, while frowning, "are like the connections in a neural network processor since both connect nodes."

"No, no, no," Burak said. How dense was this guy? What would it take to make him understand? Burak was getting tired of trying to explain it.

"They are completely different," Burak said. "A connection between cables is just a connection. That is all. It is completely different from electrical connections in a neural net. In a neural net processor, interconnections between nodes are used to detect patterns, like the human brain. If more is input at one connection, the node there is weighted higher. It is like an image, where the light is brighter, the node will have a higher weight."

"Weight?" Roger asked.

"Weight simply means the amount of amplification," Burak said. "Just think of it as *amount* or *value*."

Zenko's hand suddenly appeared an inch in front of Burak's face, waving back and forth. "Why don't we take a break?" Zenko broke in.

Burak recognized Zenko waving his hand as the agreed signal that Roger was up to no good, and that Burak should stop talking and think about what Roger was trying to do. But when Zenko had said he'd wave his hand as a signal, Burak hadn't realized it would almost hit him in the face. He pushed Zenko's hand away. He didn't see any problem. It was clear that cables and neural nets were completely different, and that Roger didn't understand this. He was confident that he could explain this to Roger.

"I think it's early for a break," Roger said.

"So do I," Burak said. "I am okay, and I would rather just get this over with."

"So Burak," Roger quickly said, "let me see if I understand this. The term *weight* confuses me. I think I understand you to say it means the same as *amount*. So is it correct that your neural net processor basically strengthens connections in accordance with an amount at a node?"

"That is —," Burak started to say, but this time Zenko didn't just wave his hand in front of Burak's face, he put his hand over Burak's mouth.

"Let the record reflect," Roger said, turning to the court reporter, "that Mr. Kamisaka is putting his hand over the witness' mouth."

Zenko removed his hand from Burak's mouth, grabbed a highlighter, and highlighted a clause in his blown-up copy of claim 41 of the AutoSmart patent. He slid the copy in front of Burak, who looked down to see highlighted: "*means for strengthening said connections in accordance with an amount detected by said sensors at said nodes.*"

Burak quickly realized what was going on. Roger was trying to get him to describe Telekinetics product using the exact language in the claim. Roger would then assert that Burak had admitted that Telekinetics infringed.

"I need to use the restroom," Burak said. "So now is a good time for a break."

"Okay," Roger said. "I only have two more questions on this topic, and then we'll be done with it and can break."

Zenko stood up and grabbed Burak's arm to pull him out of his chair. "We're breaking *now*," Zenko said. Roger protested loudly, accusing Zenko of interfering with his deposition and prejudicing his case. But Zenko ignored him as he led Burak out of the room. They went down the hall to the restroom. It still had the smell of the detergent the janitor used to clean it last night. While Burak stepped up to a urinal, Zenko checked the stalls to make sure they were empty, then stepped up to the urinal next to Burak.

"Do you see what he's doing?" Zenko asked.

Burak nodded.

"He went on for an hour about stuff he in reality doesn't care about, just to wear you down and get you off guard," Zenko continued. "Then he tries to slip in a question putting words into your mouth, getting you to describe a feature of your product using words from a clause in the claim. The claim has 5 clauses, so guess what he's going to do?"

Burak shrugged. He felt sheepish.

"He almost got you to say the first clause described your product," Zenko continued. "If you had, he would have gone on for another hour with a bunch of other irrelevant questions, then he'd try to sneak in another question to get you to use the language of the second clause of the claim to describe your product. After 5 hours, he'll have gotten answers to 5 questions that have you using all 5 clauses of the claim to describe your product. Then he'll put together a petition for preliminary injunction, and quote all 5 answers in one column, with the claim quoted in the other column for comparison. Bingo, he's just gotten you to make an admission of infringement."

"But I was just trying to explain to him," Burak protested over his shoulder as he zipped up. "He clearly does not understand the technology. Once I explain it, I am sure he will make his client drop this crazy suit, since it will be clear that they cannot win."

"Give me the chance," Burak pleaded, as he turned on the faucet. "I know I can explain it to him. I am an outstanding teacher."

"No, no, no!" Zenko said, accentuating each 'no' with his fist against the wall. "Don't you understand? He already knows the difference between cables and a neural net. He probably knows it better than you by now. He does his homework, and probably spent days with an expert until he understood it backwards and forwards. He's *pretending* not to know to get you to explain. The more you talk, the more of your words he can take out of context and quote. And he can try to put words in your mouth by pretending to be grasping what you are teaching, but needing to understand it in his own words. Which happen to be the words in the claim."

"They don't care about the truth," Zenko continued. "A deposition of a witness is not taken to learn the truth. It is taken to try to put words in the witness' mouth that can be later quoted and used in a motion."

"How will it look," Burak asked, "with the re-cord showing you put your hand over my mouth?" He was annoyed that Zenko had done this. It made him feel like an idiot, and it probably made him look like a crook hiding something.

There was a long pause before Zenko answered. "I don't know," Zenko said, betraying uncertainty for the first time. "I made a split second decision that it would be better than an admission on the record."

"I guess we'll find out what Roger thinks in a mo-ment," Zenko said. "Roger may ask again, or may decide to leave it with the deposition transcript showing me putting my hand over your mouth. He might figure I'm telling you to say no, and he doesn't want a no on the record, so he'll leave it and argue to the judge that you were trying to say yes, and I was trying to cover up the truth. But if he does that, I'll ask you his question when I get a chance for cross-examination at the end of the deposition, so you're on the record as saying no."

Burak suddenly felt drained as they returned to the conference room. He sat down across from Roger, and glanced at the court reporter. The room didn't feel friendly anymore. It felt dangerous.

"OK, let's start again," Roger said calmly, as if nothing had happened. "Let's move on to the output circuit."

Roger turned to a page in the Telekinetics manual. "Burak," Roger said, "can you explain to me what this signal labeled CNT is doing?"

Burak picked up the data book printout and looked at it. "CNT selects between the output paths of the output buffer," he quoted from the data book.

"Oh, come on!" Roger said, pushing his chair back and flinging both arms in the air. "What are you guys trying to pull? That is not an answer. I already have the data book; I can read it myself. I need you to explain it. I object to this obvious coaching of the witness."

"Well I object," Zenko said coolly, "to your quoting of the claim and trying to put words in my client's mouth. We have the claim; we can read it. Burak has already told you we don't do it. So if you can't come up with anything else to ask, we should just end the deposition now."

Burak put the data book down, and slid it back to Roger while the two attorneys argued. Normally, all this arguing would have made him nervous. Now it made him comfortable. He liked having his attorney step in and fight for him while he just sat back.

Burak and Zenko rode the elevator to the Turner, West offices early that evening after the deposition had ended. Zenko wanted to go over strategy with Burak. He wasn't prepared for what he saw when the doors opened. There was not only no receptionist, there was no receptionist desk. A trace of dust on the floor outlined where it had been. He could see why the elevator had taken so long. The other elevator was locked off, and movers were loading furniture into the elevator. He walked down the hall to his office. There was literally an army of movers packing up furniture and computers. Attorneys and staff were packing up personal belongings, and he passed by two knots of people arguing, both apparently over the contents of computers. It must have been a surprise visit by the movers; the staff didn't seem to be prepared for it. It had the feel of an evacuation.

Sidney and Joe were sitting cross-legged on the floor in Zenko's office, calmly going through piles of paper when they walked in. "Ah," Burak said, "the unpretentious décor. I like it."

Zenko looked around with a pained expression.

"Yeah," Joe said, "it does have a certain charm. The best part is that it's finally okay for me to be in the office, now that everyone is joining the ranks of the unemployed."

Burak waved his hand toward the hall. "A surprise attack?"

"Yeah," Sidney said. "They hit the partner's offices first. I guess that the bank figured that's where the most valuable furniture and computer equipment would be. Well, not first. They went into accounting and the computer room initially, and shut down our network. I called Joe to help salvage the Telekinetics documents. "

"Well, I can sympathize," Burak said. "The same thing happened with my first company."

Zenko wearily sat on the floor. The Telekinetics case could be his last chance to redeem himself, and he felt it slipping away. Now this. Everything seemed to be spiraling out of control.

"I saved your liquor stash," Sidney said, grabbing the sake bottle from a box on the floor and pouring Zenko a drink.

Zenko took one sip then got a call on his cell phone.

"They're hauling the University of California into court," A.J. said. "Not all of my customers. Just UC and a few others who have placed orders for the Retinal Screen."

"Hauling them into court?" Zenko asked, thinking for a minute. "Do you mean with a 3rd party subpoena?"

"Yes, I think that's what it is," A.J. said. There was an audible rustling of paper. "I have a copy of one here, and it does say subpoena on it. How can they do this? This will scare off the rest of our customers. What can we do?"

"We need to object to the judge," Zenko said. "I'll get right on it."

"Zenko," Sidney said after Zenko hung up. "I heard about the bank calling the loan and called around to some friends. I found an office you can use a couple blocks away, on a month-to-month basis. I took the liberty of saying you wanted it, and was able to move a couple computers and other equipment and files. I figured you could always cancel, and say I had no authority, if you didn't like it."

"No, that's good thinking," Zenko said. "Why don't you guys move what's left over there. Give me the address, and I'll meet you there later. I want to talk to some of the people here first. It may be my last chance to say goodbye."

Sidney handed Zenko a large manila envelope from Peterson, Malone and a paper with the new office address. "You might want to look at this right away. I'll take the rest of the stuff and see you there."

After the rest had left, Zenko sat back down on the floor and poured himself another glass of sake. He opened the envelope. It had their answers to his discovery requests. He skimmed through them — they hadn't answered a single one. They objected to all of them. They also wanted to postpone the depositions of the inventors until the day before the Preliminary Injunction hearing. Zenko had agreed to their deposition of Burak and others, and now they were refusing to reciprocate.

Zenko pulled out the bottle of Johnnie Walker Black Label Scotch Whiskey. He poured a big shot and downed it. He then opened a bottle of Effexor antidepressant pills and tossed a handful in his mouth. He poured another shot of whiskey and slowly sipped it with his eyes closed.

———————————

Joe could feel the perspiration bead up on his forehead in the judge's chambers the next day. He had never been in court before, and certainly not in a judge's chambers. He had long ago specialized in the transactional work, not litigation. But Zenko had been taken to the hospital after a drug and alcohol overdose last night. Joe had to cover this appearance for him.

Joe heard the judge grunt, and looked over at him, with the President looking back at him from his portrait over Albert's shoulder. The judge finally sat back, took off his reading glasses and looked over at Joe. "So why are you bothering me with this?" Judge Albert asked. "I thought I told you boys to work this stuff out among yourselves, and not just come running to me. I'm a busy man."

"Your honor," Joe started. "Mr. Borland is subpoenaing customers of my client in a clear attempt to intimidate them into canceling orders."

"Your honor, I object!" Borland interrupted, getting to his feet. "We are doing no such thing. We are simply trying to obtain evidence of infringing activities."

"If that's the case, why have you only targeted customers who haven't canceled orders yet?" Joe asked. "No one who already canceled an order was subpoenaed."

"Obviously there is no infringing sale if the order has been canceled," Borland answered, looking at the judge instead of Joe.

Joe was watching the judge out of the corner of his eye during this exchange. The judge was nodding when Borland spoke, and frowning when Joe spoke. Not a good sign.

"You know as well as I that there is no difference," Joe said. "There hasn't been a sale in either case."

"Sure there has," Borland answered. "The canceled orders are sales, but your client has elected not to sue for breach of contract. So we're simply honoring that decision."

"And why do you need their testimony right away?" Joe asked. He regretted asking this as soon as the words left his mouth. He could feel that he was losing this argument, and an open-ended question like that was just an invitation for Borland to spin things his way. Zenko would have done a better job.

"Certain information about customer contacts just came to my attention," Borland answered. "Due to the closeness of the preliminary injunction hearing, and the fact that one of the customers was leaving on a trip today, we couldn't afford to wait another day."

"Oh for Christ's sake!" Joe exploded out of frustration. "That is such a bunch of crap! You give me one day and I bet I can prove . . ."

Judge Albert rose halfway to his feet, with his hands on his desk, as if supporting his weight. "I will not have such language in my courtroom!" Judge

Albert barked. "This issue is closed. Move on to your next issue or I'll hold you in contempt right now."

Joe said nothing, looking down at his notes to try and contain himself.

"Go on to your next item, Mr. Nile," Judge Albert said again. "I don't want to hear anything more about these customer subpoenas."

"Uhm," Joe said, trying to remember what next issue Zenko had.

"The next issue is your motion to compel Mr. Borland to answer your interrogatories," Judge Albert said, apparently tired of waiting. The judge put down the motion papers he had picked up and looked at Joe. "Why are you bothering me with this? Like I said, I told you boys to work out these things between you. I'm feeling like a broken record here."

"Your honor," Joe said, winging it, "I'm only coming to you as a last resort because we can't get cooperation from Mr. Borland."

"Can't get cooperation?" Judge Albert interrupted. "Did you call Mr. Borland after he objected and try to come up with language that wasn't objectionable?"

Joe didn't know if Zenko called. He guessed Zenko hadn't, but only because Borland's response was so outrageous there was no point. And how did Judge Albert know? Borland must have talked to him.

"Your honor," Joe quickly continued, "we responded promptly to *their* interrogatories even though we could have made the same objections and more. It was clear to us... "

"Well, wait a minute," Judge Albert broke in. "I understand from Mr. Borland you only answered questions that you felt like answering, and even those you only partially answered. Seems to me as if you are hiding something."

"Your honor," Joe said evenly, restraining his anger. He knew the answer to this one, Zenko had complained about it. "Mr. Borland's questions and document requests would require us to hand over every piece of paper ever produced by my client, and to produce answers the size of a book about each one. My client didn't want me to object, so I gave them what was relevant. That's not a partial answer, that's a complete answer."

Joe picked up the pace of his words, fearful of another interruption by Albert. "Mr. Borland waited until the deadline for his answers to object, he could have objected much earlier. He was clearly not attempting to be reasonable at all. If we had called, I know Mr. Borland would have given some BS about changes he wanted, then would have asked for more time, then would have objected again. If we waited until then to make a motion, we'd be out of time."

"So you admit you didn't try?" Judge Albert said sternly, staring at Joe.

———————

Shortly after the conference with Judge Albert, Joe climbed the two steps from the Telekinetics parking lot to their front door. He wasn't looking forward to explaining what happened to A.J. and Burak. Two men were in animated discussion by the door. It sounded like one was a potential customer, and he overheard mention of a "patent problem." He announced himself at reception, and then signed the visitor book and his badge, pealed the back off his badge, and pressed it on his shirt. He smoothed the badge again as he sat to wait, the edges were already trying to peel back.

After 2 minutes A.J. herself showed up to escort him in. "So how'd it go?" she asked, as she extended her hand.

He put down the Telekinetics brochure he had been leafing through, and shook her hand as he stood up. "It could have gone better," he said.

A.J. just nodded. She gestured toward the door of the conference room and continued on to get Burak.

A.J. returned with Burak. "Where's Zenko?" A.J. asked.

"He was preoccupied with another matter today," Joe said. He quickly went on to explain how the session with the judge went.

"Joe," A.J. said, "we were discussing these issues this morning, and Burak has convinced me that we need a different strategy. Your report confirms that. We seem to be playing into their hands by cooperating. We can't afford it, and your firm couldn't afford it. It is no good to us to have our attorneys driven out of business. What can we do?"

Joe thought for a moment. "Well, there is a strategy."

"What?" Burak asked.

"We stonewall and object to everything from now on. We minimize our costs and distractions — do only the minimal work needed, and don't give them anything if we can.

"I think that you will win the preliminary injunction. There are risks, but the odds are in your favor. The judge won't want to make a preliminary determination early on, before all the evidence in. This is in our favor for the preliminary injunction. Since they don't care about a trial that is years away, we shouldn't either. Instead of dealing with this lawsuit, you put all your efforts into marketing. If you win in the marketplace, you can worry about the lawsuit in a year or two. If you don't win in the market, you're dead anyway."

"I like it," A.J. said. "What are the details of this strategy?"

———————

Meanwhile, at Neuropt, Erika carefully looked around then opened her briefcase to look at a D & B report on one of Gage's companies. She had printed it out at home; she didn't dare use her computer at work. She was sure it was being monitored. She had been suspicious about Neuropt's rush to hire her, which was only heightened by the fact that since she arrived she hadn't had much real work. She had been given a busy work project recording stock certificates for several of Gage's companies. Curiously, the stock certificates showed Gage had formed the company just before the virus broke out. She had thought he formed it just after, to go after a treatment. Did he have some sort of inside information, or was he just lucky?

The job offer actually erased the last doubts she had about Joe's theory on Neuropt. She decided to turn the job into an opportunity to investigate them on the inside, and prove Joe right. She didn't tell Joe or Zenko for fear they'd try to talk her out of it as being too dangerous. Plus, Joe or Zenko might give it away with their body language at some inopportune time. Men could be so oblivious about things like that. But it was killing her that they thought she was bought off.

She focused on the D & B report. She was trying to decipher Gage's web of companies. She looked up as she saw someone down the hall open the combination door to the center of the building. That was the biggest curiosity, where Gage Booth and certain other managers had offices. There were jokes among her coworkers that there was a spa or bar in there.

She had gotten friendly with the Information Services guy, and found out a little about the combination door. He had volunteered, for example, that any time there is a power outage, the electronic lock goes back to a default code. He was complaining about having to come in late one night and reset it from the service computer in the electrical closet.

One engineer had opened up about the Neuropt product development not being far enough along for him to work on it. The high level design needed to be completed before he could start work on the circuits he was hired to design. In the meantime, he was working on designing modems for another company. Contract work. Neuropt got paid for it, and he stayed busy, yet available to start work as soon as needed. And he did spend some time keeping up to speed on the Neuropt design.

She had the feeling someone was constantly watching her. Immediately after the engineer talked to her about not having work to do, Harold Walsh, a manager, asked her not to talk to the engineers — it distracted them from their time sensitive work. Right.

A new message popped up in her e-mail. It was from Cassia. She scanned it quickly. The Russians apparently had an antidote to the virus, and Cassia asked Erika to go public with the attachment if anything happened to Cassia. Erika would know if she didn't get an e-mail from Cassia every day. Erika was to tell absolutely no one in the meantime, or Cassia would end up dead.

What was Cassia up to? Why was she putting her life in danger?

She was about to click on and read the attachment when she suddenly became aware of a presence behind her. A quiver went up her spine. She quickly closed her briefcase, and brought up an employee handbook on her monitor. She pretended not to be aware of someone behind her, and started scrolling through the document.

"You must be Erika," said a voice behind her.

She forced herself to jerk her body upright. "Oh," she gasped, turning around in her chair and looking up at the man standing there. "You startled me."

"I'm Gage Booth," he said, moving forward until he was standing right over her, and extending his hand. She couldn't get up without brushing against him, so she stayed seated and took his hand and gave it a weak shake. She was suddenly self-conscious about her blouse. Although it was buttoned high enough, he was looking straight down at it, instead of at her face. When he shook her hand, he held it a little too long. He must be enjoying the view. She took an instant dislike to him.

"I run this place," Gage said, grinning at her as he put a hand on her shoulder. "You must be the new paralegal?"

She nodded and looked over at her computer screen; it was doing a periodic back-up. That used to seem innocent, even comforting. Not anymore.

Gage talked to her for 20 minutes, mostly about himself. He also seemed to like looking at her. Anytime she looked away from him, she could see out of the corner of her eyes that he was going up and down her body with his eyes.

"I understand you used to work at Turner, West," Gage was saying. "Was Joe Nile a friend of yours?"

"I knew him," she said, intensely aware of Gage studying her face as she spoke. "We didn't work together much. He was in prosecution, I was in litigation."

"I see," Gage said. "A real shame about him getting fired, but he had some wacky ideas. Did you hear him talk about Neuropt?"

"Not directly," Erika said. "But it seems he was a little paranoid. I don't know why he would expect anything different about Neuropt compared to any other start-up going public."

"So you didn't agree with his assessment?" Gage asked.

"I'm working here, with stock options that depend on the success of the company," Erika said. "That should answer your question."

Gage flashed a lascivious smile. She wanted to smack him.

"Roger Borland is waiting in the conference room," Sidney told Zenko the next Monday morning. Zenko had given Sidney a job at his new office. There was a common conference room and copy room he shared with other solo practitioners. Zenko had gotten out of the hospital, and no one mentioned the overdose.

"I know," Zenko said. "I just want him to keep cooling his heels a little longer. While he's waiting, I'll answer his supplemental interrogatories."

"Won't that take quite a while?" Sidney asked.

Zenko smiled at him.

Zenko checked his stocks on the Schwab web page, and then looked over some e-mails before walking out to Sidney's cubicle and handing him the interrogatories and his handwritten instructions.

Sidney glanced over them, and then looked up at Zenko in disbelief. "Are you sure you want me to do this?" Sidney asked. Zenko just smiled.

Before he got to the conference room door, Zenko could hear Roger Borland talking loudly and officiously on his cell phone. As he stepped in, Roger was standing in the corner, his back to the wall, apparently talking to some client. An associate was sitting at the table, using her laptop. Two others, perhaps attorneys, were reading though some papers. A paralegal was making himself busy rifling through a box of documents.

The court reporter was the first to notice him. She was reading a magazine, but put it down as soon as she saw him. Zenko introduced himself to the court reporter, and gave her his card at her request. He then introduced himself to the others, while Roger acknowledged him with a glance and a nod, but kept talking.

"So where is the witness?" asked the court reporter.

"I just got word he came down with a bad case of the flu," Zenko lied.

Roger turned and stared at Zenko. "Gotta go," Roger said into his phone, and hung up.

"What kind of bullshit are you trying to pull?" Roger snarled.

"I've been busily trying to find out where he was while all of you were waiting here," Zenko said quietly, with a shrug of his shoulders. "I'm afraid we'll have to cancel the deposition. I wish I had known this earlier."

"This is bullshit!" Roger said. "We're rescheduling for tomorrow. And if the witness isn't here, I'm going to the judge."

Zenko shrugged. "You can show up if you want, but we won't know until the morning if he's any better. And you know the judge wants us to work this stuff out between us."

Two days later Ned was uttering barely audible curses. He had bypassed the news on the virus and clicked on his stock website. Two-thirds of his stocks were losers so far today. He knew they were still way up for the year, but he just didn't like seeing that red. He had taken to reviewing his stocks several times a day.

Roger Borland rushed into his office, clutching a stack of papers. "Look at this crap," Roger said, slamming them down on the table in front of Ned's face. Ned looked down at them. It was Telekinetics answers to interrogatories.

"All evasive, bullshit answers," Roger continued. "They were answering before, and now this. Something is going on."

Ned looked at a couple of the answers. "Why," Ned said, "they look like just the sort of answers and objections you'd provide."

"Not just *like*," Roger replied, "they *are* my answers — the ones that I gave to his interrogatories. The sonavabitch copied them."

Ned couldn't help but smile. It was okay when Roger was doing it to them, but he went ballistic if they did it back to him.

Roger's cell phone rang.

"Yes?" Roger answered. There was a pause while he listened. "You're kidding," Roger said, and paused some more. "No, go ahead," Roger said. "And try anything you can think of. Not too overboard, since the court reporter will record it and the judge will see everything. But try to put some words in his mouth."

"Well, now Zenko isn't bothering to show up," Roger said as he closed his phone. "That was one of my associates. He's taking the deposition of a Telekinetics customer. Telekinetics is waiving having a lawyer present. It's going undefended."

16.

Erika watched two days later, on Friday, as the monitor out on the table in the parking lot changed from 32 to 34. A loud cheer went up from the crowd and the group of 6 engineers surrounding her momentarily looked away. She felt numb. Her stock had nearly tripled in just a few hours from an opening 12 dollars per share to 34. Her seventy-five thousand dollars of stock options was now worth over two hundred thousand! If only there weren't restrictions on employees selling it for 90 days. At least that was better than the founders having to wait 6 months.

She looked around at the engineers, and pretended to listen to one of the engineers encircling her. No work would get done today. Half of them were nearly drunk already, and it wasn't even lunch time yet.

The company had decided to set up the celebration outside in the parking lot, to give that start-up feel. It seemed odd to be standing out on the asphalt. An area was roped off with a line, and red, white and blue streamers hung down from it. Card tables covered with white tablecloths had a variety of snacks — cheese and crackers, bagels, a variety of vegetables and dip, chips and nuts. Lunch was about to be barbecued — steak and ribs.

Several coolers were filled with beer and soft drinks. One of the tables was covered with champagne bottles and glasses. That's where Gage was holding court, entertaining a small group huddled around him.

She felt frustrated as she nursed her glass of champagne. She had yet to see evidence of the product they were supposed to have in 6 months, but how could she show that was intentional? She had yet to be given any important work, convincing her that she had been hired to take her off the Telekinetics case. Little did they know that not only was she helping Joe and Zenko in the evenings, she was sneaking in documents in her briefcase and reviewing them during the day.

That night Erika logged onto her computer at home. There was an e-mail from Cassia asking her help to track the ownership of a Saudi company selling generic Adbil over the Internet. Apparently, Cassia's people had hit a dead end. Cassia was also livid about her government, the bureaucracy in dealing with other countries. Erika presumed that meant there was some problem in getting the antidote from the Russians. She decided to do the tracking for Cassia after she did some checking on Gage's companies that she had been recording stock certificates for.

Two hours later her eyelids were drooping. She had been surprised at the number of companies owned by Gage. In one branch alone, there were over 100 companies. Most seemed to be shells — she was puzzled as to why he needed so many shells. For a break, she worked on Cassia's request, tracking the ownership of the Saudi company, Abdulla Al-Jameel Pharmaceuticals, which had a surprisingly long string of convoluted ownership.

The last company in the Saudi chain sounded familiar. She checked the string of Gage's companies, then leaned back in her chair and stared at the screen. The two strings met.

The following Wednesday, Burak walked slowly back to his cubicle, annoyed that he had been paged. He studied the circuit board in his hand as he walked.

"Hello?" Burak said.

"We won!" crackled the familiar voice of A.J. from her cell phone. "The judge denied the preliminary injunction — we can continue selling the Retinal Screen while the lawsuit proceeds."

"This is terrific news," Burak said.

"Let's go full speed ahead on the Retinal Screen," A.J. said. "Get the press release out and on our web site. Then we should start contacting customers who have canceled orders. I'll call the University of California myself. I want to jump on this to get as much of a surge as we can."

Word spread quickly through Telekinetics, and everyone was celebrating. Soon, there were a group of engineers in and around Burak's cubicle.

Burak clicked on his browser to check for news on the Internet. The first thing he found was a press release issued by Royaltec.

> "Royaltec Enterprises, encouraged in the strength of their case against Telekinetics by a judge's ruling today, filed suit against one of Telekinetics' customers, Sunworld BioMedical. Royaltec

attorney Roger Borland said that they didn't expect the judge to grant a preliminary injunction. Borland said that rarely happens. Rather, they requested the hearing on a preliminary injunction to do a dry run of their case. The judge confirmed that they had evidence of infringement, and that they could prevail at trial."

Burak stopped reading, and leaned back in his chair and groaned. The masters of spin had beaten them to the punch.

———

A few days later, Friday morning, Burak slouched in the chair in A.J.'s office.

"Thanks for the effort," A.J. said, putting down Burak's report. "But it won't be enough."

Burak had proposed some layoffs and other actions to cut expenses. Telekinetics efforts to make hay out of the Preliminary Injunction ruling had fallen on deaf ears. Even the success with the Sheath in Brazil didn't give them momentum. Customers wanted to wait until the patent battle was sorted out. When Burak had explained that could take years, one customer explained that no, he expected Telekinetics would be out of business and a stronger company would acquire the technology within a few months.

Burak knew the Board of Directors was ready to pull the plug on the Retinal Screen at their meeting this afternoon. In normal times he would admit they had a point. But the Retinal Screen was critical to treating the virus. Could they not see that? But the investors were not inclined to put more money in the company, and they could not launch an IPO with the litigation pending and lackluster sales of the Retinal Screen. Burak had proposed a design-around, but that would take extra cash for both the design and for keeping the company going during the estimated six months it would take. They were running low on options.

Zenko checked his messages after getting out of a meeting later that morning. A.J. had called; it was urgent. He called her back.

"What can we do to get rid of this lawsuit now?" A.J. asked. "They are just killing us with their legal weapons. Is there any hope I can give to our Board this afternoon? How about summary judgment?"

Zenko sighed. He had explained this before. A summary judgment was a mechanism that allowed a judge to decide a case without having a trial in front of a jury. But it required that both sides be in agreement on the facts, so that the jury wasn't needed for that. The judge could then decide what the law required. It was used where facts weren't in dispute, and the two sides were arguing over what the law was. The summary judgment could be based on prior art showing the same invention and making the patent invalid, or it could be based on showing that the Telekinetics product didn't have all the elements of the patent claim, and thus didn't infringe.

"We have to have more discovery first, A.J.-san," Zenko said. "I could file a summary judgment motion as soon as I accumulate enough evidence from discovery or otherwise to support it. The usual way to show the facts aren't in dispute is to get one of their witnesses to confirm in a deposition what the facts are. And they want to delay, so they'll insist on dragging out discovery to keep us from being able to file a summary judgment motion any time soon."

"Of course, this all assumes we have something to make a motion on," Zenko added. "And we just don't, at least not yet." Zenko paused to let this sink in.

"The other problem with doing a summary judgment motion this soon," Zenko continued, "is that we haven't done the Markman hearing yet. Until we have a Markman hearing, the judge won't want to decide a motion."

"What's a Markman hearing again?" A.J. asked.

"That's a hearing where the scope of the claims is decided," Zenko answered. "Basically, they argue why the claim terms should be broadly defined, we argue why they should be narrowly defined, and the judge decides. So until it is clear how the claims are to be interpreted, it is difficult to do a motion based on what the claims cover."

"Right," A.J. said. "So when is the Markman hearing?"

Zenko sighed. This was not going to make her happy. "The judge hasn't even scheduled it yet. It usually doesn't happen for at least 6 months, and I've seen it dragged out to a year or two."

"We'll be out of business long before then," A.J. said.

————

Erika was still working after 5 PM that evening. With the discovery of Gage's ownership of a Saudi company, Erika was beginning to suspect there was more going on at Neuropt than even Joe had guessed. She read between the lines of Cassia's e-mails and figured that the virus must be some bioterror weapon distributed in generic Adbil pills. But why would Gage be involved? Either Gage didn't know about what the Saudi company was doing, or there must be a lot of money to be made, she decided.

She looked around. The other employees there sure didn't seem to be acting like they had some hot design that was near completion. If they did, they were certainly pretty blasé about it. Here it was, only 5:30 on Tuesday, and most everyone had left already. Perhaps inside the combo door there was more activity. She looked at the door again. She would sure like to get behind it.

She picked up the phone and dialed Gage Booth's extension. He was there.

"Sorry to bother you, Mr. Booth," she said. "Do you remember me? I'm Erika, the new paralegal."

"Yes," Gage said. She could almost hear him grinning. "I remember you."

"I was wondering," Erika said, "if you might have a project I could work on. I'd like to get some variety of work, and it would be a thrill to work for the president. I'm good with numbers, perhaps you have something like financials or something I can work on."

"I have just the thing," Gage said. "Come over to the combination door, I'll let you in."

She unbuttoned the top button of her blouse, grabbed a notepad and some pencils, and just waited by her cubicle. In a moment Gage opened the door and looked down the hallway.

"Coming!" Erika said, taking a step, and then dropping her stuff on the floor. She got on her knees and bent over to pick them up, taking her time. She figured Gage would come over to get a peek down her blouse, and he didn't disappoint. She stayed on the floor for a moment to make sure he got his look.

"It's been a long day," she said, leaning back on her knees. "It's actually nice to have a little rest here!"

She held up her hand, and Gage put out his to help her up. She followed him to the combo door.

She watched Gage punch the numbers. It was almost too easy to see what numbers he pressed. They passed through an inner hallway with desks on one side and interior offices on the other. It was remarkable how ordinary it looked. She had expected something different, but it seemed like any other office. She was surprised not to see anyone at all. She had envisioned it as buzzing with activity until late in the evening. It made her even more nervous to be there alone with Gage.

He was asking a lot of questions about her personal life. She twisted her wedding ring as she explained how happily married she was.

The pattern of the pictures in Gage's office struck her immediately. He was in every one. He had his picture with quite a number of celebrities that she recognized, and a few politicians. His desk looked like it belonged in some stuffy men's club. He had a box of cigars, and too many gaudy desk accessories, including a pen with a huge white and gold feather.

He motioned to a chair, and she sat down. He grabbed a binder and pulled up a chair next to her, so that their arms touched. It felt really gross, but she didn't move her arm. He leafed through the binder, frequently touching her arm when he was making a point, and holding his hand there too long. She finally started lifting her arm to turn some pages and get his hand off her arm.

"I could really use a latte," Gage said. "Would you be a good girl, and get me one?"

"I'll get you one from the Starbucks next door," Erika said, leaping to her feet, anxious for a brief respite. "I guess I can call you on my cell when I get back, so you can let me back through the combo door?"

Gage nodded.

After Erika returned with the latte, Gage showed her to his secretary's desk where she pulled up on the computer the analysis he wanted checked to make sure the numbers added up — clearly busy work. Thankfully, he went back to his office, and she started comparing the numbers with those in the binders. She looked through the secretary's drawers and noticed a Post-it with what appeared to be a password stuck to the inside wall of one drawer. It was new — she guessed Gage made the secretary change the password every day, and she used the Post-it so she could remember.

She glanced at Gage and quickly looked back at the computer. He was on the phone, but he was watching her through the glass panel in his office. They had made eye contact, and it gave her the creeps. She smiled at him as she lifted and waved a pencil from the drawer. He nodded and looked away. She pulled up his secretary's file directory — time to see what else was on his secretary's computer.

———————

At that moment in São Paulo, Cassia was pursing her lips and digging her fingernails into the chair arms to keep from shouting out in anger. It had taken over a week for her to be able to come to the Russian embassy, and now her government's trade officials were doing all the talking. Apparently, there was some sensitivity to jeopardizing trade with Russia. All this while people were dying and Russia had an antidote. The Retinal

Screen was working, but they could only handle a fraction of the victims.

"I'm sure you can appreciate this is very sensitive," the Russian ambassador was saying. "We have not been able to confirm if the virus came from any of our labs. And if it did, we would want to track down the terrorists who took this, and publicizing where it came from would hurt that effort."

"You mean it would hurt Russia's reputation," Cassia blurted out. "Especially when the world finds out you sat on an antidote. Why didn't you give it to us immediately? What kind of animals are you?"

"This is a sensitive situation," the Russian ambassador continued.

"It'll be more sensitive when I tell the press you've been sitting on an antidote," Cassia said.

"You have no evidence," the Russian ambassador said. "Just the word of some nut who claims to have worked for the KGB. You can't even give us his name, or let us talk to him."

"Suppose we let the public decide how believable it is?" Cassia said.

The ambassador's eyes narrowed as he leaned back in his chair and folded his hands across his stomach. The Brazilian trade officials had looks of horror on their faces. "That would be extremely dangerous," the ambassador said.

"Look," Cassia said standing up and walking over to the ambassador's desk, then leaning over it. "Suppose the antidote just happens to find its way to me. I can publicly claim that we developed it. There is no need for the world to know the source, or that an antidote was held back by Russia."

Cassia studied the ambassador's face. He showed no reaction.

"Oh," Cassia said, taking a step back, "I forgot to mention. The terrorists would not be tipped off that you are on to them, so your vigorous effort to track them down won't be jeopardized."

Cassia turned and walked briskly to the door, spinning around when she reached it. "If the antidote isn't on my desk within 3 days, I go public with this. If I should have some accident before then, a number of other people around the world have this information, and know to release it if something happens to me."

——— —— ——

Burak walked into Zenko's office the next day to give Zenko the bad news. Zenko was working with Joe. Burak handed Zenko a press release.

Burak explained the press release as Zenko read with Joe looking over his shoulder, "Our Board decided we cannot fight Royaltec. We are announcing that we are canceling our Retinal Screen product. They want you to prepare the papers to get us out of the lawsuit."

Joe started shaking his head. "But — "

Burak cut him off. "They know we do not have much chance as a company without this product. And I personally believe we will be out of business in couple months because of this. But they say we will be out of business tomorrow if we do not do this."

"I'm afraid it's not that simple," Zenko said. "You can't just tell Royaltec to drop the suit. Being the assholes that they are, they will ask for damages, trebled, for the few prototypes you shipped. That won't be much money, but they will ask for attorney's fees too, and claim that by violating the injunction and shipping it to

Brazil, you enabled its manufacture there. They may not get all this, but you'll have to spend money and effort to fight it. And they'll be able to keep the suit alive, with all its bad publicity, for awhile. Don't forget, Burak, they want Telekinetics out of business completely. They want a dead body."

"Between you and me," Burak said, "A.J. had gotten strict orders from the Board of Directors. But if there is anything you can do, do it. But it has to be done right now."

———————

Ned stood up and walked over to look out the conference room window that afternoon, while Gage continued to congratulate Roger Borland.

"This is what I call delivering the goods," Gage was saying. "Those Telekinetics bastards are abandoning the Retinal Screen. I can't imagine they'll last more than a month or two without it. You've killed them."

"Almost," Roger said, swirling the shot of scotch that Gage had poured for him. "The body is still breathing. But we have a few more slugs to pump into it. We're not going to dismiss the suit, we'll argue consequential damages and other things, and force them to keep spending on their attorneys."

"That's my kind of talk," Gage said. "Finish them off."

"What about the Retinal Screen and the Sheath?" Ned asked.

"What about it?" Gage replied.

"It seems to me you could force them to hand over the technology now," Ned said. "Then Neuropt could continue developing it, or you could sell it to another company to develop; with heavy royalties to Royaltec, of course. That way you wouldn't have to wait a few months to get your hands on it, and the Retinal Screen can be used to put the Sheath into use against the virus sooner."

"That is the plan," Gage said. "You know that. No need to move it up. We have enough on our plate for the next month or so."

"But they need it in Brazil now," Ned said.

"Yeah?" Gage said. "What kind of money can we make in Brazil? The damned Brazilian government won't let us exploit our patent there. You saw how they threatened to impose compulsory licensing on AIDS drug companies at minimal royalties. So screw them. We'll make money here in the US."

"But people are dying every day this waits," Ned protested.

"So?" Gage said. "Unless you can tell me how I can make a lot of money off of that, I don't see why I should care."

17.

Bernie Sloan couldn't sleep again that night. He put on his bathrobe and ambled over to his computer. There was a mailbox full of e-mail, again. He clicked *delete* time and again on his e-mails without opening them. Almost all of them were either for Viagra, to enlarge his member, or were from hot, naked girls eager to date him. It was the modern day snake oil. The ring of the phone startled him. It was Joe Nile.

"Joe," Bernie said, "what are you doing, calling me at this time of night? You might have wakened me up."

"I saw the e-mail you just sent me," Joe said. "So I knew you were up. You must be pretty busy. I keep seeing these e-mails from very late at night."

"I do whatever it takes for my clients," Bernie said. Bernie's business had actually dropped off as more law firms went to younger, more computer literate searchers. The only reason Bernie was working late was that he couldn't sleep. But Joe didn't need to know that.

"I'm just stumped on this Royaltec searching," Joe said. "I thought maybe we could compare notes on the neural network articles we've found. I've searched everywhere I can think of, but can't find prior art to knock out the Royaltec patent. But my instincts tell me I should be able to find something. I've looked for everything — neural network prior art, sales by AutoSmart, you name it."

"To be honest," Bernie said, "I hate this complex neural network technology. I wish you'd let me search for cabling and robotics prior art. After all, that is what the patent is supposed to be about."

There was just silence from Joe.

"Joe?" Bernie asked. "You still there?"

"Of course," Joe said. "Why have I been so focused on searching for neural network prior art? That's what Royaltec is trying to twist the words of the claim to cover. You're right — we should be searching for prior art relating to cabling and robotics. That was what the invention was in actual fact about."

"Yes," Bernie said, "and I suspect there is more likely to be prior art on cabling and robotics in that time frame."

Besides the fact that he could understand that technology better.

"Remember," Bernie said, "the patent will be just as dead no matter what kills it."

———————

Joe stretched his neck as he awoke the next morning. He had fallen asleep on the floor next to a pile of papers, and his neck was crimped. He rubbed his eyes as he made his way Zenko's laptop computer which he had borrowed. The computer clock showed 6 A.M. There was an e-mail from Bernie with some French article. Bernie had attached a crude automatic translation. It didn't make sense in some places, but combined with the drawings Joe was able to figure it out. It was too good to be true! Autosmart hadn't been the first to invent this robotic cabling system after all. And the date of the article was plenty earlier than the Royaltec patent.

He went to work on preparing a summary judgment motion Zenko could use with the French article, and e-mailed the article to a translator for an official translation to use as an exhibit. Summary judgment was possible before the Markman hearing to interpret the claims since the French article didn't require interpretation of the claims. It would apply under any interpretation of the claims. He'd like to see Royaltec wiggle out of this one.

But just in case — he picked up the phone to call Bernie about pursuing another angle.

The next day, Zenko was relaxing in his tub mid-afternoon. He had edited and filed Joe's summary judgment motion that morning. It was time to relax now. He had never seen a clearer case for summary judgment. He was sure the judge would grant it.

Joe was correct. The prior art would invalidate the patent under any interpretation of the claim. So there was no need to wait for a Markman hearing. This case was over.

Just before lunchtime the following day, Burak was smiling as he went through his prayer ritual. Allah had answered his prayers. He had been ecstatic when Zenko told him what Joe found, and that they had filed a summary judgment motion.

He saw A.J.'s unmistakable plain pumps come into view as he lifted his head off the floor. She dropped a print-out on the floor in front of him. It was a Royaltec press release. He read it while bowed down.

> *Royaltec Enterprises moved to strengthen its patent on neural network microprocessors. It will file a petition with the Patent Office to confirm the patent in light of prior art asserted in the litigation with Telekinetics. The prior art relates to robotics, and Royaltec believes it is only by stretching the description of the robotics art that it could be asserted to correspond to claims on a neural net processor.*

> *Royaltec will be asking the Patent Office to reissue the patent with additional limitations in the claims that make it clear that it covers a neural net processor, but not the cited robotics art. Royaltec obtained a stay of the lawsuit pending the Patent Office examination, except that limited discovery should continue to aid in assembling materials for the Patent Office's consideration.*

> *Royaltec is confident it will prevail in its lawsuit against Telekinetics as soon as the Patent Office reissues the patent. It should be noted that a stay of litigation does not apply to any customers of Telekinetics, and Royaltec intends to vigorously enforce its patent rights if there is any new infringement.*

> *Royaltec is a company dedicated to advancing technology and protecting the intellectual property rights of individual inventors. Royaltec has helped dozens of inventors reap the benefits of their inventions, and has brought a variety of technologies to realization in the market.*

Burak couldn't help but laugh. Talk about Orwellian doublespeak. The patent was on a robotics cabling system, and Royaltec was trying to twist it to read on a neural network processor. Now Royaltec was making it sound the other way.

He got up, and A.J. had Zenko on the speaker of her cell phone. "What is this filing with the Patent Office they are talking about?" A.J. asked. "Is this the *re-examination* you mentioned before as a risk?"

"Similar," Zenko said. "It's a reissue. That means they're changing the claim language. The court granted Royaltec's motion for a stay of the court proceedings to give the Patent Office time to re-examine the patent in light of this new prior art. I called the judge and tried to get him to rule on the summary judgment motion, rather than stay the case, but he refused."

"Why?" A.J. asked. "He doesn't need this Markman hearing you mentioned. As you and Joe said, it is invalid under any interpretation of the claims."

"The judge doesn't want to do any work," Zenko sighed. "He'd have to think about it to verify that no interpretation would avoid the prior art. And he agreed with Borland's argument that they should have a chance to submit Markman briefs. Borland claimed that there was an interpretation that avoided the claims."

"Borland's lying," A.J. said.

"I'm sure he'd come up with some B.S. argument," Zenko said.

"Well, then," Burak said, "the Patent Office will throw it out, no?"

"Maybe," Zenko said. "The problem is that the Patent Office may not make a determination for a year or two."

"I would hope," Burak said, "that this time our customers would be savvy enough to look at the prior art and see that the patent is clearly invalid, it is just a matter of time before the Patent Office throws it out."

"I'm not so sure," Zenko said. "I hate to bring this up, but there is a chance they could win in the Patent Office. You see, in court we get to argue against whatever they present. But in the Patent Office, we get one chance to submit papers, and after that it's an *ex-parte* proceeding."

"Ex-party?" Burak asked. "I am not sure what that means, but it sounds like the party is over for us."

"It means," Zenko said, "that they can make all the arguments they want to the Patent Office and we don't get to hear them or argue against them. I've seen the most amazing things come out of re-exam or reissue. They can come up with some convoluted argument and convince the examiner, since there is no one there to point out why the argument is wrong. It's really not a fair fight, a big law firm against one government employee. They oftentimes just beat down the examiner. It's like a trial where the defense gets to present opening arguments, but then is excluded from the courtroom for the rest of the trial."

"I think," Burak said, "that it's more like . . . ."

"No more analogies!" A.J. said, cutting him off. "As long as there is some legal proceeding pending, our customers won't buy. We're back to the Board decision to quit."

———

An hour later, Joe met Erika and Zenko at Moe's. He had called Erika, hoping to talk to her about what it was like inside at Neuropt. He was pleasantly surprised when she readily agreed. He had also gotten his friend Hank to agree to look at the Neuropt prospectus and join them. He was hoping Hank could shed some light on what Neuropt was doing, and ask the right questions.

Joe felt butterflies in his stomach when he saw Erika there. She was wearing his favorite knit dress. He sat next to her, his shoulder brushing against hers as he sat down. It sent a shiver down his body.

Shortly after they ordered, Desoto appeared with their lunches on a tray, which he set up near their booth. "Here," Desoto said to Joe, "you pass out meals." Desoto handed Joe the steamed rice, which Joe set down in the middle of the table. Next came the spinach with bean sprouts, which Joe turned up his nose at and handed to Erika, who stuck out her tongue at him. Joe kept the sweet and sour pork for himself and passed the hamburgers to Hank and Zenko.

"I can't believe you ordered hamburger in a Chinese restaurant," Joe said.

"I can't believe a Chinese restaurant has hamburger," Erika said.

"American food is an exotic treat for me," Zenko said.

"We Chinese American restaurant," Desoto declared. "Hamburger good choice, we make real good." Zenko gave Joe a knowing nod.

"The spinach and bean sprouts are also house special," Desoto continued, flashing a broad smile at Erika. "Very traditional, honorable Chinese dish. Very good choice by the lady." Erika beamed.

"How about the sweet and sour pork?" Joe asked, stirring it with his chopsticks.

Desoto turned to Joe with an exaggerated scowl. "Tourist food," Desoto announced, "no self-respecting Chinese would touch it." Desoto walked away with his nose in an exaggerated tilt toward the ceiling.

"I did some snooping on Gage Booth's secretary's computer," Erika said. "Did you know that they have drafted press releases going several months into the future on developments they haven't made yet? It's like a movie script that has already been written."

"So you believe me now?" Joe said.

Erika nodded as she struggled to balance some beans on her chopsticks. "I always did. That's why I joined Neuropt."

"You shouldn't be telling us this," Zenko said. "You are a Neuropt employee. You have an obligation of confidentiality."

"That's why you can't attribute anything to me," Erika said. "You are the only ones I can trust, and can talk to. I also found a couple other things that are interesting. This is extremely confidential, of course. Cassia told me she suspects a Saudi company of shipping Adbil pills tainted with the virus."

Joe, Zenko and Hank exchanged glances. "You mean the virus is a terrorist attack?" Hank asked.

Erika nodded. "Also, I found that Gage actually owns, through a maze of corporate shells, the Saudi company that was shipping virus-tainted Adbil pills."

Joe looked at Zenko — his face was blank at this news. "Do you think that's a coincidence?" Joe asked. "Or did Gage create a market for Neuropt by planting the virus?"

"I don't know," Erika said. "It gets more interesting. I found out Gage is speculating against the US dollar," Erika said. "Big time. He's doing it through literally over a hundred companies. I'd estimate he has about a 100 billion dollar bet."

Hank whistled softly. "He must be leveraged to the hilt. I thought his net worth was only about 10 billion. He must have other investors with him. When are his currency contracts due?"

"About six and a half months after Neuropt's IPO," Erika said. "I'm stumped. What do you guys think all this means?"

"He's trying to make money," Hank said. "A lot."

"Duh," Erika said. "What does he know that no one else does about the dollar?"

"Did you know," Hank said, "that the current account deficit for the United States is now over 600 billion dollars each year, with the total accumulated debt exceeding eight trillion dollars?"

"I'm no economist," Joe said. "But that's a lot of money."

Hank nodded ominously. "We're vulnerable. The dollar is vulnerable — there is no reason it has to stay the currency of choice for trade forever. Did you know that the *daily* volume of currency exchanges is nearly 2 *trillion* dollars? By comparison, the daily volume of the New York Stock Exchange is about 60 billion. Currency speculators have helped ruin economies around the globe, driving currency values into the ground. That happened in Mexico in '94, the Asian crisis of '97 and Brazil in '99. The hedge funds are so big, they can drive the price of the currency by their activities. It's like gamblers buying off a ballplayer — they control the result. You have to be a big player to play; usually the smallest transaction is 10 million dollars. But these hedge funds, which combine assets of a lot of rich investors, are so big that they affect the market by their own actions."

"Yes," Joe said, "but how do you explain our economy doing so well right now? We're in the middle of a boom. The virus has spurred all kinds of companies trying to find cures and therapies. The government is throwing something like 50 billion at it. And those companies will need to buy test chips to test their stuff, chemicals and drugs to experiment on finding a vaccine, tools for the surgery itself, there's a whole infrastructure being built up. And when they find that cure or therapy, hold onto your horses. It'll be a huge market — huge. Those were your words to me, remember?"

"Yes, Hank-san," Zenko said. "If the virus was deliberately planted to bring down the dollar, it backfired. As Joe said, the economy is booming with all the companies going after the virus. Companies are investing and forming like mad to develop a cure or vaccine. And that stimulates other industries to provide the tools, supplies, etcetera. I think Gage miscalculated and is going to lose a lot of money."

"Booms have a tendency to become bubbles," Hank said. "Which have a tendency to burst."

"But the U.S. is different," Joe said. "Those other countries all had debt denominated in dollars, which was different from their currency."

"That's right," Hank said. "Our debt is in our currency, so there wouldn't be a technical default. But it will be the same as a default. All those countries that bought US debt in dollars will see the value evaporate as the currency crashes. They won't invest in dollars or us anymore, and our economy will collapse. We won't be able to import goods because no one will take our worthless dollars. It will be the end of US dominance in the world. We won't be able to pay for new weapons systems, or even pay our soldiers, so our military will collapse too. And don't forget we're vulnerable on housing prices, too. Those are overvalued by at least 20%, and with a general bust of the dollar, who knows how low they'll go."

"So why does Gage think the dollar will go bust now?" Joe mused aloud. "All the things you mention have been going on for some time. It could be years before it catches up with the dollar."

18.

Bernie looked at his watch again at that moment in Alexandria as he sipped his coffee in a café near the Patent Office. Al Chan was late, as usual.

Joe had asked him to try to find a copy of the missing pages of the file history of the Royaltec patent. AutoSmart had been shopping its patents around, trying to find a buyer to raise money before Royaltec bought them. It occurred to Joe that some other law firm might have gotten a copy before the pages were "lost."

Joe had contacted AutoSmart and found the companies AutoSmart had talked to, and then contacted them and their law firms. All the ones that had ordered the file history were dead ends. Some "consultant" for Royaltec had contacted them and paid them for all original copies of the file history. This made Joe even more suspicious that Royaltec had deliberately destroyed the pages. Somehow, they must have gotten the Patent Office pages as well, perhaps by bribing a clerk.

Bernie had taken on the task of contacting his searcher buddies. Bernie had hit nothing but dead ends until he talked to Al Chan. Some firm had been in the process of ordering it when Royaltec bought the patent, and the law firm cancelled the order with Al. But Al said he had already copied it. Al remembered because he hadn't charged the law firm, hoping he could use the copy if someone else ordered it and cover his costs that way.

Al finally showed up. He waved at Bernie, and headed to the counter to order something first. Something was wrong. Al wasn't carrying anything. After a few minutes he joined Bernie at the table.

"Where's the file history?" Bernie said. "Don't tell me someone got to you?"

Al smiled. "Nice to see you too, Bernie." Al took a bite of his doughnut, and then leaned back in his chair to take a sip of his coffee and survey the people walking by.

"Do you have the check?" Al finally asked.

Bernie pulled the check out of his tattered wallet and laid it on the table. Al reached into his coat pocket and pulled out a CD, and slid it across the table to Bernie.

"What's this?" Bernie asked.

"You have to get into the twenty-first century, Bernie. It's the file history. I always copy them onto CDs now. I don't know about your clients, but mine have computers. I don't even order a paper copy anymore, I just get a CD. You can also download the newer ones from the Patent Office website. Get with it, Bernie."

———————

Joe grinned when he saw the FedEx package leaning against the door of his apartment the following morning, Saturday. He tore open the package, sat down on the floor and inserted the CD into his computer, quickly locating the section with the missing pages. They were there.

The missing pages were an office action and response. To get around the examiner's rejection, the patent attorney for AutoSmart explicitly argued that the claim was limited to a robotic cabling system, and wasn't any broader. The patent attorney had admitted in writing that the claim could not be interpreted to cover other technology.

It just got better as Joe read. The AutoSmart patent attorney had agreed that the claim should be interpreted to cover only a robotic cabling system as described in the patent application, and nothing else. The examiner had complained that the language was so vague and broad, it could even read on electronics, such as a neural network microprocessor. Wow — this examiner was sharp to see that. The AutoSmart attorney had responded that it was certainly "not intended to cover a neural network microprocessor, for example."

Joe leaned back and smiled. This time, Royaltec was dead.

———————

"How the hell did they find these pages?" Gage asked, as he flung the missing file history pages across the granite conference table the next Monday afternoon.

Ned glanced at Roger Borland, then spoke. "Don't know. That was your responsibility, if you recall. You had some specialist in this. I had explained that we couldn't know anything about it. If the pages were missing when we got the file history, and we didn't know what was in them, or where they went, we could pursue this patent."

"Yeah, yeah, yeah," Gage interrupted. "Save me your sanctimonious bitching. A few days ago these assholes were dead, and now they have *us* by the balls. How do these guys do it? They keep coming back to life, like the living dead."

"Not to worry," Roger said. "I've got a wooden stake we've been holding in reserve."

————————

Zenko shot another glance at the Peterson receptionist as he sat down late the next afternoon. He looked around at the ornate surroundings — reminding him of his new drab office. Zenko had wanted to deliver the news of the missing file history pages in person, but Roger Borland would not agree to a meeting unless Zenko told him what it was about. Roger had been at a loss for words when Zenko told him. It was a delicious moment, even if it wasn't quite as savory as it would have been if Zenko could have seen Roger's face.

Roger didn't keep him waiting long this time. He said a curt hello and ushered Zenko into the main conference room. Roger quickly sat down and slid some papers across the marble table to Zenko.

"Take a look," Roger said. "We filed it with the court an hour ago."

Zenko didn't like the smile on Roger's face. He shouldn't be smiling. He looked at the papers. It was a complaint, file stamped by the court that day. Royaltec had filed another suit against Telekinetics. Royaltec had acquired a patent from some company called Virtual Net, and was suing Telekinetics for infringement of it.

"We have Telekinetics stone cold on this one," Roger said. "No need to stretch things as for the

AutoSmart patent. This covers exactly what Telekinetics is doing in their Retinal Screen. The Virtual Net people bought one and took it apart, and their code was copied. The patent is solid, it's specific to this method, and we're not trying to interpret it broadly, so there won't be any prior art issues. Plus, we have a continuation pending, so any prior art or smart arguments to get around it that you come up with, we'll put before the Patent Office Examiner. And since you don't get to be present in those proceedings, we'll get it to issue again. So Telekinetics is dead in the water."

Zenko thumbed through the patent, pretending to read it.

"Here's the deal," Roger finally said, "I think you realize we can still put Telekinetics out of business. Well, we've decided we don't want to do that. We're not animals; we think the Retinal Screen and Sheath are needed. So instead of putting Telekinetics out of business, we'll give them a license for both patents. But the price is seventy-five percent of the stock of Telekinetics. In addition, you round up all existing copies of the AutoSmart file history and give them to us and agree not to talk about its contents. Instead of bankruptcy, Telekinetics prospers. We even let the employees and investors keep their stock. It will be diluted, but even with that dilution, it's more valuable than the alternative. Of course, if anyone talks about these missing file history pages, everyone loses their stock. That's the only reason we're letting them keep anything — so they have motivation to keep the agreement."

Zenko couldn't believe Roger had found a way to slip out of this. He thought he had Roger dead to rights. Now Royaltec wanted to make money on the Sheath. He wondered if that what this was about from the beginning. It was ironic, by raising a lot of money, they could use that money to hire lawyers and steal technology for a song through litigation, without having to buy the technology.

"I tried to talk Royaltec out of taking ownership of Telekinetics instead of money," Roger said. "They're taking a big risk. But they want to make sure mankind has the benefit of the Sheath."

Zenko just stared at Roger.

"We've put a deal on the table," Roger said, smiling broadly and standing up. "I expect an answer. By the way, there's something in it for you if you convince Telekinetics to accept. When we own Telekinetics, we'll make sure your bill gets paid by them."

Erika answered her cell phone as she was leaving Neuropt midday the following day. It was Joe.

"Erika, I know it's incredibly last minute," Joe said. "But can you meet me for lunch?"

"I'm not having lunch today," Erika said. "I'm heading out on an errand right now. I brought in lunch to eat at my desk."

"I'll join you on your errand," Joe said. "Where are you going?"

"Can't we do this later?" Erika said. "It's kind of a personal errand."

"I can't wait," Joe said. "We're still good friends, aren't we? How personal can the errand be?"

"It's lingerie," Erika sighed. "Okay, meet me at Stanford Shopping Center. Call me when you get there."

"If Ray left you, why are you buying lingerie?" Joe asked.

"It's for me, I'm splurging on myself," Erika said.

"I don't understand," Joe said. "What good is lingerie if there isn't someone to see it?"

Erika groaned. "I like to look at myself in the mirror with it on," Erika purred. "And caress my body at the same time. And think about how you'll never see me that way."

When Erika arrived at the mall, she rushed into the mall and hurried toward the store.

"Erika!"

Joe hurried up to catch her. She hadn't beaten him there like she hoped. Joe grasped her elbow and guided her through the door when they reached a new lingerie store.

"So now that you believe me about Neuropt," Joe whispered, "and both of our marriages have fallen apart, how about if I help you pick out some lingerie?"

"I thought you'd want to buy some for your slut Alicia, so you could replace what she gave you?" Erika said. "And I had Victoria's Secret in mind, not this place."

"Alicia is history," Joe said. "She just wanted to get information out of me, and I let her so I could get information out of her. I haven't seen her since I found out you were leaving Ray."

"That's brave of you to make such a sacrifice," Erika said.

"Since I didn't know Ray and you had broken up," Joe said, "I didn't know it would be a sacrifice."

A saleswoman walked up to them. "A little gift for your wife?" she asked Joe. What was she talking to him for? Well, Joe could handle her then.

"Actually, she's someone else's wife," Joe said. Erika stifled a snicker.

"Oh," said the saleswoman, pausing for a moment. "Well, let me know if you need any help."

"So can I pick something out for you to try on?" Joe asked, grinning as he took a few steps inside the store, picked up a thong panty and spun it around his finger.

"No, but you can pick out some suggestions if you want," Erika said.

Joe stopped. "You want me to help you pick out this sexy lingerie, knowing that I won't see it on you. Do you really expect me to subject myself to such frustration?"

"Yes," she said, leaning close in to Joe's face and whispering, "I do."

"Okay," Joe said.

She browsed through a few racks quickly and picked out a black lace teddy. She held it over herself and walked over to Joe. "Joey," she said, "envision me wearing this and tell me what you think."

"Hmmm," Joe said, touching the hem and slowly running his hand up inside the teddy. "It's hard to tell without seeing you in it."

"Uh-huh," Erika said, jerking the teddy away from his hand and spinning around. "So what did you want to talk to me about?"

"I want you to put a bug on the glass wall of Gage's office," Joe said.

"How'd you know he has a glass wall?" Erika asked. "Have you been there?"

"No," Joe said. "I have my ways."

"So I have to get inside his office?" Erika asked.

"No, you can just put it on the outside of the glass," Joe said. "Remember Gosonar?"

She remembered — she had helped with a project at Turner, West involving licensing Gosonar. It was an electronic bug invention that looked like an MP3 player with headphones, and could attach to the outside of any window.

Gosonar had a transducer that could attach to any piece of glass. It then used the glass like a flat panel speaker. When the transducer was vibrated, it would vibrate the entire glass, and it would generate sound waves and act as a speaker. The transducer would generate sound waves that weren't audible, and then switch to receiver mode to detect the echo of the sound it had just generated. Using the echo, Gosonar would then detect the characteristics of whatever glass — such as a window — that it was attached to. Using this calibration information, it could later detect any sounds hitting the window.

"I think we can catch Gage admitting Neuropt is a fraud," Joe said. "That will vindicate me, and stop them from being false competition to Telekinetics."

"And cost me my stock," Erika said.

Joe handed her the transducer, then held up some panties. "How about these?" Joe said.

She widened her eyes in mock surprise. "But Joey, there's no crotch in those panties." She put her hand through the crotch to demonstrate. "See?" she said, wiggling her fingers in Joe's face, with the panties up near his nose.

Joe put the panties back.

"Where's the rest of Gosonar?" Erika asked.

"I'm keeping it," Joe said. "I'll monitor it from outside Neuropt." He held up a leather thong with matching bra.

"But it has a limited range," Erika said, and poked a finger through each of the two holes in the front of the bra. "You'd better give it to me so I can monitor from my desk."

She wiggled her fingers through the holes. "Same problem with these," she said.

Joe shook his head. "Too dangerous."

"And placing the bug isn't?" Erika asked.

She had turned her back to Joe, and was busily going through one of the racks. She pulled out a full-length red silk nightgown and held it over herself, looking at Joe. Joe shook his head, and held up a beige, ribbed corset with sheer cups and garter belts.

"Do I get the rest of Gosonar?" she asked. Joe handed over the rest of Gosonar.

Erika grabbed the corset and put it back on the rack. "I'm not buying anything here anyway," she said. "I just have something to pick up at Victoria's Secret."

"Then why are we in here?" Joe asked.

"You're the one who led us in here," Erika said.

She led Joe over to Victoria's Secret, where the saleslady pulled out of a box a purple merry widow made of see-through lace with garters, and matching G-string and nylons. Erika quickly pushed it back in the box. "Yes, that's the one," she said, blushing as she glanced over at Joe.

When Erika returned to Neuropt, her heart jumped. An IS guy was in her cubicle, dismantling her computer. Had they discovered the research she'd been doing?

"What's up?" she said, flashing her biggest smile.

"We're upgrading computers," he said. "We brought a lot over from Mr. Booth's old company, and now we're upgrading."

She chitchatted while he finished his work, and found out the old computers were being donated to a local school. After he left, she pulled the Gosonar out of her purse.

Gosonar had a limited broadcast range to keep the battery small, but her desk was close enough. It wasn't until after 5 PM that she had an opportunity to go inside to Gage's office. He had asked her to go over a memo she had done. She unbuttoned two buttons this time. She felt her heart beat faster as she followed him to his office and sat down. She pulled out her notepad, and kept her eyes focused on her notes. That way she didn't have to see him leering, and maybe he wouldn't see how nervous she was. Her heart was racing now, and she was starting to sweat. Calm down. She told herself she could do it another time, when she was less nervous. That was it; she'd put it off. Her heart calmed down.

Gage went on for 15 minutes, on something that could have been done in two. Finally, the phone rang. He picked it up, and said he'd have to take it. He turned sideways away from her. She took the hint, and got up to leave. As she was going out the door, she looked back at him. He wasn't looking at her. If she moved quickly, she could do it now after all. She wouldn't have time to be nervous. She pulled the transducer out of her purse and touched it to the corner of the window, watching him as she did this.

Gage suddenly swiveled around and stared at her. Had he seen what she was doing? She leaned forward against the door jam, knowing her blouse would open up. He looked angry. She felt her legs get weak. Gage stared at her breasts for a few moments, then put his hand over the receiver and called out, "Please close the door." She nodded, and grabbed the door to close it. After she closed it, she walked by the window and looked in. His back was to her again. She gently pressed the transducer against the corner of the window. She had decided to put a smiley face on both sides, and then double sticky tape, to disguise it in plain sight.

She took a deep breath as she got back to her office, and opened the drawer to turn on the monitoring system for the bug. She admired her new computer for a few moments, and then an idea hit her. She wondered if Hal, her friend from Turner, West's information services group, would be interested in volunteering to help set up computers at a local school.

Zenko looked at his sake the next evening as he slowly swirled it in his glass. Burak had confirmed that the Virtual Net patent was a problem for Telekinetics. Burak had been worried that Virtual Net might sue. Joe had looked at it, and had an argument that Telekinetics did not infringe if a design change was implemented. But it was not as good as the argument they have against the AutoSmart patent. Burak's words still rung in his head: "And we all know what good that argument has been."

A.J. and Burak felt they didn't have any choice except to take the Royaltec offer. To do otherwise would be to condemn their company to extinction. And it was the only way more Retinal Screens would be sent to Brazil. Both A.J. and Burak felt that was more important than their ownership of the company. They needed to continue the development, they couldn't afford spending more time to fight, or look for investors to fight. They even agreed to the terms that required them and others, as key employees, to agree not to quit and continue to work for 2 years. Slave labor.

Zenko drained the rest of his sake and headed for the door. He didn't want to drink alone; there should be others at the bar by now. He needed someone to gripe with. He couldn't believe Royaltec was going to get away with it, and there was nothing he could do. Roger's offer to get him paid just made it sting even more.

Erika tossed her purse on her bed that night, walked by the card table in the corner and clicked on the computer. She sat on her bed while looking through the mail. Bills went in one pile, things to get to in another, and the rest she tossed toward the recycling box under her desk. About half made it in. Her computer finally finished coming up, and she started her e-mail program. Immediately after it came up, an Instant Messenger box from Joe popped up.

Nilesan: *Erika – Find anything?*
EErika2: *I found out that Neuropt is making license payments to KUSTA, a lobbying group– Keep US Technology in America. KUSTA in turn is making payments to Royaltec for a license. KUSTA is just a trade organization – they don't need a license because they don't make any products. It's clearly being used as a funnel for providing funding to Royaltec.*
Nilesan: *That's odd. I thought Royaltec earned plenty of money from litigating its patents. There*

was an article recently that said Royaltec has $450 million. They don't need funding.

She thought she heard a cry. She slowly walked up to Jeffrey's room and peeked in. He was asleep. He had run her ragged since she got home. Her punishment for picking him up late, she guessed. She hadn't even had a chance to change out of her work clothes. She walked to her bedroom, kicking off her shoes toward the closet as she went through the door, while she pulled her sweater over her head. She checked herself out in the mirror as she unclasped her bra. She wiggled out of her skirt and pulled down her panties. It felt fabulous to be naked. She went over to her closet and dropped her clothes in the hamper, and grabbed an extra-large T-shirt and pulled it over her head. She then stepped into some sweat pants and pulled them up under the T-shirt.

She sat down with her feet crossed under her on the chair and picked up the beanbag turtle and rubbing it across her lips as she held her finger on the mouse for a moment.

Nilesan: *So how is Jeffrey doing? Is he asleep?*
EErika2: *He just went to sleep. I had to work late, and he made me pay! I was only able to change out of my work clothes a few minutes ago.*
Nilesan: *So, if we had connected a few minutes ago, I might have caught you naked?*

She smiled.

EErika2: *Yes. Completely.*
Nilesan: *Why don't you turn on your camera?*
EErika2: *You first.*

Nilesan: OK, *we're at a standoff. So what are you wearing now? Just curious.*

She looked down at her sweats.

EErika2: *the lingerie I bought — a purple merry widow made of see-through lace with garters, and matching G-string and nylons. I can't keep from caressing myself.*
Nilesan: *It's apparently contagious. Why is Gage using Neuropt to put more money into Royaltec? Doesn't he have enough money to fund Royaltec directly?*
EErika2: *Bingo. I found a few letters to Royaltec from Gage in his secretary's recycle bin on the computer. I also believe greed knows no end with Gage — he apparently has gone into hock for those currency contracts. I think he wants to leverage as much as possible to make as much as he can. He must be short on liquid cash, and it must be killing him that Neuropt is sitting on a pile of cash. You find this more interesting than my lingerie??*

———————

Zenko wobbled down the street — walking home when drunk was one of the advantages of a condo near downtown. It had been a good Thursday night of Royaltec bashing. He just wished that they could do more than trash talk. There had been a surprising number of former Turner, West attorneys there. More than when Turner, West was still in business.

The lights were all on in his condo. He looked at his watch. 2 AM. And Joe was still up? He hoped Joe didn't want to talk. He was so tired, he just wanted to crash. It had been a long time since he had this much to drink, and now he remembered why.

Joe was sitting on the couch, reading some papers. He looked up and frowned. "Out getting drunk again?"

"Go piss on yourself, Nile-san," Zenko said.

"Well, while you've been out getting drunk," Joe said, waving the papers in his hand, "I've been coming up with a plan."

"Well good for you," Zenko said as he struggled to his feet and made his way past Joe to the kitchen.

"Erika has gotten some information that will completely discredit Neuropt," Joe said, following him into the kitchen. "What do you think will happen when we make that public?"

"How'd she get it?" Zenko asked.

"A little old fashioned bugging," Joe said, "and she talked our old IS guy, Hal, into some volunteer work at a local school. It's amazing what e-mails you can recover from a disk drive even after it's been completely erased."

Zenko popped six aspirin and took a long drink of water.

"Erika unwound Gage's maze of corporate shells," Joe said. "And all of Gage's liquid assets are in Royaltec. The rest is long term investments and currency futures."

Zenko leaned against the counter. He just wanted to go to bed.

"Now, what happens to Neuropt if we discredit them?" Joe asked.

"OK, I'll bite," Zenko said. "Their stock plummets."

"What if Gage were to use all his Royaltec money to buy the rest of the Neuropt stock on the open market just before it plummeted?"

Undue Diligence

Zenko just blankly looked at Joe. "And how do you make him do that? Hypnotize him?"

Joe started to explain something, but Zenko groggily waved him off. "In the morning, Joe. I need sleep."

19.

Joe was sitting at Zenko's desk in his condo two days later, on Saturday, swiveling the chair from side to side as he studied the materials he had assembled so far on Neuropt. Zenko came over and sat on the edge of the desk. Zenko brushed a new-looking scratch on the desk, then wet his finger and rubbed it again.

"Are you sure you can trust Hank?" Zenko asked.

"Absolutely," Joe replied. "Even if I could do this myself — which I can't, because Gage would recognize me — Hank would do a better job in any case."

"So how long do I have to put off Telekinetics?" Zenko asked. "They called again; they want this thing settled today, tomorrow at the latest. You said it might take a few days to a week. Which is it?"

"It's going to take at least a couple weeks," Joe mumbled, bracing for Zenko's reaction.

"A couple weeks?" Zenko shouted, hopping off the desk, and then bracing his outstretched arms on it, with his head down, as if he were trying to move it. "Why didn't you tell me in the first place? I can't possibly stall that long. We're going to have to give them the file history pages."

"I was waiting for the right moment to tell you," Joe said, lifting his head and looking sheepishly at Zenko. "We can't give Royaltec those pages."

"No way," Zenko said. "I'll have to declare under penalty of perjury that I've given them all copies. No way I'm going to risk disbarment over this."

"Well, you can't," Joe said, as he returned to scanning the papers on his desk. "Telekinetics doesn't have the right to give them all copies."

"Sure they do," Zenko said. "Have you forgotten they're our client?"

"No," Joe said. "QuadStar is our client. They are the ones who paid for us to obtain the file history."

"Quadstar?" Zenko asked. "What do they have to do with this?"

"Nothing," Joe said. "I just put their name on the invoice when I paid for a copy of the file history. I'm not going to bill them, since they didn't ask me to do this — but we have documentation that I got the pages on behalf of another client, not Telekinetics."

"Okay, that will buy us some time," Zenko said. "But Telekinetics is going to be pissed — they'll see what's really going on. Plus, they might buy off QuadStar. They could pay QuadStar to order us to release all copies. This might not buy us enough time."

"That's our opening delaying tactic," Joe said. "They'll have to deal with new counsel for QuadStar. Quadstar doesn't have the copies — we do, as Quadstar's counsel. We'll say we have a conflict, representing both QuadStar and Telekinetics. Royaltec will be having a fit about getting more people involved who will know about this. And after they nail down a deal with Quad-Star, we tell them we as attorneys have a right to keep a copy to protect us against a possible malpractice claim in the future. I'm sure we can drag this out for several weeks."

"Nile-san, you scare me sometimes," Zenko said.

Cassia rushed down to the conference room after getting the message that the doctor had arrived with news. Her cell phone rang on the way.

"It's Vladmir," the caller said. "So you got your antidote?"

"Yes," Cassia said. "Thank you so very much. Are you sure we can't compensate you somehow?"

"I have enough money," Vladmir said. "I just wanted to end this brutality. And stick it to my former employer. Will you be going public soon?"

"I'm about to find out," Cassia said. "But we will be saying we developed the antidote — Russia won't be mentioned."

"So did they tell you why they didn't give you the antidote sooner?" Vladmir asked.

"Yeah," Cassia said. "The assholes wanted to catch the terrorists and keep their weapon. They didn't say that, but I'm guessing that. They said they could catch the terrorists more easily if they weren't tipped off."

"They're lying," Vladmir said. "They like the economic consequences."

"How's that?" Cassia asked.

"Gotta go," Vladmir said. "I've been talking too long."

"But . . . ," Cassia said as the line went dead. What economic consequences was he talking about? How would Russia benefit from the Brazilian economy going down the tubes due to the virus?

Cassia put her phone back in her purse and hurried to the conference room.

"Well?" she blurted as she opened the conference room door.

"It appears to be working," the doctor said. "We've got 10 patients with no symptoms 24 hours after taking the antidote. All of them were showing symptoms when they first took it, and would normally be partially paralyzed or dead by now."

"Side effects?" Cassia asked.

"None we've been able to detect," the doctor said. "Of course, any side effects might not show up for weeks, months, years, decades."

"You know we can't wait to study that," Cassia said.

The doctor nodded. Cassia looked at the technician.

"With the formula the Russians gave us," the technician said, "we have two companies that should be able to start producing the antidote ourselves in a few weeks. That's about the same amount of time the Russians said it would take them to gear-up again to produce it. Since, as you know they dismantled that operation a decade ago."

"So what do we do?" the doctor asked. "We don't have enough antidote for the people that are dying today."

"We can go public now," Cassia said. "Hopefully, by warning everyone, no one will take any strange pills and we won't have new cases."

"That will tip off the terrorists and make it harder to catch them, right?' asked the technician.

"We can't help that," Cassia said.

"What if it mutates?" the technician asked.

"And I ask again," the doctor said, "how are we going to ration this?"

Ned saw his secretary standing outside the glass of the conference room door Monday, but ignored her. Couldn't she see he was in an important meeting with Gage? He frowned as she knocked on the conference room door and stepped in. "Mr. Stern," she said, "there are a couple gentlemen at reception that want to talk to you and Mr. Booth."

Ned glanced at Gage, who shrugged. "I don't have an appointment, do I?" Ned asked. "Who are they?"

"They just dropped in," she said. "They said that if you want to make any money at all on Neuropt, you better talk to them right away."

She looked nervously at Gage. "I'm sorry to interrupt you," she said, "but it sounded important, and I thought Mr. Booth might want to hear this."

Ned looked at Gage. This didn't sound good. He wondered if it had been due to Gage's looting of the company's cash. Ned had tried over and over to discourage Gage. It had taken a long time to convince him. Maybe the damage had already been done. He hoped they weren't from the SEC.

"Show them in," Gage snarled, with the hardened tone of one about to do battle.

A minute later, Ned's secretary escorted two men in suits into the conference room. One of them turned to Ned's secretary as she was closing the door. "Some coffee would be wonderful, thanks," he said.

She looked at Ned and raised her palms. He gave her a nod. Why not?

Ned and Gage sat quietly without standing and said nothing, sizing up the two men.

"Hi," one of the men said, "I'm Hank Brown and this is Fred Haskens. Fred is the CFO of Healthtronics, who you may have heard of."

Hank paused, apparently watching for a reaction that didn't come. Ned just stared at them without looking at Gage. Hank and Fred each leaned forward and placed a business card first in front of Gage and then another in front of Ned. Ned knew the company.

"I'm an outside consultant for Healthtronics," Hank continued. "I help them with their acquisitions. They are interested in acquiring Neuropt."

Ned had to check a sigh of relief. He shot Gage a glance. This was unexpected, and intriguing. Maybe they could get their money sooner than they thought. A buyout would eliminate the holding period. They hadn't thought this would be possible because of the high stock price after the IPO.

Ned leaned forward. "Go ahead, we're listening."

"Healthtronics is the second largest maker of medical equipment in the country," Fred continued, pulling up a chair. Hank sat down beside him. Fred placed a beaten-up brown leather briefcase on the table in front of him, but didn't open it.

Ned listened to Fred describe Healthtronics and the industry in general for 5 minutes, then cut him off. "According to my secretary, we had to talk to you if we wanted to make any money at all on Neuropt. Why would we not make money without you?"

Hank smiled. "We think you'll find what we have here persuasive." Hank reached over and pulled Fred's briefcase toward him. He popped the latches one at a time, opened the briefcase and pulled out a large manila envelope. He flung the envelope across the table toward Ned, who had to quickly grab it before it slid off onto the floor.

Ned slowly opened the clasp on the envelope and pulled out a stack of papers. He glanced at Gage, and then started looking through the papers in the envelope. They did have dirt on Neuropt, as he first feared! How did they get it? What was going on? Why were they talking about an acquisition?

"What do they have there?" Gage asked Ned.

"It seems," Ned said, continuing to leaf through the papers, "that these gentlemen have stolen copies of a number of your electronic files, including e-mail. It generally seems to relate to the feasibility of Neuropt's product."

"It's very interesting reading," Hank said. "It seems that there are a lot of e-mails from your engineers at Neuropt basically saying the product won't work, and even speculating that it's a fraud."

"And this?" Ned asked, holding up some technical papers.

"That's a copy of files used to prepare Neuropt's patent applications," Hank said. "It shows that a couple of public papers were scanned in and combined to generate the application that was filed. It's entirely a product of published materials, nothing new. Very interesting way to do a patent application."

Gage grabbed the stack of e-mails from Ned and started looking through them. Ned continued to look at the other materials, looking up to see Hank and Fred just sitting silently and watching.

Ned was starting to get concerned as he went through the materials. But they didn't seem to have any smoking guns. Did these guys even realize what they were on to? Could they tie anything to him? He didn't see anything that would implicate him. He had tried to be very careful in his dealings with Neuropt. So far as he knew, there was nothing in writing that would implicate him in any knowledge that they weren't completely on the up and up. As he went through all the material and didn't see anything that tied to him, he relaxed. He looked through again, more calmly now, and tried to analyze the damage.

The e-mails were very damaging, but probably not fatal. The market would react badly, though. There would be a significant price drop, but there would still be some value. Even if it went back to its original offering price of $12, Gage would still make money. After all, Gage had originally contributed only 5 cents per share, so that was still a pretty good return. Ned frowned. The stock market had a way of overreacting. It might go to pennies.

"Okay," Gage growled after a few minutes. "I know blackmail when I smell it. What's your game?"

"It's very simple," Fred said. "We think Neuropt has some real value, in spite of what these e-mails and other materials say. We want to buy Neuropt. But we think it has problems, and will require a lot of effort to develop the product. And we think the stock is way overpriced."

"So?" Gage asked. "I can't control the stock price."

"Oh, but you can," Hank said. "You can buy all the shares you don't own, and then sell the company to us."

"Wait a minute," Gage growled. "You want me to buy the stock at inflated prices, and then sell it to you at a lower price? Do I look crazy?"

"Well," Fred said, "since you'd be able to sell the stock you already own, we figure you'd still come out ahead to the tune of about $60 million. Now I know that's not the hundreds of millions you were probably hoping for, based on the current stock price. But it's better than the big fat zero you'd get if we released this information to the press."

"I don't think the press on this would drive the stock to zero," Ned said, assuming a negotiator's role. "So why are you interested in buying from Gage? Why not just release the information, and then buy the shares on the open market after the stock price dropped? If it drops to zero, as you say, it would be a much better deal for you. And why would you want a stock that is worth zero?"

"You're right," Hank said, "the stock wouldn't go to zero. But it would drop significantly. And we think the public would overreact. The stock might recover, but Neuropt's reputation would be irreparably sullied. We take a more objective approach. We'd rather buy from Mr. Booth."

"You want me to buy the rest of the shares?" Gage protested. "This is a bunch of crap. Neuropt has a market value of over one billion dollars. To gain control, with the other founders, I'd need to buy the 60% of the shares in the public's hands. That's $600 million dollars. Why would I spend that cash to sell it to you?"

"We are willing to pay 600 million for the whole company," Fred said. "There is no way it is worth a billion in light of what we found."

Ned quickly did some rough math in his head. Gage had 25% of the stock, and the other founders had 15%. If Gage bought the remaining 60%, he'd have 85% of the company. If they paid 600 million for the whole company, which happened to be what Gage would have to pay to buy those shares; Gage would only get 85% of 600 million, which was around 500 million.

"It doesn't make sense," Ned said. "Gage would lose plenty, plus his existing investment in 25% of the stock."

"Not if the stock price dropped before Gage bought," Hank said.

"I thought you didn't want to release this information?" Ned said. He had an idea where they were going with this. But he wanted to hear *them* suggest stock manipulation.

"We don't," Fred said. "But you can make the stock price drop. We understand you have a meeting with the analysts the day after tomorrow."

"Are you suggesting we manipulate the stock price?" Ned asked, standing up and putting on his best outraged look.

"Not at all," Fred said. "I think we'd both agree it's currently overvalued. And you know how sensitive analysts are. If you even give them body language, without saying anything, suggesting that things aren't all that rosy, the stock price will drop. As a matter of fact, we figure you could cause it to lose a quarter of the value, down to 750 million, if you give the right impression to the analysts. At 750 million, you can buy the 60% for 450 million. Then you get 85% of the 600 million we pay you, which is $510 million. You clear 60 million. Not bad. Do the math, you'll see."

"And what makes you think I have the cash on hand to do this?" Gage growled. "I may be rich, but it's in long-term investments, not liquid."

"You can use your Royaltec money," Hank said.

Ned involuntarily froze, but resisted the temptation to look at Gage. He didn't want to give away his surprise. He slowly sat back down. How the hell did they know how much money Royaltec had? Almost to the penny. Who were these guys?

"I'm afraid you're mistaken about Royaltec," Ned said. "Royaltec doesn't have that much cash."

"We know," Fred said. "So don't try that bullshit on us."

"How do you know?" Ned asked.

"We just know," Hank said, staring at Ned.

Ned waited to see if they would offer more explanation. Sometimes it paid to just shut up for awhile, and see if the other side got tired of waiting and started volunteering things. They weren't doing it though. They just sat there impassively. These guys were good.

"OK," Ned finally said. "I'll play along just for the sake of argument. Suppose Mr. Booth did have the money. If he tried to acquire control, he would have to file a statement to that affect. And that would drive the price back up."

Hank was shaking his head. "We figure you are smart guys. If Gage releases a statement that he's buying back to take it private, because he doesn't want the public risking its money in light of the latest stock drop, it could temper the rise. It would also allay any SEC concerns. Besides, if you cause it to drop enough in the first place, you can absorb a little increase."

"Well, you guys are simply full of shit," Gage said. "Get the hell out of here."

Hank stood up, and Fred followed suit. Fred put another stack of papers on the table. "Here's the proposed purchase agreement. We think it's very fair. We wrote it so that the terms don't favor either side because we don't want to waste time haggling over terms. We want to keep the present personnel if possible. Look it over. It's not quite 'take it or leave it.' But since we think its fair, we're not going to agree to any changes. We'll take anything more than minor proposals for changes as an indication that you don't want the deal."

"This is blackmail!" Gage shouted, slamming his fist on the table. Ned cringed. There went any hope of finding out if they were bluffing.

"Call it what you want," Hank said. "But if we don't have a positive answer in 24 hours, we release this information to the press. And if we don't sign the deal within 3 days after that, we release the information to the press."

"That's impossible!" Gage bellowed, getting to his feet and walking around the table, apparently eager to start a fistfight. "I can't raise that money in 3 days! And I won't be bullied like this!"

"And *you* can't close a deal like that in 3 days," Ned added with his best tone of indignity. "You'd have to do a Hart-Scott-Rodino filing and wait for a minimum of 10 days. And we'd need time after that to do the stock purchases."

"We didn't say close it," Hank answered. "We want an agreement signed in 3 days. The closing would be later, and conditioned on Hart-Scott-Rodino approval, of course. It's all in the agreement." Hank pointed at the documents.

"We're not interested," Ned said. "But out of morbid curiosity, why not just 51%?" Ned asked.

Fred shook his head. "With 51% we'd still have to hassle with the minority shareholders, so that is clearly out. No, we want to take Neuropt private. That way, we can take our time investing in the technology and developing it without being under the glare of Wall Street and having all the SEC reporting requirements. We don't want pressure from public shareholders to make a profit before the product is ready. We think that Neuropt has potential to be profitable if proper long-term planning is done. We don't see how you guys could ever have thought you'd have a product ready to go in 6 months, unless it was a complete kludge."

"We will," Gage lied. "We *have* to. The Amazon virus will be all over America by then. Our people are extremely motivated. They'll get the job done."

"What about the employee stock options?" Ned asked. "How do you propose to deal with them? All these people are counting on public stock. You may lose a lot of them if you go private."

"It's all spelled out in our proposed agreement," Hank said. "Read it."

Hank and Fred turned and left. These guys were sure cheeky, Ned thought.

"You won't get away with this, you bastards!" Gage yelled after them. "I'll have your heads!"

As soon as they left, Ned grabbed some paper and started doing some calculations.

"I can't believe this just happened!" Gage said, pacing the room. "Where the hell did those assholes come from? What just happened here?"

"I don't know," Ned said, looking at the materials they had left. "But I got to tell you, those guys were good. They sure had done their homework."

"Dammit!" Gage growled, slamming his fist on the table.

"I guess we should have figured something like this might happen," Ned said thoughtfully. "With all the hype you've been putting out, we focused on the effect on investors. We didn't count on competitors buying our line of hype. But I think that at least this one did."

Ned continued his calculations as Gage sank into his chair. He punched numbers into his calculator to verify Gage's holdings. Some he knew from memory, for others he had to consult different files on his laptop.

He finally closed his laptop and put down his pen, looking up at Gage. "Their numbers are right. You would clear 60 million. And they are eerily close on how much money you have to buy stock with."

Gage waved his hand impatiently. "Any fool could figure that out with a little effort. How about all that other stuff about controlling the stock price? Is that right?"

Ned turned it over in his mind. It made sense. He thought their estimates of how the stock would react were right, and there was flexibility built into the scheme so Neuropt could control the press to get the stock to where they needed it.

"Yes, I think they were probably correct about how the stock would react," Ned said. He was surprised at how sanguine he felt about this development. Although Gage was certainly angry, he strangely felt almost relieved. Here, they could still make a lot of money, and without having to tough it out another five months with the very real risk that the lack of any development would drive the stock price even lower.

When he looked at Gage, he wasn't prepared for what he saw. Gage was grinning ear-to-ear, and then started laughing.

"Didn't you originally project we'd get 50 million," Gage asked between laughs, "before the stock market surprised us all and drove the price way up?"

"That's correct," Ned said warily.

"So we're still getting more than we hoped for," Gage said, "and these suckers are paying for it, and we're getting out earlier. Besides, Neuropt was always a sideshow to the main action, and the stock price would probably have dropped before I got out anyway."

Ned nodded.

"These clowns truly think Neuropt is worth something!" Gage said. "This is actually fantastic luck — we have a sucker just falling into our laps." Gage continued laughing. Ned felt a wave of relief wash over him.

"And I called *them* the extortionists," Gage howled.

While he was typing an e-mail, Joe anxiously glanced at his phone in Zenko's condo that morning, like a cat ready to pounce on a mouse. When was Hank going to call? They were supposed to keep the meeting short and sweet.

Zenko had been on his cell phone with A.J. for 5 minutes. It wasn't going well, from what Joe could hear from Zenko's side of the conversation. He imagined A.J. must be going ballistic. Zenko was maintaining his cool, trying to calmly answer, but Joe could tell A.J. kept cutting him off.

Joe's phone vibrated. It was Erika calling him back.

"There's one other thing I need from you," Joe said. "Do you think you can get Cassia to send you a pill with the virus in it, and a dose of the antidote?"

Erika was silent for a moment. "You're serious? I don't know why you want them, but that is sure asking for a lot. They don't have enough of the antidote to go around, you know."

"I know," Joe said. "I'm sending you an e-mail right now that you can send to Cassia. I think she'll spare a dose when she sees this."

"Any other impossible requests?" Erika asked.

"Yes, actually," Joe said. "I want you."

"Well, I'd love to see the e-mail you're sending to convince me of that," Erika said, then hung up.

"I've been fired," Zenko said, narrowing his eyes at Joe. "They're going to hire other counsel, and she's threatening a malpractice action."

"Don't worry, Zenko," Joe said. "It'll never get that far. Royaltec will be toast shortly."

"I hope you're right," Zenko said. "What do you think the odds are — 90 percent?"

"More like 50-50, I'm afraid," Joe said. "But that's a slam dunk for a litigator."

———————

Ned wiped his brow as he watched the Neuropt CFO performing on Wednesday. The CFO could have been an actor. The CFO was wearing a dark gray suit and matching tie instead of the casual clothes he usually wore for these meetings — he looked like he was going to a funeral. He was now carefully looking at his hands after finishing his dry presentation to the analysts. Of course, the analysts participating by conference call couldn't see this, but those present could.

"Is there any new projection on when the Optospine will be ready for shipment?" one of the analysts asked.

The CFO sighed. "We don't have enough information yet to make any change in that prediction."

"You don't sound very confident or upbeat," the analyst said, looking around at her fellow analysts. "And *not enough information* sounds like bad news you aren't ready to deliver yet. Would you care to comment on that?"

"No," the CFO said, "I can't say anything more at this time. I'm sorry. And I'm afraid I have to go now, I have another meeting."

Ned put on his best somber look as he made a point of quickly pushing his chair back to get up and follow the CFO out of the conference room. When he looked back, he could see the analysts anxiously whispering among themselves. This was easier than he had thought.

Things were working out perfectly. It had also been fairly easy to consolidate Gage's money and the Royaltec cash. And they had a bank lined up to loan money based on the collateral value of Gage's Neuropt stock, since they might fall a little short on the cash. After all, they would be using the loan to buy the Neuropt stock, which was certainly worth the money Neuropt had raised in its IPO and had sitting in a bank account, which Gage would have access to once he acquired all the stock.

20.

Over a week later, Joe took a deep breath to calm himself as he sat impatiently in Zenko's condo. It was finally showtime. It had been 11 days since Gage signed the agreement for the purchase by Healthtronics. Gage had delayed signing until they could see the stock reaction to the analysts meeting. After Gage was satisfied it had dropped enough to make the deal feasible, he signed. The Hart-Scott-Rodino filing was then made. The 10-day waiting period expired without any action by the FTC, so it was approved by default. Gage had then started buying stock.

Joe picked up an article from the table. He still got a kick out of reading the quote of Gage Booth on why he wanted to take the company private so soon after going public.

> "Certain investors have asked that we go private after seeing that the pressures put on us as a public company are distracting us from our long term goals. Going private will give us the chance to make long range decisions about how to run the company without the pressure of short-term earnings expectations. Without the distractions of Wall Street, we can concentrate on research and development of follow-up products."

He was just waiting for Zenko's call to send out the press release and supporting materials. He had contacted all the major brokerages, and they were ready for whatever Joe was going to send them, and they would post it on their web sites for their customers. He also had contacted a respected Internet reporter and given her an exclusive, in exchange for keeping it quiet until Joe released the press release. Her article was already written, and ready for distribution. It would add legitimacy to the press release, and make sure it was taken seriously.

Joe turned to one of the front page articles in the paper. More companies that had gone after the virus were shutting down and laying people off. It was having a ripple effect on their suppliers. The stock market had headed south for the third straight day, and some predictions were that the worst was yet to come. It was already being compared to the collapse of the dot-com bubble. However, it would have been much worse if the truth about the virus hadn't come out for another six months. The dollar was headed south. Joe hoped it wouldn't crash as much as Gage wanted, but that remained to be seen. Either way, Gage would make a lot of money.

Instead of more riots over rationing in São Paulo, another article talked about the lawsuits being brought by the heirs of virus victims who had been denied the antidote. The rationing had been on the basis of age — younger patients got it first. Cynics speculated that was because the damages would be less for older victims, since they had less of a lifetime of earnings lost.

———

Meanwhile, over at Neuropt, one of the engineers was approaching Erika's cubicle. She started typing frantically, her eyes fixed on the screen. She wasn't about to make eye contact and give him an opening. It didn't work. But he just wanted to grouse about the stock. No one was happy since it had dropped and Gage had announced his plans to take the company private. A number of them had their resumes out and were interviewing elsewhere. Very few had held out much hope for Gage's promise that he would be able to announce a substitute stock option plan they would be happy with. They all wanted stock in a public company, not a private one.

He said rumors started flying that morning when word leaked of a meeting that Gage and the CFO were going to. The speculation was that the company would be sold. Maybe they'd get stock options in another public company. That could be even better. Everyone was running around whispering their own theories.

The engineer finally walked away.

"How's it going, Erika?" said a voice she knew. She jerked her head around. This was bad. He wasn't supposed to be here.

"Good morning Mr. Booth," she said. He seemed very relaxed, as if he were enjoying a private joke. "I'm surprised to see you here," she said, recovering quickly. "I heard a rumor you had a meeting to go to?"

"Oh, that little thing," Gage said nonchalantly. "That's why we have a CFO with signing authority. They can call me in my office if they need me. I'm too busy to be attending every little meeting. Besides," he smiled at Erika, and leaned forward as if letting her in on a big secret, "I wanted to announce the results of the meeting to everyone in person the minute it's concluded."

He pulled back and walked toward his office. She watched as he disappeared through the combo doors. She had to tell Zenko! She could use her cell phone to avoid the possibility the phones were tapped, but she was worried they might intercept the cell phone as well. There was a pay phone at the convenience store across the street. She grabbed her purse and started to head out, when a thought occurred to her. She clicked on her browser to bring up a stock quote on Neuropt, and printed it out.

———

Zenko looked around at the hotel lobby as it disappeared from view. He looked down the escalator at the wide hallway leading to the meeting rooms. He supposed the hallway had to be wide proportionately to the size of the meeting rooms. It was wider than some churches he'd seen, and with a ceiling just as high.

He saw a lot of people in front of one meeting room. There was a table in front, covered with pamphlets, with different lines for registering. Other than that group, there were very few people around the other rooms. He wondered which of those people were working for Hank, guarding the meeting room.

Hank was waiting for him at the bottom of the escalator. Zenko's phone buzzed just before he reached Hank. It was Erika.

"Zenko," Erika whispered. "Bad news — Gage's here at Neuropt."

Zenko relayed the information to Hank. They had planned to keep the key players isolated so they couldn't check the stock during the closing, and see that it was falling. With Gage at Neuropt, he'd certainly be constantly checking the stock price. Hank's face fell. "Any ideas?" Zenko asked.

Hank shook his head. "I'm thinking."

"OK," Erika said. "Here's the plan. Come up with some last minute change you want in the deal. Get Gage on the phone to talk about it, and keep him there as long as you can. As soon as he's on the phone two minutes, release the information. I'll go by his office, and keep everyone away from him. We'll just have to buy as much time as we can and hope it works. Okay?"

"How will you keep people away?" Zenko asked.

"I'm working on that," Erika said.

———— —— ——

Ned walked slowly around the room, waiting for Hank to return. He found himself more relaxed without Gage there. At first, he had been dismayed at Gage's rash and inexplicable decision not to show up. But Ned also realized he wouldn't have to worry about Gage saying something stupid, or poking fun at him, as Gage liked to do. And the CFO was easy to get along with — all business.

The main meeting room table had folders all around the edges. Two of his associates were busily rechecking the closing documents in them. They had gone over them before, but as always there were some last minute changes. And when the other side was controlling the paperwork, he liked to have it checked. Besides, it gave the associates something to do at the closing.

Hank appeared back in the room. "I'm afraid there is a problem with the deal," he announced to the room.

Ned stiffened into a ramrod posture. Shit. Now what?

"My people tell me," Hank said, "that they are worried about whether Gage's proposed buy out of the employee stock options will hold up. I'd also like to hear from Gage how his employees are reacting to it."

Ned relaxed. This was only a hiccup, and one he was sure could be dealt with. But no need to cave-in early.

"We have a signed agreement," Ned said, "that spells out the stock option plan. It's too late to raise this."

"But there have been some changes since then," Hank said, "as you well know."

Ned looked at the CFO. "Let's get Gage on the speaker phone."

Erika wiped her clammy left hand on her skirt while she held the latte in her right, and punched in the combination. She jerked involuntarily at the loud clicking sound of the lock opening, then took a deep breath and walked through the combo doors to the inner offices. She walked into Gage's office and put the latte down. He looked up while on the phone and nodded, picking it up and taking a sip.

She walked around the perimeter to see how many people were there. About 10. How would she keep them from watching the stock reports and then interrupting Gage? Gage's secretary was there, playing solitaire on her computer. She stopped to chat with her for a few moments about the rumors. She found her very willing to talk.

Finally, she saw Gage's line light up. The secretary answered, then announced to Gage a call from the CFO at the hotel. This was it. Erika excused herself, and walked back through the combo doors. An idea had come to her. It wasn't very elegant, but it was a plan.

She walked to her cubicle and grabbed her coffee mug. Then she walked over to the nearest fire alarm. But there were a few engineers in sight. She walked to a second one. There were people around there, too. She didn't have much more time. She should just go for the next one. She didn't see anyone in sight.

She didn't need to use her mug to break glass or anything. She just pulled on the handle. The alarm immediately went off. It was an extremely annoying, piercing sound. Apparently designed to get people out of the building even if they thought it was a false alarm. She started walking away but was startled by an engineer popping out of his cubicle and looking at her. "What did you do?" He exclaimed.

"I'm so sorry," she said, forcing some sobs. "I tripped and grabbed for the wall, and my hand hit the alarm. Am I going to get in trouble? Can we shut it off?"

The engineer said a few consoling words, and said they would have to just leave the building, and promised not to tell on her. She said she had to get her purse, and rushed back to her cubicle. She grabbed her purse and the stock quote printout. She looked around as she walked to the combo doors, and quickly entered. She wasn't prepared for what she saw inside.

Half the people were still there, ignoring the alarm. It took her a few moments to realize what was different — the alarm wasn't that loud inside. Maybe they installed less annoying alarms inside. She had to do something. She walked up to one of the administrators in sight of Gage's office. How could she get her to leave? She smiled at her, then turned around and walked over to Gage's office. She discreetly unbuttoned the top button of her blouse and opened the door.

Gage looked up with annoyance. Gage's cell phone was on his side of the desk. She had to get it. She walked over to his desk and leaned over it. Gage was using the video feed on his computer — so he hopefully wouldn't be checking e-mail.

"There's a fire alarm," Erika said, leaning over his desk so her cleavage showed.

"I can hear it," Gage said. "It's a false alarm. It always is."

As he was looking at her, she grabbed his cell phone with her left hand and slid it into her purse.

"I'm on an important call," Gage said. "So just close the door. You're letting in the alarm sound."

"OK," Erika said. "I just wanted to tell you it definitely is a false alarm."

Gage looked away as she closed the door. She walked over to the administrator, who had been apparently watching her the whole time. Had she seen Erika lift the phone?

"Gage said everyone is to go outside," she said. "Apparently there was some trouble last time with the fire department because people were ignoring a false alarm. Gage's on an important call, so he has to stay. But everyone else should go outside. Can you help me tell everyone?"

"Consider it done," the administrator said, leaping to her feet. "You go that way, I'll go this."

Erika walked the other way. She looked at Gage's cell phone and turned it off, then stuffed it into her purse. She started telling people to leave. Everyone complied when they heard that Gage had requested it.

Erika started to close the combo door behind her as she and the administrator were the last ones out.

"Oh," Erika said. "I left my purse inside. It'll just take a second."

Erika went back in and walked over to the equipment room. It was sometimes left unlocked during business hours. She let out a deep breath when she got there — it was unlocked. She reached behind the security computer and pulled the plug. She hoped it would work. She remembered the IS guy telling her before that if power was lost, the locks would still hold, but the combination would automatically change to a default code.

She walked back to Gage's secretary's desk. She stiffened as she looked at the secretary's phone. She had forgotten that Gage's desk phone had two lines. Someone could try to interrupt him on the other line. She picked up the phone using Gage's other line. She rifled through her purse for a moment, and found a 900 number one of the tacky engineers had given her. She dialed it, and then set down the handset.

She checked off everything in her head. How else could someone try to reach Gage? She thought she had it all covered. But had the combo lock in fact changed? She had to know. She walked over to the combo door and opened it. Holding it with one hand while it was open, she leaned over and tried the combo. Good — it didn't work. She closed the door and stared at it for a minute. She looked around. Gage couldn't see it from his office. She looked around for a regular chair. One not on rollers. She finally found one in the computer room. She carried it to the combo door, and wedged it against the door handle. A little extra insurance.

She went back to Gage's secretary's desk and sat down. She looked over at Gage's office. He hadn't noticed her. He was focused on the video conference. She could hear him yelling over the fire alarm. She leaned back in the chair and took a deep breath. Nothing to do now but wait.

———————

Joe took one last look at Neuropt's stock price before hitting the send button on his e-mail. Neuropt's stock had shot up to $90 a share on rumors Gage was selling the company. It was volatile because there was so little stock left to trade. Only about 3% of the company's stock was still in the public's hands. They were the greedy ones, Joe thought, holding out for more money, so they deserved what they were about to get.

Joe's e-mail broadcast went to a large group of brokerages and news organizations on a pre-programmed group he had put together. He had contacted some key ones ahead of time and given them the answers they needed to verify the authenticity of what he was sending. Attached to the e-mail were copies of internal e-mails Hal had lifted from the disk drives of computers donated to the school. The e-mails said the product wouldn't work, and speculated that it was a fraud. The internal grousing had been quickly stopped, probably because the e-mail was monitored, but Hal had been able to extract the deleted e-mails. Joe also included the Neuropt patent application and the articles it copied from. But the coup de grace was a voice attachment of Gage Booth's phone call Erika had picked up with the Gosonar bug. Gage could be heard laughing about the scam he was pulling off. Hank hadn't shown that one to Gage and Ned.

Joe monitored the Internet. Nothing was happening yet on the Neuropt stock. He checked the headlines while he waited. The stock market was continuing to drop precipitously, with more companies announcing layoffs or shutdowns. The dollar was taking a nose-dive. Ten minutes later a grin escaped his lips — the first news sites had started to carry stories. He watched these continue to appear, while the stock ticker on Neuropt at the bottom of his screen showed the stock price start to drop. Fifteen minutes after he hit the send button, the stock had dropped from $90 to $75. In another 10 minutes the stock was down to $20. If trading wasn't halted soon, it might free-fall to under a dollar.

He didn't like the idea of Erika being near Gage. Especially if Hank was working Gage into a rage just before they dropped the bad news on him. He grabbed Zenko's cell phone and the keys to Zenko's other car. Time to drop the other shoe.

Erika glanced over to see Gage looking at her through the glass wall as she checked the Neuropt stock price on the computer again. She smiled at him. He didn't change expression. He appeared too involved in his conversation, gesturing as he talked.

At least the pounding on the door had stopped. The IS guy with the default code must not have arrived yet. She was sure they must have called him. Or maybe they hadn't figured out that the power had been cut off? She might be giving them too much credit. She wondered if they had wanted to warn Gage or strangle him. Or maybe just wanted to get back in.

Gage had gone to the door of his office earlier, and she had rushed over to intercept him. Gage wanted to know about the pounding on the door, which he could faintly hear in his office. She explained that somehow the alarm had screwed up the door lock. She couldn't even open it from the inside. She assured Gage that she had called maintenance, and they had told her it would be fixed in 15 minutes.

She saw Gage heading for the door again, and rushed over. She was relieved when he just asked her for the current stock price on Neuropt. He apparently didn't want to switch off his video, or reduce the video window. Maybe he just didn't know how to reduce the video window? Or maybe he just wanted to look down her blouse.

She went back to her computer and clicked on her mouse a few times, aware that Gage was looking at her. She hit print, and then picked up the printout. She moved so her back blocked Gage's view, and switched it with her previous stock price printout. She walked through his door and handed it to him. He snatched it from her hand, startling her. She noticed he was red in the face. He was getting real mad. He looked at it and nodded absentmindedly before launching into a tirade against someone on the videoconference.

———————

Zenko hit the end button on his phone. He had just warned Joe he was about to go in. Trading in the stock of Neuropt had been suspended; there was nothing Gage could do now. It was finally showtime.

He grabbed the handles and swung back both of the double doors of the meeting room, swaggering in as if he was a gunman heading into a bar in an old west town. The eyes of all the attorneys and paralegals turned to him. Hank stopped talking when he saw Zenko. Hank knew that if Zenko was in the room, there was no more point in talking.

Ned was frowning as he tried to work his cell phone. Hank had set up electronic devices which interfered with wireless communications in the room. Ned looked up and saw him. "What are you doing here?" Ned asked with suspicion. "You don't represent Healthtronics, do you?"

Zenko just grinned. "Where's Gage Booth?" He looked around, feigning surprise not to see Gage. There was no need for such theatrics, but he couldn't resist.

"Right here," boomed a voice from the speaker-phone.

"I'm afraid there's a problem with the deal, Mr. Booth-san" Zenko said, moving around the table to be in the view of the camera, and bowing slightly. "We are going to have to cancel because you've breached the condition that there not be undisclosed problems."

There was dead quiet for about 5 seconds while this sunk in.

"What the hell are you talking about?" Ned growled. "We've complied with all the conditions. It's your guys who are raising new stuff. We should have had all the closing documents signed and the money wire transferred by now. I'm getting tired of these 11th hour negotiating tactics. We have a done deal, let's close it!"

As Ned spoke, Zenko handed out copies of the press release that had been released.

"Jesus!" Gage said. "What's going on there?"

"Zenko has just handed us a press release," Ned said as he scanned the document.

"A press release?" Gage said. "Whose press release? What's it say?"

Zenko saw realization dawn on Ned's face. Suddenly Ned put down the press release and leaned into the microphone. "Gage, you've got to sell the Neuropt stock, now! We've been set up!"

"What do you mean, sell?" Gage asked.

"Tell them to dump everything you've bought!" Ned yelled. "Or you'll lose everything. You can't sell the restricted stock you already had, but you can sell everything you just bought. Do it now, don't worry about the price. As soon as this press release gets around, you won't be able to give it away! Now! Now!"

———

Erika could hear shouting through the glass as she tapped her pencil on the desk, trying to keep her eyes on the computer screen. Was Gage just complaining again, or had he gotten the good news? She sorely wanted to be out of there, but she thought she might be needed again. She checked the stock price again. Trading had been suspended — there was no longer a need to stall. Time to leave.

As she stood up, she was startled by a loud clanking sound and shattering glass. She looked and saw that he had thrown a mug against the glass wall of his office. Gage walked over and picked up the Gosonar bug, which had fallen in plain view. Then he looked at her. Their eyes locked for a moment.

She ran toward the combo door. As she was wrestling with the chair, she yelped as her arm was grabbed and she was spun around.

"Where are you going in such a hurry?" he said. He looked at the chair. "So the door is broken, huh?"

He started dragging her away from the door. She screamed, but only got half out before a big hand clamped down on her mouth and he started choking her. "Shut the hell up, bitch, or I'll break your neck!" he barked.

He dragged her back to his office in a headlock, with his hand over her mouth. He was too strong; she couldn't pry his arm free. Gage was cursing at her the whole way. He slammed her roughly into his chair. He slowly walked over to the door of his office, as if in a trance. He was blocking her escape. When he turned to glare at Erika, his face was bright red again.

"You bitch!" Gage screamed. "You bitch! You're part of this, aren't you?"

He approached her and she frantically pushed with her legs to roll the chair back into the corner. He grabbed her by the shoulders and shook her. "I'm ruined! I'm stuck with owning this worthless piece of crap company. And it's all your fault, isn't it? Isn't it?"

Gage stood up and backed away from her, leaning against the desk. It appeared as if things were slowly dawning on him. "What else did you do? You put the chair against the door, didn't you? You disabled the door, I bet. What else? Was that fire alarm part of your plan?"

She watched as Gage started pacing. "This whole last minute negotiation was just a distraction, wasn't it?" He looked over at her. She turned her head toward the wall.

"And you were conveniently here," Gage said, "keeping everyone from telling me what was happening to the stock. Who put you up to this?" Just when she didn't think he could get any redder, he did. He looked almost purple in his face. She thought his face might explode.

After a few moments of silence, Gage's face returned to his normal color, and he started chuckling. It quickly turned into a loud laugh. "I bet you think this is going to hurt me?"

Gage said. "You have no idea. I'll make so much money off another investment I have, that this will seem like peanuts."

Erika smiled. "You mean your currency speculation? Won't do you much good when you're dead from the virus."

"Ha!" Gage said. "I don't intend to catch it."

"You already have," Erika said. "It was in the latte. I have a friend at the federal health agency in Brazil. She sent me one of the virus pills."

Gage just had a blank look on his face. Erika's cell phone rang. "Yes? Okay, I'll be right there."

"It's the man with the antidote," Erika said. "Okay if I let him in?"

Gage still didn't say anything. He just stared at Erika, then slowly stepped aside.

Erika went over to the combo door, removed the chair, and returned a few moments later.

"Jesus H. Christ," Gage said. "Joe Nile!"

Gage sneered at Joe. "How's it feel to be disbarred, asshole?"

Joe leaned in toward Gage and smiled. "How's it feel to lose 600 million dollars?"

"I'll have your ass!" Gage said.

"Brave talk from a dying man," Joe said.

"I think you're bluffing," Gage said. "Besides, even if I did have it, I could be on a flight to São Paulo today and get the antidote there."

"Good luck with that," Joe said. "They don't have any more there, haven't you been reading the papers? I'm sure you know about your own disease. There is only one dose of the antidote left, and I have it hidden."

"You are full of it," Gage said. "Get out of my office."

"That was quite a plan you had," Erika said. "If you can somehow make the economy go bust big time, the dollar plunges and you make a ton of money on your currency speculation. Ideally, you'd like another Internet and telecom bubble. Billions of dollars chasing overvalued companies going after a market that just isn't there yet. You just need to dangle the right false market in front of American business, and let greed do the rest."

Erika paused.

"And how do you do that, you ask?" Joe asked. "You fake an epidemic. Make it look natural — put a virus in a vaccine. Also put some in pain pills to make it hard to trace. Do some in other countries to make it look like it's spreading. Do it in a country far from the US, where verification of the cause is difficult. Count on panic to make it difficult to get data. Sabotage containment efforts by bombing a CDC office."

"So what would happen?" Erika continued. "The US would rise to the challenge. Billions from the government, companies investing and forming like mad to develop a cure or vaccine. And that stimulates other industries to provide the tools, supplies, etcetera. A big bubble of business builds up to take on the virus. And then, it is revealed, or discovered, that there is no plague. The culprits are caught, or delivered. The bubble bursts. Currency speculators pounce. The dollar nose-dives, foreign investors pull their money out, the US is faced with onerous debt payments and no growth to finance it anymore. It's the Second Great Depression. But you are filthy rich, what do you care?"

"You should have gotten the Russians to pay you too," Joe continued. "You lucked out there. You didn't know they had an antidote. They figured out your scheme and decided they liked the action, so they didn't offer the antidote. After all, they knew it was a fake virus, it wouldn't spread around the world. It would only kill ten or twenty thousand Brazilians. A small price to pay to bring down their archrival."

Joe looked at Gage's hand, and Erika's eyes followed. Gage didn't have to look — he could feel it. He pushed his hand against the desk to try to stop the shaking.

Joe and Erika started to leave. All of them knew Gage only had about 8 hours to take the antidote before it was too late. Gage slowly eased into his chair, holding his shaking hand.

"What do you want?" Gage said.

"It seems you are about to have guilt pangs and an attack of patriotism," Erika said, pulling a contract out of a folder and putting it in front of Gage. "You call your lawyer and get him over here right now. We want witnesses to your signing this contract giving all your gains from your currency speculation to the U.S. government. That ought to ameliorate the effects of this bust on the dollar. You can paint yourself as a patriot, and use it to plea bargain when fraud charges are brought for this Neuropt business."

"There are also a few other things in the contract," Joe added. "You agree to have Royaltec to withdraw its lawsuit against Telekinetics, and to have Neuropt drop its malpractice suit against me. The suit won't succeed, since we've demonstrated I was right, but this makes it happen sooner so I don't have to pay some damned lawyers."

"You know such a contract won't hold up," Gage said. "I can prove it was signed under duress."

"Sure," Joe said. "You do that, and we go public with your role in the virus. You end up going to jail, and losing your fortune paying off virus victims."

"That could happen anyway," Gage said.

"Perhaps," Joe said. "But Brazil already made a deal with the Russians to keep quiet in order to get the antidote. The only others who know the source of the virus are us, and if you sign the contract and give up your currency gains, we'll keep quiet. We're letting you keep your other investments so you have incentive to play ball with us, and not challenge the contract later."

Gage picked up the phone with his shaking hand. "Some very smart people badly misjudged you, Nile."

———

That evening Joe and Erika were joined by Zenko, Burak and Hank at the Rose and Crown.

Burak gave him a bear hug. "Joe, you dog!" Burak said. "You are just like a Turk. I am proud of you. That sting was like an old Turk trick —"

Joe laughed as everyone moaned to cut Burak off.

"The sting worked superbly," Zenko beamed, mixing regular and light beer in a glass and handing it to Joe. "I just wish I could have been there with you, Joe, to help kick Gage's ass."

"That press release you made Gage issue is already working," Hank said. "The dollar has edged up a little on news that Gage would be donating his gains. The dollar took a big hit from the news about the virus being deliberately planted. But it looks like the devaluation of the dollar has bottomed at 25 percent. Hopefully there will be a soft landing for the economy. It helps that there are some other potential uses for many of the virus solutions from all these companies."

"And Telekinetics is back in business," Burak said, clinking his mug with Joe's. "Now that these lawsuits are gone, the Retinal Screen will sell! It won't be used for the virus, but it was always planned for other uses. Even the government is showing an interest in the Sheath, now that they realize Neuropt was a fraud. A.J. has gotten a number of calls this afternoon. It looks like we've got some huge momentum building."

"So who was it that fired Zenko and I, and was ready to give up?" Joe asked.

"Yes, rub me in it," Burak said. "Go ahead, you cannot change my joy at this fantastic result."

"I heard the SEC is already starting an investigation of Neuropt and the Peterson, Malone firm," Zenko said. "And of course, Ned Stern won't be collecting on his receivable from Neuropt. So it looks like some rough justice there."

Zenko got a call and started talking on his cell phone.

"Guess what?" Zenko interrupted. "Borland just filed papers petitioning the court to withdraw from representing Royaltec."

"That didn't take long," Erika said. "We've got bubbles bursting all over."

The waitress popped open a bottle of champagne and started pouring glasses.

Half an hour later, Joe put his hand on Erika's shoulder and whispered into her ear.

"Now why would I want to go back to your apartment with you?" Erika said loudly. "You're out of a job and still have bar and SEC investigations against you."

"How about the fact that you're married?" Zenko asked.

"Separated," Erika corrected, waving her ringless hand.

"When did this happen?" Zenko asked. "Why did Joe hear about it before the rest of us?"

"Joe needed all the help he could get," Erika said, taking Joe's hand and standing up. "So I let him know first."

Erika paused at the door, looking back at the group at the bar, who were loudly complaining about Joe and Erika leaving. She smiled at Joe.

"You know," Joe said, "I should have had Gage give me some money. You realize we're both out of jobs now?"

"Yes," Erika said, "but don't forget, you made Gage buy my Neuropt stock, so I have some cash. If you're good, I might buy you breakfast."

Joe smiled even more as he grabbed Erika by the shoulders and placed his lips on hers, tenderly at first, then vigorously. A wave of warmth washed over him as she pressed her body against his. She kissed back just as forcefully. Joe's hands started to slowly work their way down her back, and she worked her hand inside his shirt against his stomach.

The End

Printed in the United States
47594LVS00001B/7-9